Attraction and Repulsion

"Here in the span of a few tumultuous days, in the heart of Paris, being the only theater that could stage this resplendent play on sudden love, we find a dreamed love that becomes real with quick edges, a purported ménage à trois that is not a threesome, a plotted death that is not murder, where death's sanctuary becomes a playground, and where actors become characters and characters become actors. We realize this could only happen on a romp in magical Paris at the hand of Robert Scott Leyse."—Tom Sheehan, author of *Epic Cures* and *Brief Cases, Short Spans*

"Ah, to be a young man in Paris with two lovely, liberated ladies in a very contemporary ménage à trois and with a colorful crew of international misfits for friends—picnicking gourmet-style in Montsouris Park, sneaking into Père Lachaise cemetery after dark to cavort amid a thunder storm, partying all night in the City of Light, delighting under the playful spell of Eros—all of it good fun until true love and jealousy intrude, and their lives take a serious turn. Robert Scott Leyse gives us a Parisian romantic comedy with a well-earned happy ending and repartee as sparkling as the champagne. À votre santé!"—William T. Hathaway, Rinehart Award winning author of *Summer Snow* and *Radical Peace*

"Add a love triangle and a love-hate triangle together in Paris, mix in some festive adventures and crackling dialogue, and *Attraction and Repulsion* is the entertaining result. Page-turning fun, love, duress, and triumph: true happiness doesn't come cheap in life, or in this novel."—George Fosty, ESPN featured author of *Black Ice*

BY THE SAME AUTHOR

Self-Murder

"*Self-Murder* is a fascinating and excellent psychological thriller readers won't be able to put down."—*Midwest Book Review*

"A phantasmagoria of unbridled lust, sexual obsession, and stealth madness, *Self-Murder* is a dazzling indictment of desire that brims with sensory imagery and moments of exquisite verbal beauty delivered by a narrative voice that is baroque but disturbing and more than a little reminiscent of Edgar Allan Poe." —Gary Earl Ross, Edgar Award winning author of *Blackbird Rising*

"Robert Scott Leyse channels Baudelaire's Queen of Spades and Jack of Hearts, speaking darkly of dead loves, in this new book. He also reminds me of James Purdy's notorious eccentricity. There's plenty of middlebrow stuff if you want it. *Self-Murder* isn't that."—Kris Saknussemm, author of *Private Midnight*

"After his first novel, *Liaisons For Laughs*, which took *Sex and the City* to new heights and depths, Robert Scott Leyse's second one, *Self-Murder*, explores broader, deeper, and darker territories. Leyse achieves a striking stylistic gallimaufry: Proustian memories underpinning thoughts, words, and deeds; obsession treated in a way which evokes *Lolita*; romps that Henry Miller would have enjoyed; a finale that delivers a blow to the solar plexus."—Barry Baldwin, Emeritus Professor of Classics, U. of Calgary, Fellow of the Royal Society of Canada

"*Self-Murder* is lush sensuality of language injected with menace. A vivid portrait of mental disintegration and an explosive picture-show. Hallucinations without substance-abuse. Overwrought nerves and insomnia are *Self-Murder's* drugs of choice."—George Fosty, *ESPN* featured author of *Black Ice*

"Here is a psychological struggle and sensual breakout where you best get a comfortable seat, grab the joy stick, and hang on. *Self-Murder* is a delicious look at the mystery of self-psychoanalysis, sensual release, acceptance of gifts of the tallest order, or the lowest."—Tom Sheehan, author of *Epic Cures*

Attraction and Repulsion

Robert Scott Leyse

SHATTERCOLORS PRESS
NEW YORK, NEW YORK

Copyright © 2011 by Robert Scott Leyse

All rights reserved under the International and Pan-American Copyright Conventions. Except for use in review, no part of this publication may be reproduced, stored in a retrieval system, or transmitted in any form, by any means, including electronic, mechanical, photocopying, recording or otherwise, without prior written permission from the publisher and author.

This book is a work of fiction. All names, characters, places and incidents are a product of the author's imagination or are used fictitiously. Any resemblance to actual persons, living or deceased, and events, past or present, is entirely coincidental.

Book Cover Design and Layout
by Cathi Stevenson / Book Cover Express

ISBN 978-0-9821710-5-9

Library of Congress Control Number: 2010917990

First Edition

ShatterColors Press
New York, New York

For those who know *falling in love
is the most important experience in life.*

Attraction and Repulsion

CHAPTER 1

It's a Friday evening in late May in Paris when our hero's pacing back and forth in front of the main entrance of the Père Lachaise Cemetery, at the intersection of Boulevard de Ménilmontant and Rue de la Roquette—frequently glancing north towards the Père Lachaise metro station, scanning the sidewalks of the boulevard, in the hope of sighting the two young women for whom he's waiting. No matter that he's arrived a good ten minutes before their meeting time of 5:15 PM: he continues to wonder whether his friends have failed to counter the influence of jetlag and overslept or become lost in the metro or run into complications regarding their mission to purchase two bottles of champagne. At the same time, he's literally tingling with exhilaration, gazing at his surroundings with unconcealed delight: the high white stone wall, curving away from him concavely in a semi-circle, of the cemetery's entrance; the view of the cemetery's interior, its jumble of sepulchers and greenery, through the gate; the buildings across the street, their architecture markedly different from those back home; the wide walkway island in the center of the boulevard, planted with a double row of trees; the shimmering brightness of this sunny spring day. Again he glances north; still failing to detect his friends, he consults his cell phone for the time and laughs. *It's not their fault I'm early*, he says to himself.

But let us describe our hero: although of twenty-three years he's often mistaken for a teenager, mostly on account of his fresh youthful appearance but also on account of his playful and mocking disposition—his persistent refusal to admit he takes much of anything seriously. His height measures at six feet one inch and his weight's never far from one hundred fifty-five pounds. He has a higher than average forehead on a handsome face of even features, fine light brown hair just long enough to betray its tendency to curl, dark brown eyes, a fair complexion, and long tapering fingers. At once quick and graceful in gait and gesticulation, there's often an air of being lost in daydreams about him; this quality of abstraction somehow carries a mood of intentness with it, as if it's maintained out of defiance or reflects a desire to be in possession of a vantage point, deal with others from a position of once-removal. He's wearing a black cotton dress shirt with rolled up sleeves and blue denim pants: the untucked tails of the former flap below the waistline of the latter in the lively gusts of breeze. He's an American, born in San Francisco, who's been a resident of Manhattan for over six years on account of having attended New York University. His name is William Bergen.

It's not William's first visit to Paris; he's been here twice before, for a week when he was fourteen and for three weeks during March and April of the previous year. He doesn't recall too many particulars of Paris from his first visit, when he accompanied his father on a business trip, because he was more interested in getting to know the Italian girl who was staying with her family on the same floor of their hotel; what he clearly recalls is the girl and frame of mind he was in. Paris during that visit was but a blurred backdrop to an adolescent infatuation that was happy to content itself with flirtation, kisses, and caresses—a stirring chapter of his emotional education. He feels he came to know the city fairly well, though, during his last visit: he rode on virtually every metro line, exited at stops in each arrondissement and went for lengthy strolls in them. He was bound and determined to map out Paris in his head because he'd decided to make it his second city—his disconnect-himself-from-responsibility-and-surrender-to-frivolity city. Most importantly, he'd befriended a number of the locals and had several memorable adventures in their company.

So here he is in Paris for the third time, breathing air that he's never breathed outside of carefree-mode; that carries no reminders of regularity of routine, any variety of commitment. How removed his surroundings and frame of mind are from the work responsibilities he put on hold less than twenty-four hours ago—when he exited the office early, picked up his luggage at his apartment, rendezvoused with his two friends at JFK, and caught a flight to Orly: goodbye New York work-grind, hello Parisian giddiness. Such is William's lightheartedness it almost as if the force of gravity's been altered: he feels as if he's floating about instead of walking about; it's as if basic self-propulsion requires less energy. It's amazing how an alteration of geographical location has liberated him from all trace of care; how quickly the inanity of office politics has vanished from his thoughts, and no longer seems real. Not that William has a bad job—far from it. If anyone ever had a cushy job, he does. He works at a large law firm, ranked in the top thirty worldwide, and his official title is Corporate Resources Associate—a fancy way of saying he performs searches in legal databases for specific documents or samples of legal phrasing at the request of attorneys. As the searches are generally easy to perform and the requests can be few and far between, his primary responsibility consists of padding his billing. His job, in fact (and one will never find this stated in the official literature of any law firm), exists for the purpose of padding billing. He's essentially being paid very well to do nothing at least 50% of the time: as long as he bills for that idle time, his salary's more than covered and the firm turns a tidy profit from his employment. Good work if you can get it and William knows it and isn't lacking in gratitude, even though he often mocks the setup.

But when people are confined to office space for hours at a time day after day and month after month they often begin to bicker over nothing, form alliances and rivalries, trade gossip incessantly, start unkind rumors and/or assist with perpetuating them. Some fling themselves wholeheartedly into office politics; others are pulled into office politics against their will; virtually no one's immune because nonparticipation has a tendency to incite all parties against one: it's a case of either choose sides and bond with a clique or suffer the consequences of having no allies. William, who's never breathed a word of gossip about anyone in any building he's ever lived in, is—we regret to admit—a primary player in the politics at his place of employment. He's told himself he ought to seek to minimize his participation in office politics, for fear it might blow up in his face, but has never been able to resist going at it full throttle: he always winds up considering it a game. He and some of his cohorts have concluded that the primary cause of office politics is the tedium of office life: it's a means of introducing adventure and uncertainty into an otherwise nauseatingly predictable environment. If there's no real adversity, people will create some; if the unexpected has gone into hiding, people will lure it into the open. When faced with boredom, people create tension: it's an instinctive form of protest.

Your humble narrator apologizes for the aside concerning office politics: again, the point is that William's been cut loose from the influence of the office and is as dizzy with delight as it's possible for a person to be. Factor in the fact his employer's granted him a six week leave of absence and the reader will understand the amount of freedom he's relishing in advance. *I'll be scamping about Paris for a month and a half*, he thinks while continuing to gaze enrapt at the scenery; continuing to dwell upon the upcoming night's adventure, that he conceived of over a month ago and has looked forward to ever since.

Bending to attend to the two bags he's placed on the ground near one of the traffic pillars—transfer items from the heavier one into the lighter one, so the latter will stop sliding across the cobblestones on account of the breeze—William hears, "Hey there, Billy!" shouted from a short distance, glances in the direction of the voice, and sees Christina Alari on the walkway in the center of the boulevard.

"Hey Chrissy," he answers with a wave of his hand as she scampers across the crosswalk to his side of the street, her long wavy blond hair swishing in the wind as the same wind flattens half of her dress against her slender frame. Her every movement radiates the natural poise of a dancer. "Where's Pas? She's coming, isn't she?"

"I left her at the metro station," laughs Christina. "She's adjusting her shoe, a pebble slipped inside it."

"And how are we this fine spring evening?" he asks, spreading his arms in anticipation of encircling her with them.

"Quite in clover, Billy," she returns as they embrace and exchange greeting-kisses. Born into a second generation Italian family and raised in Bay Ridge, Brooklyn, Christina's recently turned twenty-one, has just completed an internship as a translator at the United Nations, and resides in Manhattan's East Village, diagonally across the street from William, close to the all-night cafe where they met. A part time job awaits her at the UN in September; while using it for an income, she'll be continuing to attend voice and dance classes and go to auditions, with the aim of breaking into Broadway. She's a size two, five feet six inches in height, has dark hazel eyes, a perfect oval of an alabaster complexioned face, and—as mentioned—long waves of blond hair. She's wearing a sleeveless indigo knee-high dress, a jumble of bangles on each wrist, and black hiking boots.

After their embrace Christina backs a step away from William, flings her hands up so that the bangles jinglingly slide down her forearms, and asks with mock solemnity, "And how are you, sir, on this lovely-enough-to-die-for day?"

"Dying for love of it, of course," he answers. "As happy as those bangles are as they jangle about your arms! Such a cheerful sound, like the pinging in my senses—my springtime-in-Paris senses, racing at the speed of light! Chrissy, we're going to have so much fun—my head whirls into a zillion beautiful pictures at the thought of all the stuff we're going to do!"

"Yeah, we're in one of those go-wild-in-a-foreign-land adventure stories," she says. "Clichés can be a thrill if they happen for real."

"But who wants to be in a story?" he says, making a face of mock aversion. "Patterns of ink on a page that only come to life in the minds of readers can't reach out and do this." So saying, he caresses her neck.

"Umm," she purrs, tilting her head in the direction of his hand while lifting her chin.

"So you see," he laughs. "We're living and breathing flesh and blood New Yorkers on holiday, instead of the airy concoctions of some author's imagination!"

"I make a crack about storybook stuff and you use it as an excuse to pet me?" she smiles, pressing herself against his chest again. "Want me to reel off more nonsense? For the love of sacred springtime and all the unexpected things it makes us do as we're flooded with waves of restlessness, I'll spout all the silliness you want!"

"But that's pearls of wisdom, Chrissy! Buds are bursting into blossoms, birds are bursting into song... Springtime renewal and excitement's all around us and surging in our blood! Hail the inner fireworks that rob us of the self-control we don't want! It's..."

"So rude! No welcome!" interrupts a nearby voice. Up steps Pascale Rosetourne, the third member of the party. "First Chrissy abandons me at the metro, then both of you ignore me!" Born in Asnieres, a suburb to the northwest of Paris, Pascale relocated to Manhattan's Upper East Side with her family when she was four years old. Having spent many summers with relatives in various locations of France during childhood and adolescence, she's as familiar with the language and customs of her native country as she is with those of her adopted one and considers herself a French girl, even though she's never thought of leaving New York. A recent graduate of the Fashion Institute of Technology (FIT), she's joined her friends for a final fling before applying herself to a career in clothing design. Like William and Christina, she resides on the 400 block of East 9th Street, between 1st Avenue and Avenue A; her building is three doors east of his on the same side of the street. Pascale and William met as a consequence of springtime sunning on their fire escapes: glances were exchanged over a period of three days; on the fourth day he suggested, via hand-signals, that they descend to the sidewalk for a get-acquainted chat. Their chat, during which both were treated to an as-if-we've-known-one-another-for-years experience, lasted for approximately six hours in her apartment. William, already close to Christina, introduced Pascale to her. Thus was born a special threesome chemistry, characterized more by friendship than intimate relations (although the latter aren't lacking), which has strengthened with each passing month, nearly twelve of them now. Pascale has magenta streaks along the face-framing edges of her straight raven black hair, cut at her neck in back and longer in front, and is wearing a mid-thigh high black leather skirt, scarlet silk t-shirt, and black hiking boots. About half an inch taller than Christina, she's likewise a size two and shares the same appealing shape of face; in fact, if the two of them wished to do so, they could dress alike and dye and cut their hair alike and fool many into believing them to be fraternal twins. Pascale will turn twenty-two in September and has brown eyes.

As we've indicated, Pascale's acting offended at not having received a greeting. After chiding her friends regarding the oversight she does an about face, makes as if to walk away.

"Sorry Pas, we didn't see you there," laughs Christina, tapping her on the shoulder and inducing her to turn around again, whereupon she kisses her on each cheek.

"I sort of snuck up, if you want to know the truth," Pascale says with a grin, kissing Christina in return while extending an arm in William's direction, grasping one of his hands. "I wanted to see how close I could get before you saw me! I got pretty close!"

"Sure, prowling kitty," William says as he pulls her close, frames her face with his hands, lightly rubs her temples with his index fingers. "Good to see you, Pas! It's been nearly three hours! I was starting to forget what you look like!"

"Good to see you too, sweetie," returns Pascale, ignoring his teasing as she hugs him. Then, raising the bag that's in her hand and shaking it, she asks, "But what's the idea of us cutting our post-flight naps short and traipsing all the way up here from the 14th with some champagne? Your friends are having a big party later and have a whole case of champagne! Aren't we going to their party?"

"I'm mystified myself," seconds Christina, winking at Pascale.

"And, *especially*," resumes Pascale, "why am I wearing clunky hiking boots on my first day in Paris, when I have much cuter shoes to put on and show off? Answer me that! I mean, hiking boots? What sort of girl wears hiking boots in Paris? I feel like an outcast and a fool! And why haven't we had a bite to eat? Why the insane urgency? No time to nap, no time to eat! Just blind rush-rush while starving!"

"You're bright girls," William responds, gesturing at the gate of Père Lachaise. "Certainly you've surmised why we're here. I told you we were going to do something we can't do in New York that neither of you have done before and that, incidentally, you'll love doing and won't forget anytime soon. I've brought plenty of succulent food, three headlamps, and some climbing rope. So guess where we're spending some, if not all, of the night?"

"In other words," Christina laughs, "tombyards are where thrills are to be had."

"Smart girl," William says. "You've guessed correctly. Père Lachaise officially closes at six and we're going to unofficially stay as long as we please. Tonight's agenda is play in Père Lachaise until we're exhausted enough to swoon in a tomb, mimic the dead."

"If I wanted to be dead, I'd move to New Jersey and work in a mall," declares Pascale.

"Yeah, that's it," says William, with a light poke at her ribs. "Be difficult for the sake of being difficult! You know very well I mean glorious self-expenditure in fun and games until we're blissful inside, at peace with ourselves, happily exhausted! Such is the opposite of dead! Pure euphoria!"

"Euphoria, shmoria," Pascale scoffs. "What's euphoric about grass that's slimy with dew, getting our clothes wet? What's euphoric about swarms of insects crawling and flying all over the place, biting us? Why waste a Paris night, and a Friday one at that, on running around in a dismal park cluttered with stones marking where corpses decay?"

"So what's become of the Pascale that *I* know?" William asks. "What's become of the fearless, always-thirsting-for-something-new, girl? The Pascale that *I* know would never pull a frail flower act, whine about bugs and wet grass! She'd never kiss a unique experience goodbye because she's afraid of breaking a nail!"

"She's here, sweetie—is she *ever*!" Pascale says as she grasps his neck with both hands, gently pulls his head down and kisses him on the forehead. "And, believe it, your Pascale's eager to play in a graveyard! I *love* my hiking boots now, and to hell with pretty heeled and toeless things!"

"Being dragged out of bed after a jet lag catnap and dashing up here, with no time for more than a quick shower and cup of tea, is *priceless*!" Christina exclaims. "It's a swirly half out of my body experience, with my two favorite people on earth! On New York time, but already vibrating in rhythm with Paris! I'm already tumbling in emotional overflow, and we haven't stepped inside Père Lachaise yet! But, boy, am I starved! And I'm talking about *food*!"

"I'm with you there, Chrissy," Pascale says. "I feel like I could devour five chickens!"

"Don't worry about that," William says. "As I said, I've brought plenty of tasty provisions, as only the French can make them. Pate, brie, baguettes, the best butter on earth, and those succulent cans of tuna with the vegetables and marinade crammed in—there's nothing remotely like them back home. Plus celery and cherry tomatoes, fruit—blueberries, strawberries, figs—and three liters of water."

"And I have the champagne," Pascale says. "So what are we waiting for?"

"Just one thing before we go inside," William answers, leading them to the left of the entry area and pointing at the wall which encircles the cemetery. "The gates will be shut at six so we'll be exiting by coming over the wall, using the rope I've brought. I don't think we want to wait until eight-thirty in the morning for the gates to reopen. In fact, I insist Père Lachaise be solely a nighttime adventure."

"Absolutely," Christina says. "Aside from the nighttime factor, fifteen hours would be too long."

"Of course graveyard wanderings are best before sunrise," Pascale laughs, "if one's looking for maximum atmospherics! And we *are*!"

"OK, so here's the deal," William continues. "Unlike elsewhere, the wall here in front's only about four feet high on the cemetery-side, thus sparing us having to climb it. I'm going to stash the rope and gloves in a nearby tomb and we'll get them when we're leaving. The rope has knots in it for foot- and hand-holds and the gloves are so we can get a better grip and not get rope burns. I'll descend first, then help you down. I'll grab you before you reach the ground to minimize your time on the rope. As you can see, the wall's about fifteen feet high on this side. With your aerobics training I'm not worried about you handling the descent, but take a good look anyway and remember how it looks from here on the sidewalk."

"Petite things we may be, but we're toned and muscular," Christina says, flexing her arms. "It'll be fun climbing down."

"I'd say we're set, Billy," Pascale says, saluting him. Then, as she turns towards the gate and glances up at its twin pillars and perceives the hourglasses and torches engraved thereupon, she adds, "How uncannily appropriate! It's spring and our torches are blazing bright, but life's brief and our hourglasses are measured, so the thing to do is use our time to have fun! Let's go!"

"Here Chrissy—you can carry the lighter bag, with the headlamps," William says, handing her the said bag as he picks up the heavier one containing the water and most of the food.

"But why headlamps?" Christina inquires. "We're in a city. Street lamps are all over the place."

"No lamps in the city of the dead," William laughs, gesturing at the cemetery. "No lights in the sepulchers we're going to explore!"

"Never let it be said you're not a fun date, Billy!" Pascale exclaims as the three of them stroll through the gate.

CHAPTER 2

"First we hide the rope and gloves," William says, leading his friends to the left. They ascend a small flight of steps, stroll alongside the wall they were recently examining from the street-side, and immediately encounter a distinctive tomb with three circles on it. "Perfect landmark," he announces, slipping the rope and gloves underneath a nearby planter, raised on four short legs. Then, after he bids the girls lean over the wall (as he said, it's only about four feet high on this side) and examine their future descent from above, they return to the area just inside the entrance.

Christina, seeing the map that's posted there, darts up to it and announces, "Père Lachaise has avenues, chemins, and divisions—cute! It's a city of the dead compliment to Paris!"

"What's *chemin* mean, anyway?" William inquires. "I never thought to ask."

"A path," Christina responds.

"Anyway, I have our own map," he says, patting his pocket. "We're going straight ahead, to the end of Avenue Principale, then veering right, getting away from the main avenues and paths as soon as possible. I doubt if they patrol the whole cemetery before shutting the gates, but we sure don't want to be in plain sight. And we have to stay away from Morrison's grave: a guard's posted there, on account of the bastards who deface the area and litter it with trash. As long as we stay in isolated areas in other divisions, we'll be OK."

"Where's Jim?" Christina asks.

"Here, in the 6th," he answers, pointing at the map. "They actually tried to exhume him and kick him out of here, but discovered his site's leased in perpetuity. It's amusing that an American's the most troublesome resident, even if it's inconvenient for us!"

"Jim, shame on you," Pascale laughs, wagging her finger towards the interior of Père Lachaise. "Speaking as someone who likes your music, I'm not pleased with your posthumous antics! How dare you attract disrespectful louts who vandalize the cemetery and necessitate the installment of a guard? You give us respectful and tidy cemetery-rompers a bad name!"

"But why are we veering right, when Jim's to the right?" Christina asks.

"We're not veering *that* far to the right," William replies as they commence walking. "We're going where the terrain's rough, with hills and retaining walls, tombs so tightly packed together we'll almost have to crawl over them. We'll eat in an isolated and picturesque spot."

"The whole place looks like isolated spots—I can barely see past the first rows of tombs and trees," says Christina, gesturing at the sides of Avenue Principale. "It's as much a garden as a graveyard! In fact, it reminds me of a fairytale enchanted forest, where mysteries lurk in the shadows, around every bend! Who knows what wonderful or dangerous things will greet us the moment we step from the path? Who knows what strange phenomena await discovery? Ooooo! It gives me the tingles something fierce!"

"Sheer inner up-rushes of delight," adds Pascale. "Endless rows of ornate tombs, trees twisting in the breeze, flowers everywhere, the sweet smell of springtime air! It's a fizziness-all-over feeling!"

"Glad you approve of our humble excursion," William says, turning about a couple of times with arms spread. "I've been looking forward to this night for over a month, and it's already exceeding expectation!"

Reaching the end of Avenue Principale, our three friends turn onto the stairs at their right and ascend a hill, still heading slightly north of east, if one takes the actual alignment of Père Lachaise into account. At first the vegetation's dense enough to block their view of the sky; then they emerge into an opening, with an expanse of lawn on their left.

"I thought we were going to an out of the way place, cluttered with graves, where we can't be spotted," Pascale teases.

"Oh, be quiet," William answers. "Here, to the right."

Following another section of steps and some more veering to the right, they arrive at the corner of Avenue de la Chapelle and Chemin du Bassin and turn left onto the latter. After advancing a few more yards, William points at the jumble of tombs and vegetation to their right and announces, "Dinnertime!"

"About time," Christina says, scampering from the path without hesitation, Pascale and William at her heels. The three of them weave among a forest of monuments and sepulchers and trees and shrubs of all shapes and sizes as they descend a hill.

"Here's a perfect dining table," Pascale says, pointing at a flat-topped vault, about a yard high. "And it even has flowers!" She's referring to the concrete flowerbox at its head, planted with crimson and orange tulips.

"Courtesy of Claude Bernard," Christina says, reading the name engraved upon the front.

"So kind of Claude to provide us with a dining table and floral arrangement," Pascale says, beginning to spread napkins on the vault at the same time that she's weighing them down with food items so they don't blow away. "What are Claude's dates? Hmm... 1813-1878! He's no spring chicken, our Claude! I'd invite him to join us if he was able!"

"Poor Claude's gone the way of all flesh," says William, tearing the foil and unwinding the wire from one of the champagne bottles.

"As long as I have my flesh, I know what to do with it," says Pascale, running her hands up and down her thighs while shaking her hips. "A-Woo!"

"A-Woo!" seconds Christina, readying a plastic cup for the first frothings of the champagne.

"A toast," says William after the champagne's been opened and everyone has a full cup. "May tonight's adventure be one we happily recall for the rest of our lives! May it be the first of many in this great metropolis! May our six weeks in Paris be sheer delirium!"

"A very worthy and appropriate toast," Christina smiles as they clink their cups and exchange kisses, before drinking.

"And now we devour," Pascale says, pulling the tops from three cans of tuna. Soon our friends are consuming the cans of tuna while tearing chunks from the baguettes and smearing them with pate, brie, and butter. Nor are the cherry tomatoes and celery stalks neglected. Inside half an hour, the demands of hunger are satisfied.

After wrapping up the remaining food and placing the trash in a separate bag (William's brought extras), they set the baskets of blueberries, strawberries, and figs on their table and open a liter of water. "Snackies for while we await sunset and relish the beauty of this place," William says, sweeping an arm towards the horizon. "Some would say desolation, a disturbing reminder of our mortality, but I disagree: the presence of the dead heightens my awareness of life."

"I'm alive, all right," says Christina. "How could I not be when I'm with my best friends in an open air art museum that seems to extend for miles? The wind's picking up and temperature's dropping; my legs are goose-pimpled, shivering a bit in the wind's undulations, but guess what? The shivers are pure invigoration, mini-fireworks overspreading my skin! I'm a girl who ought to be cursing herself for forgetting to bring a sweater, but who's happy with energy instead!"

"Right," says William, "a slight oversight! We're dressed for a warm sunny day when it's a blustery evening, with the sun soon to part ways with us, not to mention we're planning on spending part of the night here. I'm wearing pants, though, and will have it easier, so listen: if anyone does get cold, become uncomfortable in any way, we'll return to town immediately. This is for fun, not discomfort. No one's going to conceal it if they want to leave, right?"

"Of course not," says Christina. "Sorry I mentioned it! I mentioned it out of joy, not distress, I hope you know! Being underdressed is going to bring me closer to the elements, where I want to be! And it's not as if civilization doesn't surround us! We're not stranded on a mountaintop!"

"Just making sure," William says. "I'm savoring the breeze too, but I don't have a dress on."

"Just being the overprotective male, as if we're frail flowers fond of being sheltered," Pascale says, whacking him on the shoulder. "You've said it yourself: you like your women fluffy on the outside, steely on the inside. You know us, so no more worrying about whether the poor girls are going to get coldie-woldie! No one's leaving before anyone else wants to! If I get chilly I'll run around, or use the wonderful age-old remedy: shared bodily warmth!" So saying, she hugs him tight.

"Whatever happens, happens," Christina giggles, joining in on the hug. "There's no plan, right Billy?"

"Leaving by the way I showed you is the only plan," affirms William. "This is our launch-party, as in launching ourselves into our six week antidote to the ordinariness that afflicts our lives too much of the time back home—that afflicts every person who's being forced, by the necessity of remaining fed, to endure the impositions of our unnatural civilization—so it's not going to be ruined with any pre-set program! Whatever happens, happens, is right!"

"And so Billy's finally gotten around to hinting at his favorite subject," Christina laughs, winking at Pascale. "Modern civilization's a hijacking of our true primal selves—a false refuge of moral abstractions, artifice by which we avoid responsibility for our feelings! Isn't that so, Billy?"

"Right," Pascale chimes in. "We're all being infiltrated by pop culture shallowness, media-dictated pseudo emotions! Religion's become meaningless sham acting, parrot mimicry! True transcendence no longer exists! Authenticity of feeling's rapidly going the way of the dinosaurs! Soon humans be little better than robots; our species as heretofore known on earth will be, for all intents and purposes, extinct: only a shell stripped of spirituality will remain! Am I phrasing it correctly, Billy? *(She brings her hands into prayer position, widens her eyes in exaggerated supplication.)* Please instruct me if I'm not! Feel free to sermonize your heart out!"

"Preach to us ignorant girls, Billy," Christina adds, likewise making prayer hands and putting on a submissive look, going one better and dropping to her knees before him.

"Tell you what," William laughs. "Just to teach you to beware what you wish for, even in mockery, maybe I *will* treat you to a fine speech!"

"Mockery? Who's mocking?" Christina says, putting on a face of innocence while tapping his knees. "I'm sincerely asking to be enlightened, and I believe the same is true of Pas!"

"Of course it's true of me! I'd never make an insincere request! I don't even know the meaning of irony!"

"Why don't you go up there?" Christina suggests, pointing to the top of a nearby sepulcher, about two yards wide, that's adjacent to an easily climbable tree. "It'll make your sermon more visually compelling, lend greater weight to your words, more effectively drive home the relevancy of your message."

"Serious messages stand on their own merit and are in no need of ostentatious theatrics, memorable locations of delivery," William says. "On the other hand, I'm rather fond of vantage points. I always enjoy a good view."

"Hurry up, then," says Pascale, grasping him by the hand and pulling him towards the sepulcher. "We poor civilization-victimized girls are in need of a quick antidote to what ails us! Our spiritual enlightenment can't happen soon enough! This city of the dead's starting to spook us! Without the medicine of your words we'll sicken with fear and turn tail and run towards the gate and..."

"Nothing like overacting," William interrupts. "As I said, be careful what you wish for! I might..."

"Oh, get on with it!"

Laughingly shrugging his shoulders, William advances to the sepulcher, ascends the tree beside it, and crawls onto its roof; then he seats himself on the edge of the roof with his feet dangling into the air. Christina and Pascale sit on one of the vaults below.

"But now it's been drained of spontaneity," says William. "How can I spout heartfelt opinions after all this setting of the stage? Spur-of-the-moment inspiration's been killed by over-preparation: I'd only be playacting, laughing at myself."

"No, no! We're eager to be harangued, be it from the heart or not," says Christina, making a pout-face. "We're starting to be afraid of goblins and ghouls because our parasitical civilization's left us unprepared to handle this unique cemetery experience! We desperately need to be restored to equilibrium by your comforting voice!"

"The build up of anticipation's taken deep hold of us, is churning in our tummy-tum-tums," insists Pascale, pointing at her stomach. "It would be inhuman to let us down—you can't back out now that we're pining for instruction! See *(She makes the sign of the cross and Christina quickly imitates her.)*, we're good Sunday school girls and won't judge or mock you! We'll be silent and respectful, gaping in amazement at the glorious edification of your words!"

"Instruction?" William laughs. "I'd say the only thing you princesses really want to be instructed about is where the latest designer clothes are to be had for bargain basement prices! Making other females foam with envy without having to break the bank is the real path to contentment, right?"

"Pas, we've been found out! We've tried in vain to fool Billy into thinking we're more than ditzy dollfaces! We thought we'd duped him into believing we can see beyond the clutter of makeup on our vanities, but we haven't! He's figured out we only care about being consumers of slickly packaged fashion products, are suckers for trendy trinkets—that we're the dream-stuff of Madison Avenue demographics studies!"

"Right, Chrissy! Of course we're interested in nothing but endlessly posturing, idling about in stylish vacuousness, frittering away our expensive educations on the latest ways to preen ourselves and be seen!" chimes in Pascale, before uprooting a weed and tossing it—along with the soil clinging to its roots—at William.

"A hit, girl! A palpable hit!" shouts Christina as the weed strikes his upper thigh and dirt sprays onto his shirt. Then she uproots a clump of grass, tosses it just over his head.

"Missed!" taunts William, retreating from the edge of the roof. "You're a bad shot, but Pas isn't! She filled my shirt pocket full of dirt!"

"I won't miss next time! I'll fill your *mouth* full of dirt!"

"I'll bet you think there's no ammo up here and I'm defenseless," William says. "Think again!" He peels a mat of moss from the sepulcher's roof, tears it into palm-sized chunks, begins raining them down.

An exchange of spiritedly thrown botanical specimens ensues: Pascale and Christina are racing about the base of the sepulcher, attacking from all sides with clumps of grass and weeds, and William's alternately approaching and retreating from the edge of the roof while flinging moss and, once that runs out, twigs torn from the tree. Finally, they're all lying on their backs laughing.

"And so," William says while the girls are still catching their breaths, they having run around a great deal, "we're already slipping into the psyche-healing spontaneity that we've come here for, well on our way to washing away civilization's will-immobilizing influence! There's nothing like frivolity for flushing excess clutter from our thoughts, restoring us to our rightful selves!"

"Spontaneity *was* healing us until you opened your mouth, and chased it away!" exclaims Pascale, sitting upright. "Now, we're reduced to *thinking* about it! Words kill feelings! Thoughts kill emotion! Analyzing things is a surefire loss of innocence!"

"But didn't I say be careful what you wish for?" responds William. "Did you think I'd forgotten? You wanted a sermon, so here... *(He breaks off laughing, attempts to fight it off.)* Girls, we find ourselves in a vast playground, a... *(He's laughing harder, slaps the roof of the sepulcher, doubles over on his side.)* My stomach hurts!" he manages to shout.

"Cry cry for poor Billy!" mocks Christina. "He's laughing too hard and his tummy hurts! Poor poor Billy!"

"Serves him right," Pascale says, standing and extending a hand to Christina, pulling her to her feet. "He wounded sweet spontaneity by speaking its name, and so deserves to suffer! As for me, I'm not about to endure one of his silly sermons! I say we leave!"

"Absolutely," Christina says, following Pascale to their makeshift table. After each of them grab a handful of fruit, they scamper away giggling and soon disappear in the jumble of tombs.

"Fine," William yells as he begins climbing down the tree from the roof of the sepulcher. "You two hide out! I'll pop the top of the second bottle of bubbly and have it to myself!"

"Thanks for the warning, Billy!" Christina laughs, darting forward from behind a monument with a large cross affixed to its top. She easily reaches the table before he's finished descending the tree, seizes the bottle of champagne, and runs off with it.

"Hide it, Chrissy!" Pascale yells, clapping as she rises from where she's been crouching. Then she darts out of sight again.

William, jumping to the ground from the lowest limb of the tree, runs to where he last saw the girls. Of course they're gone by the time he arrives there, it not being difficult to remain hidden among the tombs and foliage. "Yoo-hoo!" he hears, the sound coming from ahead of him; and so he proceeds in that direction, being obliged to turn sideways to wedge himself between a couple sepulchers as he does so. "Yoo-hoo!" is heard again, along with some giggling, not too far to his left. When he emerges from behind a sepulcher festooned with ivy he sees his friends are sitting with their backs to the railing of a retaining wall, smiling from ear to ear, as the ground drops from sight behind them.

"What took you so long, darling," Pascale laughs, holding the bottle of champagne out to him.

"You didn't really think we were going to start without you, did you?" Christina asks, sliding forward onto her knees and raising her lips for a kiss.

"Of course not," he responds, bringing forth his hidden hand to reveal three cups, before kissing both girls.

"Here's your seat, Billy," Pascale says, scooting a couple feet from Christina.

William, sitting between them, sets about opening the champagne as they rest their heads on his shoulders.

"So cozy-wozy," Pascale says once their cups are full. Then, scrunching more insistently against William, she raises her cup and says, "To shared bodily warmth!"

"To shared bodily warmth and friendship and cemetery romps!" Christina adds as they touch their cups.

"Beautiful toasts from beautiful girls," William says, rubbing his head against the heads of each in turn. "I couldn't possibly improve upon your wise words!" And, with that, they drink while gazing at the sky.

Soon they turn around to admire the view below them: the railing, being constructed of bisecting metallic tubes a foot apart, allows them to pass their legs through it and dangle them over the wall. Speaking little but still snuggling close, they take their time draining the bottle while gazing over the tops of the sepulchers as the hillside falls away before them. After close to an hour of quiet contemplation they return to their dining table, finish packing everything up, and set about exploring more of Père Lachaise. When they toss the bag of trash into a receptacle on Avenue Transversale 1, sunset's approximately an hour away.

CHAPTER 3

It's been dark for at least half an hour and the absence of sunlight hasn't hindered our friends in their explorations of Père Lachaise. Their lightweight LED headlamps, purchased by William at a New York sporting goods store and designed for camping, are in place on their heads and emit bright wide beams. Far from missing daylight, they're enjoying the swishings of the light beams against the darkness; and dark it is, for the cloud cover's such that there's no trace of moon or star. They might be in the center of Paris, but the city illumination's for the most part blocked by the cemetery's enclosing walls, as well as by the trees and tombs. Likewise, are the city's sounds muted: our friends are amazed at how quiet it is.

"Where are we now?" asks Christina as they pause to admire three or four rows of tombs, arranged one above the other on a terraced rise bisected by a row of steps.

"I don't know exactly," William answers. "Aside from a couple quick looks to make sure we're staying away from Morrison's grave and that annoying guard, I haven't checked the map since sundown."

"You could check it now."

"What for? Why not let this scene remain mysteriously locationless, as if glimpsed in a dream?"

"It *is* a dream," Pascale says. "Look how the silver light of our lamps flits among the tombs, scatters patterns of brightness and shadow in all directions—ever restless shapes, as if vapor's coming to life!"

"Ghosts you mean," laughs Christina. "Of all the tombs surrounding us, these—for some reason—seem arranged in a sinister pattern, as if the dead have taken over the earth and built their homes on every hillside and there's no room left for the living! And I *love* it! I arch my back, think of ravening spirits of the night—ghouls, vampires, succubae—and shimmer with unease-tinged delight! It's *fun*!"

"A sinister pattern?" asks Pascale. "How so? I see neat rows, without any space being wasted."

"Not really sinister," answers Christina. "It's a passing mood of mine that twists it into being sinister, because such suits my pleasure. I was afraid of heights as a girl and would seek them out so I could shiver deliciously in the face of my fear. Alas, I'm no longer afraid of heights, but sometimes I can taste a hint of vertigo by indulging in mental tricks and that's what I'm doing now."

"Speaking of mental tricks," William says, gesturing towards their left. "Look at the green-stained bronze sculpture. Now, whisk your light beams back and forth across it—faster, that's it! The two women come alive, the folds of their robes splash about, as they raise the wreath! Such swirling symmetry soaring skyward! The one's holding an urn, the other a...it looks like a thyrsus. The Greek and Roman influence is obvious! Beautiful!"

"Famille Crespin," Christina reads after the three of them approach the sculpture. "And here it says Crespin du Gast. Why two names? Or is Crespin du Gast a family motto? I'm ashamed to admit it, but I don't know what Gast means."

"It's not a word, Miss UN translator," Pascale laughs. "It's a name variation within the family. But who cares? Look at the flowers among the tombs, the shouts of color in the gray. Geraniums, chrysanthemums, and lilies in our light beams, liquid crystal dreamglow! Quicksilver highlights juxtaposed with shadows, and blossoms spilling about in the breeze! And the curly-cue patterned gates and gingerbread eaves of the tombs—the Doric columns of that one up there! So ancient seeming, a scene from a bygone age!"

"Take away the crosses and what do you have?" William asks. "Think of the facades of the Roman tombs in the Met—the fundamental designs haven't changed much. And these two beauties aren't Christian women! They're Pagan women in all their glory! No one's dressed like this since the Roman Empire collapsed!"

"The Romans are gone, but their designs and fashion live on," Pascale says. "I wouldn't mind having a robe like that, in purple or scarlet! And they sure knew how to do their hair!"

"The Romans are gone, and someday this too will be buried and built upon by another civilization," William says, sweeping an arm across the scene before them. "They'll have some of these tombs in their museums!"

"And they'll copy the designs all over again," Pascale says. "They might have a different government and religion, but they'll still have the designs! We still copy Egypt and Greece and Rome and everyone else, and future societies will copy us! Fashion lives forever!"

"Sure," laughs William. "Do we have the slightest idea what fashion was like fifty thousand years ago? The span between the Egyptians, Greeks, and Romans and us is a very small sampling of time! Fifty thousand years from now will anything of the Romans or us be around in any shape or form? All will be as obliterated as chalk drawings on the sidewalk after a rain!"

"Yes, dear," Pascale answers, patting him on the back. "We're all aware that time will eventually demolish all trace of our presence! We're very aware of our mortality, the mutability of existence!"

"Look," William continues, pointing skyward. "Aim your light beams straight up and watch them vanish in the embrace of the night! That's where we're headed, utter oblivion! We'll be joining the dear departed in the blink of an eye!"

"I blinked and we haven't joined them yet," Pascale says, swatting his shoulder. "Shows what you know, Mr. Know-It..."

"Speaking of the fragility of us humans," Christina interrupts as she folds her arms across her chest and jumps up and down. "This breeze is passing straight through my dress and making me feel naked—I might as well be naked! Brrrrr! I could do with a little warming up, and guess where?"

"What?" scoffs Pascale. "You want to leave?"

"Of course not," Christina counters. "Let's find a tomb to examine on the inside, it'll be a break from the wind. And we'll be up close and personal with the residents. Why visit a place if one's unwilling to mingle? I'm very willing to mingle with the dead, contrast my living muscles with dry bones! I'll gaze inside an open casket if it gets me out of this breeze! Brrrrr! Come on!" She rapidly strolls to the stairs that divide the rows of tombs and begins climbing them.

"Chrissy might rhyme with prissy, but Chrissy's no prissy!" William yells as he and Pascale watch Christina turn from the stairs and vanish behind the second row of tombs before they can catch up with her.

"And Billy rhymes with silly, and Billy *is* silly!" Christina yells back.

"It truly is a separate city," Pascale says as they follow Christina onto the second terrace. "Row upon row of mini-houses, with their own landings and flowerboxes! Yummy flower-scents, sharp sweetness and tingling pungency! Umm! *(She bends to pick a couple scarlet chrysanthemums, places them in her hair.)* One for me and one for Chrissy! Hey Chrissy! I have a flower for you!"

"In a moment," Christina answers abstractedly, trying the handle of the gate of one of the larger sepulchers.

"Our light beams are more concentrated here, bouncing off the tombs and bending the air, giving it a thick velvety quality," Pascale continues, turning to William—who's behind her—and stopping. "Look how the light ripples over us, transforms our skin into radiant effervescence! Ghostly platinum light's caressing me! Look at my legs! *(She lifts the hem of her skirt, extends a leg towards him, taps his belt buckle with the toe of her boot.)* I love being here, where I'm reminded life's a miracle that isn't to be wasted! The dead remind us to make the most of what they no longer have, and relish the fireworks in our senses! Thanks again, sweetie, for this beautiful night!" Bringing her upraised leg back to the ground, she steps to William, wraps her arms around his neck, presses him against one of the tombs, briefly kisses him, then springs away laughing.

"Anytime," William says, saluting her. "Life's a miracle, all right, and those who fail to realize it are to be avoided like the plague! Just think: a year ago we were strangers, now we're running around after dark in Père Lachaise! Try to predict that or anything else in life! One girl crawls onto her fire escape, another girl's having a salad in a cafe, and now the three of us know each other so well we might as well have been born under the same roof!"

"A-Woo!" Pascale yells. "Life, sweet life! And flowers!" She bends towards a vessel that's overflowing with multicolored snapdragons, gently runs her hand through them while inhaling their scent.

"I found one!" Christina calls. "Come on!" She pushes open the gate of a sepulcher a few yards further down the terrace and vanishes inside it.

"Be my doorman, Billy?" Pascale laughs when they reach the sepulcher. She puts on an air of exaggerated sophistication—lifts her chin, brushes her hair from her temples with her forefingers, takes high steps.

"The honor's mine, ma'am," he says, holding the gate open.

"It's not as big on the inside as on the outside, but I think it's the best we can do," Christina says once all three are within what's about a five by six foot space, wider than it is deep.

"The better for bump and grind," Pascale says, rubbing against William.

"And bump and grind's the best for warming up," Christina adds, rubbing against his other side.

"And beautiful hair's my favorite toy," William says, gathering their hair and spilling it into their faces; as he does so the chrysanthemum blossoms fall from Pascale's hair onto the floor. "Sorry, I knocked your flowers off," he says, bending to pick them up.

"You definitely get punished for that," Christina laughs, winking at Pascale as she pokes him in the ribs on both sides at once.

"Ow!" William yells, jumping upright. "Alright girl, you want to play games? You mentioned the thrill of picturing vampires in your head: you ought to be careful what you picture, because the pictures might come to life! Open your skin and give me the liquid crimson I crave!" He grasps Christina by her shoulders, fastens his mouth on her neck, makes slurping sounds.

"Ha ha ha!" shrieks Christina. "You're just tickling! Stop!"

"Tickle you both!" chimes in Pascale, directing her fingers towards their stomachs. Christina and William instantly spring apart, slap her hands away.

"Vampires aren't choosy!" William says as he backs Pascale up to the wall and pins her against it. "Any girl's blood will do!"

"Turn your back to me, will you, as if I'm a negligible threat? What an insult!" Christina cries as she pokes at William's ribs again, causing him to release Pascale.

"Got a stake, Chrissy?" Pascale asks, taking advantage of the opportunity to circle around to William's back as he reaches for Christina's wrists. "We must rid all good people of the scourge of the undead! Hurry! The stake!"

"I stake my claim on you, tasty maid!" William says, twisting around and planting his mouth on Pascale's breastbone.

"Careful, Billy," Pascale says as she slides her hands under his untucked shirt, lightly draws her nails across his chest. "Wildcats are as dangerous as vampires, especially when they need to sharpen their claws!"

"Is that supposed to be a scratch?" William taunts. "Just can't bring yourself to follow through and claw me, can you? All empty threats and bluster, no cutting edge!"

"Is that so?" Pascale counters while positioning all ten nails upon his skin with arched fingers. "Just say one more word, and the tearing starts! Mock me again, if you dare!"

"Maybe I'm a cat too!" Christina laughs, slipping her hands under the back of his shirt. "I don't need to sharpen my claws—they're ready to go!"

"Christ! Look at that hairy spider!" William yells, shaking with revulsion. As the girls freeze and glance about in alarm, he laughingly scoots from between them.

"Oh, ho ho!" Christina shouts. "Big man scaring girls with fake sightings of spiders! What a cheap cowardly trick! Don't be too proud of yourself!"

"You should've seen your faces—ha ha ha!" William's laughing too hard to be fully coherent. "Pas almost—ha ha! What a picture—the worry! And—ha ha! because of a little spider! As if you're squeamish grade schoolers! Just like—ha ha! the time..."

"Don't get too comfortable," Christina cuts in, narrowing her eyes. "We'll make you regret that shoddy cry-wolf tactic, get'cha good and proper, before the night's over! Count on it!"

"May the dead rise and devour us if we don't!" adds Pascale

"Oh, I'm soooo scaarrred!" William mocks.

"Why you..." Pascale begins.

"But, wait—just listen! It's funny! I want to tell it before I forget!" William interrupts, criss-crossing his hands by way of asking for a pause in their gaming. "That time—ha ha! Adrienne Heidion, in the third grade... I caught a big moth on the playground, brought it back to class! She's sitting at her desk, pretty and serene, in a frilly light blue dress with billowing folds! 'Hey Adrienne!' I say, 'Look at this!' and toss the moth into her dress—it's furiously beating its wings, trapped in the billows—looks like a big brown bat! And did she scream! Ha ha ha! I can still hear her! Finally the moth flew up at the ceiling, flapped against it! Adrienne treated me to a priceless look of fury and reproach!"

"You evil child!" says Pascale. "Picking on girls! You sure haven't changed!"

"Well, I got in trouble for it—had to stay after school for a week. Rather severe for a harmless prank."

"Adrienne's fright wasn't harmless—she probably saw big brown scary flying things in her dreams for a week!"

"Her dad was our dentist—treating her to that prank could've been risky. I'm sure she told daddy all about it."

"Her dad was your dentist, and you *pranked* her?" says Christina, widening her eyes. "Say hello to stealth malpractice!

Daddy would know how to set up a delayed tooth problem, as in undermining their foundations with a number of hairline cracks! Don't be too surprised if your teeth crumble to dust someday!"

"It's not like anyone else is exempt from the same fate," answers William. "The family that's interned here, for instance. *(He traces his fingers along the names engraved on one of the walls.)* What do you think they look like now, when the last one—let's see—departed for the great beyond in 1909? Dust is our shared destiny!"

"Oh, no you don't!" Christina laughs. "I get to sermonize this time! I want to do a temporality-of-life lecture! a better-live-now-because-a-body-doesn't-last-long lecture! a futility-of-outdistancing-time lecture!"

"I wasn't going to give any lectures, but obviously *you* want to—the floor's all yours," he says, bowing.

"Sure, Chrissy," Pascale says. "If you want to preach, we'll be your congregation. Just don't be boring, or..."

"Or what?" Christina cuts in, flicking at Pascale's hair.

"All right, I apologize," Pascale says, curtsying to Christina with something of an evil grin. "It's just that we were playing, and now there's this lecture interruption!"

"Hey!" Christina shouts. "You listened to Billy's story, so you're going to listen to me! Both of you are! I invoke the right we all have to halt our goings-on when one of us wants to be heard!"

"Point taken," Pascale says, erasing the grin from her face. "Besides, this tomb's a nice chapel, appropriate for a sermon—it even has an altar." She's referring to the high white marble lid of the vault that spans the width of the tomb opposite the entry gate. A figure has been sculpted upon it, that of an aged man in eternal rest on his back with his wrists crossed over his stomach.

"As you said earlier," William laughs, "advantageous placement heightens the impact of lectures. Why not climb onto the altar?"

"Good idea! Boost me, please?" Christina says, placing her hands on the vault. Assisted by William, she climbs onto the sculpted figure's stomach, where she positions herself in the cup formed by the crossed arms. "Alright, pay attention kids! This man upon whose likeness I sit could be the founding father of this family—maybe he purchased this tomb. He's buried at or near the bottom of the heap, depending on who passed on first, and is literally the foundation of succeeding generations—the bodies stacked above his body."

"How do you know that?" Pascale asks. "That could be anyone on the lid."

"Quiet!" Christina yells. "It doesn't matter if it's him or not, I'm assuming so for the sake of making a point concerning the brief amount of time we have to live, and our unavoidable destination! Every moment is the most precious thing we have and should never be taken for granted, because in a flash all our moments will be taken away! We're here tonight, confronting our mortality while having fun! The juxtaposition of the dead with our fun makes us appreciate our fun all the more! As in times past when symbols of the dead, or the dead themselves, were present at banquets to help people appreciate the time they had together!"

"That still happens," William says. "A friend in college worked in a funeral home, and held a Halloween party there—he had the key, let everyone in after midnight. At one point he wheeled a body out of the freezer, one that hadn't been prepared yet, wrapped in clear plastic, all scrunched up on a wheelchair—a very compelling representative of death. Some girls started screaming."

"Is your whole life one long persecution of girls?" Christina asks, swinging a leg in his direction.

"Only the high points," William laughs. "Anyway..."

"I don't want to hear it!" Christina yells. "Now, to continue... This man here, who I'm assuming is the founder of this family: what's he now? Exhume him and open his box: what's to be found? A skeleton—moldering dust! And this man once walked proud, worked hard to establish his family—perhaps fought in a war, started a business. While among the living he took measures to ensure that future generations would be able to come here and see his name and those of his loved ones engraved upon this wall. But what's his grasping at posterity availed him? Posterity's an illusion, false consolation for our temporal state! This man's the stuff of dirt now, as we will be sooner than it seems! My great grandmother says the years whirl by with increasing speed the more they add up and that the older one gets the more it seems like childhood happened yesterday. 'Time's a deceptive beast!' she says. 'Flaunt it while you've got it!' she says. 'Life's too short to fret about what others think!' she says. She's... "

"My God!" interrupts Pascale. "The eloquent Miss Alari's weighty words affect me to such a degree I'm compelled to feel for my arm to confirm I'm still a creature of flesh and blood! Her superior wisdom inspires me to take advantage of this arm while it's still young and athletic, firm with muscle-tone—inspires me to pick up this twig, and pelt her! *(She retrieves a twig from the floor, tosses it into Christina's hair.)* And, following more of wise Chrissy's advice, I'm *not* going to fret about what she thinks about it!"

"Think about this!" Christina shouts. Gathering a handful of the leaves that have accumulated between the lid of the vault and the wall of the tomb, she springs to the floor and stuffs them down the front of Pascale's t-shirt. "Are you still *not* fretting, Pas?"

"Leaves bulging out of the top, sticking to your hair! You're a wood-nymph!" laughs William.

"Let's see how fast time whirls when I'm...!" Pascale yells, her voice dissolving in mirth. She's shaking the leaves from her shirt, semi-dancing, laughing; she's makes as if to attack Christina, but starts laughing harder instead. Finally, she says amidst giggles: "I like how her great grandma appeared from out of nowhere, and hijacked her lecture!"

"Alright, Miss Oration, you have a go!" challenges Christina. "Show us what you've got! *(She mockingly bows to Pascale, extends her arms towards the lid of the vault.)* The chair's all yours, honey!"

"Sitting up there's too contrived," says Pascale. "Too false and stagey!"

"What's the matter?" taunts Christina. "Can't put your mouth where your mockery is? Going to wilt under pressure, try to wheedle out of it with a transparent excuse? *(She imitates Pascale's voice and manner.)* Going on the tomb's too fake! It's *stagey!*"

"Pas, certainly you're not going to let that pass?" asks William.

"Either have at it, or apologize and concede victory to me!" says Christina, slapping at Pascal's shoulder.

"Think you can bait me into it? Think I'm a manipulable fool?"

"Pas surrenders!" announces Christina, making self-congratulatory gestures.

"Of course," answers Pascale with a dismissive wave, turn towards the gate. But then she wheels about. "Look!" she shouts as she tousles her hair, then lifts her t-shirt to her neck. "Listen! There are women asleep in these tombs who were once fit and toned nubiles, like yours truly! They were once able to slip their shirts over their heads and slide their skirts down their legs, like this! *(She removes her t-shirt and skirt.)* They were once able to gaze fondly into the eyes of their men and brighten with desire; once able to join their lips to other lips and drink of bliss; once able to... Ooooo!" She breaks off, backs up to give herself enough room, then executes a couple eye-high kicks. "OK," she resumes speaking, "so where are these women now? Worms have gotten the better of them! Time's erased... But this is silly! Come on, let's go back to playing!"

"And so the Pascale School of Oration is: excuse to do a tease-routine!" William laughs. "A-plus for visuals, C-minus for consistency of subject matter!"

"What subject?" asks Christina. "All I heard was blather about glances and kisses, a middling mention of dead girls, and a highfalutin' opinion of herself! *(She pauses to loosen the thin fabric-belt at her waist, then pulls her dress over her head.)* As if disencumbering oneself of a dress is a big deal!"

"Here, have your leaves back!" shouts Pascale, bending to gather some of the leaves scattered about the floor.

"Nah, nah! None of that!" says William, yanking her upright. "Forget about your differences, you two, and focus on what you agree on!"

"What I think we both agree on," Christina says, slinging her dress across the legs of the figure on the vault, "is that if we're going to strip to our underwear, you are too! None of this double standard fully-clothed-male-surrounded-by-skantily-clad-nymphettes stuff! Let her go, and get that shirt off!"

"Why is it no nighttime visit to Père Lachaise can be considered complete without a disrobing?" William asks, as if genuinely puzzled, while starting to remove his shirt and pants.

"It's contamination from gothic novels," Pascale laughs, also tossing her skirt and shirt onto the vault. "It's because we all like *The Monk*! It's because nothing drives home the contrast between us and the dead more than us showing off our attributes, that the dead no longer possess! It's because it's *fun*!"

"Actually, I think it's healthy rebellion against being systematically separated from awareness of the natural world by civilization," William says. "It's another way of reminding ourselves we're perishable and that we'd better live full lives, uncontaminated by media infiltration! The commercial interests that regard us as little more than sources of income, raw resources to be exploited for labor and money, are doing their best to distract us from our mortality and addict us to the distraction! Facing off with death undermines their glitter-show, frees us from needing it! We have better things to do than be blinded and victimized by the conspicuous consumption treadmill!"

"OK, sweetie," Pascale says in a sympathetic tone, patting him on the back as he bends to put his hiking boots on again, his pants having been removed. "Now that you've gotten the obligatory lambasting of the evil modern world out of the way, you can surrender yourself to a good time, right?" Then she turns to Christina, begins combing her hair with her fingers, and says, "Let's get those kinks out, sweetie."

"In all seriousness, darling, you put Demosthenes to shame with your speech," says Christina, returning the finger-comb favor.

"Yours was a very vivid, entertaining, and enlightening lecture," says Pascale, kissing Christina on the cheek.

"You both scaled the heights of eloquence!" William adds.

As if the three of them are hearing the same silent voice they cease speaking and join hands in a circle, gaze upon one another with deep affection. For a couple minutes they savor their mutual regard, communicating solely via gentle hand-pressure and the looks in their eyes. Then, still as if with a united will, they slowly unwind their fingers, allow their arms to drop to their sides, and step apart smiling.

"Look how our shadows flit about the vault, tremble on the walls," says Pascale, breaking the silence. "Think they're speaking to the shades of the dead?"

"Ooooo!" Christina exclaims. "The thought of our shadows talking to ghosts without our knowledge is good for a nice shiver! I like that! As for the more physical variety of shivering, it seems I've forgotten to be cold—never mind that my dress is on the patriarch instead of me! Ha ha ha!"

"Speaking of our host," Pascale says, bending to retrieve the trampled chrysanthemum blossoms from the floor, "I think we should thank him for his hospitality with a flowerpetal shower!" She hands one of the blossoms to Christina, who imitates her by pulling the petals from it and tossing them onto the vault.

"We need more flowers!" William shouts. "Let's carpet the floor!"

"A flower ceremony!" Pascale yells, clapping as she follows Christina outside while William holds the gate open.

"We're wearing next to nothing in the open air," Christina laughs, facing the wind and thrusting her chest at it while fluffing her hair. "And guess what? This is too wonderful for chilliness to get in the way! My blood's racing, keeping me warm!"

Laughingly darting from one planter to another on the terrace of tombs, as well as pilfering from a few recently placed bouquets, they gather an assortment of flowers—snapdragons, tulips, lilies, marigolds, chrysanthemums, geraniums—and return with them to their temporary shelter. "A kaleidoscope rain!" Pascale says as they start tearing the blossoms apart, throwing them in all directions. Soon the floor's covered with multicolored flowerpetal confetti.

No sooner are they finished dispersing the petals, than they're scooping up handfuls of them and flinging them at each other. Shortly Christina and Pascale, giggling like little girls and constantly brushing their hair from their eyes (it falls into them each time they bend down for more ammo), gang up on William, who begins frantically raking at the floor with his fingers, scattering whirls of petals in their direction. Finally, fairly winded, they're seated in a circle on the floor. William starts laughing.

"What's so funny?" Pascale asks. "Are you laughing at us?"

"Absolutely not—don't think that for a second," he responds. "I'm laughing because I can't believe I'm here doing this stuff—that I'm in a tomb at night with two nearly naked beauties, and with flowers all over the place! It's laughter of appreciation and wonder! Listen: you've said in the past that you're happy being girls, and don't envy men one bit? I say that if for five minutes you could be a man looking at girls like yourselves, then you'd never want to be a girl again, because it's as close to heaven on earth as anyone can get!" Leaning forward, he softly caresses their cheeks.

"This is why we love you, Billy," Pascale says, grasping and squeezing his hand.

Dearest reader, we shall respectfully withdraw and allow our friends an interval of privacy. About half an hour later they reclothe themselves and bid the tomb adieu. They stroll to the stairs which bisect the terraces, complete the short climb to the top, and turn left onto a path. Noting that the wind's not only stronger, but punctuated by frequent gusts, William says, "We could be in for a storm."

"Let it come," Christina smiles, lifting her arms to the sky. "I'm ready!"

CHAPTER 4

William's observation concerning the likelihood of a storm has been proven accurate: lightning's slashing across the sky, thunder's booming, and it's raining furiously. Where are our friends? They're on their backs on the circle of lawn at Rond-Point Casimir Perier, one of the largest open spaces in Père Lachaise; the bronze statue of Casimir Perier towers above them from its place atop his massive white stone tomb, situated in the center of the circle of lawn. In fact, the Rond is a circle within a circle within a circle: a wide cobblestone walkway, then the lawn, then the wrought iron fence which surrounds Casimir Perier's tomb.

"Ooooo!" coos Christina as she twists against the grass while making slow snow-angel movements with her arms and legs. "How the splash of the rain tickles and excites me—such an invigorating touch, at once electric and ethereal, the raindrops have! What a stirring lover the storm is! It's like the boundaries of my body are dissolving and I'm about to soar into the lightning flashes, unite with the storm's elemental beauty, whirl forever in charged mist!"

"A-woo!" Pascale yells, flinging her arms outward as she lifts her legs towards the sky, rhythmically opens and closes them; then she folds her legs against her chest and wraps her arms around them, grasping opposite elbows. "Sir Storm's reaching through my clothes as if they aren't here, spinning wind and rain over every inch of my skin, massaging me to the ends of my nerves and turning me inside out, flowing me across the lawn! Tingles whip through me in time to the wind's undulations and it's like I'm about to drift into an unending sigh! Ravish me to your heart's content, Sir Storm! Molest me until I forget my name!"

"Thank you, Sir Storm, for deeming us worthy of your attention!" Christina continues, running her hands up and down the sides of her torso while continuing to massage her back against the lawn. "Thank you for expending your delicious fury upon us and energizing us! I'm naked before my God, and my God's the infinite sky!"

"Wee-o!" Pascale cries, rolling onto her right side in fetal position. "I'm a baby again, Sir Storm, so take advantage of me! Plunder me, consume me, use me up! I'm all yours!"

"Ever your willing suppliant maidens, Sir Storm!" Christina adds. "Baptize and rebirth us! In the healing power of unexplored vistas we trust!"

"But you're very quiet, Billy," Pascale says, turning towards him. "Have you fallen asleep?"

"You're kidding, right?" William laughs, stretching his arms towards the sky. "I'm admiring the storm's beauty, and the lightning in particular—thrilling to the magnificent show Mother Nature's putting on! I was thinking what a windfall of the unexpected, icing on the cake, the storm is! Here we are in Père Lachaise on our first night in Paris, and we're treated to an unforeseen bonus! The Gods truly love us tonight!"

"Bonus is right," Christina says, rising to her knees and flinging her soaked hair in front of her; then she tosses it behind her head, shakes herself, and happily gazes about. "Immeasurable power and stunning visuals in equal measure! The lightning's shattering the dark so steadily we don't need headlamps! What energy!"

"Look at the grass writhing in the splintering light," William says, turning his head in all directions while remaining on his back. "Look at the trees dancing insanely around us on the perimeter of the circle! What strength in those branches swiping at the sky! What a roiling ocean of motion! And the gusts are getting stronger! This is what I call medicine!"

"Shimmy-shimmy trees, dance to the beat of the rain!" chimes in Pascale, also rising to her knees. "Come lightning-light, shimmer in our hair, bathe us in silver! You two look like flickering ghosts!"

"And so do you!" Christina laughs. "But we don't feel like ghosts, do we? Ghosts don't have surging blood, sparkles racing up and down their spines, energy tingling to their fingertips!"

"Speaking of ghosts," William says, pointing at the statue of Casimir Perier. "Look at the president's robes swirling to life in the shifting light! It's like he's about to float down on the wind and join us!"

"Maybe he can join us in a game of tag," Pascale says, rising to her feet. "The lawn-circle's the boundary!" She taps William, gleefully says, "You're *it*!" and races giggling to the other side of the tomb.

Christina, eager to avoid being tagged by William, stands and begins to run too abruptly and slips on the rain-soaked grass, although she manages to remain on her feet. William, quick to capitalize, lunges towards her while rising from his back, shouting, "Now you're it!"—a premature declaration, on account of the fact he also slips and finds himself sprawled on his side: she just manages to elude his outstretched hand.

"Aw, did we fall down?" Christina laughingly calls over her shoulder as she hastens to join Pascale.

William, rising to his feet and circling around the fence that encircles the tomb to tag one of his friends, finds himself again stunned by the beauty of the scene: the tombs flicker-flashing on the hill beyond as trees writhe about them; the figure of Casimir Perier towering above him; the wind flattening his friends' dresses against their lithe bodies as they regard him with charming looks of apprehension, ready themselves to flee. "I still can't believe we're here doing this!" he yells. "It's all exaggerated, wild and ancient and strange! It's Paris and Père Lachaise and we're Americans, in here running around! And you two are gorgeous, illuminated by the lightning!"

"Why thank you," says Christina, warily watching him while curtsying. "We're your rainstorm girls, and... Oh no, you don't!" she shrieks as William darts at her.

"He almost suckered you with flattery!" Pascale shouts from about ten yards further away.

But no sooner is William closing in on Christina than a loud crash, different from that of thunder, is heard; turning in its direction, our friends perceive a large branch has been torn from a tree by the storm and landed partially within the circle of grass, not far from where they were running moments ago.

"My God!" Christina yelps, stopping in her tracks.

"Silly us, we haven't been paying attention!" Pascale says, joining the other two as they back away from the perimeter of the lawn, huddle near the fence at the base of Casimir Perier's tomb.

"Stupid us, you mean," William says, "and stupid me most of all! I brought you here, and am responsible for getting you out! I shouldn't have been too busy playing to be mindful of the danger of these storm battered trees! Look at the size of that branch—it's over half a foot thick! We could've been standing there! The Gods love us tonight in more ways than one! They've let us off with a warning, one we'd better heed! We should think about leaving, going back to Steph's! You'd be insane to trust me again if I didn't get you out of here safe!"

"Of course we trust you, Billy," Christina says with fervor, "and always will!"

"Don't doubt it for a second," echoes Pascale. "We know we're in good hands! We wouldn't be here otherwise, and we know you know that! And, besides, don't exaggerate: we all knew better than to stand under those trees! If I'd tried it, you would've told me to stop being a fool! A limb fell on the edge of the grass? We weren't exactly lingering there! In fact, I don't think we ran that close to the edge! I don't think you were correct when you said we could've been standing there!"

"Good point, Pas," Christina says. "We weren't running that close to the edge! So Billy, don't be berating yourself for failing to look out for us when it's unwarranted! And as far as that goes, you know better than to think of Pas and I as helpless little girls, unable to be as responsible for you as you are for us! We're *all* equally responsible for each other! We trust you implicitly, as I'm sure you trust us! Shame on you for seeking to appropriate all the responsibility! We're *all* going to get each other out of here safe!"

"Exactly," Pascale says. "Thanks for spelling it out, Chrissy! Billy, we love you to death and appreciate the chivalry, but we're adults and are here of our own accord and watching out for you too!"

"Of course I trust both of you, as I'm honored to be trusted by you, and know we're in this together," William says, bowing. "I could never be best friends with helpless little girls: I've never considered you such, and never will! But you already know that, right?"

"Yeah, we know that," Christina laughs, curtsying.

"And you're right," William continues, "we weren't brazenly ignoring the perils of the tossing trees. And as for peril, when it's intermingled with beauty: what's more invigorating? The storm's a miracle in the sky, an onrush of delight, but it feels no kindness towards us and doesn't care if we're alive or dead! Look at all the debris that's scattered about! I don't mind conceding victory to Mother Nature! There's no dishonor if *she's* the one that shortens our stay!"

"I agree one hundred percent," Pascale says. "I say we go out on a high note, before we start to get cold!"

"Exactly," William says, "The thrill of riding our energy, being sustained by excitement, can only last so long. We're puny humans, and sheer emotion can only extend our physical limits so far. Face it: we're soaked to the bone, in wet clothing, with no means of drying off, so let's not be idiots. Hypothermia can strike quickly and it's a stealthy beast—one isn't always aware of it taking effect. And, besides, leaving during the storm will be more fun than leaving after it's over, right? Plus we have no idea how long it's going to last."

"Why don't we fortify ourselves with food and water, then get going?" Christina suggests.

"Absolutely," Pascale says as they, while warily watching the tossing trees, advance to the small tomb where they've stored the remainder of their provisions. The tomb's situated close to where the circle of the Rond intersects with Avenue de la Chapelle.

There's only room for them to stand inside this second tomb, at best a three by three and a half foot space; the one distinguishing feature of its interior is a cross, engraved on the wall that faces the entrance. Despite the tight squeeze they remain inside it while sharing a wedge of brie and having a handful of strawberries and figs apiece. While eating, they take turns draining a liter of water. After they finish their snack William extracts the soaked map of Père Lachaise from his pocket, unfolds it, and flattens it against one of the walls. "Hey, not bad," he says, "the ink's barely running. Anyway, here's our route: down Avenue de la Chapelle that's right outside here, then left on Avenue Latérale du Sud and down its stairs until we're able to cross over to Avenue Principale, where there won't be any danger of being brained by falling branches."

"And then straight to the wall, and right on over it," Pascale laughs. "I'm going to enjoy negotiating mist obscured pathways, keeping out from under huge trees, on our way out of here!"

"The last phase of our adventure," Christina smiles, "during which we show deep respect for the forces of nature while enjoying the show nature's putting on! A graceful bowing out, while our blood's racing for sheer joy! We'll be as alert as rabbits being hunted by coyotes, and also as delirious as rabbits helping themselves to the bounty of an unguarded garden! As you said, Billy, what's more invigorating than danger intermingled with beauty? Not much!"

"Right," William says. "We're not being chased out of here, we're electing to leave so we can experience the thrill of doing so during the height of the storm! And also because Steph's throwing a party, and his parties are worth attending! Are we ready?"

"I sure am," Christina says, opening the gate and stepping outside.

"Yeah, I'm getting claustrophobic and need open space," Pascale says, not hesitating to follow.

After tossing the last of their trash and what little remains of their food in a nearby dispenser (there are several at the Rond), they turn onto Avenue de la Chapelle and begin their journey. Wide by Père Lachaise standards and for the most part flanked by small trees, Avenue de la Chapelle is an easy leg of their journey. It's not until they turn left—that is, south—onto Avenue Latérale du Sud that they're faced with large trees, a row of them on their right.

"All right," William says. "I say we go right under these trees, from trunk to trunk. Branches are less likely to fall close to the trunk, because the other branches deflect them."

Immediately tending to business they dart under the trees. At the third one, they stop and survey their surroundings.

"An optical illusion," William laughs. "In the lightning splintered darkness and rain this row of trees seemed to go on forever, but there are only three of them! I *love* this wild disorientation!"

"Our headlamps are next to useless," Christina says. "The rain reflects the beams back at us, same as car headlights in dense fog! If it wasn't for the lightning we'd be close to blind!"

"Here," Pascale says, "hug the tree trunk! Feel the power of the storm coursing through it? Hear it creaking? It's as if it's about to be torn out by its roots!"

"Unfortunately, that's not far fetched," William says. "The steps start here—let's go! But crouch low, the gusts are really whipping through this opening! *(He gestures at the bare plot of grass to their right.)* We don't need to be blown down the stairs!"

"More trees ahead," Pascale says. "See them?"

"I see them, all right," he answers. "No choice. We go down these stairs first, then under those trees until we can cross to the main avenue. We'll soon be in the clear."

The stairs turn out to be two stairways, neither of them longer than fifteen steps, separated by a flat area of three or four yards. Once the bottom of the second stairway is reached William's laughing again, albeit while continuing to advance at a quick pace. "Talk about sensory distortion—short distances seem like football fields!"

"It's the churning mist effect," Pascale says. "Because we can't see far through it, we overcompensate and add features and distance that aren't there!"

"How much further ahead before we cut over?" Christina asks. "We're under the worst kind of tree, you know!" She's referring to the tall trees on both sides of the path at this point, the thick limbs of which don't begin fanning from their trunks until about fifteen feet from the ground and loom directly above them, swaying wildly.

"Very aware of it, dear—straight ahead a bit more, then it's through the tombs on the right to get out from under these monsters!"

Following ten or so more yards, they turn from the path and are soon surrounded on all sides by tombs; taking care to avoid the larger of the trees on their way through, they shortly emerge onto the wide and safe Avenue Principale.

"Damn!" William exclaims as soon as they're standing in the center of Avenue Principale, not far from where it intersects with Avenue du Puits. "These gusts are whirling part of the storm skyward, flinging it back at itself, before it hits the ground! The rain's spinning in whirlwinds instead of streaking!"

"Whirlwinds is right," Christina says. "No sooner do I lean into the wind than it switches direction and shoves at me from behind, in the direction I'm leaning! It's swishing in all directions, trying to knock us down! And yet if I twist hither and thither and keep moving, like this, the wind has a harder time grabbing me! I can dance with it, slide through it like a rudder! Wee! I love rolling with the wind's contours, sweeping through the moving architecture of the air! The wind's the perfect dance partner!" She skips sideways a couple yards, twirls about, then skips in another direction and continues doing so, steadily moving in the direction of the front gate.

"Sir Storm knows how to dance, all right!" Pascale says as she extends her arms over her head, widens her stance, and undulates her hips while gazing skywards. "He grabs me all the way to the marrow of my bones, unites my heartbeat with the churning sky! He... Ahh!" she yelps as a gust nearly knocks her backwards and she scampers to remain on her feet. "But Sir Storm can get a little rough!" she laughs, proceeding to execute a sequence of kicks while turning in all directions. "You're right, Chrissy! We have to keep an eye on him! He doesn't want us to stand still!"

"The storm's shortened our stay, but intensified it," William says, turning away from the front gate to face the larger part of Père Lachaise, "and I'll take quality over quantity anytime! Seeing the lightning flash in the forest of sepulchers, being intoxicated by the storm as it seeks to cut us to the bone and break us—not to mention our trip here from the Rond, negotiating wind-tossed trees as debris flies in blinding rain! How many people have had a night like this?"

"Not many," Pascale says, sidling up to him and wrapping an arm about his waist. "I know I speak for Chrissy too when I say you've treated us city girls to a stirring taste of raw nature in the most beautiful cemetery on earth! It's a night we'll never forget, and we thank you!"

"From the bottom of our hearts, we thank you," Christina affirms, stepping to his other side and likewise wrapping an arm around him. "And just think: of all the people in Paris, we might be the only ones here! I don't know for sure of course, but I tend to doubt Jim's guard stands watch in this kind of weather! Who else but New Yorkers would be nuts enough to still be in here? We're in the center of Paris, but on our own against the elements! How *healthy* it is!"

"It's an inoculation of strength like no other!" William yells, raising a fist to the sky. "A vacation from falsity and lies! We humans aren't supposed to spend our lives in a state of constant isolation from direct perceptions of natural forces! For most of our species' time on earth, before this modern civilization aberration, we tasted of the untamed majesty of nature every day and were stronger and wiser because of it! Only strength can come from taking our true measure against nature, and the fury of a storm! And we'll get over the wall safe, count on it! We'll be careful, and... All right, let's go!" After kissing each on the cheek and extracting himself from their arms, he turns about and starts walking towards the front gate again.

"A-woo!" Pascale shouts, dashing ahead.

Soon the three of them are on Avenue de Boulevard, the walkway which hugs the length of the front wall of Père Lachaise, at the point where it intersects with Avenue Thirion: the main gate of the cemetery is less than fifteen yards away. William's retrieved the rope and gloves from where he concealed them under the planter near the tomb with the three circles, and is tying the rope around the trunk of the small tree that's in front of the same tomb.

"This is going to be interesting," Pascale says, glancing up and down Avenue de Boulevard. "The wind's stronger here!"

"Fierce and beautiful!" Christina exclaims. "The gusts are slamming into the wall, carrying the rain over it in tight spins! It's like a river's flying over the wall!"

"Yeah, it's *so* beautiful!" says William, having finished securing the rope to the tree and tossed the other end over the wall. "Beautiful and deadly! So listen: we're out of range of tall trees here so there's no worrying about falling branches and we're going to take our time. Once it's your turn to go over and you have the gloves on you keep both hands on the rope at all times, including leading up to when you're straddling the wall and preparing to descend. *(Seeing that Pascale's rolling her eyes and about to speak, he places a finger across her lips.)* Look, I know I'm stating the obvious but I'm covering it anyway, as much for myself as for you. You said it first: the gusts are fierce here. We're not taking any chances."

"Right," Pascale says. "I'm listening."

"OK, first," William resumes, extracting a plastic bag from his pocket, "Chrissy, give me your bangles and rings and, Pas, give me your rings and watch. I'm putting them in this bag along with my wallet so they don't limit our limberness or otherwise get in the way when we're descending the wall. After I'm down you'll toss the bag to me."

"Good idea," Christina says as she begins removing her bangles.

"Might as well add the credit card and our IDs," Pascale says, extracting them from the pocket of her skirt.

"All right," William continues. "I'll go down first, so I can both steady the rope for you as you descend and grab you once you're within reach. I'll throw the gloves back up here after I'm down. The rope has knots in it for foot- and hand-holds and you cling to it for dear life, grip it as firmly as you can, the whole way down because these gusts will be doing their damnedest to blow us off. OK, I know you know that. Are we ready?"

"Absolutely," Pascale says.

"Yes, sir," Christina echoes.

"Good night, Père Lachaise," William says, turning to gaze down Avenue Thirion and saluting. "I thank you for tonight's adventure! Until next time!" Then he places the gloves on his hands, grabs the rope, goes to the edge of the wall, and straddles it. "See you on the sidewalk," he smiles as he swings his leg over and commences descending. In less than ten seconds he's on the ground.

"It's easy!" he announces. "I'm putting rocks inside the gloves to weigh them down so I can toss them up there without the wind blowing them away! I'm going to throw them at the front of the three-circle tomb, so stand to the side! Ready?"

"Ready!" Christina shouts.

"One! Two! Three!" William yells, and throws the first glove. Then he repeats the process for the second one.

"Got them," Christina says. "I'm coming down next." She appears at the wall's edge and drops the bag containing their belongings to the ground; then she straddles the wall, swings her leg over, and begins her descent.

William barely has time to say, "Chrissy, be careful and take your time!" before he's enfolding her in his arms and easing her to the ground.

"Wee! That was fun!" she laughs, clapping. "Can I go back up and do it again?"

"No, you'll stay put!"

The gloves are thrown to Pascale and she's soon descending the rope. "Ooooo!" she squeals when she feels William's hands upon her, sliding towards her waist. Then she's on the ground, smiling from ear to ear, saying, "Let it never be said our Billy's unprepared! Coming down the rope was a breeze! Hanging suspended and knowing I was safe as the wind buffeted me... It was over too soon!"

"Glad you enjoyed yourself."

"And now we cross to the treeless side of the boulevard before walking to the metro, don't we?" Christina says. She's referring to the fact that Boulevard de Ménilmontant, like most boulevards in Paris, is lined with trees; in this case some of them are quite large. Curiously, although there are two more rows of trees on the traffic island, there are none on the boulevard's southern side.

"You got that right," William laughs, gesturing at the trees further down the sidewalk from where they're standing. "Not a chance are we running that gauntlet! Look at the downed limbs, all over the sidewalk and in the street!"

"At last," Christina says once they've crossed the boulevard and are huddled in a doorway, extracting their belongings—bangles, rings, IDs, watch, and wallet—from the bag and returning them to their customary places. "A breather!"

"Look out!" William yells as he thrusts himself between the girls and the sidewalk, presses them against the door of the building with his arms spread as gusts of wind spin around them. As he does so a rasping clattering sound is heard, then the sound's gone as quickly as it appeared. "Damn!" he continues, after releasing the girls and turning towards the sidewalk. "That umbrella's a deadly weapon! Smashed to pieces, but the webbing's a sail, and it's sailing around trying to stab people with the ribs! No sooner do we escape falling branches than city litter sets its sights on us! Time to hop on the metro, then you'll have your breather, Chrissy!"

"Sorry for speaking too soon and jinxing us!" Christina says.

"Don't be silly," Pascale says. "The storm doesn't care what we say or think! Anyway, we have plenty of time to catch the metro—it stays open until two fifteen on Fridays. It's only eleven forty-two."

"What about finding a cab?" Christina inquires.

"Think finding a cab's hard in New York on a rainy Friday?" Pascale laughs. "It's nothing compared to here, especially considering we're not exactly in the center of town! It could take hours!"

"Everyone have their stuff?" William asks.

"Every last piece," Christina smiles, lifting her arms and shaking them as her bangles side down her wrists. Then she darts from the doorway as William and Pascale follow.

Alternating between an extremely rapid walk and spurts of running while shielding their eyes with their hands, our three friends are soon stepping up to the Père Lachaise metro station entrance on the traffic island in the center of Boulevard de Ménilmontant, where it intersects with Avenue de la République and Avenue Gambetta.

"God, it's beautiful!" Christina says, running to the front of the traffic island and gazing out across the open space of Place Auguste Métivier. "I've been transported to an ancient city swathed in mist and rain! How is that the designs of the buildings and features of the streets—this café here, the entire atmosphere—pierce my nerves through and through, feel so close to the bone? How can it be so eerily familiar, when I'm a Brooklyn girl? I'm in a waking dream, surrounded by recollections from another life! Europe's always haunted me, been in my head!"

"Same here," says William. "All the reading I've done, from Boccaccio onwards: those stories stir recollections I'm not supposed to have, strum strings of recognition that..."

"Hey tourists!" Pascale interrupts. "Why don't you turn around and admire the *real* scenery!" When William and Christina do so they see she's opening the door of an empty cab on the north side of the boulevard with a wide smile on her face.

"It just pulled up to the light!" Pascale exclaims, bouncing up and down on the seat once they're all inside the car. "An empty in the 20th during a storm! What are the chances? The Gods are *definitely* on our side tonight!"

CHAPTER 5

Within twenty minutes our friends are entering the circa 1960s building at 225 Rue d'Alésia, near the western boundary of the 14th arrondissement. They take the elevator to the eighth floor and as soon as its door opens they hear music and boisterous chatter emanating from the apartment to the immediate left of it, number 811.

"Sounds cozy and toasty," Pascale says, jumping up and down. "I can do with some thawing out!"

"I don't mind admitting the exhilaration that kept me warm in Père Lachaise can do with reinforcements, as in a hot shower," William says as he inserts a key in number 811's door and turns it.

"Definitely," Christina agrees, vigorously shaking herself. "I was soaring on adrenalin in Père Lachaise, and now it's the crash landing! Brrrrr! Goose pimples and frozen bones!"

"Good thing we're wearing dark colors," Pascale laughs, glancing at Christina.

"Right! We're soaked, but not see-through!"

When our friends step inside the apartment what first catches their eye among the sea of people in the huge living room is the tall sinewy shirtless young man gyrating on top of the heavy oak dining table, champagne bottle in hand. The young man is their host, Stephan Fleury, an understudy at the Comédie-Française. William met him the previous spring, on his second visit to Paris. In William's words, as told to Christina and Pascale before their trip, they met as follows: "I'm on a chair by the circular pond in the Jardin des Tuileries, staring at the water. Steph comes up to me as if we're already acquainted, says in English, 'Why so glum, my friend?'—laughs at my surprise, says my nationality and frame of mind are as good as written in red letters on my shirt. Then he's saying, 'Mind if I sit here? I'm doing it whether you mind or not, because soon you won't mind.' I shrug my shoulders while glancing at the empty seat, uncertain if he's going to pester me for a handout or try to sell me something. But as soon as we're talking all apprehension's swept away in about two minutes; inside of an hour we know a great deal about one another, are carrying on as if we've known each other for years—it's such instant and easy camaraderie I'm not even surprised at the private things I'm confiding to a person I've just met. Then he's asking me if I'd like to attend a party in the 16th, and by then there's no question of me not embracing the suggestion. We bond further at the party, a tedious affair thrown by rich patrons of the arts who've invited members of the Comédie-Française: the actors—all friends of Steph's to whom I'm introduced—are their conversation pieces, means of breaking up the banality. During this party my new friends explain we have a right to extract payment for putting up with bores, and begin stuffing their coat pockets and a couple bags with food and drink. Happily imitating them, I pilfer as much as I can—we've thrown our coats in a corner near the front door and it's easy to add victuals to their pockets and the bags hidden underneath them while others of us form a human shield to prevent direct observation. Afterwards, we have our own party in the Bois de Boulogne with the filched delicacies; courtesy of the well-to-do dullards on Avenue Victor Hugo we enjoy a feast of smoked fish, caviar, salami, assorted cheeses, tropical fruit, and pastries under the stars in the forest, wash it down with cognac and single malt. Two days later I move from my hotel into Steph's place, and the rest is history."

As for Stephan, he's twenty-two years of age, six feet three inches in height, and has a curly brush-top of brown hair and dark jolly eyes. One of his guiding principles in life, regardless of whether he's aware of it, is to imbue the ordinary with the theatrical, lift the everyday towards a realm that's larger than life; given to frequently and vividly gesticulating as he speaks, he has a loud booming voice that carries well and easily fills up a room. Another of his guiding principles, of which he's very much aware, is to spend as much time with girls as possible, among whom he's immensely popular. At present he's keeping company with Lucinda Junot, who will be introduced later, but in general his bedroom door's a revolving one: seldom does a girl have an exclusive claim upon his attention for longer than a fortnight. Stephan's father, a state-funded artist, obtained apartment number 811 at a subsidized rent and unbreakable lease while raising his two sons; he has since moved to another neighborhood, leaving the apartment—two floors, living room, four bedrooms, three bathrooms, and kitchen—to his offspring. The other son is Didier, four years younger than Stephan. Didier presently sits with his girlfriend Antoinette on one of the living room couches, oblivious to all but her pretty face, which he's showering with kisses. They've been together for two years, with no sign of abatement. Didier has his brother's build but, at barely over six feet, not his height; likewise his hair's a bushy mop, but it's jet black instead of brown; he's about to complete his final year at the lycee.

"Welcome, my American friends!" Stephan shouts, handing the champagne bottle to William, who drains what little remains. "Damn rain ruined an excursion—we've got to compensate for being chased indoors, thumb our noses at bad luck and laugh!" Then, spreading his arms towards the assembled company, he yells, "Under the table, one and all! I won't hear of anyone sitting out the bout! Drink up! Drink all!" Then, after blowing everyone a kiss, he turns to the short chubby young man idling by the kitchen door, and says, "Panclerc, more wine! Yeah, you Panclerc! Fetch another soldier, bring him here! Line 'em up, shoot 'em down! Lots of dead soldiers tonight, bottles piling sky high!"

Panclerc reaches inside the kitchen door, grabs a bottle from the tub of ice on the floor, and brings it to Stephan, saying, "Another soldier, sir!"

"So what are you waiting for?" Stephan responds. "Open it, sir! Christen the bottle and have a swig before you hand it to me! Dead soldiers, Panclerc! That tub's going to be empty by dawn! All of 'em have a date with the firing squad!" Then, glancing at our friends and slapping his forehead he shouts, "Forgive me! The bubbly distracted me! At last we meet, my dears!" Jumping from the table, he embraces Christina and Pascale while kissing them on their cheeks. "Who's Pascale and who's Christina?"

"Pas here," says the owner of that name, lifting her hand.

"And I'm Chrissy."

"Chrissy and Pas, let's understand each other straightaway," Stephan smiles, placing a hand on each of their shoulders. "Any friend of Bill's is automatically a friend of mine, especially if they're as gorgeous as you are! You're not to be shy about helping yourself to my hospitality, or I'll be insulted! Is that clear?"

"Thank you," Christina says. "You're very kind."

"Thank you so much," Pascale says.

"The honor and pleasure's mine," Stephan continues. "Just remember you're part of the family, and take it in stride! There's..." His eyes suddenly widening, he interrupts himself, "But you're drenched like mice coughed up by cats! I know it's raining, but this is insane! You look like you fell in a lake!"

"Ha ha ha! Took you awhile before you figured it out!" William laughs. "How much have you had?"

"At least a bottle—maybe more!" Stephan answers, quickly adding, "But how long have you been sopping about?"—and again, while gesticulating towards the hallway, "Get back there! Hot showers and dry clothes will do you wonders! No one gets sick on my watch! I *refuse* to allow it!"

"But aren't you wondering how we got this way?" William asks.

"You can tell me after your showers," Stephan says. "Get changed first!"

"We were in Père Lachaise when it started raining," William says with a grin, "and stayed for awhile!"

"If it wasn't for the falling branches we'd still be in there," Christina chimes in, flicking her hair.

"Playing in the rain among the dead's a kick," Pascale adds, "but it's not something to do when the trees are being torn apart! Play leads to distraction, and distraction's not a good frame of mind to be in when limbs are crashing down all over the place! We didn't want to leave—we *had to* for safety's sake!"

"Highly annoying to have to wave bye-bye prematurely," Christina continues. "I had more respects to pay to the dear departed, and didn't get to see an exhumed body!"

"Ha ha ha! You're *still* playing!" Stephan laughs, looking the girls up and down with unaffected surprise. "An exhumed body! I'm half inclined to think you'd take evening tea beside one without batting an eye!"

"I didn't get a chance to find out," Christina responds. "The storm, though, *was* fun in its own right—I don't want to subtract from its brand of thrill! We had a nice run for it in the wind and rain and mist!"

"Debris flying every which where, trees groaning, furious gusts trying to blow us over!" William says. "We didn't plan it that way, but we'll take it! Oh, yeah! The perfect first night in Paris!"

"Your night's not over," Stephan says. "It's not going to be over until sunup at the soonest, and might last until noon! We don't waste our nights around here! But tell me more about Père Lachaise: how long were you there?"

Suffice to say that Stephan, curious enough to forget about chasing anyone into the shower for the time being, fires off a number of pointed questions; in answering them, our friends provide him with a vivid summary of their adventure. "Americans come to town, and they do something I've never done on their first night!" he laughs; then, turning to face the group and fanning out his arms, he yells, "Hey, everyone! Your attention please! First, I'd like to introduce you to three special bravehearted people, who'll be staying here for six weeks! William Bergen, Pascale Rosetourne, and Christina Alari—Bill, Pas, and Chrissy—from New York! Do please greet them! *(Shouts of approbation are heard.)* Second, I'd like to announce that they win the Wild Adventure Prize!"

"The Wild Adventure Prize?" asks someone in the crowd. "First I've heard of it!"

"Silence!" Stephan commands. "Speaking out of turn doesn't become you, Gui, especially when you're ignorant of the facts! Do not shame me, and dishonor our guests, again! Now, listen up everyone! These three were in Père Lachaise as the storm raged, while we stayed indoors! Huge branches were falling from the trees! Look! They're sopping wet, soaked to the skin, and will soon hit the showers! But before they temporarily leave us congratulations are in order! They were playing tag at Rond-Point Casimir Perier in the rain when a massive limb was ripped from a tree and just missed them! They were weaving among tombs in the stormy dark, then descended the wall close to the main gate on a rope! These girls did that! New York girls! Their reputation precedes them, and doesn't do them justice! I've never been in Père Lachaise at night during a storm! Has anyone? Hey, I'm asking! Has anyone been in Père Lachaise at night during a storm? *(Heads are shaken, a number of 'No!'s are heard.)* I thought not, so that's why our American friends get the Wild Adventure Prize, and I dare anyone to naysay it! I, for one, am in awe of their exploit and I don't awe easily, you all know that! Lift your glasses! Honor Bill, Pas, and Chrissy! *(Glasses are raised.)* Now I want to hear it loud and clear! Repeat after me: well done, fearless ones!"

Well done, fearless ones!

"Brave of heart and steadfast of soul, you consorted with the dead as nature raged!"

Brave of heart and steadfast of soul, you consorted with the dead as nature raged!

"For equanimity in the face of adversity in a foreign land, we unanimously award you the Wild Adventure Prize!"

For equanimity in the face of adversity in a foreign land, we unanimously award you the Wild Adventure Prize!

"Now, tip those glasses and do them honor! Hear! Hear!"

Hear! Hear!

Then, stepping behind our three friends and huddling them together as he wraps his arms around them, Stephan continues, "Look! The storm's rattling the windows! Heavy rain, thunder repercussions, high winds! It's no paltry sprinkle! It's a full-out tempest! Our dauntless three refused to call it quits when the skies opened up and wind howled! Alone in a storm in Père Lachaise! Again I say I'm stupefied with admiration!"

On account of abruptly sweeping his arms towards the ceiling in the heat of his emotion, Stephan loses his balance and stumbles sideways; righting himself with large stomping steps, he resumes, "Yeah, I've had some bubbly, but not enough! And you, my heroic American friends, have had none! So take your showers and put on dry clothes and rejoin us and guzzle! You'll meet everyone, I'll introduce you to your new admirers; and I'll be damned if we're not all doing sloppy sing-alongs by dawn! No rain spoils my night! All right, everyone, another round of applause for our graveyard scamps before they go!"

Cheers erupt as William, Christina, and Pascale stroll towards the hallway that leads to the bedrooms. Unable not to be self-conscious to some degree on account of the amount of attention they're receiving from people they don't know, but also undeniably elated, the girls content themselves with scampering down the hall laughing. William, to whom not all of the faces are unknown—he having met a number of those in attendance the previous spring—salutes the company before following the girls. As they reach their bedroom, one of the two largest, with an attached bathroom, they hear Stephan yell, "Holy bubbly! Drink up! Drink all!"

CHAPTER 6

We rejoin our three friends after they've showered and put on fresh clothes. The girls are wearing silk summer dresses—lavender with pink and dark purple floral patterns for Christina, scarlet with indigo polka dots for Pascale—and open toed pumps. William's wearing blue denim pants and an untucked black and gray striped dress shirt. They now reenter the crowded living room and approach Stephan, who's standing engaged in conversation with his back to them.

"The modern world's nothing but vicarious pseudo-life, the slick packaging of artificial experience!" they hear the young man, unknown to them, with whom Stephan's conversing half-shouting as they approach. "We're considered to be little more than zombie-entities to sell stuff to! What equal opportunity really means is that we all have an equal opportunity to be enslaved by an occupation, addicted to materialistic trash, and parasited upon by the media-corporate conglomerate! What equal rights really means is that we all have an equal right to be severed from our cultural roots, stripped of our individuality, and made desperate to fill the void—

an equal right to be tossed into the consumer-mix, conned into mistaking the purchase of useless trinkets for emotional fulfillment! I ask: what atrocious crimes did I commit in a previous life, such that I've been punished by rebirth into this nightmarish present, where organized psychic hijacking of all that's worth living for is the norm?"

"There's a new friend for you, Billy," whispers a bemused Pascale, referring to the young man.

"Hey Steph," William says, clapping a hand on Stephan's shoulder from behind.

"Hey hey!" cries Stephan upon wheeling about. "My cemetery romping friends, welcome! Hey Claire!" he calls. "Glasses for these three! Quickly, if you please!"

A tall redhead of voluptuous physique—with the appealing inward smile of contentedness which often characterizes such amply endowed women (as if they're serenely immersed in life's subsurface currents, happily overflowing with nature's bounty)—glances over and nods, deftly gathers three glasses from a long table alongside the wall, and cheerfully advances to distribute them.

"Sweet Claire, I present to you three fearless New Yorkers!" Stephan says, waving a bottle of champagne. "Claire the fair hasn't a care in the world!" he declares amidst the introductions, as embraces and kisses are exchanged. "Claire of the kind muted stare is as soft as her hair—and what hair, I do declare!" He gathers up a handful of Claire's wavy mid-back-length hair and swishes it across his face.

"Steph, you're embarrassing me," half-whispers Claire in a sensuous purr.

"Claire with-the-world-in-your-hair, I do not embarrass you!" he counters. "All small feelings drown and disappear in the bottomless well of your kindness and generosity! You can neither be embarrassed nor angry nor baffled! All that's paltry and unpleasant is disarmed by your sweetest of tempers, rendered harmless by your infinitely loving disposition! All..."

"Nice to meet you," interrupts Claire, addressing our three friends and dispensing smiles upon each, along with parting hand-clasps. "I must go!" She does a rapid one-footed about-face, prances off while raising her hair above her head and letting it fall.

"A wee bit proud, be our Claire the fair!" Stephan calls after her, before filling the three proffered glasses of our friends—a task he's no sooner completed than he announces, "All right, I'm off to the couch! Lucy's waiting! See you in the morning!" But then he checks himself and, seizing the arm of the young man he was originally conversing with, pulls him closer and says, "Before I go, my friends, please do make the acquaintance of Jean-Marc de Traille! Jean-Marc, do please warmly greet our guests of honor: William Bergen, Pascale Rosetourne, and Christina Alari! *(Hands are shaken and cheek-pecks are exchanged.)* And now, most respectfully, I bid you adieu!" he finishes with a bow. Before he's taken two steps, though, Stephan whirls about, hands the nearly empty champagne bottle to William, and says, "Respectably, Bill, I leave you this! Religiously, Chrissy, I leave you this! *(He kisses her.)* Reflectively, Pas, I leave you this! *(He likewise kisses her.)* Remarkably, Jean-Marc, I leave you this! *(He grasps him in a bear hug.)* And you too, my friend!" He hugs William forcefully enough to cause the latter's glass to tip and spill its contents—noticing which Stephan backs away with a look of shock, brings his hands to the sides of his head, and shouts, "Holy hell! The precious elixir's lost! Woebegone is me!" Still staring at the spilled champagne in apparent horror, he continues to clench his head and twist about; then, returning to himself to some degree, he yells, "More lifeblood elixir! More!" as he dashes to the kitchen and plucks a fresh bottle from the tub of ice on the floor. Returning while frantically undoing the wires at the bottle's top, he yells, "May the Gods forgive and bless us! May Dionysus return to rain his benevolence upon our humble gathering! Please Dionysus, I beg of you, do not forsake us! The insult was unintended! The spillage of the nectar was an accidental consequence of human frailty and imperfection, certainly forgivable! Please overlook our mortal shortcomings! Please vouchsafe us a second chance!" Stephan's really screaming at this point, such that many heads are turned in his direction—a circumstance of which he's perfectly aware and that he's certainly been endeavoring to bring about, as he doesn't hesitate to capitalize upon it by turning to face the room, lifting the bottle over his head, screaming even louder, "May Dionysus spring forth!" as the cork pops off and the fizzing overflow showers upon his face. "Yes! The good God forgives, shows forbearance! The good God infuses this room with his divine spirit and healing essence, drowns us in cheer! Hail the golden grape fluid, miraculous intoxication, holy revelry! I taste of it, I slurp it, I shout its glory! Drink up! Drink all! Honor our lord and master, Dionysus!" He bows to acknowledge the applause and shouts of approbation and is soon at William's side, refilling his glass. "And so," he yells anew, "the wrong has been rectified! The glass from which the precious balm was wastefully ejected is again filled to the brim, ready for quaffing! Drink up, my friend! *(William does as instructed.)* Yes, it's Godly and good and great! It's magnificently enlightening, multifariously glorious!" Then addressing our three friends and Jean-Marc in lower tones, "But now, fellow revelers, I must be off!" Stephan hands the bottle to Jean-Marc, wheels about with an arm raised in farewell, and strolls to the couch where Lucinda awaits him.

"So much for being introduced to everyone," observes Pascale.

"Lucy's trumped us!" laughs Christina.

"Assuming he can see straight enough to focus upon the said Lucy," says William.

"Steph never has courtship difficulties," contributes the recently met Jean-Marc. "He's gifted with courtship auto-pilot, unfailing in all circumstances. Drink never obscures the girls, and the girls never obscure his love of drink. The one feeds the other—a perpetual-motion machine."

But let us describe Jean-Marc: he's perhaps four inches shorter than William, about five feet nine; twenty-three years old, slender with bright lively brown eyes, high cheekbones, a wavy mane of black hair that reaches to his shoulders; of a pale complexion, as if he seldom sees much of daylight; extremely animated during conversations—constantly shifting from one foot to the other, gesticulating pronouncedly, occasionally stomping by way of emphasis; inordinately given to (as he's phrased it himself) "the gentlemanly occupation of putting bores out of countenance"; equally devoted to doing whatever he can to make the lives of his friends more amusing and the lives of his enemies more miserable. He's recently completed his law degree at Université de Paris 1, is presently undecided as to how to best apply it, and plans on having his mind made up by the end of the summer. Such is he whose observation regarding Stephan has caused William to laugh to the degree that he's unable to make an immediate reply.

"It wasn't that funny—merely an observation of fact," says Jean-Marc, beginning to laugh on account of William's laughter.

"Not as funny as people who take our emotionally whitewashed civilization seriously," William says with a grin.

"So you overheard me!"

"Indeed, I did, Mr. Traa... What was your last name?"

"de Traille. Hopefully, you won't regard my inclusion of the 'de' as being pretentious. Aside from the fact it's my real name, it's also a way of reminding myself of previous centuries, specifically the pre-revolutionary 18th, when aristocratic refinement hadn't yet been stamped out by puerile money-grubbing repression, value systems based upon capital gain."

"Yay!" exclaims Christina. "Billy's found a comrade-in-arms!"

"Right, male bonding in progress," chimes in Pascale, tugging on Christina's arm. "And as Steph's reneged on his introductions, let's find someone more obliging—Genevieve's over there. Bye Billy! Good to meet you Jean-Marc!" She starts pulling Christina towards the other side of the room.

"A pleasure!" Christina calls over her shoulder, having already been yanked a couple of steps.

"Good to meet you too!" Jean-Marc says before turning to William to hear his response to his explanation of the "de."

"Did Steph prep you on how to best bait me into believing I've encountered a fellow right-thinking individual, play a prank?" William asks. "Because I've also always felt I've been born too late to be at home in this world, get past an on-the-outside-looking-in frame of mind. I detest the see-a-film-instead-of-do-something manner of pseudofying experience—detest it like debilitation, disease! All this anti-life, emotional fraudulence!"

"Maybe Steph's briefed you for the purpose of setting me up for a joke!" laughs Jean-Marc. "After all, it's extremely rare to encounter our way of thinking in this atmosphere of share-all/share-alike anti-sophistication! Atmosphere of anti-refinement-of-taste! Anti-aristocracy-of-the-mind! Anti-cleverness! Anti-uniqueness!" he concludes at a volume just short of a shout.

"This atmosphere of enslavement to endlessly generated and manipulated information!" William also nearly shouts, thoroughly enjoying himself. "The tyranny of *being informed*, as if cramming one's head with inherently worthless facts is the equal of being overcome with wholehearted feeling! As if *being informed* is anything besides emotional corner-cutting—the means by which bloodless slouches persuade themselves they're caring and enlightened individuals when all they're doing is shallowfying experience, avoiding intensity as if it's the plague!"

Jean-Marc, also enjoying himself immensely, starts shouting in earnest. "This enervating atmosphere of easy-offendedness, the constant hedging of forthright expression! This disgraceful blandification of social interaction, triumph of emotionally sterile non-speak! Language is being systematically stripped of its emotional roots, redefined to carry zero reference to feeling! Instead of saying 'Drop dead gorgeous cutiepie!' we're supposed to say 'Appearance advantaged woman!' Instead of saying 'The maid's scrubbing the floor!' we're supposed to say 'The domestic engineer's managing the upkeep of my residence!' The sorry souls who spout such *approved* language are terrified of spontaneity and directness and are as good as dead!"

"What's the agenda of the powers that be?" continues William. "It's to systematically subject us to the spiritually anesthetized insipidity known as pop culture—dupe us into adopting stand-in personas dreamed up by ad agencies, media-fabricated self-images! It's to standardize our personalities, swindle us into trading our depths for an anti-existence of false-bottomed experience! It's to turn us into scared lemmings—make us want to sever ourselves from authenticity, fling ourselves to our psychic deaths! And as for sex and its glorious eruptive unpredictability... The powers that be want to reduce sex to mental masturbation at the feet of airbrushed fairytale creatures on billboards and magazine covers!"

Already delighted with one another's company (echoing their ideas off each other is like playing with a new toy), William and Jean-Marc become aware of having come to the notice of a number of the others, and start playing to the audience: it's icing on the cake.

"Sex?" shouts Jean-Marc. "The glorious extremes that the sex-drive thrives upon gravitating towards have been pared down to shoddy and mean-spirited marketing techniques—subverted to cheap product-endorsement come-ons! And pornography, far from being the atypical shadow-activity we're meant to believe, is the biggest multi-billion euro lust-poisoning sham there is! Pornography? Pah! What healthy hot-blooded male could possibly be titillated by patterns of light on a screen, fleshless photography on flat paper? I find it incredible grown men can be swindled into getting hot and bothered on account of such contrived moneymaking! As for me, I like to grab a real live ass of flesh and blood and shake it, like this! Shake-a! Shake-a! Shake-a! *(He acts out seizing a woman's posterior with his hands, jerks his arms up and down.)* Yeah, that's what I like—a real live panting female! Umm! Umm! Tits! Luscious tits! Plunge your face in, thrill to their softness, and blow bubbles! Bbbbb! Bbbbb! Bbbbb! *(He acts out grabbing a woman's breasts and thrusting his face between them, twists his head from side to side.)* I ask: how can pathetic films vaguely approximate real life touch and friction, a living and breathing girl's flushed body? Wave bye-bye to overt love of lust, rapture via sex-ritual! Intone a eulogy for the experience of dizzily turning inside out at the sight of your loved one naked, being overcome with joy at the thought of what divinely perverse impulses lurk below the beautiful contours of her face! Yeah, that's what pornography's designed to rob us of! Give me the pre-media world! Give me the pre-electronics world! Give me the 18th century, the art of seduction, rampant libertinage, de Sade!"

"De Sade!" William exclaims. "*Juliette's* one of the three books I've reread the most! And de Sade practiced what he preached—he'd lure girls to his basement, whip them senseless while in priest's garb! During his time the entire aristocracy was immersed in seduction-projects, swooning with inflamed imaginations—living for the moment when unbridled yearning would twist in their guts, scramble their nerves, drive them half insane! Imagine a whole ruling segment of society devoted to the noble activity of putting restraint to rout! How I'd love to lick the neck of an 18th century ingénue—as honey-voiced and doll-faced as she is ravenously focused on pleasure—on a swing in the winding maze of one of those manicured gardens; and then pull her to the lawn and unlace her whalebone stays, watch her slip deft as a cat from the voluminous folds of her dress; and then tickle her with a feather from her hat and further fire her up with a playful spanking; and then... Ha ha ha!" William's laughing too hard to continue.

"Such finely tuned pleasure-hungry refinement!" yells Jean-Marc. "As you wisely observed, an entire ruling sector of society devoted to the art of stimulating the opposite sex! The heights achieved by the 18th century in the language and practice of seduction have never been equaled! Just think: phones and email didn't exist! There wasn't any technology intruding on the exquisite agony of a drawn-out siege! Poor us, we'll never know what it's like to romance a girl with hand-delivered letters: the meticulous composition of turns of phrase designed to entice and entrap; the suspenseful wait for the post to arrive, desire being delayed for days or weeks on account of delivery difficulties! We'll never experience an epistolary pay-off, after enduring anticipation sharp enough to scramble our reason and untold storms in our imaginations! Imagine what one-on-one with a cutie in the 18th century would be like! Just think: there wouldn't be any Information Age chatter in our heads! No Internet, TV, or radio—broadcasts of any kind—would've tampered with our senses at any point in our lives! To bed down with a girl that free of modern manipulation, before electrical apparatus existed, and to be as free of such manipulation myself! I'll never have that experience, and it haunts me! I'd sacrifice virgins to have that experience! I'd feed newborns to lions to have that experience! I'd trade the rest of my life for one night of 18th century copulation!" Jean-Marc's jumping up and down when he concludes this speech.

"Hear, hear!" William shouts, pausing to quaff the last of the champagne in his glass; then he begins yelling with an upraised fist. "The aristocracy answered to no one and made their own laws, as only the truly great do! Consider the Marquis de Grenadine! He'd hire a carpenter to repair the roof of his love-chamber, then enter it to show his girl a good time: as the moment of consummation approached, he'd raise a pistol and shoot the carpenter through the roof—would yell in triumph at the sound of the pistol's report, as the room filled with smoke! The said carpenter's body would go *Klunk! Thunka-thunk! Thunka-thunk!*—fall on the shingles, and roll off the roof! The Marquis, experiencing heaven on earth, would be enjoying his girl in time to the sounds of the dead carpenter rolling off the roof! Now, I ask: is it possible for such exquisite refinement of taste to exist in a boring democracy? It isn't! No such laudatory expression of individuality has a chance to thrive in a demeaning government-by-peasantry! No originality! No genius! No fun!"

"Long live de Grenadine!" Jean-Marc shouts; then, eager to provide an example of his own, he continues, "And long live the Count de Sero-Laure! de Sero-Laure would—ha ha ha!" He wheels sideways with the force of the hilarity which overtakes him, clutches at the edge of the dining table, grabs a chair, and sits doubled over in it; then just as suddenly jumps up again, attempts to resume. "He'd—ha ha ha! Priceless!"

"Priceless!" William repeats, followed by several among their audience.

"Wait!" Jean-Marc calls out, raising his palms and placing them flat against the air in front of him, as if by this act to stabilize himself—a maneuver which apparently works, since he immediately succeeds in, so to speak, swallowing his laughter. "The Count de Sero-Laure," he recommences, "would dress himself in lion skins, with lion's paws for mittens and a big lion's head for a mask, and enter a cage—would crawl about in the cage while roaring, snarling, acting the part of a fierce angry hungry lion! Upon the deliverance of a prearranged signal, an attendant atop the cage would raise the door, after which the fun-loving Sero-Laure would race from the cage and pounce upon naked girls tied to stakes distributed about the room—untie them, wrestle them to the floor, take his pleasure with them one after another while still roaring! After amusing himself in this manner for a few hours he'd traipse off to the dining area, eat and drink himself into a stupor! The following afternoon he'd awaken eager to repeat the performance—he'd carry on thus for days on end! Just think! An endless enthralling cycle of expenditure and recovery—a new bevy of beauties every evening for him to run wild in, nights spent in delicious post-satiation dazes with the pleasure-moans of a dozen girls lingering in his senses! What I wouldn't give," he yells louder, "to be a man of wealth and privilege in that enlightened age when genius was still the high ideal, before dim-witted mediocrity overran valorous accomplishment and plunged civilization into its present darkness of tacky social responsibility crap!"

"But you've told about something Nero used to do, not the Laure guy, whoever he was" says a blond young man in a pompous tone, stepping forward. "We read about it in Roman history class, in Suenonius. Nero was one of the Emperors..."

"So you've caught me!" Jean-Marc interrupts, briefly pantomiming a look of panic; then he looks the blond young man in the eye, and says, "Of course I know who Nero was, he's one of my heroes; and, by the way, it's *Suetonius*, not Suenonius! And the other ancient sources that detail the enlightened doings of Nero are Tacitus and Dio, in case you need to be told! I've read them by heart! Have *you*?" He's noticed the blond young man lurking in the background on previous occasions and has never paid him much mind; now he's aware of heartily disliking him, and not caring to conceal it.

As for the blond young man, he's Baptiste Grashelle, student at Sciences Po, twenty-one years old, about five feet ten inches in height. He has close-cropped blond hair, sparse eyebrows, pale gray eyes, a pinkish complexion that easily reddens; pudgy cheeks, a chin that will doubtless be a double-chin before too long, a belly that's already hinting at concealing his belt buckle. He has a habit of endlessly adjusting his clothes, particularly tucking in his shirt, and caressing the band of his ostentatious watch. He also has a habit of demonstrating to others how clever he is, despite the fact that he's seldom able to provide the evidence. Easily annoyed and flustered, he'll readily tell any lie that he feels will cast him in a favorable light or conceal his frequent behavioral miscues. He's often envious of others, and always willing to do his best to attach himself to authority figures and shamelessly flatter them. Such is he who Jean-Marc's looking up and down with mocking eyes.

Unease and distaste grapple for ascendancy in the features of Baptiste's face. For an instant his eyes flash threateningly and he's on the point of speaking, but then he's flutteringly glancing sideways, under the influence of cautionary instincts. Finally, he loudly exhales, shoves his shirttail further inside his pants, and says, "I was letting people know that the person who you said did that stuff isn't the one who did it. I..."

"So what's the difference?" Jean-Marc cuts him off. "18th century libertinage, Roman extravagance: both are high points of history! Both offer prime examples of commendable behavior! What does it matter if I flip the timelines, when the examples stay true?"

"It's plainly inaccurate," states Baptiste, smugness overspreading his face. "I'm also wondering, and I think other people are wondering the same thing too, how much truth there is in all that you're saying. I'm wondering if you both personally believe any of your bold statements."

"Personally believe?" scoffs Jean-Marc. "That's..."

"In other words," cuts in William, making an ease-up signal to Jean-Marc, "are we acting, putting on a show? Do we really and truly embrace what we've been expostulating? *(He shrugs his shoulders, makes a dismissive gesture.)* Who cares, as long as the material expostulated is appropriately novel, entertaining, and contemptuous of the ordinary? Authentic or playacted belief on my part, I've never troubled to bother with the boundary! Do I even know what I genuinely believe? Do I care? It all depends on what mood I happen to be in at the time and my moods whirl like leaves in a storm! If I embrace any consistency whatsoever, it's *The Aristocracy of Nondeclaration*! One must be multifaceted enough to be unknowable by others and oneself alike! One must studiously avoid being entrapped in a single mindset! Human beings are *not* meant to be categorized, pigeonholed, typecast! Human beings *cannot* be pinned down by psychological profiles and demographical statistics! Yes," he concludes, giving into an urge to overtly provoke Baptiste—the very thing he sought to dissuade Jean-Marc from doing—and looking directly at him in a manner bordering on contempt, "moodiness and capriciousness—beautiful unpredictability—is the means by which to keep mindless herd-instinct-driven dolts at a distance, outside of our lives; the means by which to enjoy our limited amount of time on earth without interference! To hell with full self-disclosure, plebeian forthrightness—the familiarity that masquerades as honesty in the eyes of morons! We're better than that!"

The smugness has drained from Baptiste's face; he's twitching with pronounced irritation, again wrestling with an impulse to give way to anger—it's fear that's holding him back. Again, he audibly exhales, then speaks. "But how..."

"But how, what?" interrupts Jean-Marc, taking a couple rapid strides towards Baptiste, stopping when he's about a yard away. "How can we champion insincerity, playacting, deceit? Is that what you were going to ask? My illustrious friend *(He makes a palm-up gesture towards William, like an emcee announcing a performer.)* and I champion these things for the purpose of keeping idiots guessing; for the purpose of remaining slippery, impossible to grasp ahold of; for the purpose of maintaining our God-given measure of inner freedom in the face of this monstrosity of a civilization that would like nothing better than to transform us into trained monkeys yapping politico garbage! Ha ha ha!" Dissolving into laughter, Jean-Marc gazes at Baptiste with a broad grin on his face.

Baptiste's eyes are now ablaze in earnest. "Are you mocking me?" he demands. "Do you want to go at it?" he continues, half-hesitantly shoving Jean-Marc's shoulder—the gesture's something of a desperate attempt to save face, conceal his fear.

"Whoa!" Jean-Marc exclaims. "What a blow was there delivered! My-oh-my, I'm *very* impressed! Go at it? Go at it how? I was having you on, my friend! We're all friends here, aren't we?"

"Troublemakers!" shouts Stephan as he steps between Jean-Marc and Baptiste. "We *are* all friends here, and I'm not happy about having to forgo Miss Junot's company *(He gestures towards Lucinda, who's lying on the couch.)* to remind you of it! Now shake and make up! I insist!" So saying, he seizes the non-glass-clasping hands of each and brings them together—a gesture not nearly as effective as he would wish, on account of the fact he's seized a left and right hand—a shortcoming no sooner noted than he commands, "You, Baptiste! Set the glass down! *(Baptiste irritably does so.)* No! None of that!" continues Stephan. "We're going to have goodwill here, Lucy's waiting! And it's improper to keep a lady waiting! And if you two keep me away from her for a minute longer, then you're both expelled! Yes, *both*!" he accentuates, upon catching Jean-Marc's surprised glance. "Why would either of you think I had a preference? That's it, grasp firmly and shake! Be hearty! I insist!"

Jean-Marc and Baptiste, taking Stephan at his word, make a show of good-greeting. Stephan, satisfied, says, "Lucy and I want privacy, and if I have to step away from her again... You get my drift?" Without awaiting a response, but nevertheless sneaking in a wink to Jean-Marc, he turns to escort Lucinda from the couch to his bedroom.

"Yeah, it was just silliness," puts in Jean-Marc as he releases Baptiste's hand. He begins to turn towards William, intent upon avoiding further tension—for Stephan's sake.

But Baptiste doesn't want him to turn away. "It was dumb," he hastens to say, "I shouldn't have bluffed you guys." Seeing Jean-Marc and William are exchanging questioning glances, he continues, "You're not the only ones who do acting stuff. I'm not as one-dimensional as you think. I was faking the whole time and pretending to disagree with you."

"So you were shamming it too," says William, smiling. "Good for you!"

"I guess Bill and I aren't the only ones who know how to have fun," laughs Jean-Marc. "Sir, I'd like to shake your hand of my own free will!" He shakes Baptiste's hand again.

William, following Jean-Marc's example, comments, "Another prankster nondeclarative! Steph surrounds himself with the right people!"

"To all scampscalions unable to resist a jest," Jean-Marc adds, raising his glass. "To all stranded nondeclaro Aristos seeking to eke out an emotional living in these passion-impoverished times!"

"Hear, hear!" shouts William.

"Yeah," says Baptiste.

"Take care, sir," William says, addressing Baptiste. "We'll catch you later. We need to check in with the girls." He and Jean-Marc raise their hands in farewell as they begin strolling away.

"If he was pretending to disagree, I'm in Bangkok," Jean-Marc says in an undertone the instant Baptiste's out of earshot. "The little prig told that lie because he got in over his head and is scared to death."

"Obviously," answers William, "but who cares? Forget about him."

Our two new idealistically bonded friends approach the couch where Christina and Pascale are chatting with three other girls. One of the other girls is Claire Gabriel, who's already made a brief appearance in our narrative. The other two are Genevieve Clouitier and Carole Marsolet, who will figure prominently in our narrative and be introduced in the next chapter.

CHAPTER 7

Now let us turn the clock back about half an hour, to the moment when Pascale and Christina take their leave of William and Jean-Marc. They spot Genevieve, the one girl they know to some extent (she having been at the apartment and assisted them with settling in when they arrived before noon), among a group of girls in a corner and hasten to join her, intent upon being introduced to more people. Genevieve, at five feet ten the tallest girl in the room, has long amply curling black hair and dark intelligent eyes. She tips the scale at one hundred forty pounds and every square inch of her musculature is proportionately distributed from her toes to the top of her head. She's wearing a lightweight aquamarine cashmere sweater, as tight-fitting as a t-shirt, and pleated white skirt with her hair tied in a ponytail and could easily pass for a teenager; love of life radiates from her fresh complexion, vivacious gestures, gaiety of disposition, and sensual voice. At the same time, perhaps because of her imposing physical attributes, she's possessed of an air of self-assurance and maturity that people seldom acquire by their twenty-first year, for such is her age; the fact that she's from a wealthy and indulgent family (She's presently pursuing a degree in French literature, and may take her parents up on their offer to set her up in business—a clothing shop or restaurant—at some point in the future.) and under no pressure to earn a livelihood may also contribute to her effortless ease of manner and inner equilibrium. Genevieve's love of teasing and laughter, the readiness with which she gives way to girlish giggling at the slightest pretext, cannot dispel the impression of maturity; if anything, her inclination towards fun only serves to contrast with and accentuate it. Almost as if despite herself, she's always looking after her friends, whether they be older or younger than she, in a maternal manner.

Instantly perceiving that Christina and Pascale are mildly uncomfortable, Genevieve says with a smile, "Everyone knows who you are and where you're from and about your adventure, but you don't even know their names! That's *not* how it should be, so we'll remedy that!" Stepping between them and grasping each by the hand, she escorts them about the room. Following nearly two dozen introductions, she brings Christina and Pascale back to the original corner, where Claire's chatting with a girl unknown to them.

"Girls, pay attention, please," Genevieve cuts in, "this is Pascale and this is Christina, friends of the household who'll be staying here for six weeks. Chrissy and Pas, this is Claire and this is Carole, two of my dearest friends."

"I know," Claire says. "I brought them their glasses! Hello again!"

"I'm honored!" Carole exclaims, enthusiastically embracing and trading cheek-kisses with Christina and Pascale. "It's not everyday I get to meet girls who play among the dead at night during storms! And petite, like me! Us petite things make up in courage and spirit what we lack in height, right?" As Carole's stated, she's petite—five feet four at the most, and barely over one hundred pounds. The predominant expression of her face is that of good-natured mischief; there's also much of willfulness in her eyes and manner—it's obvious she drives herself hard. As dismissive as she is with people she considers "sloucho," she's as appreciative of people she considers lively and intelligent; strong in her emotions, she recoils in something resembling terror from those who are not. She's studying dance while supporting herself as an aerobics instructor; she's a popular instructor who makes the euro equivalent of about forty thousand dollars a year by working a mere eleven hours a week. She's wearing a backless short-sleeved scarlet dress with black trim, seamed black stockings, and silver heels. There's a red rose attached to the pearl barrette in her long curly brown hair.

"You got that right," Pascale says, looking Carole up and down with smiling eyes and instantly warming to the force of her personality. "Petite's another way of saying firebrand!"

"Petite's another way of saying limitless energy, and dancing!" Christina laughs, fairly certain she's detected the aura and physical intentness of a fellow dancer in Carole.

"Absolutely dancing!" Carole says, clapping. "I'm flattered you saw the signs! I see them in both of you!"

"You see the yoga and aerobics maniac in me," Pascale responds. "I'm focused on fashion design, but always enjoy a good standing split!"

"Carole and Claire teach aerobics," Genevieve laughs, "and I've taken their classes! It's obvious we're all going to be best friends!"

"It's in the stars," Claire agrees. "And I'm sorry for dashing off like I did earlier, but Steph was being a brat. I didn't think he'd desert you, leave you hanging. He was *supposed* to be a good host, and tour you around." Claire's appearance has been described. A year older than Genevieve, she's completed college and is no longer sure why she bothered to do so. Her revised ambition in life is to find a man with whom to settle down, and have children—lots of children, as her Catholic faith dictates. In the meantime, she's, as Genevieve stated, working as an aerobics instructor: she met Carole at the gym where they're both employed. It's on account of Claire, a native Parisian who's known many of the people present since childhood, that Carole's now a part of the group.

"Steph's caught a case of Lucyitis," Carole says, gesturing towards the couch where Stephan and Lucinda are cuddling, "and isn't able to see past her pretty eyes!"

"I suppose he can be excused on those grounds," Claire smiles; then, turning to Christina and Pascale again, "You're going to remember Paris very fondly, we'll see to that! Aerobics girls stick together!"

"And Claire and I'll give you passes to our classes," Carole says, "so you can kick and sweat when you're not running around in cemeteries!

"Thanks sweetie," Pascale says as she and Christina embrace the French girls anew.

Another girl, who's just strolled up to introduce herself, is Suzanne; but before she can say two sentences, a young man embraces her from behind, covering her eyes with his hands. "Guess who?" he asks. She responds with giggles and some playful shaking of her hips.

"It's time," the young man says.

"So it is," Suzanne answers; then, addressing Christina and Pascale, "Welcome to Paris! I'm sure we'll see more of each other, I look forward..." She's unable to say more on account of being tickled by her admirer. "Will you wait!" she admonishes him.

"I will *not* wait!"

"Shush you!" commands Genevieve. "Susie's just met our guests, so you need to be a little patient and show you know the meaning of courtesy." The young man shrugs his shoulders and falls silent, albeit while gently tugging at Suzanne's wrist.

"I look forward to getting better acquainted," Suzanne says. "Here's my number—give me a call." After handing Pascale her card, she scampers away in the boy's company.

"Susie's such a slut!" laughs Carole.

"But she's not as much a slut as you are, is she?" says Genevieve, flicking Carole's hair. "It's a wonder you still have your dress on, with all these males about! You're neglecting your reputation!"

"Later will do just fine," returns Carole. "Besides, the truth is...hate to disappoint you, but I might be contemplating monogamy, assuming he is too." She gestures towards Jean-Marc.

"Now, there's an admission I never thought I'd hear," responds Genevieve, "despite the fact I was starting to suspect as much! The evidence..."

"Oh, were you?" interrupts Carole, narrowing her eyes and placing both hands on her hips. "How clever you are!"

"Hey, Jean-Marc!" shouts Genevieve. "You might want to hear what Carole's saying about you! Jean-Marc!"

"Quiet, you nut!" says Carole, placing a hand over Genevieve's mouth. "Private information, OK?"

"You needn't worry," Genevieve says after removing Carole's hand. "He's too busy listening to himself give speeches to heed me!"

"Too busy bonding with our Billy!" Pascale smiles. "Try to tear two politically aligned males apart! It's impossible! Look at them, working overtime to impress each other! It was love at first word!"

"Isn't that the truth," says Claire. "Be as pretty as you please, shake some leg *(She raises her hem halfway up her thigh, turns out a heel.)* and lick your lips and flick your hair *(She executes these maneuvers.)* while they're carrying on like that, and they won't notice a thing! Ha ha ha!"

"Right," Genevieve says, mirth dancing in her eyes. "Carole, I dare you to go over there and try to pry him away from William! You'll discover the true measure of where you stand in his eyes! Monogamy? Dream on!"

"Look who's talking big," counters Carole, a mischievous grin overspreading her face. "Girls, take a look at what our esteemed Gen dragged to the party! It's her childhood sweetheart, *Bap!*"

"Shh!" says Genevieve, a trace of embarrassment and shame instantly appearing in her expression. "He was at dinner tonight, I couldn't shed him. I didn't want to bring him, you know that, but..." she trails off, making a gesture of irritation.

Carole, unaccustomed to seeing Genevieve—one of her two closest friends, the other being Claire—lose her composure, immediately stops teasing and grasps her hand. "But, why, Gen? It drives me crazy that..."

"Carole, please," Genevieve says softly and urgently. "Our American friends...it's a party! They..."

"Please," Christina quickly says, "don't be uncomfortable on our account! If it's none of our business, fine, but..."

"What's a Bap?" Pascale interrupts, directing the question at Genevieve. She's being consciously pushy, but there's profound kindness in her eyes—it's her way of furthering their budding friendship, and asking for trust. "Who's this Bap?"

"Pas," begins Christina in a mildly chiding tone, "maybe we shouldn't..."

"Chrissy and Pas," Genevieve breaks in, having overcome her embarrassment as quickly as she acquired it. "I didn't mean to imply I was shutting you out! It's just that the person being referred to isn't worth your time and attention! But the cat's out of the bag, thanks to darling Carole *(She smiles at Carole)*, so take a look. That's him over there, the blonde one with the displeased look on his face. I've known him since birth, his family lives in the same building as mine; our dads are friends and business associates; our moms go to the opera together and are in the same social clubs. Our families have taken ski trips together, have next-door vacation homes in Normandy. Baptiste..."

"*Bap!*" corrects Carole.

"Bap," resumes Genevieve, silencing Carole with a look, "was a great kid and we grew up together and were close, but now he's changed and is getting worse by the week—I swear he's caught a mental disease. I was in an awkward situation earlier, it was his mom's birthday dinner with my parents, and I didn't have the heart to tell him I didn't want him coming here. Not on his account, mind you—he's becoming insufferable, I'm getting fed up—but on account of it being his mom's birthday celebration. I would've unsettled both sets of parents, sabotaged the party. I had to grit my teeth and smile and allow him to accompany me. Now, though, I realize I'm going to have to bring the matter up with my parents. But the thing is, I'll be breaking an association that's an integral part of both our families, assumed by all concerned to be permanent! Bap and I used to ice skate together, swim in the sea together!"

"That's the Bap?" asks Pascale, pointing at him. "The one who's acting like Billy and Jean-Marc are insulting him, even though they don't know he's alive?"

"That's him, all right," answers Claire, "in all of his creepy, negative, depressing..." Then breaking off to address Genevieve, "Gen, your parents *will* understand! It's hardly your fault if Bap's turned bad, and the last thing they'd want is for you to suffer because of it! I encourage you—I *command* you *(She seizes Genevieve's arm, squeezes.)*—to tell them tomorrow and end this nonsense!"

"I'll be telling them..." Genevieve trails off.

"For Christ's sake!" exclaims Carole, flinging her arms up in exasperation. "I don't care how long you've been forced to know him because of family ties—skiing, skating, swimming... Pah! He's starting to entertain notions, as insulting as they are disgusting, and you've got to disabuse him of them! Smack him *down*!"

"And he's unfit for hauling about," adds Claire, becoming uncharacteristically heated. "He's a social liability! No one can stand him, he doesn't like anyone! It's all envy and petty conflict and insecurity with him! And sick possessiveness where you're concerned, delusion that makes me retch! I'm surprised, by the way, that he isn't over here pestering you! The stuff you've already told us... How on earth can *you*, of all people, put up with it?"

"I haven't wanted to burden two families with it," Genevieve answers. "You simply can't imagine the history! Bringing pain to my parents—not because they won't support me every step of the way and accept what I say without question, but because the revelation itself will pain them—isn't something I've been able to do thus far, but now I see I'll have to. I've been telling myself that Baptiste—I mean, *Bap*—wasn't aberrant until recently, and hoping it would go away; but, unfortunately, it isn't going away."

"You bet it's not," says Christina, casting a look of excessive distaste at Baptiste. "Take the word of someone who's just walked in on the situation, and is seeing with fresh eyes: that boy is nuts in a very bad way, resentful of the happiness of others because he'll never be so himself. It gives me the chills to look at him."

"I second Chrissy," says Pascale. "That is one sick puppy and, if you need to burn down a building to be rid of him—much less speak to who I gather are truly wonderful parents who deeply care about you—then you must do so at once! If fact, if I may be so bold, I'll join Claire *(She smiles at Claire.)* in *commanding* you to shed yourself of him right away! *(She notes the mild surprise of the three French girls.)* OK, I'm being too familiar. Sorry...I'll back off."

"No no no!" says Carole. "No apology! Please don't insult us! We're all friends here and we adore you!" She embraces Pascale.

"Maybe I showed some surprise—maybe we all did," Claire says. "I can assure you it was pleasant surprise! As in how swiftly and unexpectedly people—nice people—can come to an understanding, and how wonderful that is!" She embraces Christina.

"Pas and Chrissy," Genevieve hastens to say, "I appreciate your words of insight and encouragement. It's a bad situation that can't be allowed to get worse, and I'll do as your observations dictate. Thank you for your good sense, and for giving me courage."

"Which is thoroughly insane to hear from the lips of Gen," Carole says, addressing Christina and Pascale. "You don't know it yet, but she's our rock of Gibraltar, the strongest and best of us! The sanest, and most unselfish! It breaks me apart to see her in this situation, and it's going to *stop*!" she concludes, pecking Genevieve on the cheek. The three other girls likewise peck Genevieve on the cheek.

"Thank you again," Genevieve says, grasping Christina and Pascale by the hand. "But enough of Bap—he's not going to poison our night. New friends is what tonight's about!"

"Absolutely," Carole agrees. "Tonight's about new beginnings with fearless graveyard rompers! Parisiennes and New Yorkesses, Franco-American relations!"

"Tonight's the first of many more," Claire adds, "during which we'll get to know each other as well as we know ourselves, and I look forward to that with all my heart! Like I said, Chrissy and Pas, we're going to make sure you love our town! It's our mission!"

"We already love it," Christina says. "Paris is buried memories come alive, a waking dream! I still can't believe I'm here!"

"And I still can't believe you've consorted with the dead during a fierce storm," Carole laughs. "You've already trumped us in the escapade department, and haven't been here for a day! Talk about making a splashy entrance!"

"Yeah," Pascale says, "we were dripping and splashing all over the place, drenched to the skin! We were lucky we had dark stuff on, to keep us from being exhibitionist city! Ha ha ha!"

"That didn't stop the boys from craning their necks to catch a glimpse of your outlines," Carole grins. "Your dresses might not have been transparent, but they were clinging as tight as your skin! You were perfect teases, suggestive without being ostentatious!"

"Mostly we were cold," Christina laughs. "Only thinking about thawing out in the shower!"

"When the water hit me in the shower it was a fresh injection of energy," Pascale says. "Instant insanely invigorating relief! Sometimes the most magical drug on earth is *heat*!"

"Speaking of relief," Claire says, suddenly darting towards the left, "I *do* like to get off my feet now and then! Come on!" She's referring to the fact that one of the two couches has just been vacated, the other still occupied by Stephan and Lucinda. Reaching it before anyone else, she claims it for herself and her friends.

"So now that we're cozy-wozy," says Genevieve once they're seated on the couch, "I can ask what all the girls have been wondering. What's the story with you two and William? Does he have two girlfriends?"

"Now you've given yourself away," laughs Christina. "That's what you three have been scheming all along, maneuvering us into spilling it!"

"Right," says Pascale. "And the second we've told everything we'll be discarded! We'll be nothing but a solved mystery, former curiosity! You'll triumphantly spread the news, boast that no secret stays a secret for long when you're on the case!"

"Oh, stop it!" from Carole.

"Pointless delay tactics!" from Claire.

"Cough it up girls," says Genevieve. "Enough teasing!"

"Did you know French hussies were so pushy?" Christina asks Pascale.

"I *am* a French hussy!" answers Pascale. "That's right, fellow French girls, it's not by accident I have this name—my parents aren't Francophile Yanks! I was born in Asnieres!"

"A lot closer to Paris than Carole!" laughs Claire.

"Oh, shut up!"

"A hick from Lille!" Claire continues to tease.

"A lily from Lille!" shouts Carole, grabbing a handful of Claire's hair and flinging it in her face.

"Now, now!" says Genevieve. "You're letting these two off the hook! Do you want the lowdown on William or not?"

"Right," says Carole. "Fess up to us pushy French hussies!"

"Happy to," Christina smiles, her urge to tease having run its course. "The three of us live on the same block, and met because of it. First Billy and I, at a café on the corner. Then a couple months later Billy and Pas because they were crawling onto their fire escapes for some sun, and started to look each other over and signaled to meet on the sidewalk. So then Billy introduced me to Pas, and guess what? There wasn't any jealously *at all*! Instead of each of us wanting Billy to ourselves, we wanted him and each other—each other as friends, mind you."

"So it was you two who initiated a threesome?" asks Claire. "I know that sounds shoddy, but... How else am I to say it?"

"A threesome!" shouts Carole, giggling.

"Threesome!" Pascale echoes. "No way to make it sound less than silly! We're aware of the dubious nature of the beast, improbability of making it sound—for lack of better words—decent and above board. Long story short, Billy was worried about doing a juggling act. He'd become acquainted with me without Chrissy being aware of it—not intentionally, it just happened—after having been with her for a couple months. He was afraid of losing both of us, so he took a chance and introduced us. In the first place, he had to because Chrissy's building is across the street from his and mine's three doors down and we would've known about each other pretty fast. Plus he didn't want to poison things with dishonesty. So he introduced us and didn't say much, allowing us to figure it out—which, of course, we did in a second."

"He thought we might spring on each other like wildcats!" laughs Christina. "Or on him! He didn't know what to expect! He didn't dare suggest dividing his time between us! He was actually pretty paralyzed!"

"I can imagine," says Claire. "So how did it resolve itself?"

"Oh, I don't know," resumes Christina. "Billy has a way of being friends with a girl first and treating sex like a privilege of friendship. He really likes women as *people*, and cares, so that helped. But the kicker was how well Pas and I hit it off from the get-go—we liked each other and wanted to continue to know Billy, so it all just fell into place of its own accord, without any ickiness. So Billy, fearing the worst, ended up being part of a threesome instead of three acrimonious ones."

"It was as much what he didn't say," adds Pascale, "as what he did say. He didn't presume anything, or try to sell it. Billy knows when to keep his mouth shut and let his eyes and body language do the talking."

"But doesn't he get crazy sometimes, dealing with two girls? And haven't either of you ever thought a preference was being shown, and reacted unfavorably?" asks Genevieve, quickly adding, "I don't mean to pry, I'm simply...let's say very respectfully curious."

"Please, Gen," says Christina, "we're friends, so no standing on ceremony. As for your question, it's not like that—the three of us deal with each other equally. Squabbles erupt, sure—we're humans, after all—but usually over trivial getting-on-nerves things: someone wants a window open when the others don't, another is annoyed about music one of us is playing to death. But it's never been a case of the girls against the boy; if anything, it'll be boy and girl against the other girl. And Billy's always quick to end *that*! We each have our own lives, and want to keep it that way."

"Best friends who sleep together," continues Pascale. "What's preposterous about it? Being three counters jealousy instead of fostering it. You might wonder if it's love or not. Sure it's love. OK, so it's probably more like love between siblings: what's wrong with knowing we'll always know and support one another? What's known as, quote-unquote, *true* love—uncontrollable life-altering attraction: maybe it awaits us with other people. In fact, I'm sure it does. So what? We three are friends first; when one of us enters unfamiliar waters, the other two will always be there to proffer advice—dispense sanity, if need be. Maybe I'm being naive? I don't think so. It's not like there *always* has to be war between the sexes. I sincerely believe—and, more importantly, feel—the three of us have achieved a truce. We're bound far more by our friendship—

the trust between us, our knowledge of one another—than by the sex."

"People see us together, arm in arm," Christina laughs. "Billy's in the middle, trading off kissing us, and they gawk. They're thinking it's some jokey free-love thing between immature idiots who don't know what a real relationship is. They're wrong! It's a deep, for-the-rest-of-our-lives, relationship based on mutual respect. We know it, and that's all that matters."

"Our present accommodations notwithstanding," says Pascale, "we prefer to and *do* live alone. We're on vacation and have a nice place to stay and there's one available room so we're sharing. It's the exception, not the rule."

"Do you sleep with others?" from Carole.

"A slut will ask a slut's question!" cracks Genevieve.

"As if you're not wondering the same!" retorts Carole; then, readdressing Pascale and Christina, "So?"

"Well, yes, that's been done," answers Pascale. "We're not out to impose restrictions on one another. We're not prison guards, chaperones. Friendship is always first—*always*."

"Girls," Genevieve smiles, "I think we can leave them alone now—we don't want to be *too* pushy!"

"Speaking of pushy," says Pascale, "it looks like the Bap's decided to interfere with Billy and Jean-Marc's male bonding party." All turn in the direction of William and Jean-Marc.

"Oh, great," Genevieve says, exhaling with annoyance. "It's *so* pleasant to watch the little man make a fool of himself when I'm the one who brought him here! First thing after I wake up today, it's straight to mom and dad to lay down the law! I cannot and will not endure being in the same room with him again! Grade school's ages ago, junior high's ages ago...I don't owe bygone versions of Bap anything! Actually, last month's ages ago when it comes to the lunacy that's overtaken him!"

"Puerile intellects *will* seek to get noticed, and start squeaking," says Carole, adding with pride, "Jean-Marc will tear him apart!"

"Billy will squash the worm, count on it!" says Christina.

"Why, that little bastard!" Genevieve cries, upon seeing Baptiste shove Jean-Marc's shoulder. "And here comes Steph to break it up—he's none too happy and I don't blame him! I could die of shame!"

"Sweetheart," Claire says tenderly, caressing one of her shoulders, "we don't want to hear you berate yourself. It's not like you met Bap on your own and misread him and took him into your confidence, temporarily lost your sanity. He's like an insufferable cousin who's been forced on you by family. You will *not* beat yourself up and blame yourself, especially when you're going to be rid of him soon!"

"Certainly not," Carole says. "You're not the first person to be stuck with an insufferable loser on account of ties to the past, and everyone understands that. He won't be at any parties after tonight, and that's what you focus on! Count on it, your mom and dad are going to want to kill him after you describe his behavior! You *are* going through with it, right?"

"Every fiber of my being's thirsting to be rid of him," Genevieve says. "I'm so focused on what I'll be doing as soon as I wake up it's like I'm only half here. Don't worry about me!" She straightens herself and brings composure into her face.

"Too bad Steph's broken it up and made them shake hands," Pascale comments. "I'd enjoy seeing Billy or Jean-Marc knock Bap on his ass!"

"Wouldn't *that* be fun?" Carole agrees.

"But maybe Bap's good for something after all," Pascale adds. "Our men have stopped impressing each other, and are coming to see us!"

Sure enough, William and Jean-Marc are approaching the girls, as they were doing at the conclusion of the last chapter. What they're unaware of is that Baptiste is glancing after them and at Genevieve with a highly unpleasant look on his face: he's on the point of resolving to follow them.

CHAPTER 8

"So are you two going to dump us and live happily ever after in Male Bond Land?" asks Pascale once William and Jean-Marc reach the couch.

"What?" responds William, pulling a baffled look; then, turning to Jean-Marc, "Looks like Pas has overindulged in bubbly! She's babbling nonsense!"

"She is not," says Carole, joining in on the game. "Your budding buddy-love's obvious—we're wondering if you're going to toss us aside so you can yak all night."

"That's females for you," laughs Jean-Marc, winking at William. "Jealous of *everything*! A guy can't have a discussion with anyone else—it's perceived as competition! That's how secure girls are!"

"Leave females unattended for an hour," adds William, "and this is the sorry outcome! Their possessiveness becomes maniacal!"

"Jealousy's foreplay to a girl," says Jean-Marc. "They can't wait to get some kind—any kind—of tension in the picture, so we'll be obliged to calm them! They always want make-up cuddles, for imaginary offenses!"

The girls exchange incredulous glances, make dismissive gestures, look William and Jean-Marc up and down with narrowed eyes.

"Uh-oh!" Jean-Marc laughs. "The kitties are baring their claws! They want to jump on us for speaking the truth!"

"Don't flatter yourself," says Claire. "You're not worth a serious reaction! We don't waste our time with bombastic fools, and are going to ignore you!" She turns to the girls and begins complimenting them on their clothes.

"Why are you still here?" Carole says, looking at Jean-Marc. "We have important wardrobe matters to discuss! We... Ha ha ha!" With mirth dancing in her eyes she scoots forward on the couch and extends her hand to him—a hand he readily grasps, and affectionately squeezes.

"Come here, you!" says Pascale, addressing William and pointing to the width of couch between herself and Christina.

As William's seating himself in the indicated spot Baptiste lumbers forward and, uncertain how to proceed, abruptly turns to Jean-Marc and mutters, "Hi."

"Oh, it's *you*," Jean-Marc observes witheringly.

Baptiste, taken aback by Jean-Marc's response (because he was sure he'd fooled him with his false declaration of pretended anger a minute ago), is unable to prevent himself from sputtering, "A bad mood? Don't take it out on me!" as hatred flashes in his eyes. But then, recalling such displays are distasteful to Genevieve, he passes his hand across his face, and says, "Whew! I'm a little dizzy! That champagne's sorta potent!" by way of offering an excuse.

"Baptiste," says Genevieve hastily, eager to ward off a possible altercation, "it's only a party!" Then, catching Jean-Marc's eye, she bids him be more tactful with a slight shake of her head. Having firmly made up her mind to permanently remove Baptiste from her life, she wants the process to go as smoothly as possible, with no advance tension. She wants to avoid displays of bad feelings at all costs.

William, in the meantime, quickly suspects that the girls, including Christina and Pascale (who somehow already know him), have no fondness for Baptiste, such is the collective wave of recoil that passes through their bodies. All five of them, moments before relaxed, are tense and on guard. To further confirm this impression, he springs up from the seat he's just taken, stands facing the girls, and looks them in the eye. *That's right, he's poison!* is what their eyes say. So he turns to Baptiste and says, "Yeah, it's only a party! Relax, sir! Why not help yourself to some food? Plenty of tasty stuff over there!"

"A nice party...good food," Baptiste mumbles, glancing about nervously; then, resting his gaze upon Genevieve and addressing her while pleading with his eyes, "My mom's birthday was nice, wasn't it?"

"It was very nice, Baptiste," answers Genevieve in an even, and careful, tone. "She loved the sapphire your dad gave her. It was beautiful. I'm glad she had a nice party." Then she turns to Claire, grasps her arm, and asks, "What were you were saying about the new boutique?"

"A divine place," gushes Claire, immediately taking her cue to shut Baptiste out of the conversation. "You'll love it! It has..."

But Baptiste, encouraged by having spoken to Genevieve and been replied to, and also driven by the fact he's getting more uncomfortable by the moment, interrupts Claire. "Gen...Genevieve," he stammers. "Maybe...it might be time to go, isn't it? I have studying...I might've had enough wine. Maybe we could go now?"

"Baptiste," Genevieve responds, smiling at him as if he's a child, "it's too early. I'm here with my friends."

"We're not letting her go!" exclaims Carole, reaching across Claire to seize Genevieve's hand. "Are we Claire?"

"She *can't* leave!" Claire affirms, wrapping an arm around Genevieve. "The night's young, and she's not going for a *long* time! Put that thought out of your head!"

"If you have studying," Genevieve continues, "I'll understand if you need to leave. I won't be offended. Thank you for escorting me here."

"N...no," Baptiste says, only semi-aware of what he's saying, "I didn't mean...I mean the studying's not extreme, and I...I don't want to pull you away or anything. As long as we've known each other...you know I always stick by you, and..."

"But we'll look after her," Claire interrupts, smiling an exaggerated smile in which irritation is apparent. "Rest assured, Gen's in good hands and we'll get her home safe. Please, go ahead and study. We wouldn't want a failed exam on our conscience."

"I think I'll...I'll stay here after all," Baptiste mutters abstractedly, while staring at the wall; then, stepping to Genevieve's end of the couch, he stands a couple feet from her shoulder uncertain what to do next.

"Gen," Christina says quickly. "Pas and I want you over here *now*! *(She points to the space between herself and Carole.)* We want to see the picture in your locket bracelet!"

"You said you would!" says Pascale, backing Christina up. Both have already seen the picture: it's of Genevieve at her confirmation.

"Yeah, get over there—hurry and satisfy the curiosity of our American friends, so we don't have to hear it anymore!" says Claire, pulling at Genevieve's arm.

"Alright, alright," Genevieve says. "Sheesh! You'd think the future of civilization was hanging in the balance!"

No sooner is Genevieve relocating than Carole pulls at Jean-Marc, saying, "Sit down, you fool!" He seats himself in the spot vacated by Genevieve at the same time that Carole trades places with Claire.

"And why are *you* standing?" Christina says to William. "Sit here!" He seats himself at the other end of the couch, next to Pascale.

These maneuvers, designed to move Genevieve away from Baptiste and to make certain the couch is too crowded for him to attempt to sit, are executed within seconds. It may not be of importance, but the order of our friends on the couch, from left to right, is: Jean-Marc, Carole, Claire, Genevieve, Christina, Pascale, and William. Baptiste is standing to the left of it.

"Come on," Christina says to Genevieve, "don't be bashful! Show us the goods! *(Genevieve flips open the locket on her bracelet, extends her wrist to display the picture within it.)* You're so cute!"

"I don't know why you were hesitating," says Pascale. "It's a heavenly picture, hair and a dress to die for!"

"Thank you," responds Genevieve; then, whispering in Christina's ear, "I'm issuing an official fun-directive. Everyone's to ignore Bap, and carry on. Please don't be rude to him, though. Act as if he isn't here. Pass it on."

In half a minute all are aware of Genevieve's wishes. Carole, for her part, first tickles Jean-Marc, then plays at kissing his ear while imparting the message. Soon the couch erupts in a flurry of teasing, both verbal and physical.

"Crazy girl!" Jean-Marc shouts the moment Carole's done whispering. "She licks my ear, then tells me I'm spending the night alone! Can't live with 'em, can't live without 'em!"

"How original! I've never heard *that* before!" answers Carole, slapping at Jean-Marc's leg.

"Help!" Jean-Marc calls to Claire, reaching across Carole to pat her thigh. "Claire the fair, will you rescue me from this minx? Dare I entertain the hope?"

"No, little one, you may not," replies Claire, batting his hand away. "You know I'm spoken for and, unless you learn to mind that mocking mouth of yours, I'll see to it my man tosses you in jail on a trumped up charge and buries you in all the paperwork our wonderful French bureaucracy can come up with!"

"In jail? How?" asks Christina, her hair being tousled by William.

"She's dating a cop," announces Carole. "A lieutenant, in charge of homicide investigations."

"He is not," counters Claire.

"He is too a cop!"

"He's a cop, but isn't in homicide. He's in vice, which makes it all the easier for him to frame men who bother me!" She reaches behind Carole to smack Jean-Marc's shoulder.

"I'm bothering you? Not likely!" laughs Jean-Marc.

"Yes likely—highly likely!"

"But you love it to death, Claire the fair—I know it and you know it! After all, I've been doing it since grade school!"

"Yes, you have, and now the time has come for you to stop! One of us is an adult now, and that would be me!"

"And if I stopped *flattering* you, what then? You'd fall into a deep black hole of depression and aimlessly wander about with lifeless eyes! Because, Claire the fair, you adore being flirted with and teased by me! You can deny it in front of the others, but we both know it's true! And one of these days, Claire the fair, I'm going to show you no one knows you half as well as I do and, when that day arrives, you'll be mine! In fact, why wait? *(He stands and kneels in front of Claire.)* Will you marry me, Claire the fair? Pretty please?"

"Raving lunatic!" laughs Claire, tapping his forehead as she rises to her feet; then, addressing Christina and Pascale, "Girls, I know we'll be seeing a lot more of each other, and the pleasure will be mine. I've got to go, my boyfriend's shift is almost over." Baptiste, eager to appropriate Claire's place on the couch, makes a movement in its direction; but she quickly places her palms flat against the air in front of him, saying, "Baptiste, there just isn't any room! We were all dying with me sitting there! Now *my* friends might manage to breathe! Sorry, but you're just going to have to stand! It's Steph's fault for not bringing more furniture from the neighbors!"

"I didn't know," Baptiste says sullenly.

"Well, now you do," responds Claire, not bothering to conceal her irritation. "Shoo! You need to go back there! You're in my way!" Then she exchanges farewell kisses with everyone, excepting Baptiste, saying with emphasis when she reaches Genevieve, "You have my cell number, and you have Armand's. Any trouble, ever, you give us a call. Just because Armand's off-duty doesn't mean his friends won't do him a *favor*. Any trouble, anytime, do you hear?"

"Why Claire," laughs Genevieve. "What on earth...? You'd think I was being *stalked*!" This last phrase sends a jolt through Claire and everyone on the couch. Genevieve can't believe she said it—is annoyed with herself for saying it, because of the stir it's caused and because she feels it borders on crying wolf—and shifts her weight uncomfortably. Finally she says, "You have a good time, sweetie!" while standing to embrace Claire, who looks at her intently and questioningly. Indicating that all is well with a smile, Genevieve whispers, "Claire, I'd rather you left on a light note."

Claire, heeding Genevieve's request, sticks her tongue out at Jean-Marc, who's reseated himself beside Carole, and yells "Lunatic!" Then she walks to a nearby closet, wraps herself in a long black raincoat, and exits—not, however, before turning to cast Jean-Marc a last mirthful glance while waving her phone aloft.

"Did you see that?" Jean-Marc shouts. "That look she gave me, full of earthy joy, as if life itself were smiling at me? And while waving her phone! Does she really want me to call her when she's with her *police lieutenant* boyfriend?" Extending a hand in the departed Claire's direction, he opens and closes it suggestively.

"That's just what a girl wants to see!" exclaims Carole. "You have the gall to wrap an arm around me while making eyes and grab-gestures at someone else? I don't think we're going to be doing what you want to do tonight! There are plenty of others, sir, who'll be happy to show me I'm the only girl for them! But it was nice of Claire to give us her *police lieutenant* boyfriend's number, wasn't it? A girl always likes to feel *protected*! In fact, I think I'll phone Claire's police *lieutenant boyfriend* and get the number of a good-looking cop who'd be happy to offer me more *protection*! I'm done with frittering away nights on rude, disrespectful, uncouth children! You've got a lot of cheek, buster!" She unwraps Jean-Marc's arm from her waist.

"But my cheeks aren't as lovely as yours," Jean-Marc answers, bringing his hands close to Carole's face, pausing them in the air. "Your cheeks are as fresh as lilies on a sunny morning—the petals dripping with dew, translucent in the light! As for Claire and I... That's our flirtation routine, started in grade school and honed in junior high—no different than any other vaudeville act! We've done it in half the cafes of Paris and, before we die, will probably do it in the rest! For you to get jealous and riled on account of a comedy act, just because it involves a member of your own sex, is stupid!

I'm sure her *police lieutenant* boyfriend understands our game, because he's a man instead of a flighty female!"

When Jean-Marc ventures to caress Carole's cheeks, she slaps his hands away and says, "Claire takes off and you think pretty words and lies are going to melt and dupe me? Do you think I'm a standby, an idiot with no pride? I *will* call Claire's *police lieutenant* boyfriend, and get me some manly *protection*!"

"Are you listening to me?" Jean-Marc asks; as absorbed as he is in playing, for a second or two he's aware that Baptiste's glaring at him, and adjusts his words accordingly. "Do you honestly think I'd risk angering Claire's *police lieutenant* boyfriend? That guy's ex Foreign Legion, a nightmare if you get on his bad side! God help anyone who threatens or otherwise makes uncomfortable Claire or any girlfriend of hers! He lives for thrashing men who cause women distress! So not for the world would I take undue liberties with Claire! I repeat: what you witnessed between Claire and I is a comedy routine, and it's nuts for you to be jealous! Claire and I are childhood buddies, and that's it! Believe me, Carole, when I say you're the only woman in the world for me!"

"I'm not a woman, I'm a *girl*! A girl who's often unreasonable and capricious, on principle, because that's what girls do! A girl who's way too hot for you to handle! Claire's *police lieutenant* boyfriend will set me up with a *policeman* who can handle me!"

"A girl!" Jean-Marc concurs. "An extraordinarily beautiful girl whose moods swirl like the sun on windows at midday and who has the most delightful petite figure in all of Paris and who, as a crowning glory, is possessed of the finest crystalline blue eyes!"

"There you go!" Carole shrieks with delight, clapping. "Finally, you've hit upon the right way to flatter me! The color of my eyes is a source of everlasting joy to me! Think how fortunate that I, with my dark brown locks, am to have blue eyes! You win, sir!" She flings her arms about Jean-Marc's neck as they dissolve into laughter.

Such is what's transpiring on the left side of the couch; on the right is a similar scene, but your humble narrator will not trouble to detail. Suffice to say William's exchanging hair flicks, waist tickles, and thigh slaps with Christina and Pascale at the same time that they never cease to chat and laugh with Genevieve.

As for Baptiste, he persists in attempting to catch Genevieve's attention from where he's standing at the left side of the couch—casting insistent glances in her direction, snapping his fingers, venturing to speak. All of his attempts are foiled by her friends—they shout louder to drown out his voice each time they hear it; Jean-Marc and Carole bounce up and down in their seats and shake their arms over their heads to create interference and obstruct his line of vision; Carole and Christina, being seated next to Genevieve, grab her shoulders and squirm against her; in short, they make sure Genevieve has plausible reasons to be oblivious of him. It should also be pointed out that Jean-Marc and Carole's intentional use of the words "police lieutenant," "policeman," and "protection" is lost on Baptiste: although able to stare at Genevieve's friends with distaste, he's incapable of listening to what they're saying, so exclusively is his attention focused upon her.

Baptiste's increasingly being drawn into a state where the evidence before his senses contradicts his thoughts and inclinations: Genevieve wants nothing to do with him, but he's incapable of seeing it. After all, he's here at her invitation, right? Therefore, he's *with* her, right? She's his date, right? How could it be otherwise? The fact that she's choosing to socialize with others instead of him is a temporary aberration, right? How could she dislike him? Even in the unlikely event that she's angry at him for some reason, how could she be so for long? There's the inescapable reality of the years of memories they have in common, right? There are dozens of photos of them side by side in their strollers, right? They were born together, raised together! So close are their families, they're as good as related! Genevieve's simply taking some time away from him to socialize with people he doesn't happen to like, right? But the more Baptiste pursues such lines of reason, the more he finds himself twisting in a void without knowing why.

Obviously, Baptiste ought to walk away—take a few deep breaths, mingle with others, seek to relax and clear his head of troubling thoughts. He literally *cannot* do so. He's as fixated upon keeping an eye on Genevieve as if he's been hypnotized. He's as if standing in a dark tunnel, gazing at Genevieve who's sitting in the light at the end of it; the more he gazes at her from this inner distance the more tension tears at his nerves and the less he's able to stop hating her friends. He's informing himself he's going to persuade her to be less sociable with others, at the earliest opportunity.

As we've indicated, Genevieve's for the most part carrying on with Christina, Pascale, and Carole; what we've left out is that she's also keeping a wary eye on Baptiste, from the corner of her peripheral vision—with her very nerves. She wishes she could wholeheartedly surrender to the fun that surrounds her, but dares not: she can feel Baptiste's gloomy presence at the end of the couch; feel his anxious hovering, the twitchings of his facial expressions; feel his eyes following her every move: it's as if she's being driven towards uneasiness, forced to be constrained. We hasten to state that, while ordinarily she's the last person to allow depressing people to intrude upon her well-being—a strong, self-assured, balanced woman who unfailingly favors all that's positive and cheerful in life, and avoids negativity like the plague—it all comes back to the history between herself and Baptiste, the extent of their family ties: she can't help but feel sad on his account. What a waste! Why has he changed into a resentful, small-minded, mean-spirited shadow of his former self? In short, although on the surface Genevieve's chatting in her blithe voice and often giggling, there's much missing from her customary vivacity: it's because she knows her lifelong association with Baptiste has ended and that he's unaware of it, and because she fears he might not allow her to go her separate way without causing trouble. Why won't he realize their friendship's over on his own, and leave her be? Why must she be placed in the position of having to broach the subject to her parents, force a separation? Why must she be the one who'll be upsetting two families who've been close since before she was born? Genevieve's becoming angry despite herself, which further fuels her uneasiness.

Such are the activities and frames of mind of our friends and their unwanted observer when Stephan excitedly bursts from his room, where he's been happily socializing with Lucinda, and shouts, "Friends! Revelers! Countrymen! Your attention please! *(He windmills his arms, shouts louder.)* Hey! Pay attention! Benevolent Dionysus has answered our prayers! The great God's cleared the weather, abated the rain—approved and blessed our excursion! Honored ladies and gallant gents, prepare..." But then he interrupts himself, yells "Hey Jean!" to a young man at his right, obviously befuddled by drink, who's staring blankly into the air. "What time is it?" Without awaiting a response, Stephan seizes the young man's wrist, jerks it close to his face, and checks the watch strapped thereupon. "One thirty-nine!" he yells. "There's time to burn! To Montsouris Park we go! To Montsouris!"

Several of those present, having resigned themselves to remaining indoors on account of the weather and become comfortable with their resignation (like someone who's climbed into bed early due to a party being cancelled and isn't overjoyed when the phone rings and he's told another party is being held in its place), aren't eager to follow Stephan outside. Our friends are not among them. "Hip hip hooray! Hail mighty Dionysus!" Jean-Marc yells, leaping from the couch and pulling Carole after him as the others follow.

Genevieve's more than happy to vacate her place under the oppressive gaze of Baptiste and fling herself into activity. Clapping enthusiastically, she approaches Stephan and inquires, "What can I do?"

"Organize the kitchen," Stephan says, patting her on the back. Then he addresses Carole, Christina, Pascale, and a couple other girls, "You're Gen's assistants! She's your boss! Obey her! Cram the coolers on the kitchen counter with food! That's your assignment!" Then he starts circling the room like a drill sergeant, yelling "Get ready!" while nudging sundry individuals on the floor with the tips of his shoes, slapping those standing on the back. "Montsouris beckons! The open sky, trees, and lake call us outside!"

"Steph, I'd like to sit this one out," says a young man who's seated on a windowsill. "I have to go to work at noon."

"I don't care if you're on the point of death, you're coming!" Stephan screams; then, addressing everyone, "Anyone who doesn't march to Montsouris will *never* cross my threshold again! I'm not kidding! No lazy bastards allowed—they're not fit company for anyone but themselves! I don't care if you have to crawl, you're going to Montsouris!"

"I love this guy!" yells William.

"You love me, do you?" responds Stephan. "Then get over here! You too, Jean-Marc! Panclerc, where the hell are you?"

"Coming!" answers Panclerc, emerging from the hallway with his round and perpetually smiling face.

"All right, you guys," Stephan continues, "help me with this stuff in the closet." He extracts two large rolls of clear plastic and a number of blankets, distributes them among them. "I'll handle the bubbly and juice and water and you three will help!" he calls to some actor friends. When one of them—the tallest and heftiest man in the room, muscular from head to toe—hesitates, Stephan steps up to him, and says, "Sergio, you know I respect you—I've learned a lot from you, and will probably never learn as much as you already know! You're my senior at the Comedie and always will be, and I acknowledge that with heartfelt humility! It will always be an honor to work with you! But, dammit, this my party and Dionysus has blessed it! So, please, offer thanks to the God and join us!"

"Shut up, you loon," Sergio laughs, reaching for a heavy canvas bag and starting to stuff bottles of water in it. "I just wanted to hear you bluster." Then, setting the bag aside, he grabs Stephan in a bear hug.

"Everyone!" Stephan yells when Sergio releases him. "Did Xerxes balk at bridging the Hellespont? Did Caesar run from the Rubicon? No! Are we going to balk at climbing the gate of Montsouris? No! We're going to climb that gate, and do Dionysus proud!"

As for Baptiste, his reaction with regard to the excursion is decidedly mixed. On the one hand, he's glad of having been rescued from his unflattering position at the side of the couch and hopeful of being able to speak to Genevieve; on the other hand, he's alarmed at how she's already busy in the kitchen, seemingly oblivious of him. At first he's hesitant to approach her on account of her being surrounded by other girls; finally, his torment gets the better of him and he enters the kitchen, touches her arm to get her attention, and says, "After you do this here, could we talk?"

"Baptiste, there is no after," she answers, wincing at his touch. "The girls are counting on me to help them carry the coolers to the park, I'm going to be busy. Then there's the setting up in the park, and... Actually, I don't appreciate the way you touched me, Baptiste! It jolted me! I'd rather you didn't do that again!"

"I..." he begins, his eyes turning every which way. "Sorry, I...I just thought it would be nice to be talk alone without with all these people around." He's on the point of grasping her wrist, then quickly pulls his hand back.

"You don't like these people?" Genevieve spits back with unmistakable irritation. "These are my friends!" She stomps to the far side of the kitchen without awaiting a response. The other girls, alert to what's going on, hasten to occupy the space between Genevieve and Baptiste, making it look like the tasks they're performing is the reason.

"I didn't say that!" Baptiste calls out to Genevieve. "I just..."

"What's going on here?" interrupts Stephan. He's poked his head in the door to ascertain the state of the preparations and witnessed the latter part their exchange. "If it's a quarrel, guess what? No quarrels allowed! Baptiste, you're the man, so listen! I don't care what she's done or what you think she's done! She's a woman, so forgive and forget! I won't have our excursion ruined by bad feelings! Get it?"

"Don't worry about it," Baptiste says, glancing away.

"That's a man!" Stephan says, clapping Baptiste on the shoulder hard enough to make him wince. "Now, come with me! I can use a strong guy!"

Baptiste, casting a last desperate glance in Genevieve's direction and finding her to be busy with her back turned to him, is reluctantly led away by Stephan. As for the latter, he's never liked Baptiste; on the occasions that he's seen him, he's put up with him for Genevieve's sake. He's aware of the family history; he's made cracks to the effect that Baptiste's taking advantage of the said history to break into circles he'd otherwise be unwelcome in, by being Genevieve's lackey. All in all, though, Stephan's never paid Baptiste much mind; he's not one to trouble overmuch with noticing bores. Tonight, however, he's seen very clearly that Baptiste's being possessive in a manner that's anathema to Genevieve. He's known her since his sophomore year in college and considers her to be one of the most extraordinary women he's ever met, which is saying a lot (In fact, he's never tried to bed her, for fear of jeopardizing their friendship: it's an ongoing joke with them.), and has always been mystified at her tolerance of Baptiste, regardless of their family history; but now that tolerance appears to be ending, and he's smiling at the thought. Long story short: Baptiste had better behave himself, or Stephan's going to do more than clap him a bit roughly on the shoulder.

But enough of this chapter: we need to get our merry band and gloomy tagalong to Montsouris Park, where they'll be at the beginning of the next.

CHAPTER 9

Our group—with food coolers, canvas bags full of beverages and dinnerware, rolls of plastic, and blankets—has walked east on Rue d'Alésia to Avenue René Coty, then turned south onto the latter and followed it to where it ends at the northwest entrance of Montsouris Park, at the intersection of Avenue Reille and Rue Nansouty. Although some individuals were cursing under their breaths at the commencement of the excursion, by the time Avenue René Coty was reached all were shouting and singing as they marched down the tree-lined walkway in its center, between the two directions of traffic. The spirit of adventure is difficult to resist when one's tramping about in Paris after 2:00 AM.

As Montsouris Park maintains regular hours, the entrance gate is closed—a minor inconvenience when strong men are available to assist everyone over the wrought iron fence. Stephan's already climbed the fence and is on its park side while Sergio's still on the street side, and they have something of an assembly line going: Sergio's lifting girls to the top of the fence, making sure they don't get snagged on the spikes, then Stephan's grabbing ahold of them and easing them to the ground. Soon a number of people are on the park side of the fence, receiving the picnic supplies from those still on the street side, after which they help them over. Within five minutes, the entire group's inside the park: when Stephan's supervising an excursion, maneuvers of this nature are executed with military precision. And he has reason to be efficient: there are residential buildings across the street and someone could see them climbing the fence and inform the police, so the quicker they climb it and get out of sight the better.

Your humble narrator wishes to point out that when he refers to the group, he's not including Baptiste. In excluding Baptiste from the group, your narrator's following the inclinations of the group itself; he's also following the inclinations of Baptiste, who dislikes everyone not named Genevieve. Standing ignored on the sidewalk as the group climbs the fence (and particularly distressed because Genevieve's the first girl Stephan and Sergio lifted over it and she's about to vanish from sight under the trees), Baptiste points out the illegality of entering the park after hours to Stephan, because he can think of nothing else to say that will get anyone to pay him any mind.

"And your point is?" Stephan asks impatiently.

"It's against the law," Baptiste answers. "It's a fact."

"What of it?" Stephan scoffs. "At least half the stuff that's illegal isn't fundamentally wrong: its sole purpose is to keep sheep in line, the better to fleece them! Haven't you figured that out? *(Turning away from Baptiste, he addresses those who are in the process of climbing the fence.)* Are we doing any harm? Absolutely not! We're having a picnic, running around! Every scrap of litter will be accounted for and put in the trash! Every flowerbed will be treated as if it's the property of Dionysus! I have the greatest amount of respect for the park! If anyone fails to pick up after themselves, or so much as snaps a twig from a tree, they'll answer to me! We all know the park's officially closed! Official closure's a prejudice of daytime people! Our schedule differs, that's all! We're not going to behave differently than we would if it was noon, right? And if the cops come and we're hauled to the station—it *is* a possibility—then remember this: the *only* law we've broken is coming here after dark! The cops will hear from us how much we love the park, right? How we wouldn't so much as smudge the windows on the kiosks with our fingers, right? And we'll be released in the morning with a warning, nothing more! And then we'll do it *again*! *(He turns to Baptiste, who's uncomfortably staring at the sidewalk.)* Thanks Bap—sorry, I mean *Baptiste*—for reminding me to remind everyone to behave, even if that wasn't your intent! And if you really are worried about breaking the law you can always go home, right? Why bother us with it?"

"Uh..." begins Baptiste.

"Nothing more to say," Stephan interrupts, criss-crossing his hands in a desist gesture; then, addressing the always cheerful Panclerc and paying Baptiste no further mind, "We're breaking a useless law and won't lose any sleep on that account, because our behavior in the park's going to be exemplary, right?"

"My mother raised me to respect nature and not be a slob," Panclerc grins as Sergio boosts him to the top of the fence.

"Well spoken, Panclerc," Stephan laughs as he and Sergio steady him from both sides at the top of the fence, enable him to turn around so he can descend it. "All set?"

"As ready as I'll ever be!"

"Good, put your feet on my hands, down we go."

"Many thanks," Panclerc smiles once he's on the ground; grabbing a canvas bag full of bottles of juice, he strolls towards the park's interior.

"Everyone's over, Serg," Stephan says a couple minutes later. "Your turn." He waits for Sergio to negotiate the fence, then the two of them race away laughing, raising their arms in salutes as they pass under the winged figure on the pedestal.

As for Baptiste, he decides to break the law after all: unable to forgo the chance of interacting with Genevieve, he climbs the fence and goes to look for her. But enough of Baptiste for now.

After briefly chasing each other about under the trees in the light of the upside down belljars of the park's lamps, the group prepares their picnic. On the grassy hillside on the southwest side of the lake, a few feet from the lapping water, they unroll several yards of clear plastic; upon the plastic they arrange blankets; the food coolers, canvas bags of beverages, plates, napkins, and silverware are unpacked. Soon everyone's seated upon the blankets or standing in their vicinity, eating, drinking, and chatting. William, Christina, Pascale, Jean-Marc, Carole, and Genevieve are sharing one of the blankets, consuming pate, cheese, bread, and fruit, as well as juice and a lesser amount of champagne. Genevieve, though, soon moves to an adjacent blanket, where she busies herself with assembling platters of food in company with two other girls, for passing around. Stephan and Lucinda gather a couple plates of food, then interlock arms and begin strolling around the lake at water's edge, occasionally pausing to assemble sandwiches or embrace. The sky, clearing and beginning to be besprinkled with stars, is still dotted with clouds on its eastern side.

"What an amazing night," William says. "First, Père Lachaise, now Montsouris, a park I've never heard of—talk about an abundance of riches! It's a setting from a Manet painting, dream scene frozen outside of space and time! On a lawn glittering with a storm's rain, after the storm's past and has purified the air, by a lake in the AM in Paris! Before us the lake's whispering water, mirroring the tops of these trees along with those buildings over there, inverting everything! Those buildings that are unlike any we have at home! Paris rising heavenwards, looking like a city of two hundred years ago! Most of the people are asleep, and we're out here! I *know* I'll remember this for awhile!"

"You're not supposed to gush like a hick," chides Pascale. "You're supposed to take it casually, act like it's no big deal, lest our Parisian friends start to get the idea you don't belong here! It's like a guy who get flustered when a girl flashes some leg: the girl starts to think he doesn't deserve to see the said leg, and *unflashes* it right away!"

"You're a New Yorker," puts in Christina, "and you shame us by getting goo-goo eyed! Of course it's beautiful, but so is Central Park and we've been there at night a zillion times, as the fireflies flashed; and we've been by Bethesda Fountain, gazing across The Lake, hours before dawn in falling snow! Stop acting like we never do anything in parks at home!"

"You *are* starting to sound like a tourist," Jean-Marc can't resist saying, grinning from ear to ear.

"Look," William persists. "I don't care what any of you think! The fact that we've brought real china plates and steel knives and forks here, instead of plastic ones; and cloth napkins, for Christ's sake, instead of paper! It's so French, and it's beautiful! We don't have that sense of permanence in America! We don't have that ingrained sense of order! Look how everything's arranged as if it's a buffet in a restaurant! The napkins folded, plates stacked! I've seen construction workers in Paris setting up tripods in the middle of the street and attaching kettles and heating up their cassoulet with real fires! You'd never see that *anywhere* in America, because it would be considered too much bother! In America ritual's for the most part sublimated beyond recognition! We Americans are aimlessly adrift in a sea of disposability by comparison!"

"All right," answers Jean-Marc, "I'll grant that it's quaint and cute to you—that an arrangement of real plates, a picnic put together by scamps, is a *novelty* to an American! Ha ha! And you're enamored of our sense of order, as you call it? If you lived here, and had to *live through it* you wouldn't find it so appealing! Consider your situation: you've just stepped off a plane in a foreign land, you've neither attachments nor obligations here, no job to go to—there's no one here who's able to meddle with your life, because your life's in New York! You're on vacation, free from the necessity of earning a living and the associated annoyances! That alone has put you in a benign, all-forgiving, seeing-the-world-through-rose-tinted-glasses frame of mind! But newsflash: I can personally attest that tedium and pointless backbiting and jealous judgmental fools are *very* plentiful on this side of the Atlantic! And I've known more than one American who started feeling claustrophobic after being here for awhile; started whining about feeling the weight of centuries bearing down upon and smothering them—saying the stuff about how Europe's a monstrous bureaucracy, rife with papers to fill out to qualify you for filling out the papers that will qualify you to eventually—if you're lucky—fill out the papers you need to fill out in order to obtain something you probably won't get! You might admire our sense of order now, just wait: maybe you'll start to think it's a disease! Because the fact is we can't help our sense of order, and often wish we could! What our sense of order really means is that we, being born into a civilization that's far older than yours, have that much more accumulated oppression sitting on our shoulders! In a word, we're *trained*!"

"Gently, Jean-Marc," Carole jumps in. "Can't you see Bill's enjoying the state of childlike naivety Americans feel the moment they touch down in our town? Let him be! Let him discover our version of the grind for himself! Let's see whether he can stand being here for a month!"

"We're going to be here for a month and a half," Pascale says, "and relish every second! Sense of order or not, real or fake plates... Who cares? But I agree with you on one point, Billy: this is one glorious night! I'm all fizzies of delight inside!"

"I would certainly hope so," says Jean-Marc. "I doubt if there's anyone here, aside from Gen's shadow *(He contemptuously gestures at Baptiste, who's seated three blankets away and constantly sneaking glances at Genevieve.)*, who isn't in heaven! Anyone with a pulse can't help but love this! But I'm telling you that if I spent every night for the rest of my life like this it wouldn't compensate me for having served a year in the military! There isn't a picnic that's been held in history, by Cleopatra or Sardanapalus or anyone else, that would make up for that! So what do you think? Does knowing you'd be forced to spend a year in the army if you lived here yank you down from your starry-eyed heights? It's a sad truth: tedium and stupidity doesn't exempt a single geological location from its oppressive rule! The ruse inherent in civilization holds true for all societies equally! We've all been cast out of Paradise, banished from life's fountainhead, and *enslaved*!"

"The moment the first Narcissus was born," William says, taking up the thread, "is also the moment boredom was born! That poor woebegone soul who, by the act of discerning his reflection upon the water's surface, immediately lost his inner unity and stopped living in rhythm with life and doomed us to subjugation to vanity! Vanity is thought, and thought is the true essence of hell! When..."

"Just what we need," interrupts Carole. "Another male bonding fest!"

"Billy's off on another fallen from grace speech, and now he has a friend to aid and abet him!" Christina says. "It's our worst nightmare!"

"To roll this back to a more relevant subject," Pascale says, frowning at William and raising her voice. "Travel's a delightful thing! The transitional state one experiences upon arrival in an unfamiliar place *is* like a return to childhood! Of course the new place is as rife with inane gossip, pointless hostility, and insipid customs as the old place; but one hasn't had an opportunity to encounter these things yet; and couple this with the mood of joyful expectation with which one's overcome; then add in the profound sense of liberation, on account of having left the familiar place's annoyances behind: tally it all up, and it's heaven on earth! It won't last forever but, while it does, the only thing to do is savor it to the utmost! But no more talking about transitional states! I just want mine to pierce me through and through! *(She spreads her arms towards the sky, falls onto her back, squirms on the blanket.)* I salute you, sweet surrender! A-Woo!"

"Well, said, sweetie!" exclaims Carole, clapping. "Pearls of wisdom!"

"The girls win!" shouts Christina.

Jean-Marc, watching as the three girls embrace and cheek-peck, says, "The palm of victory goes to the women! Never mind that I was unaware of any contest!" He seeks to join them, but is repulsed.

"Of course there was a contest," insists Carole, "and since you won't admit it, no kissies for you!"

"There was a contest, and we lost," says William, attempting the diplomatic approach.

"Phooey!" scoffs Pascale. "You don't think there was a contest either! We see through your transparent attempt to—ha ha ha!" Laughing, she grasps William's hand and kisses it.

"I said there were no kissies for you?" Carole asks Jean-Marc as she embraces him. "I lied!"

"So how about another contest, such as throwing this Frisbee?" asks William who, not awaiting a reply, rises to his feet, runs a distance off, and tosses it towards the other four.

Jean-Marc leaps to his feet and runs forward and catches the Frisbee, quickly pivots, and tosses it towards the girls. Carole lunges sideways to snatch it, misses, yells, "Get out there, Pas! You too, Chrissy!" while picking it up, then throws it to the former. In less time than it takes to tell, all five are arranged in a circle, relaying the Frisbee clockwise from one to the other.

Apparently, the Frisbee-tossing of our five friends is the opening Baptiste's been waiting for; apparently, he's apprehensive enough concerning Jean-Marc and William—and perhaps the three girls as well—to refrain from approaching Genevieve as long as they're in the immediate area. Within a minute of the commencement of the Frisbee-tossing, Baptiste's demeanor changes. His furtive manner of watching Genevieve—pretending to look at objects in her vicinity while actually looking at her, scratching his forehead in efforts to conceal the direction of his glance—changes to unveiled eagerness as he rises to his feet, actively seeks her eye. But then caution bids him pause and observe our five friends again; obviously, he's seeking to confirm the degree of their absorption in their game. As far as he can tell, they're too busy focusing on catching and throwing the Frisbee to concern themselves with anything else. So he rather abruptly, with a jerky stride, crosses the distance between himself and Genevieve; soon he's crouching at her elbow, hesitantly tapping her wrist. "Genevieve, please," he says in a pleading tone. "What have I done? I'm sorry if I've done a wrong thing! I'm sorry!"

Genevieve winces at Baptiste's touch—at the sound of his voice. Her first instinct is to repulse him in no uncertain terms and she turns to confront him; but then she perceives the amount of pain and bafflement in his eyes and something of her former feelings for him as a friend stir in her breast. Without being able to check herself she finds herself being diplomatic, in an effort to spare his feelings. "Baptiste," she says in a not unpleasant tone, "it's not that you've done anything. It's just that I came to this party with the understanding I'd be helping. I'm manning the coolers, getting food ready, instead of socializing. So don't take it personally."

"But I can help you!" Baptiste exclaims, his expression immediately shifting from hurt to hopeful to happy. "Just tell me what to do! I..."

"I'm fine, thank you," Genevieve cuts him off, every muscle in her body stiffening. She's instantly alarmed at how he's thrust his body closer to hers—at his emboldened look; instantly feeling oppressed again, recalling his suffocating behavior; suddenly she knows that, by seeking to spare his feelings, she did so at the expense of her peace of mind. She must remember not to, under any circumstances, show him any sympathy: he's become a bitter shell of his former self, is no longer a remotely pleasant person, and is probably only going to get worse. "I do *not* need, or want, any help," she adds, scooting a couple yards away.

As it turns out, Baptiste's miscalculated with regard to the Frisbee-game. There's a reason our five friends have remained within earshot of Genevieve, maintained a tight circular formation, instead of freely running about while throwing as they'd ordinarily do: they've been standing watch. "Come on, Gen!" Carole yells, dashing towards her with the other four at her heels. "What's holding you up? I thought you were going to play!"

"I think Genevieve's busy, if you don't mind," says Baptiste, to such heights has his delusion already climbed as a result of her ill-advised foray into sympathy. He hasn't yet ascertained that she regrets the said foray, is mortified by his familiarity, and wants him gone.

"I am *not* busy!" Genevieve exclaims, visibly starting, and blanching with shame. She rises to her feet, darts Baptiste a look of disbelief, and strolls to Carole.

"It doesn't look like she's busy to me!" Carole hisses at Baptiste, not only unwilling to conceal her contempt but eager to make it plain as day. "And who do you think you are? Who are you to keep her from her friends? Who are you to dictate whether she can speak to me?"

"Enough of this!" yells Pascale, flinging her arms up. "Gen, I've got to speak to you—it can't wait!" She seizes Genevieve by the wrist and leads her away, with Carole and Christina following.

"But I...I didn't mean," Baptiste stammers, addressing William and Jean-Marc, who've remained behind to ensure he doesn't follow the girls. He's half-glancing from one to the other, panic flailing on his face; he confusedly seeks to shake hands with them, then jerks his arm back upon realizing they're not returning the gesture.

"Didn't mean what?" William asks with a sneer.

"Of course if it's an emergency, she...I can't know everything," Baptiste mumbles, ignoring, or possibly not hearing, the question. "And I've known her since we were little, you know. She can talk to Carole anytime, I wouldn't try to stop it. I've..."

"We all need to speak to her," interrupts Jean-Marc in a vaguely menacing tone. He's seeking to stare Baptiste in the eye, but the latter won't look at him.

"Women!" Baptiste exclaims, shrugging his shoulders. Apparently he feels this sentiment will miraculously endear him to Jean-Marc and William. In the meantime, he's staring at the ground with scitter-scattering eyes, shifting his weight from foot to foot.

"And what does that have to do with anything?" asks William. "Four friends need to speak to each other and they happen to be women: so what?"

"I..." Baptiste begins.

"You what?" Jean-Marc cuts him off. "Please do tell me, I'm eager to hear!" He catches his anger rising; it occurs to him he might give into the urge to physically interact with Baptiste and that, if he does so, he'll be acting against the wishes of Genevieve. So he lowers his voice, saying, "Hey, I'm sorry—we really don't know each other, right? I was out of line, OK? I just want to chat with my friends."

"So come on—they're waiting," William says, leading the way as he and Jean-Marc go to join the girls, Baptiste not daring to follow.

"Gen, I'm starting to get concerned," Carole's saying as Jean-Marc and William reach the girls, where they've assembled at the sculpture, *Drame au Désert*. "Since when do you pass up a game of Frisbee, or have worry stamped upon your face? And because of that parasite? He's not worth a second of worry, Gen! And sorry, but I'm getting annoyed at you! You're just about the most spirited, energetic, non-taker-of-garbage person I've met in my life! And our American friends don't even know it—they haven't met the real Genevieve yet! You've got to snap out of it, sweetheart! Enough is enough!" She embraces Genevieve.

"You know I grew up with Baptiste," Genevieve says softly, "how entangled our families are. It's not easy!"

"I know—I know!" says Carole impatiently. "I thought we'd covered that—settled he was gone gone gone, over and out! I mean, what's gotten into you? I don't care what he once was, he's vermin now! I don't understand this business of veiling our dislike of the creep, whispering when he's near, taking care he doesn't catch on, looking out for the welfare of his feelings! And what did you say to brighten Bap up, anyway? We all saw it—it was revolting!"

"I admit that was stupid," Genevieve answers. "I didn't say much. Only that I was busy and he shouldn't take it personally."

"What?" Carole yells. "You tossed Bap a bone out of pity? He deserves no pity, only contempt! What? That *thing* who's glued to your every move, hates all your friends, and is always in knots of resentment? That sullen, negative, sick *thing*? Tossing Bap some pity's the same as giving him the green light to *ruin* your life!"

"Speaking as someone brand new to the situation who's looking at it with fresh eyes," Christina says, "I can honestly say I have a very bad feeling about that guy. I was observing him earlier—he didn't know I was doing so, he was looking with glazed eyes at the ground. His lips were moving as if mouthing words, but he wasn't speaking to anyone; at the same time, he was fitfully clenching and unclenching his hands and his arms and shoulders were quivering, almost shaking. I don't think he knew his lips and hands were moving, no one in their right mind would want to be looking like that in public. I don't think I've seen accumulated frustration showing through in anyone like that before, and I know I don't want to see it again. I'm not exaggerating when I say a shudder stabbed me in the chest! I can honestly say the sooner he's gotten rid of the better, before whatever inner conflicts he's caught up in become more entangled with Gen *(She grasps Genevieve's hand.)* and he starts stalking her! I mean, not that he really would—I'm imagining things, I know," she makes haste to qualify, feeling she may have been needlessly alarming.

"All right, Miss Melodrama," William says, "we all know Bap's nuts, but that's his problem. Maybe Gen can do without an extreme interpretation."

"She's right, Bill," Genevieve says, wrapping an arm around Christina. "Things are getting ugly! I've let it go for too long, been willfully blind! Matters will be put right today when I sit down with mom and dad! No more weak moments! No more Bap in my life! I still can't believe I was too nice to him minutes ago! Thank you all for watching over me!" She takes turns hugging everyone.

"Like this fierce mommy panther who's about to tear this snake to pieces for slaying her young," says Carole, pointing at the sculpture, "we're going to tear Bap to pieces for slaying your good cheer! We're going to channel the energy of this cat and go over there, and smack him around! Maybe only verbally, but the saying's wrong: word's *can* hurt, sometimes as thoroughly as sticks and stones!"

"No, Carole," Genevieve says. "I don't want to engage him, that's not the best way. I don't want to give him anything to cling to, good or bad, and fuel his...whatever it is. I think the best thing would be to discreetly ditch him, not humiliate him."

"What, we're still handling trash with kid gloves?" Jean-Marc exclaims. "Why? He of the bile-swollen cheeks, with hatred glittering in his eyes? When he started listening to Bill and I at Steph's it was like he was in torment, on the *physiological* level, simply because we exist! I'll be more than happy to knock him to the ground and stomp my boot in his face!" He lifts a leg, slams his foot down.

"You're not listening to me," Genevieve responds. "Here, look at me. *(Jean-Marc does so.)* Now, listen: the last thing I want is chaos among the parents, and our families irreparably torn apart. If possible, I want to be rid of Bap without direct engagement. I don't want to give him anything to cling to—no nasty looks or bad words. If we were to do him violence, verbal or otherwise, his parents might hear about it first and then family chaos could erupt before I have a chance to speak to mom and dad, and make me look like the cause of everything. I want our separation to go as smoothly as possible, get it? I want him to be spoken to by his parents, informed he's to stay away, and for it to end there, with the minimal amount of lingering resentment. Now, will you help me give him the slip unobtrusively or not?"

"But haven't we already given him the slip?" asks Pascale. "He's not here, right? Let's just leave!"

"You don't know him," Genevieve says. "He's watching us right now through the branches of an evergreen—no, don't look and give anything away! Act like I'm not telling you! The tree's in the distance, he's afraid to come too close with you here. I know this because he made a point of stepping from behind it for an instant when I was facing in that direction and no one else was. He wants me to know he's there."

"Son of a bitch!" Carole exclaims. "That measly little..."

"Please," interrupts Genevieve, "don't show that you know! Indulge me tonight and do it my way. If we exit the park now, he'll follow and make sure I know he's doing it, and maybe attempt approaching me again—my avoidance could become obvious and force the issue. Our family history gives him the courage to behave like this. But after I speak to mom and dad and tear our history down, he won't have that crutch—I'll be free. And if it doesn't work, Jean-Marc, then you can do it your way. Bap *is* a coward, after all."

"I'm not sure you should've said that," Carole can't resist saying. "You're only encouraging him to sabotage a discreet exit, so he can do what he's wanted to all night—stomp Bap into the ground! Just kidding, of course!"

"Jean-Marc, *is* she kidding?" Genevieve asks with a smile.

"Absolutely," Jean-Marc answers, grasping Genevieve's hand. "You're the one in the situation, so what you say goes. You want to ditch Bap without being obvious, and I'm with you one hundred percent. And I have an idea: why don't we take an unannounced cab ride? Someone can keep Bap distracted with hearty man talk, Steph would be perfect, and I can hail a cab off to the side and climb in with Carole, then you can hop in at the last moment, as if in afterthought, and we can zoom off and meet up with the others across town and have a nice breakfast. What do you think?"

"I think it's perfect!" says Genevieve, squeezing Jean-Marc's hand with feeling. "It not only leaves Bap in the dust, it veils premeditation! He won't be able to tell he was ditched on purpose, or follow! Simple, and perfect! Let's do it!"

"This could be overkill," says William, "but why not let us foreigners hail the cab? Bap won't give it a thought if Chrissy says it's time for us three to get some sleep because we're wiped out by jet-lag and Pas and I agree and we commence hailing; then, after we're in and the door's still open, Gen hops in—presto! Bap won't have time to blink! The cab will be leaving before his brain has time to inform him Gen's piled in with the tourists! And it also has the advantage of being less painful to the guy, seeing her hop in with the tourists instead of with the man *(He grins at Jean-Marc.)* who I'm sure he dislikes the most."

"Perfection just got a little better," Genevieve smiles. "That's definitely the cherry on top! I take off with my new American friends! It adds more innocence to the picture! Then this evening I strike the final blow, talk to mom and dad and get Bap banned, and am free! Thank you all!"

"Well amended," Jean-Marc says, shaking William's hand. "We're definitely well met: every minute affirms it all the more!"

"Right, male bonding's a wonderful thing," Carole says, rolling her eyes. "Shouldn't we be circling around to Steph and Lucy to tell them the plan?"

"Tally-ho, around the lake we go!" Jean-Marc yells; then, lowering his voice, "The long way, so we don't run into Bap! I might forget Gen's wishes and whack him after all! Just kidding, of course!"

Our six friends begin strolling to where Stephan and Lucinda are seated on a waterfront bench on the opposite side of the lake. We calculate that they'll reach them shortly after the commencement of the next chapter.

CHAPTER 10

Despite the immediate threat to the peace of mind of she who's perhaps the strongest among them (and, as the strongest, the most likely to have an influence upon their general disposition), our friends manage to recover a great deal of their natural good cheer during their trek to the opposite side of the lake. They're mindful of the presence of the enemy (Baptiste's broodingly pacing back and forth near the picnic blankets, frequently darting displeased glances in their direction.) and animated by the urgency of their mission, but this doesn't prevent them from relishing the beauty about them.

"God, it's stunning!" exclaims Christina, glancing every which way. "Please pinch me, to prove I'm not dreaming!"

"If I pinched you I'm not sure that would establish which side of dreaming we're on," answers William, "because I think I'm in the same dream! Nothing like a thunderstorm to wash the dust from the atmosphere, infuse everything with the sort of clarity that resembles a hallucination!"

"Yeah," joins in Jean-Marc, "that's how contaminated our life is by modern activity! We're so accustomed to viewing our surroundings through a veil of polluted air that when we see them as they're meant to be seen we start wondering if they're real or imagined! I cracked on you Americans earlier, laughed at your touristy gushings, but the fact is I love my town, and tonight I'm extra proud of her—happy she's put on her best face for you! I'm never bored with her and will never live anywhere else!"

"We all love our town," Genevieve says, "and don't ever let these two *(She indicates Jean-Marc and Carole.)* attempt to mask it with cynical cracks! Paris has taken my breath away from the first I can remember, and still does every day! I'm blessed to have been born and raised here! And I must say it's always a pleasure to see Paris through the eyes of new arrivals who're stunned by her beauty!"

"So kind," says Pascale, clasping Genevieve's hand. "And if you'd like me to describe what my eyes are seeing..."

"Please do."

"I see treetops swaying against the darkness of a sky that's somehow silvery, imbued with the famous light of your city that shines with its unique rich and dreamy quality, even at night; and I hear the waves of this lake whispering as they lap at the dew-besparkled lawn. And I see the buildings beyond the park seeming to lose their solidity like desert dunes in a baking sun, even though it's a bit chilly. This after-storm air's like the water of an illuminated aquarium—like gazing through a crystal magnifying glass—like... Gen, your city's so...it's just... A-Woo!"

"Well concluded," laughs Carole. "A-Woo!"

"A-Woo! A-Woo!" they all start howling; then, in the same way that war-whoops excite troops during battle, they find themselves impelled by their howling to madly dash about; and it doesn't take long for their dashing to metamorphose into a game: they're soon running a relay, whereby one of them will race ahead to catch the Frisbee and then wait for another to race ahead before throwing it and so on. In a flash they're within shouting distance of Stephan and Lucinda and Jean-Marc's sprinting ahead, yelling that if anyone touches Stephan's shirttail before he does he'll treat them to all the *bulots* they can eat at the Grand Café.

"Steph and Lucy, we've hatched a plan," Jean-Marc says as he runs up to them. "We're going to ditch that insufferable killjoy, wash away the unsightly splotch on the white of Gen's happiness!"

"You mean Bap's fallen from grace?" Stephan laughs.

"I'm not sure wining, possessive, gloom-dispensing Sci Po lackeys ever have grace to fall from! Simply put, we've all had it with the intolerable spectacle of a fair lady torn from serenity by the melodramatic antics of a mediocre nonentity who has no business being here! Honor demands mobilization, and we need your participation! But, first, if you don't mind, I need your shirttail for a second!" Grabbing Stephan's shirttail as the others approach, he says, "Too late slouches! You're buying your own *bulots*!"

"Lucy and I worship Gen as much as we detest Bap," Stephan responds, "and we'll be honored to participate! Bap's sullen mug can't be gone soon enough! But what do *bulots* have to do with it?"

"Nothing whatsoever," Jean-Marc answers, explaining the challenge he issued to the others.

"Pardon my ignorance," says Christina, now standing next to Stephan and Lucinda along with everyone else. "This is my first visit to Paris. What are *bulots*?"

"That's funny," William answers. "Miss UN translator doesn't know what *bulots* are! How are you going to further Franco-American relations when you're ignorant of one the finest delicacies French cuisine has to offer?"

"*Bulots*," Pascale says, "are sea snails—whelks—prepared the French way, cooked with spices—ginger, fennel, anise, parsley, thyme—and cider and lemon; or dipped in garlic mayonnaise. An ultra-succulent taste bud massage! Yum!" She rolls her tongue about her lips.

"Like a kiss you can eat," William adds. "Delectable, but not as delectable as *this*!" So saying, he grabs Pascale by the shoulders and kisses her for a good half-minute, before exchanging her for Christina. And then a curious, and wholly unexpected, thing occurs: when he lifts his face from Christina's and does a quick turnabout with a fist raised towards the sky and is about to proclaim his joy aloud, his eyes encounter Genevieve's eyes and he finds himself surprised into silence. She's standing quite close, regarding him with a mixed look of mirth and admiration; her eyes suddenly widen and then rapidly glance at the ground as a reddish tinge briefly overspreads her face. For a few seconds, William and Genevieve's surroundings vanish from their awareness and they're alone together, sharing an immensely appealing something that neither can put their finger on; what they're aware of is an inner shock of astonishment, caress of the nerves, coupled with a trace of embarrassment—a fleeting sensation of transparency. Apparently, their private interval passes unnoticed by the others: Stephan and Jean-Marc, having imitated William by tasting of the lips of their respective consorts, are occupied when it occurs and Pascale and Christina are located at an angle that precludes direct glimpses of William and Genevieve's faces. At any rate, no glances are exchanged among the others in reference to the episode. William, recovering himself, hastens to say, "Steph and Lucy, Jean-Marc's told you why we're here, and..."

"Thank you, Bill," Carole cuts in, slapping Jean-Marc's hands from her waist. "I was about to point out we didn't circle around the lake to discuss French cuisine! Bap's insufferable; he's a mean-spirited envious creep who's ruining Gen's night and, therefore, mine! Hopefully, my boyfriend's not indifferent to the situation!"

"Don't look at me like that!" protests Jean-Marc. "The first thing I said to Steph and Lucy was that we're ridding Gen of the parasite! Ask them!"

"She already knows, you fool!" Stephan says. "But to business. Spill it!"

"Right," says Jean-Marc. "Here's the deal: Gen's requested that we ditch Bap seamlessly, such that he neither suspects it's going to happen nor is able to realize, after the fact, that it was planned. She'll be speaking to her parents later, to obtain their assistance in permanently eliminating him from her life; at the same time, she'll be seeking to prevent unpleasantries from erupting between her parents and Bap's parents: such is why the loathsome beast must be handled with kid gloves."

"Nauseating as dealing with him tactfully is, I get it."

"OK, so we've decided you're the perfect man to distract Bap with hale and hearty talk and keep him apart from Gen. At some point Bill, Pas, and Chrissy will mention they're wiped out and start looking for a cab. Once they've piled into a cab and told the driver where to go they'll signal to Gen and she'll hop inside—quite casually, as if in afterthought—and then off they'll race before Bap has a chance to take two steps. We'll meet up with them afterwards for breakfast, at least Carole and I are. It'd be nice to have you and Luce join us."

"Absolutely," Lucinda says. "A celebration of Gen's freedom! It's long overdue!"

"Please," Genevieve says softly. "Don't count those chickens. I'm *hoping*."

"Nonsense," Lucinda says, clasping Genevieve's hand. "Your parents love you more than life itself, and justifiably never tire of singing your praises! They'll stand by you against all adversity, and this isn't much adversity to speak of! They'll give Bapso the gate without a second thought! He won't be infecting the Cloutier household anymore! Count Bapso gone!"

"It's not mom and dad I'm doubting—of course they'll support me without question, and exile Bap. It's Bap's reaction that's uncertain: will he be willing to be told to leave me alone? I have no intention of so much as looking at him again, but who knows what's in his mess of a head? He might make it necessary to do what Jean-Marc wants to do!"

"I have a good idea what *that* is!" Stephan laughs. "It's what I want to do, punch him silly and toss him in the lake!"

"Sorry I went in that direction," Genevieve hastens to say. "Giving him the slip instead of manhandling him is a way of minimizing the emotion—I want to eliminate our connection on all levels, get it? When a person's completely ignored it's more difficult for them to feel that being a pest will result in anything."

"Don't worry, Gen," Stephan says, "I understand completely. It's a good plan, and Bap's going to be ditched without a hitch. It'll be easy to keep him distracted, and... Hey, why doesn't Lucy act fed up with me? By the time we're looking for a cab, the metro will be opening soon: she could yell she's taking the metro and stomp away in a huff. I'll chase after her, but quickly return; then act upset and say women are insane, any rubbish Bap will swallow. That way, the little man won't feel he's the only one having a bad night. Not only is it a better way of covering our tracks, it'll be fun—might as well mix some gaming in."

"But what station am I supposed to stomp towards?" asks Lucinda. "Cité Universitaire? Alésia? Denfert-Rochereau? And cabs aren't exactly lining up down here."

"Good point," Stephan says, sweeping his hand through Lucinda's hair. "We'll walk up René Coty towards Denfert, best way to find a cab. Whether we find one a block away or have to go all the way to Denfert, no matter. As for what metro station, you'll stomp towards the one that's closest when a cab's found, and... OK, I've got it: Jean-Marc and Carole will follow you and wait with you at the metro until I get rid of Bap. Then we'll take a separate cab or the metro and meet for breakfast."

"Sure," Lucinda says, "it'll be fun to do the stomp-away routine. Where are we having breakfast?"

Dearest reader, your humble narrator's just realized Lucinda Junot hasn't been described yet, and will pause to remedy the oversight. She's, like Stephan, an understudy at the Comédie-Française and twenty-two years of age. She measures five feet eight, is blue-eyed, very slender, and light and supple of step. She's wearing a black kimono mini dress with a plunging V-neck and pink and scarlet flower prints; her shoulder-length blond hair's tied in a ponytail with a scarlet ribbon. It should also be mentioned that, while she's been seeing Stephan for the past three days, it's not an ongoing situation. Stephan, as has been stated, isn't inclined to monogamy; nor is Lucinda ready for a permanent relationship to compete with her devotion to acting at this point in her life. They see each other off and on without the burden of illusions or future plans. Lucinda was born on the French Riviera, where her parents are proprietors of a beach front hotel, and was seized with the desire to relocate to Paris and become an actress in the second grade; from that point on, there was never any variation in her what-I-want-to-be-when-I-grow-up essays. She's living her dream and seldom out of good cheer.

"I was thinking we could meet at the Opéra, then go to the Grand Café," Jean-Marc says, answering Lucinda's question.

"Excellent," says William. "The Opéra, with sunrise on the way! Perfect scenery for us tourists!"

"And *bulots* at the Grand," says Genevieve. "Chrissy, you'll love them! My treat, everyone!"

"Nonsense," says Christina. "We tourists are treating all of you!"

"Won't hear of a no," adds William.

"Deaf to no," says Pascale. "Least we can do."

"Opéra and the Grand it is," says Stephan. "Lucy, Jean-Marc, Carole: you're just going to have to hang around until I ditch Bap, so we can ride together—cab or metro, I don't care which. I'll first dupe Bap with talk of going to my place, then later act nuts about having been dumped. I'll say I need consolation and am heading to another girl's place, and take my leave of him. It'll be fun to feed him lie after lie! To it, soldiers! Time to circle back around, and... Jesus! Look at the little man eyeing us! *(He turns to Genevieve, clasps her hands.)* Don't worry, we'll make things right! Bap will have to go through me if wants to bother you again! No, strike that! We're going to surgically remove him very gently tonight—we'll take care that it goes smoothly. We want minimal drama, no fists in his face: he doesn't deserve a discrete transition, but you do. Rest easy, angelface: he'll soon be gone." He embraces her.

Soon thereafter, our friends are circling back to the western side of the lake, where the majority of their comrades are gathered near the picnic blankets. Baptiste's still erratically pacing off to the side, frequently darting glances in Genevieve's direction. The moment he perceives she's returning to his side of the lake, he strolls to the waterline and stares at the water.

"Deluded doesn't begin to describe that guy," Jean-Marc says. "We've made it plain we don't want his company, that Gen's with us and not him, and now he's pretending to be fascinated by the lake! We all know the only reason he's standing there is because Gen's headed in that direction, and he has no clue we know it! What an idiot!"

"Fine," says Carole, "forewarned is forearmed. Bap's not going anywhere, our plan isn't a fantasy—we'll be carrying it out for real. So are we ready? Do we know our parts? Steph, are you prepared to waylay him with cheery man-talk, pretend to take him to heart? Americans, are you ready to form a human shield about Gen with Lucy, Jean-Marc, and I, prevent would-be-loverboy from breaking through our ranks while keeping up a steady stream of casual banter?"

"Ready, coach!" says Stephan, saluting her. "Bap'll have no doubt I'm his new best friend!"

"Likewise ready," says William. "See? We've encircled Gen in tight formation, like a Roman cohort guarding an empress! No hostile force will penetrate our lines! Gen's going to be too busy listening to our wall of chatter to be expected to remember to breathe, much less spare a moment for parasitical Bap!"

"Bap, the would-be lady-killer, who's actually a groveling shoe-licker, an utter stranger to pride!" says Christina.

"Bap, who fancies girls ought to be swooning for love of him, when he's still a toddler reaching for the hem of mommy's dress!" says Lucinda.

"Bap, the pipsqueak who thinks girls have nothing better to do than distract him from his contemptible self!" says Carole.

"Shss! Quiet, the object of surgical removal's near," says Jean-Marc in an undertone, Baptiste now being not more than twenty yards away.

Pascale, not wanting to be left out of the gibe-game, quickly whispers, "Bap, the puffed up, hollow, grasping little half-man who thinks girls owe him ego-pats and adoration!"

"Bap, the thing I want to disappear!" puts in Genevieve, at the last possible moment, as she clasps Pascale's arm.

"Hey, Baptiste, where've you been?" Stephan says, strolling ahead of the others and clapping him on the back.

Baptiste, who's been brooding about the misunderstanding he feels he's a victim of—bringing the cutting tones of Jean-Marc, William, and Carole to mind—cursing Genevieve's friends in general, her inaccessibility when they're nearby—uncomfortably shrugs his shoulders, uncertain what to say. Unable to help himself, he darts a pleading-eyed glance in Genevieve's direction, but of course fails to engage her attention: she's already being lead away by those that surround her.

"So," continues Stephan, ignoring Baptiste's awkwardness, "I'm glad I ran into you! We're heading back to the apartment to watch an old American movie, *Bringing Up Baby*! Screwball comedy, and Baby's a leopard! Good fun, what?" He slaps Baptiste's back again.

"Sounds OK to me," replies Baptiste, becoming less uncomfortable. He can't help but brighten at the thought that he's being invited to go where Genevieve appears to be going.

"Plus," Stephan resumes, leaning towards Baptiste in confidential mode, as if about to impart a carefully guarded secret, "there's a stash of oysters in the fridge that hasn't been touched yet! A ten-liter cask of Falklands babies, packed alive in seawater! A virgin cask, I tell you! Untouched! From the Falklands! Fresh and alive! The best! There's nothing like slipping a knife between the shells of an oyster, prying them open, bringing the succulent organism to light! Nothing like squirting lemon on the slippery beast, lifting the half shell to one's lips, sucking the sweet meat into one's mouth! Taste bud explosion! *(He slaps Baptiste on the back twice.)* So what do you say? Are you in? Are you going help me eat those virgins?"

"I like oysters a lot," Baptiste replies. "Sure, I'll help you eat them. Lemon's a good thing, a tart flavor for oysters. I'll help you with the cask too." He's not merely more relaxed now, he's out-and-out relieved. When Genevieve and the others were on the opposite side of the lake, he was wondering if he was being talked about—especially, whether she was voicing displeasure with him. Obviously, she hasn't done so; otherwise, Stephan wouldn't be inviting him to partake of the oysters; therefore, since Stephan believes he's still in Genevieve's good graces, why shouldn't he believe it as well? The way it looks now, he's going to be wrapping up the night at Stephan's place, and Genevieve's going to be there too. So hope's definitely stirring in Baptiste's breast. Nevertheless, he's still troubled by the fact he hasn't had her to himself for a second since arriving at the party, annoyed at the extent of her familiarity with seemingly an endless amount of people. Such is Baptiste's present frame of mind.

"Glad to hear it!" Stephan responds. "It's always a pleasure to share the virgins with someone who appreciates them!" Then, gesturing towards those gathered about the blankets, "Time to roust these good people from their pastoral dream! Come on!" Seizing Baptiste's arm, he quickly advances forward and yells, "Time to break camp! We're heading back to the apartment! A barrel of oysters is begging to be devoured!"

"But we still have a good half hour left," protests Didier, checking his watch. "The witching hour's five, right? We have time before the streets start to fill up!" Perhaps the reader will recall that Didier is Stephan's younger brother. Like many younger brothers, he delights in contradicting his older brother.

"Didn't you hear me, little brother?" Stephan yells. "I said there's a cask of oysters waiting for us to pop their cherries! Virgins waiting to be slurped! I've been dreaming about their sweet meat all night, and I'm going to have at them! What's lolling in the park for awhile longer compared with the pastime of oyster-slurping? I defy anyone to inform me oyster-slurping's inferior to any other activity on earth! Baptiste, for one, agrees with me! Don't you, Baptiste?"

"Yeah, I agree with that," Baptiste says. "Definitely."

"No one in his right mind would belittle oyster-slurping," answers Didier, looking at Stephan quizzically. "But, big brother, don't you think the oysters will taste even better if we put them off a bit? Show some restraint, allow your hunger to sharpen its edge, and you'll enjoy them twofold. And what's a measly half hour, anyway?" At the same time that he's playing this fraternal game (all of Stephan and Didier's public arguments are show-arguments, opportunities to play to an audience) he's very curious as to why his brother's being friendly with Baptiste. Obviously, the latter's being set up—there's no other possible explanation. Didier's eager to know the details.

"You're forgetting, little brother," continues Stephan, "about the joys of spontaneously surrendering to intense craving! Craving for oysters that throbs in one's veins, pounds in one's head, makes one dizzy! I want oyster-meat, I want it now, and I'm going to get it! I'm going to stroll home dizzy, with pictures of available oysters in my head, and then pounce on them like a man about to die of starvation! I'm going to pry open the shells, and spread them, with trembling hands! I'm going to thrust my tongue into the moist meat, suck it into my mouth, almost faint with the thrill when the flavor explodes! Sweet sticky oyster meat is as close as we'll ever get to heaven on earth!" By the end of this speech he's yelling loud enough to be heard on the opposite side of the lake.

In the meantime, those in the know—still forming a human wall about Genevieve—have been mingling with the group and communicating the plan, so as to provide the actual reason for an early departure. In less than two minutes, everyone's busy packing.

Didier, upon being made aware of why his brother's being chummy with Baptiste (by a girl seated behind him and his girlfriend Antoinette), wastes no time in rising to his feet, and declaring, "Steph calls me little brother, but he's the real baby! We're going have to go now and slurp the oysters, before he throws a baby's tantrum! Up and out of here, everyone, for the baby's sake!" He's soon helping Antoinette fold blankets.

Stephan, perceiving that everyone knows the plan and is implementing it, switches his attention back to preoccupying the enemy. "This way, Baptiste! *(He leads Baptiste further away from Genevieve.)* Our assignment's to roll up the plastic! Glad you're here to help!"

"Uh...glad to," Baptiste mumbles.

The group packs up the picnic with a degree of efficiency the strictest drill sergeant would admire, not neglecting to properly dispose of every scrap of litter. Within twenty minutes everyone's climbed the fence at the place where they entered the park and are retracing their steps northwards on Avenue René Coty, their eyes peeled for a cab. All are united in the goal of separating Genevieve from Baptiste while keeping him from being aware of it.

CHAPTER 11

We rejoin our friends shortly after sunrise at the intersection of Avenue René Coty and Rue d'Alésia, where they're faced with a dilemma. Everyone's been diligently searching for a cab, but they've failed to find one—doubtless due both to the early hour and the fact they're still outside the boundaries, non-delineated but nevertheless real, of the center areas of Paris. What to do? The Fleury apartment is west on Rue d'Alésia, a left turn; the greater likelihood of encountering a cab is straight ahead towards Place Denfert-Rochereau. Baptiste's been duped into believing there's going to be a final gathering at the Fleury apartment: how get around the fact they have no intention of going there at this time?

A skilled general's adept at switching tactics as situations demand. Stephan, addressing Baptiste to create the illusion of consulting with him, says, "I've just thought of something—I want to see the lion! What do you think? Should we go see the lion? Be a nice way to end our excursion, don't you think? The lion brings good luck!" He's referring to the colossal statue of a lion that sits in the center of Place Denfert-Rochereau.

Baptiste is afraid to contradict Stephan. He feels fortunate that Stephan, the undisputed leader of the group, has taken him under his wing—Stephan's never appeared to like him before. At the same time, every bone in his body's yearning to speak to Genevieve, put his mind at ease with regard to any misunderstanding that may have crept between them. He feels that once they're indoors, instead of outside in these open spaces, he'll have a better opportunity of reaffirming his devotion. Going to see the lion will only delay matters. So he attempts to agree and dissuade at the same time, saying, "Yeah, the lion's a good statue and it would be OK to see it. But the lion's out of the way, and..."

"Splendid!" Stephan interrupts. "I knew it! You're aware of the restorative powers of the lion, and want to do him honor too! Your endorsement matters, and I thank you!" Turning to address the group, he shouts, "Listen up, everyone! Baptiste and I have decided our night won't be complete until we visit the sacred lion of Denfert-Rochereau! So straight ahead we go, to obtain the blessing of the beast! We've had a fine adventure tonight, and want more to follow! Offering our devotion to the lion will ensure that they do! Anyone who has the lion on his side can look forward to uninterrupted good cheer! After we visit the lion, we'll take the metro back!"

The group's well aware of why Stephan's proposing they go out of their way to visit a statue, and greet his suggestion with shouts of approbation. Crossing Rue d'Alésia and continuing north on the tree-lined traffic island of Avenue René Coty, they yell as one, "To the sacred lion we go!"

"Look at him trying to smile through it and hide his real feelings," Carole says, referring to Baptiste's obvious reluctance to visit the lion, as Stephan chats up a storm at his side. "Talk about mental constipation!"

"Only one thing's on his mind," adds Jean-Marc, "and that's to inflict his worm of a personality upon Gen!"

"Sick! Sick! Sick!" says Carole, wincing. But then she turns to Genevieve, saying softly, "Sorry, Gen—I should bury those thoughts. I know it's not easy for you. I won't..."

"Please," interrupts Genevieve, "no apologies on Bap's account! I'm a big girl and a lucky girl, surrounded by dear friends! After today I don't want a thought of him in my head, but he's here now and fair game. Sure would like to find a cab, though. I don't want people walking to Montparnasse for my sake."

"We'll walk to the English Channel if we have to," William says. "There isn't anyone here who cares how long this project takes."

"Thank you, Bill," Genevieve responds, brightness leaping into her eyes. "So sweet!" Carried away by an impulse of gratitude, she clasps his forearm with both hands, inadvertently sliding his shirtsleeve above his elbow as she does so.

The instant Genevieve grasps his arm William starts inwardly, is suffused with... With what? Benign fire, thrilling stings? His reason's unable to classify the tension that ignites his spine, fills his chest with sparkling buoyancy. At the same time, he's aware that something of his reaction's being transmitted to Genevieve, who immediately grips his arm tighter. As her body tenses in response to the disturbance within his, additional tingles erupt in his muscles and erase his sense of standing upon solid ground.

Genevieve, allow your humble narrator to stress, has grasped William's arm in a spirit of friendship—an innocent gesture; but the moment he starts and his face flushes, a more insistent impulse overcomes her and she squeezes more intimately, unable to stop. Likewise, does she feel an electric sensation course through her body—a delightfully unsettling, addictive, sensation. She plainly perceives the pleased vibrations of William's body: the aura surrounding him is almost a palpable raiment she can slip inside of and feel cozy and secure in, and she can't help but want more. Often, it's suchlike electrical reactions that bring two people together, without them seeming to have much say in the matter.

William, carried away by their shared reverberations, unfolds one of Genevieve's hands from his arm with his free hand—their fingers instantly intertwine and exchange caresses. Then he's gazing into her eyes and, such is the ineffable sweetness within them, his face and throat and shoulders shiver, are inundated with upwellings of delight. If they were alone instead of surrounded by the others they'd very likely continue intertwining their fingers; they might even spontaneously surrender to an embrace and kiss. Such speculations, however, serve little purpose at this point: they're surrounded by the others, and soon separate. Their exchange takes place in no more than twenty seconds.

The first instance of stealth sympathy between William and Genevieve by the lakeshore passed unnoticed by their friends: not so this time. Their friends, after all, are formed in a protective circle about Genevieve, as their duty requires—close enough to often brush against her. The sudden air she and William have of being in their own private world—the mutual tenseness of their bodies which, as it were, freezes the air about them, injects a charge into the atmosphere: these signs clearly broadcast their attraction. Not to mention the intertwinement of their fingers, affection darting between their interlocked eyes.

Christina and Pascale exchange knowing looks, Jean-Marc nudges Carole, Carole glances at Lucinda, Lucinda glances at Jean-Marc. Although there's amusement and wonder in these glances, there's also discomfort—on the part of those who are French, that is. Carole, although she heard the American girls declare otherwise, is afraid jealousy might enter the picture. As for Lucinda and Jean-Marc, neither know anything concerning the nature of the relationship of the three Americans, aside from the great amount of familiarity they've observed between them: they're more apprehensive than Carole. Genevieve, for her part, is as busy seeking to recover her composure as she is hesitant to meet anyone's glance. Christina and Pascale, perceiving the discomfort of their French friends, hasten to dispel it.

"So, trance man," Pascale addresses William, mischief in her voice, "do you know where you are? Do you remember your name?" She winks at the others, by way of indicating she's well aware of what's transpired and untroubled by it.

"Sure," replies William, glancing about half-absently, as if suspended between this world and another and finding it difficult to keep track of both. He'd be in a near-heavenly state, if he wasn't laboring to conceal the evidence of such. He's as if swirling into the sky between the rows of trees on each side of him at the same time that he knows its premature to believe his joy to be anything but fleeting.

"Sure, what?" Christina joins in, laughing and kicking at his feet. "Sure you know where your feet are? Sure you're not upside down?"

Carole, emboldened by the example of the American girls, tugs at Genevieve's dress. "Are you awake?" she asks.

"Of course I'm awake," responds Genevieve, slapping Carole's hand away as a blush suffuses her face. "What's gotten into you?"

"I think it's a matter of what's gotten into you," counters Carole, her eyes sparkling with glee. "It seems you're changing color, looking pinkish! Some sort of ladybug, or lovebug, color…"

"Shss!" interrupts Genevieve.

"Been bitten, have you?"

"If you don't…"

"Girls," breaks in Jean-Marc, "have you forgotten why we're walking up here, ostensibly to see the lion?"

"Of course not," answers Carole. "Gen needs to be separated from that thing *(She gestures towards Baptiste, still being distracted by Stephan.)* as soon as possible! All eyes are scanning for a cab! No one's forgotten, and I think you know that! There aren't many down here at this hour, but we'll find…"

"There's one right there!" Lucinda cuts in, excitedly pointing to the left. "At the light!" Sure enough, there's a cab waiting at the light on Rue de la Tombe Issoire, they having arrived at the point where it crosses Avenue René Coty.

"I'll get it!" exclaims Carole. "I'll have him pull up a bit ahead of us!" She dashes towards the cab while flailing her arms.

Stephan, alerted via a cat call from Jean-Marc, seizes Baptiste by the shoulders and makes as if to impart life-altering wisdom, turning him away from the proceedings. Genevieve and the Americans, immediately surrounded by additional people, rapidly stroll ahead.

In the meantime, Carole's caught the driver's attention and hopped inside the cab. She instructs the driver where to stop, says she'll be exiting and that four new people will be entering, and hands him a twenty euro bill to ensure his cooperation. Encouraged by his easygoing manner, she further explains that a nice girl is ditching a pest, and asks him if he wouldn't mind spinning the tires the moment she—Carole, that is—yells, *Have a nice sleep!* He assures her he'll be honored to help a damsel in distress.

"It was the kick of the semester!" Stephan's saying to Baptiste, still grasping the latter's shoulders, so that his back's to Genevieve. "We had a room in the hotel opposite professor Tarlot's apartment, saw it all with binoculars! We had escort girls, from different services, turning up at Tarlot's door at ten minute intervals—twice, he couldn't get rid of them before the next one knocked! Some were arguing, making nasty scenes! What we wouldn't have given to be flies on the wall! Not that watching it didn't have us dying of laughter! A couple girls told him off something fierce! Maybe some believed he didn't call them—I doubt we were the first to prank with escorts! No matter, he was catching plenty of the blame! Of course they were worried about the payments going through, and angry because there weren't going to be any tips! When the first girl turned up... That self-righteous look of his, it would've been priceless to hear the words that went with it! Can't have everything though, right? But as more girls turned up—ha ha! We saw one stomp across the room screaming! Tarlot was getting flustered, all right! No more pompous face!" Stephan doesn't stop speaking for an instant, allow Baptiste's attention to wander elsewhere; at the same time, he's following the progress of the cab from the corners of his eyes. "Of course we nixed the credit card payments later, said the services hadn't been provided! I felt a little bad about the girls, but the prank *had* to be played! Yeah, sorry escort girls, but Tarlot's a pain in the ass and the prank *had* to be played! It was out of my hands! I..."

"Hey Steph!" William interrupts with a yell. He and Christina and Pascale are standing alongside the cab at the curb ahead, Carole having already jumped out of it. "We've decided to crash at a hotel, OK? We're bushed and need quiet!"

"Leaving already?" responds Stephan, feigning surprise. "The night's still young!"

"Wrong!" Pascale shouts. "The night's over and the day's young! We're still jetlagged and want to sleep!" She makes a head-resting-on-folded-hands gesture.

"See you tonight!" says William, waving as he steps inside the cab.

"Party poopers!" says Jean-Marc.

"American slackers!" adds Carole, as Christina and Pascale follow William inside the cab.

"Yeah well...later then!" says Stephan with a dismissive wave.

The cab door's still wide open; Genevieve, suddenly dashing up to it from the middle of a half dozen people, asks those inside, "Will you drop me off?"

"Yeah, we can do that," responds Pascale, intentionally sounding reluctant. "Might as well get in!"

The instant Genevieve hops in and shuts the door, Carole absolutely screams, "Have a nice sleep!" and the car takes off as if running a race. Carole's briefed the driver well.

"Wait!" yells Baptiste, whipping around and taking a few jerky strides in the cab's direction. "Genevieve! Genevieve!" But the cab's half a block away in a flash.

For a few moments Baptiste's expression is suspended somewhere between a grimace and a scream as hate glitters in his eyes—he's frantically glancing from person to person, clenching and unclenching his hands, moving his lips without speaking in the manner previously witnessed by Christina. Then the more physical manifestations of the attack pass and he's standing immobile, his face blank and ashen: it's as if he's unaware of where he is. As for those witnessing the scene, many have an uncomfortable feeling—traces of chills are running up their spines. If anyone wondered why all the trouble and charading to separate him from Genevieve, they're not wondering now.

Lucinda, acting on cue, stomps up to Stephan, and hisses, "Guess what, you stiff? I'm leaving too! I'm sick of you talking to everyone but me! Spend the night with you? Pah! The thought revolts me, and I spit on it! *(She pantomimes spitting.)* You haven't a clue how to treat a lady, and aren't a man! I'm going to the Saint-Jacques metro, to get a safe ride home! Good night, and good riddance!" So saying, she starts to cross the avenue.

"Lucy, what's gotten into you?" Stephan says, taking a couple steps in her direction.

"Is this what you wanted, baby?" Lucinda says in a sweet poison tone as she lifts the hem of her dress, gathers it about her waist. "Did you want to touch me here?" She briefly points at her panties, then flings her dress back down and yells, "You're a loser!" Crossing to where Rue de la Tombe Issoire resumes on the east side of Avenue René Coty, she rapidly walks northeast on it without looking back.

"Good riddance, yourself!" Stephan yells after her. "Have fun with your fellow inmates in the psycho ward!" Then, turning to Baptiste, he says, "No predicting how females are going to act, what? No telling what's afflicting their nerves! But, hey, that's part of the fun, right? Girls are a roller coaster ride, and I wouldn't have it any other way! No man worth his salt lets a flighty female get him down! Plenty of other fillies in the meadow, right Baptiste?"

Baptiste, briefly twitching and his gaze glassy, can only manage to intone a slurred, "Yeaahhh."

"Damn right!" Stephan says, slapping him on the back for at least the dozenth time. "If a girl misbehaves, there's another to take her place! Let the drama queens have their drama! I just want a girl who hikes up her skirt before I know her name!"

"Rubbish," says Carole, stepping up to him. "Your bluster doesn't fool me! I know you like Lucy, and are upset! Better call her tonight and apologize!"

"I don't think I'll be doing that," Stephan answers. "It's a lot easier to see Alison in the 19th! Yeah, I'm going to find my friend here a cab so he can go to one of his cuties, then pay Alison a visit!" He winks at Baptiste.

"Yeah yeah yeah!" Carole scoffs. "Male pride's a pain, isn't it? Better cast your pride aside and live a happier life! You're no better than the prudes you revile if you let pride stand between yourself and heaven, otherwise known as Lucy!"

Our friends, aside from the fact they're becoming weary of putting on an act for Baptiste's benefit, are mindful of seeing to it Lucinda doesn't remain alone for long; therefore, Jean-Marc steps up and addresses Carole, "To tell the truth, dollface, I'm getting tired and am missing our bed. What do you say we call it a night?"

"With all my heart," responds Carole, grasping his hand. "Steph, we're going, OK?"

"Of course, lovebirds," Stephan laughs. "Enjoy your Saturday!" He exchanges goodbye kisses with Carole and shakes Jean-Marc's hand. Neither Carole nor Jean-Marc pay Baptiste the slightest mind.

"See you soon! And call Lucy!" Carole says with a finger-flutter wave as she and Jean-Marc follow the path blazed by Lucinda, up Rue de la Tombe Issoire. Lucinda's waiting for them in a nearby doorway, where they find her within twenty seconds. The three of them proceed towards the Saint-Jacques metro station, where they'll be waiting for Stephan.

In the meantime, because the goal of tactfully separating Genevieve from Baptiste has been accomplished, the group no longer has a reason to visit the lion at Place Denfert-Rochereau. Many people have already reversed direction.

"Yeah," Stephan addresses those still standing about and pointing at those who are leaving, "the lion's been cancelled! My squeeze has deserted me, so I'm off to another after I find Baptiste a cab! Go ahead and take the stuff back to the apartment, and don't forget the oysters! The best, from the Falklands! Scoff those babies! I'll be insulted if any are left! And *thanks*!"

No one needs to be told twice; bidding Stephan good night, they head south. Stephan, finding himself alone with Baptiste, is none too pleased about it. As long as Genevieve was present there was a reason to keep up the good buddies act; immediately after her departure there was still some pleasure to be derived from putting on the act in front of others; now that there's no audience, he's overcome with revulsion. Why would he trouble to find Baptiste a cab? And Lucinda, Jean-Marc, and Carole are waiting: why make them wait longer?

"You know what, Baptiste?" Stephan says as they reach Rue Hallé. "I've got to go too! I'm going to call Alison before it's too late! *(He retrieves his cell phone from his pocket.)* You're a man so you understand, right? Later!" Not bothering to shake Baptiste's hand, he crosses the avenue and strolls the short distance east on Rue Hallé, to where it feeds into Rue de la Tombe Issoire, while calling Lucinda to let her know he's on his way. As for the possibility that Baptiste might wonder why he's heading in the same direction that Lucinda took: Stephan's fed up with concerning himself with Baptiste's frame of mind, and doesn't care what he's thinking.

As for Baptiste's frame of mind, he's been directly aware of little that's transpired since Genevieve's departure: all has been seen in an out-of-focus blur, as if through a magnifying glass held close to his eyes; objects, near and far, have seemed to be looming up against his face, indistinct of outline; the words of the others have been heard as if from far away, and he's been unable to focus upon listening. He's vaguely aware that Stephan's had an altercation with Lucinda, and that he's gone to see another girl; he knows the others have departed, although he's not certain why. What he's most aware of is a sense of being smothered: it's as if the air's suffused with dark dust, pressing in on him from all angles. Instead of looking outward, he's looking inward—inward at the recollected sequence of Genevieve dashing to the cab, climbing inside it, and disappearing up the avenue; inward at the picture of her face, as she appeared at different points during the night. As he begins walking north, dread envelops him and deadens his senses, such that he can barely feel his legs. But your humble narrator, being as weary of Baptiste as Stephan is, will now switch to a more cheerful subject: the reunion of Stephan with Lucinda, Jean-Marc, and Carole.

As soon as Stephan reaches the end of Rue de la Tombe Issoire he sees Lucinda chatting with Jean-Marc and Carole under the trees in front of the metro station entrance, across Boulevard Saint-Jacques. The scarlet flower prints of her dress shimmer in the sunrise; her blond hair gleams. "Lucy!" he calls out; as she turns to greet him with an upraised arm and jumps up and down, he quickens his pace.

"Yay!" she exclaims when Stephan reaches her side of the boulevard. "Free at last!" She races forward, flings herself into his arms, and joins her lips to his. Soon he's playing with her ponytail with one hand while sliding the other up one of her legs.

"So what was it you asked me before stomping away?" Stephan teases, relishing the sight of her laughing eyes. "Right, you were wondering if this is what I want! *(He lifts the hem of her dress to her waist, then lets it fall back into place.)* I can assure you it's what I want!"

"And this is what I want," Lucinda answers, kissing him again.

"So you've made up already," laughs Jean-Marc, stepping to them with Carole at his side.

"Happy to see it," says Carole, poking Stephan and Lucinda in the ribs. "A sweet sight! But maybe we ought to catch a train so the others don't have to wait forever!"

"Yeah, the metro will be faster than looking for a cab," Stephan answers, turning towards the station.

"Metro—oh, metro! Where art thou?" Lucinda intones after they've been on the platform for about ten minutes. Within seconds the rumble of an approaching train is heard. "See," she smiles, "those who neglect to ask do not receive!"

The train pulls to a stop and our two happy couples pile in. In about half an hour they'll be reuniting with Genevieve, William, Christina, and Pascale at Place de l'Opéra, where we'll rejoin them in the chapter after the next.

CHAPTER 12

Before we reunite our eight friends at Place de l'Opéra, we'll turn the clock back about forty minutes. We join Genevieve, William, Christina, and Pascale shortly after they've piled into the cab on Avenue René Coty, as they're heading north. William turns around and glances out the back window, keeping his head down.

"Careful," advises Christina, "the last thing we need is for that loser to see you doing it and start to wonder if this was planned."

"I was being careful," responds William, turning forward again. He's seen the look of panic on Baptiste's face—his brief attempt to run after the cab, apparently while yelling—but keeps it to himself, to avoid needlessly concerning Genevieve. "Anyway, it doesn't matter, considering how fast we took off! Yee-Haw!"

"Yeah, isn't it great?" says Pascale, gesturing towards the driver appreciatively. "He's driving as if one of us is in labor! He wants to reach the hospital in time, so he doesn't have to deliver the baby!"

"The girl told me that's what you wanted," breaks in the driver. "Said one of you had to give a bastard the slip. I'm always happy to speed a lady to safety."

"Well then, Mr. Speeding-A-Lady-To-Safety, I sincerely thank you," says Genevieve, tapping his shoulder.

"Luc," responds the driver, smiling in the rear view mirror while extending his hand towards the back seat. As Genevieve and the others each take his hand in turn, they introduce themselves.

"But the bastard's history now—forget him!" says Luc. "How about I crank up the music and wash him away?" He increases the volume of the reggae CD he's playing—such that the cab literally vibrates with the soaring vocals, deep bass lines, and thundering drums—and starts pounding the empty passenger seat with his fist.

"Yeah!" shouts William, following Luc's example by stomping on the floor. Soon all five of them are tromping on the floor, whacking seats, and bouncing up and down in cadence with the beat. The cab, in Luc's capable hands, is now flying up Rue Raspail, rapidly weaving back and forth from lane to lane even though there's little traffic to dodge—the resulting pitch and roll of the car dovetails perfectly with the music as our four friends sway from side to side, laugh and yell. And when a traffic light unkindly turns red just ahead of them, Luc comes to a dramatic yet smooth stop, yells, "Hail the backbeat!" while clapping. Then they're off again with tires squealing, the scenery about them reeling as the air rushes hither and thither through the open windows.

Then it's a right onto Rue du Bac and a left onto Quai Anatole France—the Seine's now on their right, glittering in the sunrise. It's at this point that Luc asks if they'd like to circle around the obelisk at Place de la Concorde a few times before continuing to Place de l'Opéra.

"Yes! Thank you, sir!" says Genevieve, not ceasing to stomp with her feet and bump and grind against Pascale, who's seated next to her.

"Not sir—Luc!" shouts the owner of that name while accelerating to take advantage of the lack of lights on the quai.

"*Luc*, thank you!" Genevieve laughs.

"Reggae rock and roll!" Luc yells.

"Reggae rock and roll!" our friends scream.

"Ka-Chunga! Ka-Chunga!" Luc continues, pumping his fist.

"Ka-Chunga! Ka-Chunga!" echo our friends, likewise pumping their fists.

"Aaarrriibah! Aaarrriibah!" shouts Luc, reaching out the window to smack the roof of the car.

"Aaarrriibah! Aaarrriibah!" copy the others, also slapping the roof—either on the outside or the inside, depending on whether they're adjacent to the windows.

"Better than a dance floor, Luc!" yells Pascale.

"Dance floor, yeah! My cab's a concert!" agrees Luc. " Aaarrriibah! Aaarrriibah!"

Having reached the end of Quai Anatole France, where it becomes Quai d'Orsay, Luc turns right onto Pont de la Concorde, and the buildings of Paris fall away and the sky opens up and the sun broadsides the cab from the left as the Seine stretches into the distance on both sides. "Sweet infinity!" screams William, sticking his head out the window—drinking in the sight of the Seine ablaze with sunrise colors, pounding the outside of the car door with his palms.

In seconds they've crossed the bridge and are entering Place de la Concorde. "Merry go round!" Luc yells, swerving the cab to the far right side of the plaza, gunning the engine, then jerking it leftwards about as sharply as physics will permit without flipping the vehicle. Around and around the traffic island and soaring obelisk they go, with the tires squealing and our friends slung towards the right side of the car, smushed together. At one point William's leaning across Christina's lap, fighting the sling of the car, to get a view of the obelisk through the opposite window—the sun's striking its golden tip and the hair of the girls is swishing in the rushes of air whipping across his face; all are doing a sing-along with the music, clapping and shouting: moments worthy of remembering for the rest of his life.

After circling the obelisk about a dozen times, they turn north on Rue Royale—with the music still pounding, Luc still inventing new yells to which our friends play the chorus, the floor and seats and roof still being tromped upon and punched and smacked. What a blessing is this driver who's erased all trace of apprehension concerning the ditched Baptiste, propelled them into liberating physical euphoria: there's nothing like frenetic exercise and yelling for untying the knots in one's nerves, expelling troubling thoughts.

They're barely aware of the pillars of La Madeleine as they speed by and veer to the right, shoot up Boulevard de la Madeleine. When they're obliged to stop at a couple red lights on the latter they compensate by screaming louder, bouncing up and down in a frenzy; and Luc always accelerates when the light turns green with such force our friends are momentarily pinned to the back of their seat. Then Boulevard de la Madeleine becomes Boulevard des Capucines and shortly thereafter Luc's bringing the car to a stop at the southern entrance of the metro station at Place de l'Opéra.

"And so, Genevieve, that's how cab drivers play!" yells Luc. He turns down the volume of the music, leans across the back of the front seat, says, "It's been a pleasure!" and extends his hand.

"More than a pleasure, Luc—thank you!" says Genevieve, ignoring his hand and planting a kiss on his cheek—a gesture imitated by Pascale and Christina.

"An honor, Luc!" William says, shaking his hand.

"See you around town, my friends—be well!" Luc smiles.

Our four friends exit Luc's cab while returning his good wishes and receiving more. Then Luc flips a two hundred seventy degree turn, waving above the roof as he does so, and heads south on Avenue de l'Opéra.

"Luc, I salute you!" shouts William, watching the cab disappear.

"And I salute you too!" says Pascale, briefly lifting her hemline a foot or so and shaking it.

"That's about the best cab ride I've had in my life," says Christina, "and I've been taking cabs all my life!"

Genevieve, blowing a kiss in the departing Luc's direction, says, "Strangers well met; and whether we meet again or not, our time together was truly a godsend. Peace be with you, Luc!"

William, who's been obliged to take a hiatus from awareness of his budding attraction to Genevieve on account of dealing with the Baptiste problem (plus the fact she was seated on the opposite side of the cab, with Christina and Pascale between them), finds himself making a carefully considered appraisal of her appearance for the first time. The upwellings of magnetism which have occurred between them, at the lake and on Avenue René Coty, have seemed to transpire in a haze, doubtless as a result of their unexpectedness—a case of his perceptions being unable to keep pace with his emotions. It's not as if he's looked Genevieve over from head to toe and chatted with her at length and decided to pursue her: this is an instance of being ambushed by attraction, something he's never experienced before. It's happening independently of premeditation, as if other forces are at work. So he's giving her a mental going over from the side as she gazes into the distance—seeking to account for the strength of his feelings on her behalf.

How beautiful Genevieve is! Her face is straight out of a Raphael painting, suffused with a radiant flush, surrounded by light that bends the air—her complexion's otherworldly. And, also, note the clarity and sweetness of the light in her dark almond eyes. And such a body she has: perfectly proportioned, at once taut and soft, as muscular as it is curvaceous, with flawless posture—she's as effortlessly poised as a cat. And her firm round breasts, flat stomach, strong hips, long legs—the shape of her shoulders and curve of her back. Her raven black hair that contrasts with and highlights the alabaster of her visage, swishes across her back from where it fans from the ribbon that binds it in a ponytail. The white of her chest, exposed by the V-neck of her snug sweater... William's unable to gaze upon her without every muscle in his body tightening, tingles seizing him from the inside out.

As for Genevieve, she's instantly aware that William's observing her: the focused movements of his eyes are as good as darting under her skin, slipping into the flow of her blood, stimulating her nerves—at once soft as the touch of feathers and piercing as electrical pulses. Under the influence of the touch of his eyes, she arches her back and reaches behind her head, unfastens the ribbon which binds her hair; then she's lifting her hair high and releasing it, such that it splashes about her face. She immediately senses that the swish of her hair and the tension of her body's whipping through William's body, causing him to catch his breath, become invigoratingly still. She turns to meet his gaze...

If there was anything of doubt in the mind of either as to the authenticity of their attraction, it's gone the moment their eyes unite. Their eyes upwell with rapture, exchange joyful brightness, at the same time that they quaver with trepidation—trepidation that's somehow thrilling, as if fleeting impressions of weakness are inescapable when one's suddenly glimpsing an opportunity to acquire unhoped-for bliss. One inner-shock after another, agonizingly delightful, further enfolds them in desire's web as their awareness of their surroundings slips away.

William, unable to perceive (become self-conscious on account of) the discreet amusement of his two best friends, advances to Genevieve. Of unease there's no small amount: racing through his head are questions as to whether he's proceeding too hastily—as to what he's going to do next. At the same time that he's seeing mental pictures of himself embracing Genevieve, he's feeling how preposterous such would be—how impossible it is that what he most wants will actually happen. She's a yard away and it's if as he must leap over a chasm to reach her: another onslaught of trepidation informs him they're merely going to exchange embarrassed pleasantries, then part ways and suffer the pangs of frustration.

It seems to occur in sped-up slow motion, if that makes any sense: William's suddenly wrapping his arms around Genevieve, listening to her take a deep breath and sigh—softly half-moan—as her face disappears behind blurred air. Then he's aware of their lips touching, tongues intertwining; aware of the insistent pressings of her body, kneadings of her fingers at the back of his neck; aware of caressing her face with one hand while squeezing her waist with the other, winding one of his legs around both of hers. "It's happening!" flashes through his head, as if he needs to confirm it.

Their embrace feeds itself, matches strength with strength and enfolds them in waves of healing energy, as they continue to kiss; and they kiss lingeringly, greedily—as if it's what they most need on earth. As far as William's concerned, the events of last night—explorations of Père Lachaise, picnic in Montsouris Park—are pieces of a dream compared with Genevieve's vibrant presence on this sunny spring morning.

Then they find themselves separating and backing away a step to have a happy look at one another, share their appreciation. How wonderful is the blurry-stirry sensation in William's face—the shadow of the feeling of Genevieve's lips upon his combined with the rush of blood to his cheeks, emotional surge. The transparency he's experiencing as he stands before her, engulfed by her gaze: how does she know so much about him? And how does he know she knows so much about him? There's no hiding from her—she's flowing through his veins, flaring in his nerves, joined to his electrical field, the swirl of his moods. Nor can she hide from him—he can sense every quiver-shiver of her energy, read every fluctuation of the light in her eyes, shift of the lines of her facial expressions. A miracle, their understanding is: Genevieve's smile is imparting a feeling of security he's never known before, or even suspected the existence of.

But shadows of embarrassment appear on Genevieve's face, on account of the presence of Christina and Pascale, and break the spell: her gaze flickers uncomfortably in their direction. After all, how's she to know what the precise nature of their relationship with William is? The chat they had earlier at Stephan's party, in which Christina and Pascale stressed they were friends with William first and other things second, happened under far different circumstances, before anyone had an inkling of she and William becoming captivated with one another. Now that it's happened, maybe they'll change their tune, regardless of how they thought they'd feel about it? Maybe the friends first business has never seriously been put to the test, and will fail it? It wouldn't be the first time wishful thinking was usurped by an unexpected turn of events. So it's understandable that Genevieve's uneasy on their account, even as she's overwhelmingly happy.

"They're my two best friends," says William quietly, realizing why Genevieve's face has clouded. "They've never begrudged me happiness, and won't do so now." Taking her hands in his, he caresses their backs with his thumbs.

Genevieve's hands quiver uncomfortably and she makes a movement to withdraw them, as if still doubtful matters will go smoothly, apprehensive of demonstrating additional affection.

"He's right," Pascale smiles, addressing Genevieve. She's heard William's almost whispered reassurance despite the fact she and Christina are standing a few yards away. "What Chrissy and I told you earlier wasn't a false face. Nor is it self-deception, a fancy ideal. This isn't the first time someone's strayed outside our circle—we've all seen other people before. It's not a shock, Gen, so please put that thought out of your head. You have our unqualified blessing, right Chrissy?"

"Absolutely," Christina affirms. "Have no doubts on that score!"

A flicker of a smile appears in Genevieve's eyes, although she still appears hesitant.

"As difficult as it may be to believe," Pascale continues in a lighter vein, "we're always willing to tolerate Billy's antics, as good friends should."

"Of course he gets punished if he decides to be childish," Christina puts in with a grin.

Genevieve, misinterpreting teasing for gibes, visibly winces. Strong and balanced she may be, but she's never been taken by storm by attraction before, suddenly found herself feeling vulnerable and extraordinarily elated at the same time; couple that with the fact everything's been witnessed by two women she has good reason to believe have prior claims upon William and may view her as an unwelcome rival, and is it any wonder her imagination commences to flay her? Long story short: it flashes in her head that Christina considers William's present demonstrations of affection to be nothing but a childish a ploy to elicit jealousy. For perhaps the first time in her life, Genevieve finds herself at an utter loss for words.

"No, dear!" Christina hastens to say, alarmed. "I was just...I was joking when I shouldn't have been! *(She shakes her head, by way of indicating self-annoyance.)* As Pas said, we both give you our heartfelt blessing! And I know I speak for Pas too when I say I anticipate being the best of friends! I..." Abandoning speech, she steps to Genevieve and kisses her on the cheek.

"I'm sorry," Genevieve says, feeling her unease melt away as quickly as it appeared. "I'm a bit...feeling a little skittish! Put yourself in my place!" Both blushing and beginning to smile, she relaxes her hands as William continues caressing them.

"We *are* putting ourselves in your place," Pascale says, "and we don't envy you one bit! You're going to be stuck with *this* lunatic, and... All right, I won't kid! Of course it's a sticky situation for you, if you're still not sure what's between Billy and us! Please stop worrying! As we explained, we've never laid claim to one another in *that* way! Billy doesn't to us, and we don't to him! And that's the last word on it, OK?" She waves impatiently, then warmly kisses Genevieve on the cheek. Genevieve, now quite relaxed, returns the gesture, not forgetting to do the same with Christina.

"Good," says Christina, laughing. "We're square!"

"About time!" says Pascale. "We're not in Paris to suffer jealousy or begrudge Billy joy! We're never *anywhere* to do that! Leave the negatives to the negative people! The power of positive thinking's more than a book title that's become a cliché—it happens to be real! Think nice, and sweet feelings follow! A-Woo!"

"Speaking of sweet feelings," Christina laughs, "consider this: now that we're Billy-free, there'll be a gazillion more shopping sprees! No more being tied down by the boy! Wee!" She tosses her hair from side to side.

"Right," Pascale says, clapping. "Gen, we owe you a debt of gratitude! You've taken Billy off our hands, so now we've got the green light to go nuts with girly stuff! I'm going to buy enough shoes to fill a suitcase, and that's just for starters! If we were still man-encumbered, we wouldn't be doing nearly enough of that!"

Genevieve, never one to pass up an opportunity to play when she's herself (as she's rapidly becoming again), says, "Fair trade, then! You get unlimited shopping sprees, and I get Bill! Your debt's cancelled! In fact, I owe *you* for bringing him to Paris!" Stepping closer to William, she smilingly pulls her hands from his and wraps her arms around his waist; as she does so, part of her marvels at how hesitation-free and natural the gesture's already become.

"And I owe you for rescuing me from shopping sprees," William says, instantly caressing Genevieve's cheeks, leaning towards her to kiss her; as he does so he's again struck by the beauty of her face—the sweetness of her eyes and smile—and momentarily pauses, simply to relish the sight.

"Gen, you owe us nothing!" cries Christina, delighted that Genevieve's allowing herself to openly surrender to her affection for William. "Seeing a romance unfold in Place de l'Opéra at sunup's truly a treat! Pas, what do you think? Is this insanely storybook or what?"

"It's so storybook I'm..."

But Pascale isn't allowed to finish her sentence: the attention of our four friends is diverted by the unmistakable sound of Stephan's voice, rising from the base of the metro station steps. "Up we run into the light," he's yelling, "from the darkness of the underworld!" And, sure enough, soon Stephan, Lucinda, Jean-Marc, and Carole are racing each other to the top of the stairs and calling out greetings. But an event as important as the reunion of our eight friends requires a separate chapter, as shall be seen in the next.

CHAPTER 13

As Stephan, Lucinda, Jean-Marc, and Carole reach the top of the metro steps William, Genevieve, Christina, and Pascale are advancing towards them; when the two groups meet, embraces and kisses are exchanged with a fervor approaching that of family members reuniting after years apart.

"Good to see you—it's been an eternity!" Jean-Marc says.

"Yeah, a whole hour!" cracks Carole, with mirthful eyes.

"Are you sure it's only been an hour?" responds Jean-Marc. "After all, freedom of expression's been denied us for half the night, being as how dark cloud Bap was hanging over our heads and poisoning spontaneity, requiring us to be surreptitious and calculating as we focused upon ditching him!"

"And how did he take the ditching?" William asks, directing the question to Stephan.

"Who cares?" answers Stephan. "I was fed up with him then, am more so now! I took off, left him on the avenue! I don't remember what I said, and it doesn't matter! I was ready to deck him and might've done so, if it weren't for Gen's orders! He got off easy!"

"We don't need to talk about him, OK?" says Genevieve with emphasis. "He's gone—it's over, done, finito! Good riddance and good forgettance!"

"Forget who?" asks Carole. "I don't remember anyone! But *someone* did!" She nudges Jean-Marc.

"Out of mind from this moment forth," says Jean-Marc, lifting his arm in a swearing-of-an-oath gesture while counter-nudging Carole.

Our four new arrivals might be chatting uninterruptedly, but the conversation's not uppermost in their minds. What's mainly occupying their interest is the unconcealed fascination William and Genevieve have for one another. As has been described, Jean-Marc, Carole, and Lucinda were present when the two underwent their second surprise attraction-experience, on Avenue René Coty; but it occurred quickly and they placed less store upon it as the minutes went by, not to mention that the Baptiste situation was claiming most of their attention. In fact, Lucinda barely remembered to mention it to Stephan, concluding with, "Maybe something's going to happen, but probably not." But now look at William and Genevieve: it's incredible how far they've advanced in such a short span of time. Already, they can't stop staring at one another as if hypnotized or keep their hands apart: their mutual magnetism's blatantly obvious. As with Genevieve herself not long ago, our four new arrivals are also apprehensive on account of Christina and Pascale: the last thing they want is jealousy rearing its ugly head, and division within the ranks. But when they seek to assess the reaction of the American girls, they only detect good cheer: are they putting on an act, masking less happy sentiments? What's really on their minds?

"OK," Pascale says with her usual boldness, "I think Chrissy and I have had enough of being eye-probed! Yeah, that's right! We know you're wondering if we're going to throw hissy fits! Hell, you're looking at us more than *them*! *(She gestures towards William and Genevieve.)* And we can do without it, OK? We... Chrissy, you want to take this? I'm tired of explaining!"

"Why, thank you!" laughs Christina. "So nice to have the baton passed to me! All right, listen up newcomers, I'm only saying it once and there will be *no* questions! The ties that bind us to Billy are those of friendship! We're friends and want to stay that way! Friends for life! Billy's free to do as he pleases—not that we'd be able to stop that *(She likewise gestures at William and Genevieve.)* even if we wanted to! And we don't want to! Billy wouldn't stop us either, if it was the other way around! And it sort of has been the other way around before, although certainly not on the level as what's going on now! All right, that's it! End of story!" She criss-crosses her arms by way of indicating she's through with the subject.

"Girls after my own heart!" Stephan cries. "To the point, no wiffle-waffle! Hey lovebirds! *(He snaps his fingers.)* Think you can snap out of it for long enough to walk to the Grand?"

"The Grand?" asks Genevieve, with a vague look.

"Ha ha ha! Priceless!" Stephan shouts. "She's..."

"I was *faking* it, silly!" interrupts Genevieve. "What's priceless is how easily you fell for it!"

"Yay!" shouts Carole. "Our Genevie's back! Americans, you haven't officially met the real Genevie! Allow me to introduce..."

"They have too, aerobics brat!" laughs Genevieve.

"She called me aerobics brat!" Carole shouts louder. "She's back! She's back! Pardon me, Bill! *(She pulls Genevieve from William, embraces her.)* Welcome back! I missed you!"

"We all did," says Lucinda, likewise embracing Genevieve. Pascale and Christina soon join in.

"A girl syrup-session," says Jean-Marc. "It's so sickly sweet, I..." But he interrupts himself, saying, "Good to have you back, darling!"

"I missed me too," Genevieve smiles, turning her head about and blinking her eyes, pantomiming emergence from a trance.

"Congratulations, both of you!" Stephan says, looking William and Genevieve up and down and nodding his head in approval. "Bill, I'd say you're the perfect cure for what ailed her!"

"Is that a Bap reference?" chides Lucinda. "Weren't you listening when..." Suddenly realizing she's invoked the forbidden name far more assuredly than Stephan has, she claps a hand to her mouth.

Stephan's laughing too hard to reply; the others start laughing as well.

"Lucy, don't worry about it," says Genevieve. "It's inevitable that the creep's going to come up now and then as a point of reference—I was wrong to make him taboo. The second something's taboo, it becomes more noticeable, so Bap's no longer taboo—I take my no-Bap policy back. Any mention of him should carry the emotional impact of describing the reparation of a sink, and roll off our backs. I'm not going to cringe at every mention of *the thing's name!*"

"Right," says Jean-Marc, "kill him with indifference—he doesn't matter. What matters is that we've acquired a new pair of lovebirds, and it's time to celebrate at the Grand!"

"Well said!" yells Stephan. "The awning's a beckoning beacon! *(He points east down Boulevard des Capucines, at the burgundy awning.)* Yeah, Americans, it's right there! The best all night every night cafe in Paris, scrumptious oysterlings! The Falklands babies at home will be long gone by the time I get there, so I'm having a helping at the Grand! *(He swats Lucinda's behind.)* Get along, dollface! A feeding, and then some love!"

"Maybe and maybe not," responds Lucinda.

"Sure, sweetheart, whatever you say! Nice tease act! Save it for later!"

"Bye, Opera House!" calls out Pascale, waving towards it as they begin to cross the street.

"Barely got to know you, Opera House!" continues Christina. "Such a pretty pale green roof, and golden edges and angels! Colonnaded windows! Paris is an eye-feast everywhere, a..."

"Now you're embarrassing me, tourist!" interrupts Pascale. "Sorry I mentioned it!"

"And you're not a tourist? Pah! You're more goo-goo eyed than I am!"

"I hope you're not mocking each other for our benefit," says Carole. "No reason for you to put on a cynic act and ruin your fun when you don't want to! If the Opéra delights you, then by all means surrender to your delight! We like that you like our town! We get to relish our city through your eyes! We're not going to be wet blankets! Right, Jean-Marc?" She darts him a you'd-better-agree-with-me look.

"I didn't say anything!" Jean-Marc laughs. "I'm a proud resident of Paris! Thank God for Paris, I couldn't live anywhere else!"

As for William and Genevieve, they're locked arm in arm as they stroll to the Grand Café, apparently oblivious of the conversing of their friends—they're having their own subsurface conversation of surging blood. William's stunned delight's so vivid it seems to be warping sensory impressions and time. The sunlight dappled leaves of the trees lining the sidewalk are as if both swishing next to his cheeks and spinning into the sky; the building fronts are as if both pressing forward and receding into a distance that isn't there. At one and the same time, the stroll seems to be over in a flash and to have lasted for a dozen blocks. It's as if the only thing that's unquestionably real is the presence of Genevieve, the sympathy of her feelings as she winds her arm about his arm.

Once inside the Grand Café, the group makes a beeline for a large table that fronts a window. They squeeze into the booth that encircles three sides of the table, William and Genevieve snug in one of the rounded corners. Soon all of them—with the exception of Stephan, who's busy with two dozen oysters—are digging into plates of *bulots* while drinking either water or tea. We'll avoid detailing the particulars of their conversation, and simply say it's characterized by good cheer, punctuated with much laughter—no surprise there. William and Genevieve, although participating to some extent, save most of their attentiveness for one another—silently savor their state of mutual absorption. They even go so far as to fork *bulots* into each other's mouths—an activity that brings smiles to their friends' faces, but doesn't elicit a single teasing word. The new couple is so quietly joyful, as well as deadly serious, that it would be sacrilege to distract them.

Towards the end of the meal, however, as they're sharing a large salad, Genevieve begins to exhibit signs of uneasiness. Her eyes, so to speak, become wobbly in their expression; her body becomes fidgety; she starts glancing about for no apparent reason. William, tapping her shoulder, asks what's wrong with his eyes.

"It's the sit-down with my parents—it's bothering me," she whispers. "Sorry."

"Gen, there's nothing to be sorry about—please! A family history as you've described is no small matter. If you want to go home and sleep now, so you can be as refreshed and collected as possible, I'll see you to your door. We can leave this second."

"Leave already?" asks Stephan, lifting his eyebrows.

"It's the you-know-who business," says Lucinda. "What else would be bothering Gen?"

"But I don't get it," Stephan persists. "The you-know-what's been pitched aside! And I know mom and dad are going to side with their daughter! Are you kidding me? They might arrange to have you-know-what hung upside down by his heels!"

"There's no question they'll back me one hundred percent," Genevieve says quietly, placing her elbows on the table and leaning forward. "What I'm worried about is collateral damage, the possible fallout between our families from top to bottom—whether Bap's parents will be able to separate the issue from everything else. That, and broaching a subject that's not going to make anyone happy. I've got to spare our families as much discomfort as possible—avoid as much ickiness as possible—while stressing that Bap's not to come near me again, for any reason."

"OK," says Stephan. "I know you wouldn't dig up drama out of nothing. We're all here for you—you won't leave our thoughts. Please call us the moment it's over."

"Thank you," Genevieve smiles. "Thank you all. It'll be over soon, one way or another, and will probably be easier than I'm imagining. I'd still like to catch some sleep, though, and prepare. Sorry."

"No apologies!" says Carole.

"The whole thing's insane!" interjects Jean-Marc. "God, I could kill that ridiculous little pips…"

"Here's to freedom, then," Carole hastens to interrupt, raising her cup of tea. "There's no reason for anything but sweet things to happen on this beautiful day!"

"To freedom!" the group echoes, clinking their glasses and cups.

About five minutes later, as William and Genevieve are strolling to the Opéra metro station, she stops and turns to him, saying, "I deeply appreciate that you're seeing me home, honey, but I think it would be best if we say goodbye, for now, at the station. I need to gather myself for this evening, I'm not going into it lightly, I want to do it the right way. *(Seeing a flicker of worry cloud William's face, she interrupts herself.)* No, Bill, I don't mean it like that! I wish to God I didn't have to do this, I'd like nothing better than..." She trails off blushing, casts her eyes at the pavement.

"Gen, I didn't mean to press," he says softly. "I said I was going to see you to your door and that's what I meant. I just want you to trust me, I like you *so* much. I understand the gravity of the situation, believe me. We'll say goodbye at the station, *for now*."

Genevieve, raising her eyes and seeing the look of tenderness upon William's face, involuntarily gasps, "Oh!" and wraps her arms around his neck, finds her lips at his mouth. A kiss, like a picture, is worth a thousand words. She needs not speak her desire, nor does he. What leaps into their awareness is that they'll be together at the earliest opportunity, depending upon what transpires in the evening. Maybe tonight, maybe tomorrow; at any rate, soon.

"Here, sweetie," she says once they're walking again. Gently, she takes his hand and guides it under the hem of her skirt, tapping on it by way of indicating he should move it upwards. Hidden by the pleats of her skirt, his hand slides to where her thigh joins with her behind, at the edge of the lace of her panties, and lightly grips her there. As they continue to walk the muscles of her moving thigh alternate between firmness and softness in a manner that shoots tingling heat up his arm, thrills him from head to toe. As for Genevieve, she's breathing audibly while clasping his waist with both hands and rubbing her head against his shoulder. In this manner they silently stroll to the metro's gate; after briefly pausing to insert their tickets in the slot and enter, they resume their intimate activity on the platform. Their shared comfort zone is growing by leaps and bounds by the minute.

Then the train arrives—too soon to suit either of them—and they're saying goodbye. "I'll call you the *second* it's over!" are Genevieve's parting words.

She travels east to the Temple station, where she exits and walks the short distance to her apartment at 160 Rue du Temple, on the corner of Rue Dupetit-Thouars. She quickly brushes her teeth, undresses, and climbs into bed, eventually dozing off. We shall return to her when she's awake again in the chapter after the next.

CHAPTER 14

Having seen Genevieve off, William rejoins the others at the Grand Café and they complete their meal. Then they walk to the Opéra metro station and descend to the platform of the three line. Jean-Marc and Carole, though, are on the opposite side: they're headed northwest to the Villiers station, close to his apartment at 51 Rue de Lisbonne, near Monceau Park, whereas the other five are going south to the Alésia station via a transfer at Réaumur-Sébastopol. The two trains pull into the station seconds apart and our parties enter them; kisses are blown back and forth through the windows until the trains depart in opposite directions. Shortly after noon, our five friends arrive at the Fleury apartment. Stephan and Lucinda retire to his room and William, Christina, and Pascale enter theirs.

"So," says Pascale, strolling to the window and drawing the curtains, "we've been in Paris about twenty-four hours and it's already a blur! Père Lachaise, then the party, then the park—obelisk, Opéra, Grand Café! Cab rides, metro rides, the ditching of a loser! We could fly home tonight, and it would be like we had a wild dream! And one of us has had a wilder dream than the others, right Billy? Billy, are you here?" She waves a hand in front of William's face.

"Yeah," William laughs, "I'm here, although..."

"It's different now, isn't it?" Christina cuts in, smiling; then addressing Pascale, "I think we've lost our Billy, Pas!"

"He's *definitely* in Genevieve-Land," Pascale says, "and who knows when he's coming back?"

"Sorry," William begins, "I didn't plan..."

"You're not sorry one bit, nor should you be!" Christina cuts in again. "And if you try another sorry on me, then I *will* be miffed and you'll owe me an apology! I know theory can sometimes be hard to put into practice, but what's theoretical about our friendship? Sure, you're falling hard—you're already gone, actually *(She winks at Pascale.)*—and it's going to alter your perceptions, but have no doubt that we're your friends first and foremost, and happy for you! Insanely improbable, coming from a girl, right?"

"The only insane thing about it is that we're having to reassure him," says Pascale, whacking William's arm. "Falling for Gen or not, overcome with captivation-distortions or not, I would think our bond would speak for itself, and place matters in perspective! Why should we have to clarify ourselves, reaffirm what he already knows? Silly boy!" She whacks William's arm again.

"And if it was the other way around?" asks William. "I doubt either of you would plunge headlong into a new relationship—you certainly haven't before—without feeling me out first, doing a state-of-my-emotions check. Superfluous or not, feeling out my closest friends concerning a new girl's common courtesy, and expected! Don't deny it's expected!"

"Hmm," muses Pascale. "You know what, Chrissy? He's right: none of us are going to rush into a relationship without checking in first! Aside from it being friendship protocol, there's the matter of obtaining confirmation as regards the person we're attracted to! As in, have we chosen someone who's worthy? Would I feel comfortable running off with a man the two of you detested? That might get me to—definitely would get me to—question my judgment! *(She notes the look of uncomfortable surprise on William's face.)* Come on, Billy! You've got to know I don't mean it *that* way! Gen's an absolute darling, Chrissy and I adore her! We already count her as a dear friend, and have said so!"

"Have no doubts on that score, Billy," seconds Christina. "Gen's a top tier classy girl, as we'd expect from you! You go after her, and find your joy! She's worthy—we approve approve approve!" She embraces William, and Pascale immediately joins in.

"I'm the luckiest guy on earth," says William. "I'm so glad..."

"Now, don't go ruining it by externalizing it!" interrupts Pascale, squeezing his shoulder. "Keep the trap shut!" She places her hand over his mouth.

They maintain their three-way embrace for a good minute; after they separate, William asks, "So if I sleep upstairs you get it, right?"

"Of course we get it!" exclaims Christina, rolling her eyes. "You want to be alone with your Genevieve impressions! You want to be faithful! As a girl, I'd expect nothing less!"

"Yeah," adds Pascale, "we're friends first and foremost, so I do my best to keep the girl stuff—ha ha!—out of it; but sometimes the girl will be heard and right now the girl in me understands you're falling for Gen and should be staying out of this bed! *(She points at the bed.)* You wouldn't be the Billy we know and love if you were able to sleep here now! Your feelings for Gen would be a joke if you could! That's both the girl in me speaking, and your friend!"

"Having girls as my two best friends is the best of both worlds," William says.

"Externalizing again!" says Pascale, frowning. "Go on now! Get what you need and go upstairs and sleep dreaming of Gen!"

"Right," Christina says, "I'm dizzy with all the stuff we've done, and won't be able to make sense of it until after I get some sleep! It's bedtime for *all* of us! Hurry up and get out of here!"

William, after gathering a change of clothes and comforter and pillow, goes to the open area upstairs. It's about half the size of the living room on the first level of the apartment, and has two large couches—one of them a fold-out bed—against two of its walls. He unfolds the bed, already fitted with a sheet, and settles in with the comforter and pillow.

William's excitement is warring with his exhaustion; he's as eager to remain awake and bask in the glow of attraction, contemplate the qualities of she who's the cause of that glow, as he's mindful of the necessity of sleeping so he can be at his best when he sees her again. Has he ever felt this way before, in the sense he's beginning to feel he's met a girl who could never be interchangeable with another? He hasn't. There's such a one-of-a-kind tingle-inducing charm to the sound of Genevieve's voice, the light in her eyes, the grace of her step. The touch of her hand passes through his skin and swirls in his nerves and hints at supremely blissful states of being he can't put into words. The thought of the way she kisses him births a cascade of stirring images that dissolve like droplets of dye in a river the second he seeks to identify them. He's never felt more solid and centered inside; he's also never felt more as if his personality is in a state of flux, impossible to bend to his will. The way Genevieve turns him inside out with a glance, sets him to deliciously flailing inside, at the same time that she's dispensing stability and calm...

William's lying on his back, reexperiencing his moments with Genevieve over and over again: their first nerve-shock glance, by the lake; their first shiver-inducing hand-clasp, on Avenue René Coty; their first embrace and kiss, those priceless looks of rapture afterwards... Place de la Opéra will be a shrine from this day forth! And their cuddling at the Grand Café while surrounded by their friends, who've accepted their affection as a given and blessed it! Then their last caresses on the metro platform, the scene of their first goodbye; the last surge of sweet loving brightness in Genevieve's eyes as the train pulls away! He will be seeing her tonight! *He will!*

Eventually exhaustion overtakes excitement and William drifts into what can best be described as joyfully restless sleep. He's left his cell phone on and placed it near his head (something he almost never does while sleeping) in case Genevieve calls before he awakens.

CHAPTER 15

We now skip ahead a few hours to shortly past five on Saturday evening, roughly twenty-four hours after William, Christina, and Pascale rendezvoused at the gate of Père Lachaise at the commencement of our narrative. We join Genevieve as she's entering 31 Rue Campagne Première, the building where she grew up and her parents still reside. In addition to their primary residence, which comprises the entirety of the third floor, they own three small non-consecutive units—old servants quarters—on the top floor. As has been mentioned, Baptiste's parents reside in the same building; they occupy about half of the second floor.

As Genevieve steps into the lobby and approaches the stairs, the elevator being temporarily out of order, she's seeking to keep her talk with her parents uppermost in her mind. "I'm going to be dropping a bombshell," she's telling herself, "and need to stay focused! Bap needs to be exiled from the household, kept the hell away from me, but I don't want to cause a family rift in other areas! How easy it that going to be?" Why is she addressing herself thus?

Because she can't stop flushing with delight at the thought of William, falling out from under herself in shimmering waves of sensation. Her whole body, it seems, has become a conducting rod that's inundating her with delicious electricity, scattering her thoughts when she needs them the most. For the time being, she must rein in her inner fireworks. "If things go as I anticipate," she continues, "then it should be a measly hour or so before I'm free to see Bill! But, for God's sake, keep the talk front and center in my head for now! Until the Bap talk's over, there's no Bill!"

Has Genevieve oriented herself properly, succeeded in placing thoughts and feelings of William in the background, by the time she reaches the door of her family's residence? Of course not! So for at least a minute she paces back and forth outside the door, executes a few aerobics moves, in an effort to stabilize herself. "Oh, well!" she finally says. "Best to just go in and blurt it out and let the conversation follow its natural course! Once I set the ball to rolling, it'll roll, all right, and hopefully won't destroy everything in its path! Bap's the cause, but I'd still like to do damage control!"

So she slips her key into the lock and turns it; pushing the door open, she steps inside and calls out, "Mom? Dad?"

"Down here, Gen," her mother answers from what they've always called the sunken sitting room. It's to the right of the entrance, about two yards lower than the remainder of the apartment, reached via a section of marble steps with curled brass railings. It's always been the family's favorite room, furnished as it is on all sides with floor to ceiling bookcases upon the shelves of which are family portraits, a collection of Roman glassware, and assorted keepsakes, in addition to the many books—some valuable first editions, others common paperbacks—chosen first and foremost for their titles. A thick Persian rug reaches nearly from bookcase to bookcase, revealing the mahogany flooring at its fringed edges. When Genevieve descends the steps she finds her mother and father engaged in a game of gin on the long leather couch, a platter of fruit and cheese on the heavy antique mahogany coffee table in front of them.

They say that if one wants to know what a girl's going to look like in the future, look at her mother. Catherine Clouitier's such a good advertisement for her daughter she could almost pass for her older sister. Like Genevieve, she's a few inches taller than the average woman, has long wavy black hair, and a clear alabaster complexion. Slightly more filled out than her daughter, she has the same shapely, athletic-tending-towards-voluptuous, build. Her aura of centeredness and unflappability—effortless poise and serenity of expression—is such that one has the feeling she'd keep her head if car-sized fireballs were raining from the sky. As for Genevieve's father, Georges, he's six feet two, lean and muscular, with a light dusting of gray in his jet black hair. One gets the impression there's little that his eyes, brown like his daughter's but narrower in shape and with a sharper quality of light in their general expression, don't catch. His face has fine chiseled features, at once sensitive and rugged; animated in his movements and generally surrounded by an air of restlessness, Georges isn't fond of sitting still. The calmness of the wife and excitability of the husband has resulted in a very happy union: neither feel as if they're wholly themselves when they're apart.

"Down with two," Georges grins, spreading his cards on the couch.

"And I get twenty-one," Catherine says gleefully, clapping once. "I was holding this ace while waiting for gin, or for you to go down! Thanks for obliging!"

"Second time tonight—I've got to learn to be more patient," laughs Georges, rising to embrace and cheek-peck his daughter. "Gen, it's good to see you! To what... What's wrong?"

"Sorry to spoil your night," Genevieve begins, shrugging her shoulders, "but..."

"Gen," Catherine cuts in, likewise rising to embrace and kiss her daughter, "you will never be spoiling our night! Now, out with it! What's on your mind?" Then, moving the deck of cards, she pulls Genevieve to the couch.

"By all means spill it," adds Georges, reseating himself beside his daughter. "No more delays!"

"I've only been here a minute," Genevieve smiles, already calmer inside. The moment she's seated between her mother and father, cozy in the familial bond, her thoughts fall into place, dispose of unnecessary emotional noise: how ridiculous of her to have waited this long to address the Baptiste issue! Her reluctance to reveal his behavior, involve her parents, has been plain insane!

"Waiting," says Catherine, tapping Genevieve's knee.

"Alright," Genevieve says, reseating herself on the coffee table so she can face both of her parents at once, "it's this: Baptiste has become insufferably petty, jealous, and possessive—all the worst things—and has started to interfere with my life. I need to have him told to stay away from me, and not allowed to come here again. I'm not doing this lightly, I've..."

"Sweetie, we've had a feeling," Catherine cuts in, grasping her daughter's hand. "We knew something was fishy, even if not nearly as bad as this."

"He's been off his game, secretively preoccupied, testy—we figured it had to do with school," Georges says, rising to his feet and starting to yell. "Jesus Christ! Bothering you is inexcusable! Count on it, Baptiste won't cross our threshold again! I've known him since the maternity ward, and he turns out bad! I bounced him on my knee before he could walk, and he grows up to interfere with your life! I don't want to see his face again!"

Genevieve, at the same time that she's relieved beyond measure that she's finally revealed what she had no choice but to reveal (It's as if, by simply mentioning the Baptiste situation, she's relegated it to the past.), isn't happy that her father's been propelled into a rage. "Dad," she says in an effort to calm him, "I was about to say I've thought about this long and hard, I didn't want to spill bad news, cause problems; but I saw no alternative, so atrocious and demoralizing has Baptiste's behavior become, and... Hmm...sorry, I'm only making it sound worse, aren't I? Oh, hell! There's no way around it! I don't want to so much as glimpse his resentful face again, and am thrilled he won't be coming here anymore! It's a huge weight off my shoulders! I didn't want to make you mad, but..."

"What?" Georges interrupts, incredulity supplementing his anger. "My daughter—a Cloutier through and through, the pride and joy of my life and greatest accomplishment—was self-doubting herself, hesitating to speak to us? Goddammit! Why didn't you tell us sooner? And last night after dinner he left with you! Why? Because you were afraid to make waves, upset the social balance? He's the one that's upset the social balance! I didn't bring you up to put up with atrocious behavior, pussyfoot around serious matters, be afraid to make waves when they need to be made! Son of a bitch!"

"Oh, Dad!" cries Genevieve, leaping to her feet and hugging him tight. "I love you so much!"

"OK, so it's settled and over!" says Georges, who isn't known for getting straight to the point during business negotiations for nothing. "Baptiste is dead to us from now on! His parents are just going to have to deal with it! I'll cut them off along with their son if they protest!"

"But I don't want that!" exclaims Genevieve.

"I don't either, believe me," responds Georges, "but I won't hesitate to lay down the law if need be! Nobody bothers my daughter, and hears me greet them again! It's a matter for us *(He gestures at Catherine.)* to handle! If it can be worked out, it will be; and, if not, that's how it is! I won't look back!"

"Nor will I," adds Catherine. "I'll surrender Solange in a second if she doesn't understand!" Solange, as the reader has doubtless guessed, is Baptiste's mother.

"Settled," Georges says. "Nothing more to say!" Then, switching the topic, "Gen, do you smell what's cooking?"

"Of course, duck stuffed with apples and prunes; and red cabbage, mom's sauce."

"Right, so you're staying for dinner—you have no choice!" Georges declares; then, holding her at arms length, "You've outdone yourself tonight, Gen! Cathy, look at our daughter! She's stunning!"

"Of course, dear," laughs Catherine. "She's been stunning since the day she was born! And if I didn't know better, Gen, I'd say there's more to your glow than relief at getting the big talk *(She rolls her eyes.)* out of the way! If I didn't know better, I'd say a gentleman's stirred your interest; or, rather, stirred you up. You didn't have that look yesterday morning. Your eyes keep misting over, drifting fondly into space."

"I never did have a normal childhood," Genevieve smiles, "because I never had any secrets from my mom!"

"Avoidance, avoidance," teases Catherine. "Gen, you're changing the subject."

"You're right, there *is* someone. But I only met him...yesterday, actually. And when I first saw him doesn't count, because he'd just landed from New York and had to settle in and we barely exchanged two words. At Steph's, where he's staying. He's a friend of Steph's, an American. It wasn't until last night—technically today, in the wee hours—that I really met him. Less than a day ago! I know it sounds insane, but it's not! Mom, I can't stop thinking about him, and need to call him! He was a big part of the plan to ditch Baptiste this morning—he knows I'm here and why I'm here and is waiting for me! So I can't stay!"

"First of all," answers Catherine, "I know it's not insane, because my daughter's always had her head firmly planted on her shoulders. And, second, why not invite him to dinner? We'd love to meet him, and won't detain you two a moment longer than you can endure."

"To dinner?" Genevieve says, a doubtful look in her eye. "Meet the parents already? What's Bill going to think? We've known each other for less than a day, mom!"

"If he's the man he needs to be, he won't balk," Georges says. "And tell him I said that! Tell him your mom and dad are respectfully asking him to dinner, and that your dad says not to read the world into it! Tell him there's no parental approval being dished out because the only approval he needs is yours! Tell him your dad says that if he has any sense he'll realize he's going to get a great meal out of it, and have a good time! If he's a man he'll laugh, and be only too happy to come! Mostly, he'll be dying to see you—will he ever! You've dressed for him, and are beautiful!"

"Of course I have the best parents on earth, who'll make Bill feel right at home!" Genevieve says. "Of course I do! Why was I hesitating?"

"So hesitate no longer," Catherine says, "and go call him."

When Genevieve steps into her old bedroom to phone William, she's far too giddy to stand still, much less sit. How wonderful to be unencumbered by extraneous thoughts, free of the burden of the Baptiste situation—what joy's rushed in to take the place of her worries! How deliriously delightful it will be to see William again, now that's she's free to exclusively focus her attention upon him!

William's already on speed-dial and Genevieve presses his key, number seven, while pacing about the room. A couple rings later he's saying *Hi Gen! How'd it go?* What a caress of the nerves, sweet nepenthe, is the sound of his voice! All he needs to do is speak and she's instantly serene and thrilled at the same time!

Genevieve's quite the gushing little girl as she informs William of the happy outcome of her parental talk, chides herself for having put it off for so long, then listens to him say she was being a conscientious daughter every parent would be proud of; as she informs him he's been asked to dinner and relates everything her father said, then listens to him say he already likes her father and would love to come and will be on his way as soon as he takes a shower because he's still in bed because he didn't fall asleep until after one; as she informs him she can't wait to see him and show him what she's like when she's free of concern, then listens to him say he's been thinking about her every second and hears *I love you!* from his lips for the first time, when they're about to hang up; as she informs him, without hesitation, that she loves him too! My God! Already, an exchange of *I love yous!* Their mutual attraction's taking flight as if with a will of its own, and what a breathtaking flight it is!

When Genevieve enters the kitchen to tell her parents William will be joining them, Georges doesn't give her the chance, saying, "Cathy, I like the young man already! Look at our Gen, smiling from ear to ear!"

"Sweetie," Catherine says, "I'm so glad he's coming! We can't wait to meet him! Will you get the ivory napkin rings, please?"

Genevieve, amused that she doesn't need words to announce William's acceptance of the invitation, answers, "Sure, mom. And which finger bowls do you want?"

We'll leave Genevieve for the time being, happily darting between the kitchen and dining room as she assists with setting the table. William's already stepped into the shower, and will be on his way to dinner within the hour.

CHAPTER 16

We join William as he's walking east on Rue d'Alésia towards the Alésia metro station, three stops from the Raspail station that's across the street from the residence of Genevieve's parents at 31 Rue Campagne Première. Upon nearing the metro, however, he decides against it: there are some nerves in the picture, not on account of seeing Genevieve again—he's so eager to see her it's as if he's leaping from his skin into the sky—but on account of doing so with her parents present. He's going to be obliged to keep his emotions in check when he least wants to, and perhaps is least able to. Of course her parents, her father's apparent jocularity aside, have a serious stake in the matter. Their only daughter... He'd better be capable of making a good impression, even while love-distracted in a way he's never been before. So he avoids the metro, directs his feet north on Avenue du General Leclerc. A walk to Rue Campagne Première at a rapid pace will calm and center him, as exercise always does; judging from its location on his map, it looks to be about twenty minutes away.

Although William's slept for less than five hours after a highly eventful day, he's never been more thrillingly focused upon a goal and inundated with energy. He's accustomed to scanning attractive women on the sidewalk, delighting in their charm, but is blind to them now: he's become a monk as regards every woman but Genevieve. He's unable to notice the attributes of other woman on account of the pictures of Genevieve that are monopolizing his mind's eye—monopolizing his very pulse. While separated from her he's living in his imagination, because that's where she is.

Seemingly in a flash William's at Place Denfert-Rochereau, strolling by the famous lion (The one Stephan proposed visiting half a day ago, that already seems like an infinity ago.) while but vaguely aware of the fact; vaguely aware of the open space of the square, parting of the buildings. It's as if someone else is consulting the map in his hands, instructing him to stick to the left side of the square as he passes through it, then continue north on Boulevard Raspail. He's never walked the route before and will doubtless need the map again if he does so again because the only thing he's going to recall are the pictures of Genevieve in his head, the anticipation ablaze in his blood.

Then he's standing before the tall twin glass and iron doors of 31 Rue Campagne Première, momentarily taken aback due to the fact there are two identical sets of these doors situated about eight yards apart—each with a 31 above them and an oval window and face framed in plentiful curling hair above that, surrounded by tan stone with ornate designs. Genevieve's doubtless neglected to mention which set of doors to take because either will do, as the family residence has entrances on both sides of the building, but William doesn't know that. Shrugging his shoulders, he passes through the first set, ascends the wide marble steps to the third floor, and rings the bell of the only door.

When the door swings open, Genevieve—the sole inhabitant of William's thoughts and dreams—is at last standing before him again, indescribably beautiful in a violet silk sequined dress, sleeveless and scoop necked. Her gently curling raven black locks are flowing down the sides of her face and spilling over her shoulders, her smile's sending shivers of joy up and down his spine. Within two seconds he's embracing and kissing her—the gesture's already as natural as if they've been doing it for years. Instantly gone is his apprehension with regard to her parents: he suddenly knows he can do *anything* as long as Genevieve's by his side—be more tactful than he's ever been, more charming and clever than he's ever been. Such is the drug of her electric presence that all situations are rendered magically easy to negotiate.

Then he's being introduced to her parents in the dining room, beside the large rectangular beveled glass dining table. What he notices most about their features are the unmistakable signs of Genevieve: she has her mother's hair and figure, her father's forehead, the height of both of them, a combination of their suffused expressions—curls of the lips, glows and angles of light in their eyes, tones of aspect and disposition that are as readily intuitable as they are impossible to frame in words.

"That's your seat, William," says her father, indicating the spot in the center of one of the long sides of the table.

"Thank you, Mr. Clouitier."

"Please, we're Georges and Cathy," he smiles. "We're not sticklers for formality, aren't going to put you through a lot of meeting the parents rigmarole!"

"We know you two only met yesterday," says Catherine. "What must you think, being dragged over here already! Ha ha ha!" William can definitely distinguish Genevieve's laugh in her mother's laugh.

"I'll be honest," responds William, "I'm not thinking at all! I've been in Paris barely over a day, and it's already been a kaleidoscope of experiences, a year's worth! I mean, I'm thinking about Genevieve," he hastens to say, suddenly realizing his statement about not thinking is open to unfavorable misinterpretation. "I've never been more sure about anyone in my life! God, I can't believe I said that aloud, especially because it's true!"

"Truth doesn't take kindly to being spoken—only lies do," Georges laughs. "Speak the truth, and it stabs you!"

"Oh, dad!" Genevieve smiles, reaching her hand across the table to William and looking at him as she continues. "I've also never been more sure about anyone in my life, and am stunned at the miracle of it! I think we're both pinching ourselves to confirm it's not a dream! And, Bill, it's OK to say these things in front of mom and dad—they already know."

"We *do* have eyes," says Catherine, "and like to think we know how to read what they spell out to us. Enough said. Why don't we dig into the shrimp and escargots? Bill, we'll understand if you're skeptical about escargots, and would rather stick to the shrimp."

"I *love* escargots," responds William. "All the San Francisco gourmet food stores carry them and I first had them in grade school, believe it or not."

And so the conversation turns towards more emotionally neutral subjects, unpredictably switching from one to another as with a life of its own: places William's lived, his present occupation; Georges' occupation, the favorite vacation spots of Genevieve's family and a couple related anecdotes; a send-up of philosophical discussions, as in debating the "dilemma each serious home decorator faces, whether to place decorative or practical use pillows on the couch"; somehow, a mention of the architecture of Frank Lloyd Wright creeps in, as does telemark skiing and financial printers and silk scarves and English Setters and Yorkshire Terriers and the works of Celine and Tacitus and Edgar Allan Poe; and the decimation of the European population by the double whammy of colder weather and the plague during the Dark Ages, so named more on account of the onset of dismal weather and its disastrous effects upon food production than the drop in intellectual activity—a discussion on how the drop in intellectual activity was directly related to the colder climate; on how political and intellectual oppression was a byproduct of lower agricultural yields; and from there to the best way to prepare langoustine, and where an abundance of conch is to be found in the Bahamas, and the origin of the term *red herring*, and when lions became extinct in Europe, and what aurochs were, and on and on... Suffice to say that by mid-meal William's as comfortable with Genevieve's parents as they are with him. There's nothing like a lively conversation for allowing people to feel each other out, bringing them together.

As the group conversation progresses, William and Genevieve carry on their own conversation with their eyes, the gist of which is that they can't wait to be alone together. Genevieve's side of the coin is that the Baptiste situation's been resolved and William's bonded with her parents; while these are lesser considerations where the emotional sweep of love is concerned, there's definitely a discernable difference in having them out of the way. She now has nothing on her mind but William—nothing in her feelings but William. She's peeling outward from inside herself and flowing into the air, beaming sweetness and fond regard. When the conversation turns, seemingly by chance, to the family's collection of Roman artifacts, housed in one of the units upstairs, she eagerly seizes the opportunity, saying while rising to her feet, "Bill, would you like to see the collection? I'll get the key!"

"I love all things Roman," William answers, standing without hesitation, delighting in the sight of Genevieve half-dashing across the room, opening the drawer of an antique bureau—the swish of her hair and stride and dress all combining to form a breathtaking symphony of motion; as well as the smile upon her face and radiance of her complexion and brightness of her eyes. "And thank you for a fabulous dinner, Mrs. Clouitier...I mean, Cathy."

"You're very welcome," responds Catherine. "It was our pleasure."

"Until the next time," says Georges, rising to shake William's hand.

Smiling at the distraction of William and their daughter, Georges and Catherine make a point of saying goodnight, so as to turn them loose. Everything about their manner says, "You're free now—do as you will."

Genevieve, seizing William's hand, yanks him in the direction of the front door: the touch of her hand whirls straight into his spine and spins throughout him and blurs the door as they approach it. As soon as they're alone on the landing they wrap their arms around each other, squeeze tightly, and kiss again—their first since his arrival two hours ago, a much-anticipated slaking of his thirst. Then they're strolling arm in arm up the stairs to the top floor, walking down the hallway past several doors; Genevieve's soon inserting the key in one of them, and they're stepping through it. When the lights are flicked on and she begins typing the code in the keypad to turn off the alarm William finds himself surrounded by Roman busts, vases, plates, goblets, helmets, weapons, and coins—a museum quality collection of marble, glass, bronze, silver, and gold—in glass display cases along the walls, from floor to ceiling.

Despite his considerable interest in Roman artifacts, William can barely see them—as in the song, he only has eyes for Genevieve. How can Roman artifacts, striking as they are, compete with the warmth of Genevieve's hand, bliss of gazing into her eyes? An artifact cannot sigh, as Genevieve's doing; cannot spin about with innate grace, as Genevieve does—the jubilant spontaneity of the movement fills the room with vibrant waves that reach inside his chest, inundate him with delicious sensations of elevation.

"I'm going to show you my favorite place in Paris," Genevieve says, gesturing towards the skylight. Then she reaches into the narrow space between two of the display cases and pulls out a stepladder.

William assists her with unfolding the ladder and placing it under the skylight. Genevieve, ascending first as he holds the ladder, opens the skylight and climbs through it onto the roof. He shortly follows, and is greeted by the sight of Paris stretching to the horizon in every direction—it's as if the earth's covered with Paris, and its buildings and light extend forever—only the sky's larger, the dark star-besprinkled sky. Genevieve's clasping his arm, surveying his face for his response while beaming with pride—joyful awe overspreads his features, and they both start laughing.

"So this is where I grew up!" she exclaims. "Isn't it incredible? I've been coming up here since I was a toddler, first with mom and dad, then by myself since grade school when dad had stairs built to the skylight in the apartment over there. *(She points towards the front of the building.)* I used to fool other kids by going into one apartment, then coming out of another—they didn't know I was able to travel between them, across the roof, via the skylights. The third apartment has a skylight too.

"I'm in a fairytale," he says, turning about in all directions and sweeping his gaze across the skyline. "But as stunning as Paris is, it has nothing on you!" Ceasing to turn about, he frames Genevieve's face with his hands.

"Nor on you," she answers, likewise framing his face.

For a few minutes they stand in silence, gazing into each other's eyes while exchanging facial caresses. The touch of Genevieve's fingers, as they stroke William's forehead and cheeks and lips and chin, is that of electric gossamer; she's dissolving the surface of his skin, slipping inside his nerve-stream, with her touch. He's likewise barely grazing her skin while passing the tips of his fingers over her face, under her chin, up and down the sides of her neck—the responsive pulsations of pleasure in her eyes stir sparkling buoyancy into his breast. They're sharing their silent places, exchanging secrets of the heart, affirming their faith and trust in one another. Together, they're climbing the ladder of fire of love, shimmering while turning inside out. William's never felt as utterly and thrillingly transparent before; never in his wildest dreams did he imagine the *paradise* of sharing transparency with a woman as wonderful as Genevieve.

Then they're seated side by side—facing in the direction of the glittering windows of Tour Montparnasse—with hands joined, rhythmically clasping and unclasping. They sit in silence—listen to each other's bloodbeat, share the hum of their electrical fields—for over an hour, as the stars grow brighter and streets grow quieter.

It's not until after 11:00 PM that William and Genevieve return to the third floor, where they find her parents absorbed in a game of chess in the sunken sitting room as Debussy's *La Mer* ebbs and flows. Immediately standing from the chess table, they go out of their way to reaffirm their fondness for William as Genevieve returns the Roman collection key to its drawer, locates her purse, and calls a cab. At the approach of midnight the cab arrives and farewell embraces and kisses are exchanged. Soon our couple's on their way to Genevieve's apartment at 160 Rue du Temple, where they'll spend their first night together.

CHAPTER 17

Before we rejoin William and Genevieve, we'll detail what occurred while they were on the roof. Georges, acting upon his daughter's request to have Baptiste removed from her life, grabs his phone less than a minute after she and William head to the top floor and calls Baptiste's father, Alain Grashelle. When Alain answers, Georges—with little preliminary, and already irritated—first states the particulars of Genevieve's complaint, then informs him his son's to stay away from her and is no longer welcome in their home.

"Georges, there must be some misunderstanding," Alain responds, as alarmed as he is astonished.

"There's no misunderstanding," replies Georges, instantly out-and-out angry. "No ifs, ands, or buts: Baptiste is not to see Genevieve again! He's not to approach her, speak to her, bother her in any way!" He grasps Catherine's hand and squeezes—she's seated beside him—and she returns the pressure, nodding approval.

"But..."

"But nothing!" Georges interrupts, shouting now. "Where Genevieve's concerned, I don't mince words! Baptiste has lowered himself to a level unbecoming a man, and it's not going to be tolerated by my daughter or Cathy or me! He's been behaving atrociously—following Gen around uninvited, seeking to pry her from her friends, interfering with her life! None of us will tolerate that! Known him all his life or not, been visiting our house since birth or not—none of it matters! He's turned out bad and we want nothing to do with him starting *now*!"

"Georges, I don't know that your tone's called for," counters Alain, in a voice pitched in a manner that indicates he's willing himself to avoid shouting. "In fact, I'd say yelling's inappropriate—we need to talk more calmly and constructively about this! For God's sake, we've been friends for twenty-five years!"

"You think I'm going too far?" answers Georges, still shouting. "Quite frankly, I don't care if I am! Going too far is preferable to not going far enough! The situation and how I—how we as a family—feel about it must be stated crystal clear, so there's not a shadow of a doubt about how appalled we are! Gen does not cry wolf! Your son's lost all decency, and it's going to *stop*! I...I'm so angry! Bothering my daughter! Son of a bitch! I'll go too far, and more! Do you understand? Is that constructive enough for you?"

We hasten to state that Georges hasn't called Alain with the intention of being as blunt and aggressive as he's being—he's almost as surprised as Alain is when his anger increases exponentially within seconds, and he starts yelling. But once he's yelling he makes no effort to restrain himself or backtrack; in the back of his mind as he's stating his case is suddenly the clear understanding that he's willing to sever all family and business ties with Alain, throw over two decades of friendship away. First and foremost, is the need to do away with a barrier to his daughter's happiness and, come hell or high water, that's exactly what he's going to do. As the offended party, he's less inclined to restrain himself with each word that emerges from his mouth, and more willing to accept that this conversation may result in a permanent rift between himself and Alain.

"He will be spoken to," Alain says in a tight voice. "It's regrettable, I..."

"And don't bring our friendship into this!" Georges catches himself screaming. "A friend listens to what a friend's saying, no matter how unwelcome the words! A friend doesn't indulge in delay tactics, mutter distractional gibberish about misunderstandings! Think I'm making this up? Think I'd lay down an ultimatum over nothing? It *is* an ultimatum! Speaking to him? You'll speak to him? He's out of our lives! That's what you tell him! That's what you speak about! Regrettable? Of course it's regrettable! What's the point of saying that? Stop trying to shove the facts of the matter away! It's a this-is-the-problem-and-here's-the-ONE-solution situation! And I'm not going to be swayed!"

"I'm not trying to sway you," Alain says, his voice still tight, such that's it's obvious he's having difficulty composing himself. "I'm doing my best to understand, I would hope you'd try...make an effort to calm down and talk this out...that you'd make some allowan..."

"Allowances?" interrupts Georges, screaming louder by the moment. "Are you hearing a word I'm saying? I explained the matter calmly enough at the start, stated what needed to be done, and you chose to mention misunderstandings! Who's egging this on? You are! And... OK, listen: maybe you'll forgive me for yelling and being blunt, maybe you won't—I'd rather the former, but I'll take the latter if that's what it's going to take to *keep your son the hell away from my daughter*! No mean-spirited bastard's going to poison her life! Take care of it! You tell him, because if he comes here—if he pesters Gen again—God help him! You tell him! All right, I'm hanging up!" He slams down the phone before Alain can say another word.

Let us remind the reader of what Genevieve told her friends regarding the ties between her family and Baptiste's. She didn't exaggerate: they're considerable. Georges and Alain met in college, where they met their wives and became engaged and married to them within the same six-month period and were each other's best man. Both holders of advanced degrees in finance, they've been very successful in the investment banking profession, and have occasionally worked in concert in matters of analysis or when pitching proposals to prospective clients. Their spouses, Catherine and Solange, are the best of friends and serve on the board of a prominent charity together. Add in the shared vacations, cottages in Normandy in close proximity to one another, two only children who were to some degree raised in both households when of elementary and middle school age, and the reader will understand the amount of familiarity involved. This is the bond that Baptiste has jeopardized with his behavior. This is the bond that Georges finds himself prepared to break without hesitation. As long as he's known Alain, he's never spoken to him as he has tonight, nor in any manner remotely approaching it. There has been some tension between the two men in the past, occasioned by Georges being from a more established family—older money, if you will. He inherited many of his business connections and clients from his father and grandfather, they having also practiced the investment banking profession. As Alain is the first in his family to practice the profession, he has fewer such connections. Thus, Georges has occasionally felt that Alain is overdependent upon him as regards business contacts and Alain has occasionally felt a twinge of jealousy, as in feeling Georges has an unfair advantage. Never something that's emerged into the foreground, this tension is the closest they've ever come to disagreeing with one another. In short, the present situation is the only truly divisive one their friendship has encountered. As the minutes elapse following the call, Georges is increasingly viewing the matter as a serious violation of trust; soon it's no longer a question of being willing to forgo his friendship with Alain, it's the outright desire to do so for the good of his family. How dare Alain raise a son who's grown up to harass his daughter!

As for Alain, he's scared to death when Georges hangs up on him, and angry as well. At first his anger's directed at himself: "Stupid, stupid!" he's thinking. "I shouldn't have mentioned misunderstandings, instead of asking for clarification! I should've been more willing to listen, instead of mentioning regrets and how long we've known each other!" Then he's angry at Georges: "I'd think our friendship would count for something! His yelling *was* inappropriate! Was I wrong to expect more of a discussion? I sincerely don't think so!" Then he's angry at Baptiste: "He's been bothering Gen, his friend since childhood?—following her around like some low-self-esteem tagalong, an affection-thirsty dog? I didn't raise him to beg, or be a nuisance! He should know he can't force a girl to like him more than she's comfortable with, insist on friendship becoming something else! That's the gist of it, right? He's upset Gen's giving him the cold shoulder, intimacy wise, and is trying to force the issue? Bloody hell!"

Alain may have raised a viper, but he's not one himself. The above-mentioned tensions notwithstanding (and it's not unusual for friendships to contain tension; one friend's generally the dominant of the two, even if by a nearly undetectable degree—the tradeoff's seldom dead even), he's deeply attached to Georges and cannot imagine life without him: they've shared many valuable experiences, experienced life together for a long time. Granted, it's not possible for Alain to regret losing Georges as a friend without also thinking of the business connection element—as Georges wields the greater amount of influence, Alain has the most to lose—but that's not close to being his primary concern. Far from being a stupid man, Alain understands Georges wouldn't be provoked to anger by hearsay evidence. He realizes his son must have, indeed, behaved atrociously and that Georges is ready to consign their friendship to oblivion on account of it. "What the hell was Baptiste thinking?" he asks aloud, twisting his head in disgust.

Suffice to say Alain's in the foulest mood imaginable when he phones his son.

"Hi dad," the unsuspecting Baptiste answers, seeing his father's number on the display screen of his phone.

"Baptiste," Alain begins, seeking to restrain himself. "I'm very disappointed, this gives me no pleasure—I'm disappointed, and angry! Georges has told me you've become an extreme inconvenience to Gen, and..."

"Dad," interrupts Baptiste, "I don't understand. Gen's my..."

"Gen's not your anything!" counter-interrupts Alain, raising his voice. "Get that through your head right now! I don't know all the details—I'm not sure I want to know, I don't need to be more upset than I already am—but Georges described your behavior as atrocious, said you've been following her, interfering with her life! What the hell's gotten into you?"

"Uh..." Baptiste grunts, unable to make another sound. Already, darkness is enveloping the room in which he's standing; already, his vision's clouding; already, the floor's as good as dissolving from under his feet. He collapses upon the nearby couch.

"All you can say is *uh*?" yells Alain. "My God! What Georges says is true! You've decided to behave *atrociously* and might've torn our families apart!"

"Ap...art? How, I don't unders...don't..." stammers Baptiste, unable to continue.

"Apart, goddammit!" Alain resumes. "Georges, my best friend since college, was on the phone ten minutes ago telling me you are no longer welcome in their home! Do you understand? My best friend, furious beyond self-control! Screaming! Telling me to let you know you're never to see Gen again! I could cry, goddammit, I could just cry! I..." Alain breaks off, his voice cracking.

"Dad, I don't..."

"You don't, you don't!" screams Alain. "I'm tired of hearing don't! What I want to hear is you *can*! You *can* listen to me! You *can* stop doing what you've been doing! You *can* make an effort to redeem yourself! You *can* come see me in the morning, so that maybe—just maybe—we can arrange a sit-down with Georges! Maybe they'll accept an apology, and assurances of ceasing with the atrocious behavior! Georges' words! Atrocious behavior! My God!"

"I..."

"You will come here in the morning," Alain interrupts, lowering his voice. "We can try—that's all I can do. You be here by nine."

"I...I'll be there," answers Baptiste, barely audible. "I'm sorry, I didn't intend..."

"You're sorry? Sorry?" Alain cuts in again. "Why on earth did you do this awful thing you have to be sorry for? I didn't bring you up to... All right, enough for now—there's no point now. You be here in the morning. And, for God's sake, if you run into Gen, keep your mouth shut and leave her alone! Baptiste, I'm very disappointed—a father shouldn't have to go through this—but we are going to try to straighten you out and salvage the situation! And don't forget our dinner at six, that my best friend will probably *not* be attending, thanks to you! You don't deserve it, but we're going to arrange the internship at Fried! I sure hope they work you hard, so you have better things to do than tear families apart! I must say goodbye! I cannot speak now!"

"Bye dad, I'll come, I..."

"Goodbye Baptiste, I'll see you in the morning," says Alain, his voice cracking again. When he hangs up the phone he brings his hands to his face, cries for perhaps the first time in his adult life.

As for Baptiste, he drops his phone on the couch, too paralyzed with a mixture of disbelief, rage, and fear to remember to close it. He's staring straight ahead at one of the windows in his living room, unable to look beyond it at the building across the street, 45 Rue de Vouillé. The window's steadily vanishing in the yellow light reflected upon it by the overhead lamp—the light itself is somehow becoming suffused with shadows, overcasting the room in gloom. It's as if invisible hands are pressing upon his chest, squeezing tightly; tension's accumulating in the pit of his stomach, such that it's as if he's being pricked from the inside with a thousand needles; his breathing's rapid and labored. "Who's bothering my dad, telling him stuff?" he's thinking. "Gen? Impossible! But what if maybe she did? Maybe? It's those friends of hers spreading rumors, churning things up! Telling lies, spewing character assassination garbage! They want me out of the picture! They want her to themselves!"

His fists are clenched and he's pressing his back into the couch. "Aahh!" he screams, seizing his phone and throwing it at the floor, smashing it to pieces. "Bastards! They've never liked me, it's been one snub after another I've had to swallow for Gen's sake! Nasty looks all the time, snotty attitudes! And now those Americans are around her—they're in it with the others! But they're not going to win! *(He stamps his feet on the floor, pounds the couch with his fists.)* I grew up with Gen and know her better than they ever will, so they're going to lose! I can fix it by seeing her alone! She'll see the truth and understand lies are being spewed if we can talk without them around! They're always clinging to her so I can't make my case! But I'll make it! Yeah, I'll make my case, and those liars that surround her will be left in the gutter!"

Suffice to say that for nearly two hours Baptiste continues to clench his fists and seethe with anger while seated on the couch—glaring into the empty air, blaming everyone but himself for his ills. Finally, he falls into a frequently interrupted sleep with the lights still on—at first while sitting upright, then while slumped onto his side. But enough of Baptiste for now.

CHAPTER 18

We rejoin William and Genevieve at approximately 6:30 AM on Sunday morning at her apartment, after they've spent their first night together. They're seated across from one another at the small circular table in the kitchen, partaking of tea. Lightning's flashing outside the window (facing Rue Dupetit-Thouars) adjacent to the table and rain's pattering against the glass; it's almost dark enough outdoors for people to wonder if the sun's risen yet. Rain's always heightened whatever emotions are predominant within William; and so this storm's extraordinarily comforting, rich with joy. The vase of tulips on the table, the rose print tablecloth, Genevieve's white-fur-fringed emerald nightie, the purple tulip she's slipped, via its stem, under the silver barrette in her hair, the dark curls of which are streaming down the sides of her face: every detail is a source of delight so strong William's tingling from his fingertips to his toes. Holding Genevieve's hand across the table while gazing into her eyes is more than the sum total of running wild in flowered meadows, dancing about fires at midnight, plunging into breaking waves on a tropical shore. William's never felt as whole inside, or imagined such would be possible: he's flat-out amazed. He and Genevieve have united in their emotions—their very physiology—to become something larger than each of them. The night they've spent together, their explorations of one another's physical attributes and emotional responses in the muted light of a small lamp, is like a dream become flesh: the remembrance-pictures of their lovemaking stream through William's mind's eye and thrill as much as they calm; the lingering reverberations warm him as effectively as if he's sitting beside a roaring fire. Genevieve's his roaring fire, and he already knows he's going to be spending the rest of his life with her, in the same way that she knows she's going to be spending the rest of her life with him.

Smilingly forbidding him to assist her, Genevieve stands to prepare breakfast, and what heaven it is for William to watch the swish of her hair and sparkle of her eyes as she moves between the refrigerator and stove and table. And the flittings of her hands, so indescribably delicate and graceful, as she assembles the place settings and cooking implements and edibles. The curve of her back, uprightness of her shoulders, and long lines of her legs as she cracks eggs at the sink and pours them from their shells into the frying pan. Then she's chopping peppers, mushrooms, and onions, and adding them to the eggs: the carmine of her fingernails spins into the silver of the stove hood, then into the crispness of the air and his bloodstream and he's blinking his eyes as if unable to believe it's real. This domestic scene's a ballet William could watch for hours: the simple things in life have become infused with wonder, endowed with an extra dimension of feeling.

Notwithstanding that William's had his share of meals at world renowned restaurants, this breakfast is the unquestioned pinnacle of his culinary adventures. Scrambled eggs and vegetables, a platter of brie and truffle-flecked pate, a salad of grapefruit, oranges, and avocados: this is the best meal he's been served in his life because Genevieve's prepared it with love and is seated across from him as they eat while tickling each other's feet with their toes.

It's been decided that William's going to spend the remainder of his time in Paris with Genevieve, after which she'll accompany him to New York. And then? It's a toss-up as to which city they'll live in, if not both. But that's jumping too far ahead for now. What's important on this morning is that William's going to be traveling to Stephan's apartment to retrieve his belongings.

"The sooner I leave the sooner I'll be back and settled in," William says after breakfast, embracing Genevieve from behind as she places the leftover pate and brie in the refrigerator. "I can't wait for the trip to be over and done with, so we can focus on what's *important*!"

"What makes you think I'm going to let you get away from me?" she laughs, spinning around in his arms and framing his face with her hands. "I want to go with you, so I can show off my man-prize!"

"Good idea! Showing off prizes is a two-way street, my dear, and I can present my girl to the world! Your appearance at Steph's as I gather my stuff will be optimum advertising! In a flash the whole crowd will know we're an item!"

"Why not have an official coming out party?" Genevieve suggests, clapping. "I'm going to call Steph! *(She reaches for her phone, lying on the windowsill.)* But, wait: should it be an intimate gathering, our closest friends, or...? Oh, whoever turns up, right? All will be welcome, of course! I'm jumping out of my skin!"

Genevieve, wrapping a leg about William's legs while clinging to him with her free arm, calls Stephan. "Hi Steph! Bill and I are coming down to get his stuff—he's moving up here! Yup, already moving in! We're a couple now, and I'd like a couple's coming out party! Oh, it doesn't have to be a huge crowd—it's short notice, those nearest and dearest will do just fine! But if word gets around, that's OK too! Good, a Sunday brunch, early dinner—perfect! *(She's repeating an abridged version of Stephan's half of the conversation aloud for William's benefit.)* Yeah, I know it's early—I figured you hadn't gone to sleep yet! Went to bed two hours ago? Sorry to wake you! As for us, there's a lot of energy flowing around up here and we don't need sleep! Actually we did sleep a bit, but I'm not sure when or for how long! Anyway, we're coming down, OK? Of course, we'll bring food! Sunday Alésia market? Count it done, see you soon—love you! *(She claps the phone shut, addresses*

William.) We're going to grab a few items at the farmers' market, across the street from Steph's."

"Our first shopping adventure," he says, combing her hair with his fingers. "I wonder if they'll have sea urchins at the market. I haven't had any since I was here last year!"

"Not another shellfish nut," she laughs. "Steph with his oysters, you with urchins! Will I be able to compete?"

"Don't worry about that, honey! Nothing with ever compare with this! *(He kisses her.)* No shellfish or anything else will blind me to the glory of your lovely locks! *(He lifts her hair over her head, lets it go.)* Yum! Crackling hair's the music of the spheres, electricity from heaven!"

Our happy couple treat themselves to an intimate interval which, with due discretion, shall be allowed to remain between them. About an hour and a half later, after they've showered and dressed, they're scampering down the stairs of Genevieve's building.

"I think we've forgotten something," Genevieve laughs when they open the door onto the street and see the rain slanting in front of them in heavy leaden streaks. "How could we forget umbrellas?"

"Easy! We've been too busy doing *this*! *(He kisses her neck.)* Might as well be a perfect day, for all we've been paying attention to it! Hell, it *is* a perfect day!"

"I agree that it's a perfect day, darling, because you're in it! It's also a rainy day and I'd rather not get drenched! I'll be right back with a couple umbrellas!"

"What's that church?" William asks, gesturing towards the opposite side of the street.

"Sainte-Élisabeth-de-Hongrie. It dates from the early 17th century, and it's nice to have Sainte-Élisabeth closeby. I love how the cross at the top soars into the sky, and the clock's accurate—never a minute off."

"I'll wait for you in Élisabeth's doorway—I want to see those bas-reliefs. Paris is a waking hallucination on every block!"

"Sure, tourist sweetheart!" Genevieve calls over her shoulder, she having commenced racing up the steps.

William, shielding his eyes against the rain as he checks for oncoming cars, dashes across the street to the church when he sees it's clear. Upon approaching the church he discovers that the figures to the sides of the doors aren't bas-reliefs but sculptures in alcoves—the only bas-relief is above the doors, the body of Christ draped in the lap of God, flanked by two angels, under an arch of twined leaves. After a couple minutes of admiring the bas-relief, he turns his attention to the figure at his right. "Must be Sainte-Élisabeth," he says to himself, advancing to stand below it. It's when he's gazing up at her, his head turned from the prevailing direction of the rain, that he hears an angry voice shout from behind, "You ruined everything!" Before he has time to wonder if the phrase is directed at him, an object strikes the right side of his face, and knocks him off-balance—spins him towards the paving stones, such that he winds up on his hands and knees. Only then does it flash upon him: *that was Baptiste!* Rage instantly masks the pain of the blow to his face; springing to his feet, albeit while staggering a moment, he wildly glances about and catches sight of Baptiste just as he's about to vanish around the right corner of the church. Racing in that direction, William's halted by a wrought iron fence: whether on account of the rain or because he's disoriented by the attack, he's failed to notice he's within the fence surrounding the front of the church and unable to follow his assailant via a direct path. Leaning across the fence, he perceives there's an alleyway leading towards a parallel street, discerns a rapidly retreating figure that he presumes to be Baptiste, and screams, "You better run, you bastard! You better run fast and far! It's not over, you sucker-punching son of a bitch!"

"What on earth?" William hears Genevieve asking—she's returned from her umbrella mission, and is standing at his side. "Bill...? My God! Your face! Let's get you upstairs, *now!*" What's whipping through her mind is that William's been in an altercation and needs to be removed from danger. She can't, for the life of her, imagine how an altercation's come about—violent muggings are virtually unknown in Paris. And why would William be fighting? He came over here to look at the church. This thought-sequence occurs in about two seconds, as she wraps an arm around him and turns him towards her building.

"It was Bap!" William says, far more angry than aware of the throbbing of his face. "The worm was waiting out here! He whacked me with something from behind, then ran away! The bastard's *dead* when I catch up with him!"

"That sick little creep!" Genevieve hisses; then, reverting to what's uppermost in her mind as they cross the street, "Alright, upstairs we go, honey! We need to take care of you! First things first! Don't worry, the little man's going to regret what he's done a thousand times over! For now, let's concern ourselves with you!"

Genevieve leads William to the bathroom, where she examines his face from all angles. The right side of his face is swollen, from the side of his eye to his cheek, but there's no visible puncturing of the skin. "OK, we're going to clean you up," she says, retrieving a bottle of peroxide from the medicine cabinet. Bidding him bend over the bathtub and close his eyes, she lightly splashes his face with the peroxide, which imparts something of a tickling fizz—a good sign, as it confirms there's no puncturing of the skin: it would sting if there was. While bent over the tub William's still far too overcome with rage to pay much mind to anything else. "Son of a bitch!" he exclaims between clenched teeth. "Am I *ever* going to make that worm suffer!"

"Sweetie, you're going to need put that on hold until we finish here. As far as making Bap suffer, I'm with you one hundred percent, but... Hold still, please. We're going to focus on you now, OK?"

Inside of five minutes, William's face is cleaned and dried. "Hmm...I don't know about bandages," Genevieve muses. "It's tender, and I know it hurts and doesn't look pretty and is only going to look worse, but I think it would be best to let it breathe. Although unsightly, the damage is minimal, thank God. There's no open wound to protect."

"I almost want bandages so they can be a shield."

"I know, sweetie—you feel vulnerable. Because you're wounded, it seems like everything in existence is eager to brush against the wound and make it worse. But it's not, especially with me by your side. How about I have plenty of bandages in my purse, so they can be applied if needed? Good compromise, right? I'm not going to leave your side." Genevieve stuffs her purse with gauze pads and bandage rolls, along with first aid tape, an unopened bottle of peroxide, and antiseptic gel.

Wound-assessment and first aid having been tended to, William switches back to his primary concern. "I've got to get the bastard! This can't happen again! Face it: he wasn't waiting out there because of me, but because of *you*! I won't have him shadowing you! You know what he said? He said, *You ruined everything!* The deluded little worm! What was there for me to ruin? You were fed up with him before I met you! God only knows what sort of sick fancies are churning in his head! *It's got to stop!*"

"It *is* going to stop!" affirms Genevieve heatedly. "Right now! *(She grabs her phone, dials her parents.)* Good morning mom! Well, I'm overwhelmingly good and, also, not that well! Good because Bill and I...I needn't elaborate, right? Now onto the bad thing, unfortunately it can't wait: Baptiste! Dad spoke to Alain, started yelling? He gave Alain the ultimatum? *(Again, she's repeating an abridged version of the other half of the conversation aloud for William's benefit.)* OK, obviously Bap was spoken to by Alain, and that first father-son talk wasn't severe enough! It had an opposite effect! Bap attacked Bill! Yes! Smacked him from behind! He said *You ruined everything*, then hit Bill and ran away! Bill's OK. One side of his face is swelling and isn't pretty, but it's not serious, thank God! But what are we going to do about Bap? *(Her father picks up another phone, joins the conversation.)* Hi dad! Yeah, the little creep hit Bill, then ran for his life! And you told Alain that Bap was banished forever? Yeah, I heard you—I'm repeating some of this so Bill can hear it, he's standing here! Alright, good! You're going to call them again, and put the fear of God into them! So sorry about this... OK, I know I'm not responsible, I... Of course it's got to stop!"

Seeing that William's motioning for the phone, Genevieve hands it to him. "Hi Georges and Cathy," he says, "I'd like to add something. No, don't worry about me, I'm fine. What I want to say is that Bap wasn't waiting outside on my account, but because of

Gen! Please don't be insulted that I'm asking this—I'm only covering all the bases so as to map the extent of Bap's delusions—but I'm correct in assuming you didn't mention me to his parents, right? Just as I thought. I mean, I already knew that, but... OK, so the point is he wasn't waiting outside to attack me because there's no way he could've known I was here! He was waiting for Gen, and God only knows what he was planning on doing! He's one sick mixed up son of a bitch and needs to be dealt with! Right, you know that and are jumping on it! OK, that's all I have to say, here's Gen again. Bye Georges and Cathy."

"Hi again mom and dad. Yes, call us after you call them. Here's Bill's number too, an American one: 1-212-555-3768. We're heading to Steph's soon—going to have a coming out party, officially announce our relationship to our friends! Don't worry about that! We're going to have the time of our lives, no Bap incident's ruining our party! Bill and I are truly blessed, despite this mess! Thank you! Bill, mom and dad say we've made them very happy! Alright, talk to you soon! I love you too! I love you so much! Bye mom and dad!"

"They're calling Bap's parents now, to lay down the law!" Genevieve says, clapping her phone shut. "The police are going to be mentioned as an option, dad's going to say charges will be brought if they can't control the creep! And, as far as that goes, why don't I call Claire? Her boyfriend's a detective, it won't hurt to have him in the loop. I've met him—at first sight, you just know he pursues police work with a passion and isn't a man you'd want to anger; but he's also a very nice guy, a true gentleman."

Genevieve, in an unbroken flurry of activity, reaches Claire and then Stephan and Lucinda and then Jean-Marc and Carole and alerts them to the situation. All pledge immediate and unqualified assistance; all are eager to draw up plans of defense and retaliation and execute them; all congratulate Genevieve on her relationship, and can't wait to celebrate.

In the meantime, William's on the phone with Christina and Pascale, who are fairly foaming at the mouth—availing themselves of phrases such as "scratch Bap's eyes out," "rip him to shreds," and "shove him on the metro tracks"—at the same time that they're offering profuse congratulations, delighted there's going be a "Billy and Gen party." In short, his conversation's a mirror of Genevieve's. "We're leaving shortly," William winds up. "No, we don't need an escort—the little man ran away as fast as he could, he's scared to death! And he has reason! But enough of that for now! See you within the hour, I'll call as soon as we're out of the metro. You can help us shop at the farmers' market across the street. Oh yes there is—look out the window! Told you so! It's there every Sunday! See you soon! I love you!"

Curiously enough, William and Genevieve are semi-relishing this opportunity to unite against a common enemy. It goes without saying they'd rather be free to enjoy the first day of their relationship in peace, without the interference of a frustrated and resentful individual; but, because such an individual has imposed upon them, they have a golden opportunity to rush to one another's defense—show each other what they're made of. Baptiste's attack, and the threat he still presents, is a means for them to gain greater appreciation and understanding of one another, thrill to their added strength as their two wills become one.

Of course it helps that they're not alone: Stephan's proposed that he and Sergio give "Bap a roll he'll not forget!"; Jean-Marc's asserted he'll not rest until "Bap's scared enough to leave town!"; Claire's stated her detective boyfriend and his associates will "See to it Bap envisions beatings and jail time!"; Georges is already screaming at Alain, saying charges will be pressed if "that screwed up son of yours so much as looks at Genevieve again!" Plans are coming together in several heads at once on all sides of town.

It's in a state we'll term agitated elation that William and Genevieve descend to the sidewalk for the second time. They reach the Temple metro station without incident and are soon seated on a train, heading south to Stephan's apartment. A celebration's imminent, and so is revenge.

CHAPTER 19

Regrettably we must rewind the clock to about 4:00 AM, as William and Genevieve are enjoying their first night together, in order to detail Baptiste's doings after he awakens from his uneasy sleep on the couch with the lights still on. Far from feeling refreshed when he opens his eyes, it's as if he hasn't shut them yet—as if he's just finished speaking to his father, been stunned by the latter's command to stay away from Genevieve.

"It's not Gen's fault!" he says to himself as he rises to his feet. "She's being brainwashed by the enemies of mine that surround her! They know the best way to harm me is to turn her against me, and are telling lies and turning things upside down!" He's erratically pacing about the living room, half off-balance, paying little mind to surrounding objects; not surprisingly, he bangs his knee against a small table. "Unbelievable!" he screams, kicking the table and causing the lamp upon it to crash to the hardwood floor. Then he's lifting the table over his head, slamming it to the floor—two of its legs break off and a splinter of wood strikes his forehead, resulting in additional rage. He starts stomping on the lamp, shatters its ceramic base, scatters the pieces; then he's pacing again, flailing his arms, yelling inarticulately; finally, he advances to his bedroom, locates his backpack, and begins cramming books into it.

"I've got to go straighten Gen out!" he resumes saying to himself. "I have to stop the smear campaign of the people clinging to her! If I go to her place, bring my books...it's Sunday, we can spend the day together. It's insane to think she'd turn me away, refuse to listen, when we've known each other all our lives! Yeah, I'll take my books—I can study at her place all day, it'll be a good excuse to stay after I explain everything! She must be made to see that the beastly things being said about me aren't true! Those insidious people! Their envy has no boundaries! They're so jealous of me—jealous of how I grew up with Gen, and know her better! She's got to be brought around! She *will* be brought around!"

And so Baptiste, in thrall to his distorted interpretation of reality, exits his building at 50 Rue de Vouillé and walks to the Plaisance metro station, apparently indifferent to the fact it's storming and he's without an umbrella. He's on the rail platform shortly before 5:00 AM and therefore has to wait not only until five-thirty, when the trains resume running, but awhile longer for the first one to arrive. Drenched to the skin while pacing and jerking his arms erratically, he doesn't cut an appealing figure: a woman on the opposite platform doesn't believe him to be fully sane and moves as far away from him as the station's dimensions will allow.

When Baptiste emerges from the Temple metro station after 6:00 AM he dashes towards Genevieve's building, close enough to be within view. He's eager to race up the steps, knock on her door, and surprise her—how sweet it will be! Of course she'll be glad to see him, free as she is from the hangers on! Of course she'll listen when he reveals her so-called friends are doing their best to poison him in her eyes, destroy their lifelong friendship! Of course she'll sympathize with him, take his side! And then they'll spend the day studying together, just like when they were in middle school.

But when Baptiste gazes up at Genevieve's apartment from the opposite side of the street, what does he see? He sees her and William standing arm in arm on one of the living room balconies, happily gazing at the sky. Instantly he drops behind the parked car in front of him to avoid being seen. It's as if he's been punched in the gut; he's gasping for breath; his temples are throbbing and vision's blurring. He's vaguely aware of observing their outlines through one of the car's rain-streaked windows as he shivers and shakes; then their outlines vanish and the pair of window-doors that separate the balcony from her living room close.

It's not until after he's crouched behind the car for at least ten minutes in the driving rain that Baptiste realizes the café across the street—La Tour du Temple, on the ground floor of Genevieve's building—is open, and enters it to warm up. He's too exhausted to realize he's exhausted as he sits at a table dosing himself with expresso after expresso, steadily dropping sugar cubes in the cups; he's also too agitated to raise a full cup of expresso to his lips without spilling a portion of it; when he glances down at the frosted patterns on the slate gray of the tabletop, they dance about and blur. Mostly, he's gazing at the door of Genevieve's building (Like many Paris cafés, La Tour du Temple has a glass-enclosed seating area that protrudes onto the sidewalk further than the regular building line; in this case, the door to her building is right outside the glass enclosure, such that Baptiste's about twelve feet from it.), too stunned to have the slightest idea what he's going to do. He's beyond the stage of seething with anger on account of what he perceives to be wrongful deprivation of his entitlement to Genevieve's affection; he's unable to be directly aware of being enraged. His fingers, however, are clenched tight—so tight that at one point, after he's been in the cafe for over two hours, he grips a cup of expresso too tightly and it pops out of his hand and shatters on the floor. When the waiter, none too pleased, advances to clean up the mess he's struck by the fact that Baptiste continues staring fixedly in front of him as if nothing's amiss; nor does Baptiste give any indication of being conscious of the waiter's presence as he wields his mop. As soon as the waiter returns to the bar he points out Baptiste's questionable condition to the other employees: they unanimously agree that he should be left undisturbed for the time being, and carefully watched. Baptiste places no further orders for expresso; in fact, he barely moves.

It's not until Baptiste sees William emerge from Genevieve's building and cross the street to the church that he's, as it were, jolted back into awareness. In a flash, rage rises within him, propels him to his feet, and guides his hand to one of the straps of his backpack; in a flash, he's in thrall to his bottled up resentment, scowl-faced at the thought of the nefarious, backstabbing, unjust people Genevieve's surrounded herself with—cursing this American upstart in particular, vowing to put him in his place. He exits the café without paying the full amount of his bill (He placed a five euro note on the table early on, but has neglected to add to it. As for the staff, they're far more relieved to be rid of him than interested in pursuing him for the balance due.), crosses the street until he's at William's back, screams "You ruined everything!," and smacks him on the side of his head with his backpack. Then he's dashing out the gate and circling around the fence that encloses the front of the church and continuing through the small alley at its right towards Rue de Turbigo. He doesn't hear William screaming at him, is only aware of needing to run. Once on Rue de Turbigo he turns south, still running; the backpack, slapping against his leg as he holds it by its strap, becomes heavier and more inconvenient with each step; apparently forgetting that it contains over four hundred euros worth of academic books, he allows it to fall from his hand. He's slowed to a fast walk by the time he reaches the Arts et Métiers metro station but continues onwards, oblivious of its existence. It's not until he reaches the Étienne Marcel station that he descends to catch a train, which he takes to the Alésia station, in his disordered state not having the presence of mind to transfer at Montparnasse-Bienvenüe and exit at a station closer to home. Coincidentally, this obliges him to traverse the length of Rue d'Alésia and walk by the Plaisance station, which William and Genevieve emerge from about five minutes later. Needless to say, Baptiste narrowly misses receiving a beating at the hands of William.

By the time Baptiste reaches his apartment his father's deposited a half dozen messages on his answering machine, none of them kind. Among other things, his father's delivered an ultimatum: Baptiste either shows for dinner at 6:00 PM or his allowance will be restricted, or he might be cut off altogether—if not permanently, then at least long enough for him to appreciate being supported while he pursues his studies. His father's also berated him for failing to show for their morning meeting—something Baptiste's completely forgotten about. Needless to say, his father's anger and amazement knows no bounds when he addresses his attack upon William. "I'm not sure I have a son anymore! Have you utterly lost your mind? Are you *trying* to get yourself arrested?" is a small sampling of his father's commentary on the subject.

Baptiste's never been addressed by his father with such severity—his father's always been very supportive, and has never remotely hinted at withdrawing financial assistance for any reason. To say that alarm grips Baptiste's chest in a vise, seems to suspend the beat of his heart, would be an understatement. He commences pacing in a frenzy, searching for the right words to say as he works up the courage to call his father; failing to find such words, he calls him anyway. As for the resulting conversation, your humble narrator will allow the bulk of it to remain between Baptiste and his father, and restrict himself to a summary of the latter's words: 1) the Clouitier's have threatened to press charges against Baptiste and his father doesn't blame them; 2) Baptiste must report home at 6:00 PM to be introduced to the man who will provide him with an internship at a law firm; failing to do so will result in immediate financial sanctions; 3) why isn't Baptiste answering his cell phone? (As a reminder to the reader, Baptiste threw his cell phone at the floor and it didn't survive the impact.); 4) a profuse amount of avowals of shame and incredulity. One final observation regarding the conversation: Baptiste's father does at least 90% of the talking; more than once he yells for his son to be silent, saying he doesn't want to hear his voice.

As for Baptiste's state of mind following the paternal dressing-down, your humble narrator will content himself with mentioning that what little remains of his instinct for self-preservation manages to hammer its way into the forefront of his awareness. Realizing he must acquire some sleep if he's to be presentable at the mandatory 6:00 PM dinner, Baptiste staggers into his bedroom and collapses on his bed, actually remembering to set the alarm for 4:00 PM.

CHAPTER 20

Switching our narrative back to William and Genevieve, we join them as they emerge from the Plaisance metro station onto Rue d'Alésia, close to Stephan's apartment. As mentioned in the previous chapter, they do so about five minutes after Baptiste walks by the same spot. Thus the vicissitudes of chance have spared Baptiste a thrashing and William the awkwardness of administering it in front of witnesses. Why does your humble narrator trouble to mention a near-miss? (After all, it's a fact of city life that people who are familiar to one another not infrequently pass within minutes of each other without being aware of it: this is due to both the small amount of geographical area involved and the large amount of obstacles to direct lines of vision.) He mentions it because it's a ready means of establishing what the opposed parties are doing at approximately 10:15 AM on Sunday morning. At any rate, William immediately phones Christina to let her and Pascale know that he and Genevieve have arrived and will meet them at the farmers' market across the street.

Within five minutes Christina and Pascale are stepping from the gate of Stephan's building, opening their umbrellas, and crossing the street to join William and Genevieve on the curb.

"My God!" exclaims Pascale, gazing in horror at William's face. "Oh, sweetie!"

"So no skin's broken?" Christina says, closely examining the wound. "There's no internal damage? All the same, Billy, maybe you ought to get out of the rain! Why don't we go upstairs?"

"I'm alright," William answers, turning the swollen side of his face away from them. "Pretend it's not there. Don't worry: the score will be settled soon."

"That cowardly creep!" continues Pascale, shaking with fury. "To sneak up and hit you when your back's turned! I'll spring on him like a cat and rip his eyes out, let's see him hit a girl! I'll kill him!"

"We'll kill him together!" Christina adds. "Let's see him tangle with two outraged mommies! Let's..."

"With three!" Genevieve cuts in. "I've been so blind, I didn't think Bap would do such a thing! He's plain insane now, and I didn't see it! *I didn't see it!*"

It's at this point that Stephan, not content to wait upstairs to check on William's injury, strolls up to our four friends; before he can say a word, Pascale points at William and shrieks, "Look at him!"

"I'll never forgive myself for not pounding Bap yesterday morning!" Stephan yells, forming fists and punching the air. "See, Gen? With all due respect, you were wrong to take the subtle approach!"

"You don't owe me any respect," responds Genevieve, "because you're right: gentle handling was a bad idea! I simply never would've thought him capable of physical violence! For as long as I've—unfortunately—known him, I've never heard of him attacking anyone!"

"So now he's crossed that line," William says, "because he's entangled in God only knows what pathetic imaginings concerning you! But he'll find out soon enough he's stepped on a hornet's nest!

We're going to sting him so severely he won't be able to remember his name!"

"Damn right!" Stephan shouts. "Sergio and I are going to make him forget his name and his mother's name and how to tie his shoes!"

"I have to be in on it," William says. "Of course I appreciate your help, but... Where does he live, anyway?"

"Down the street, believe it or not," Genevieve answers. "Rue d'Alésia turns into Rue de Vouillé and he's on Vouillé. But seriously, honey, I'd rather we wait and consider best what to do before rashly setting off after him. He's not going anywhere, and won't escape. Shopping first, then..."

"Gen's right," Stephan cuts in. "There's plenty of time to concoct a plan of action—the day's still in it's infancy, it's not even noon. And don't worry: we'll be striking back today, not tomorrow! Bap's not going to think he's gotten away with it for long! Retribution's not going to be slow to hit him in the face! There'll be action before midnight, I swear it! I won't rest easy in my mind until I know Bap's losing his! He's going spend the night *knowing* there's no place to run or hide! That's a given! And of course, Bill, you're going to have the primary role! But first things first. *(He places one hand on William's shoulder, the other on Genevieve's.)* Bill and Gen, we've got to get your celebration underway so I'm heading back upstairs—going to get the kitchen going, start peeling the potatoes, put Lucy to work. I'll trust you to do the shopping down here. Chrissy and Pas, you know what to get, right?"

"Lucy gave us a list," responds Christina, patting her purse.

"Good, see you upstairs," says Stephan, returning to his building.

Within half an hour our four friends have purchased the items on Lucinda's list—three kilos of pre-cooked shrimp, one kilo of green beans, several onions and green peppers, two heads of lettuce, and assorted other vegetables. To her list they've added four cantaloupes, several avocados, and two large papayas; a quarter wheel each of blue cheese, pecorino romano, and brie; and, to William's delight, a kilo of sea urchins. When they reach the apartment with their purchases they find Claire's arrived with her boyfriend, Armand.

At about five feet nine, Armand's not close to being the tallest man in the room, but he's by far the most imposing. There's an air of physical compactness and concentration about him that inspires instant respect; if he were to be placed in a random group of two dozen men, and people were to be asked which man is most likely to be combat trained it's highly probable they'd point to him without hesitation. During his twenties he served in the Foreign Legion, where he quickly rose to the rank of Captain; had he not grown weary of spending lengthy intervals abroad and become interested in police work, he would have had a distinguished career in the Legion. He's now thirty-seven years of age and a lieutenant in the National Police. Having participated in active combat and had a number of harrowing experiences, the small annoyances of civilian life have little capacity to merit his lasting attention, much less involve him emotionally; in fact, his natural disposition is that of good cheer and he has an easy smile—again, with the qualification that only a highly imperceptive individual would venture to annoy him. He has a head of close-cropped light brown hair, piercing brown eyes, a somewhat angular face, and an olive complexion. Armand could also tell people he's ten years younger than his real age and be readily believed.

Claire, seeing the blemish on William's face, cries, "Oh, no! That must hurt! Armand, you see why I brought you? And you won't believe who did that! Gen's childhood best friend, who's turned into a disgusting creep! This isn't funny! Why not arrest him now? But sorry! Where are my manners? Armand, this is Bill; Bill, this is Armand. *(The two men shake hands.)* Bill just got here Friday, from New York, and he gets clocked by a coward! A despicable... So he just ran away? He hit and ran?"

Before William has time to answer Claire's question, Lucinda, overhearing our new arrivals, scampers from the kitchen to greet them and is likewise shocked by his appearance. "Bill, I don't know what to say! You're our guest, and this happens! If I see Bap again, he gets cat's claws! *(She rakes her nails against the air.)* Gen, Bap's following you? He was waiting outside your building and attacked

Bill? And we were taking care to spare his feelings yesterday, discreetly separate you from him? Why were we doing that? He needs to be squashed! But I'm so happy for you and Bill! *(She embraces Genevieve.)* I'm torn in two! What should be undiluted delight's marred by this! *(She indicates William's wound.)* A couple can't fall in love in Paris without being bothered? Insane! Bap's not fit to live here! Bill, what must you think of our town?"

"I think your town's heaven on earth," responds William. "A tap on my face is but a trifle compared to the wonder that's come into my life! *(He smiles at Genevieve, wraps an arm about her waist.)* Forget me: what's unforgivable is that Bap was, indeed, watching Gen's place and waiting for her! He didn't know we were together until he came to spy on her! It wasn't me he was after, it was her! Long story short: he needs to be made to understand that Gen's off limits—in *all* circumstances, with *no* exceptions—until the end of time! We've got to scare him out of his skin, make him wish he was never born!"

"Armand's here to help in an unofficial official capacity, if you know what I mean," Claire says. "We're in the happy situation of knowing professionals who'll handle Bap in an off-the-record way. Technically, I suppose it's abuse of authority but, realistically, it's justified self-defense. Right, Armand?"

"But he attacked me," William says before Armand can answer. "It's my girl that's being shadowed! Armand, you understand right? Of course I appreciate that you're willing to help, and I'll allow you to do so; but I've got to smack Bap first—be the primary agent of his misery! I've got to look the bastard in the eye, up close and personal, and make him *feel* it! I can't just turn it over to the police and forget about it! No creep stalks my girl!"

"Of course I understand," Armand says. "I'd insist on the same thing. You get him first—tonight, tomorrow, when it can be done. I'll have an associate bang on his door afterwards, wave a badge, mention assault charges and witnesses. I have just the person in mind. Siali, a Samoan, two hundred sixty pounds of solid muscle and intimidation. Believe me, this Bap will be peeing his pants when Siali's towering before him, doling out police officiousness with an icy mien. Siali will also state that you and Gen and everyone else here are near and dear to his heart, protected and untouchable as far as the police are concerned. Nor will he forget to inform this Bap he's on a police watch list, subject to arrest at any time. I almost feel sorry for this Bap: his sense of helplessness isn't going to be mild. He won't have any wind left in his sails when Siali's through with him. Which reminds me: what's this Bap's address?"

"50 Rue de Vouillé, not far down the street," answers Genevieve, kissing him on the cheek. "Thank you, Armand."

"Police sanctified!" yells Stephan. "Claire the fair, I do declare you've chosen the right man!"

"Shut up, you!" laughs Armand, slapping him on the back. We'll mention in passing that Armand and Claire are another couple that's met on account of Stephan, albeit in an indirect manner, since Stephan didn't know Armand at the time. Stephan and some of his fellow Comédie-Française actors were invited to a party at which Armand was present; Stephan brought Claire along; Claire met Armand and they've been an item ever since.

"I will not shut up!" yells Stephan. "Bap's going to be dealt with, we have all afternoon to plot his misery, and the cops are going to be in on it! That's cause for comfort, but not cause for celebration! Bill and Gen are hitched, that's why we're *really* here! Time to get this party going! Let's get this stuff into the kitchen, and get cracking! Where are the beans, peppers, and onions?"

"Right here," Christina says, picking up one of the bags of food on the dining table.

"That's my department," Lucinda laughs, intercepting the bag. "The potatoes are peeled and ready for them!"

The bags of farmers' market food are taken into the kitchen and the labor is divided. Lucinda and Claire prepare the green beans, onions, and peppers for addition to the pot of potatoes. Christina and Pascale clean the shrimp and make the dinner salad. William and Genevieve clean the sea urchins and cut up cantaloupes, avocados, and papayas for the dessert salad. Stephan and Armand ready the cheese and wine and set the table.

About ten minutes after everyone's busy Genevieve receives a call from her father; after a couple minutes of speaking she's heard to say, "That's very interesting. Hang on a moment, dad, I going to pass the phone to Bill so he can get the details straight from you. Yeah, we're cooking up a plan and knowing where Bap's going to be this evening might be useful. Nothing's decided yet, but it will be, count on it! Alright, here's Bill. Bye dad. I love you."

Suffice to say that Georges apprises William of the entirety of his recent conversation with Baptiste's father, including the very pertinent fact that Baptiste has been delivered an ultimatum, and is due at his parents' at 6:00 PM. No sooner does William clap the phone shut than he shouts, "I'm going to douse the bastard!"

"Huh?" from Stephan.

"Fate's dropped the perfect situation in our lap, and I'm not letting it go to waste!" William continues excitedly. "Get this: Bap has to report home at six for a dinner party where some misinformed soul's going to give him an internship, if you can believe it. He also has a lot of explaining to do to mom and dad, needs to pacify them to avoid having the pursestrings cut! Yeah, Bap's dad's so angry he told Georges he's threatened to cut Bap off for awhile! In short, it's a critical situation for Bap and he has to be at his best and his mind's going to be on it, so it's the optimum opportunity to sabotage him! I'm going to be waiting on the stairs with a bucket full of sticky and disgusting stuff and pour it on him! Then I'll run upstairs, and..."

"What you'll do is run into one of our top floor apartments," Genevieve cuts in, "but you won't stay in it! Look: if Bap doesn't start chasing you, then you get him to do it by acting afraid, or by taunting him—whatever it takes. You run to the top floor and duck into the first unit across the hall, slightly to the right. You make sure he sees you go in it, and slam the door shut! Then, my dear, you go through the skylight to the roof and cross the roof to the apartment where we were last night, with the Roman collection. I don't know if you noticed but it's near the flight of stairs on the other side of the building. Then you sneak out of the second apartment and leave the building by the second flight of stairs while Bap's still standing outside the first apartment, doing whatever he's going to do."

"Genius!" William yells. "He'll be soaked with sticky goo in the hall, waiting for me, and I'll be outside in the street laughing!

And he'll still have the dinner party to go to, where his future's apparently being decided! Let's see him keep his head straight then, and make a good impression! Priceless! Just thought of something, though: he grew up there too. Doesn't he know about the skylights?"

"He does, but he doesn't know that you know. How could he? You and I have advanced at the speed of light! In his worst nightmares he'd never suspect we've already been on the roof! His vanity won't allow it! But, OK, for argument's sake, let's say his vanity does allow him to suspect: we have three apartments with roof access, so how is Bap going to know which one of the other two you go to? And how is he going to be in three places at once? He can't stand at all three doors! Even in the unlikely event that he starts racing from one apartment to another, you'll still have enough of a window at some point to slip away without being seen!"

"Plus he's going to be far too unnerved to think clearly," puts in Christina, "assuming he's ever capable of thinking clearly."

"Exactly," says Genevieve. "We'll go there ahead of time, set up the ladder in the exit apartment, rehearse a bit. As for the entry apartment, there's a stairway to the skylight in it. In fact, I'll be waiting for you in the exit apartment! Yes! I have to be there! We'll leave together!"

"And I'll love having you there!"

"An object lesson in how loving couples work together," Pascale says. "United against a common enemy, love chemistry flies to the rescue and a plan comes together with stunning ease! Bing, bang!"

"And of course mom and dad will know what's going on and we'll call to let them know all's well once we're safe outside," Genevieve adds.

"In case this Bap starts getting any stupid ideas concerning retribution," Armand puts in, "Siali will clip his wings first thing tomorrow morning. This Bap won't be so bold after he's told he's on a police watch list and Bill's immune to prosecution. Siali's very accomplished at making people feel uneasy—all he has to do is expand his huge chest and glare. Siali's a force of nature."

"Thanks again, Armand," William says. "The harder Bap's hit the better, no sympathy for the sicko who thinks he can shadow Gen without us showing him the meaning of hell on earth!"

"No sympathy for the creep who thinks he can clock my Bill upside the head and run away and hide without us hunting him down!" exclaims Genevieve.

"And hey," William continues, addressing Genevieve in particular, "given that Bap needs to be caused some distress and we have no choice in the matter, it'll almost be fun! Having to discipline a frustrated loser's never fun, but who's to say we can't push it in that direction? We'll ad lib as the situation dictates, and you won't see me declining an opportunity to get in a gratuitous dig! But what's definitely *not* fun is that we have to cut our celebration short because of that bastard! Aside from preparing the goop and transporting it, we should be at your parents' place by four-thirty, so we can get everything ready and I can be sure I'm waiting on the stairs before Bap arrives."

"Your celebration's not going to be cut short," Stephan says from across the kitchen, where he's rummaging in a floor-level cabinet, "only postponed! What we're having now's just an early dinner, OK? The official celebration of your union will be later, after Bap's taken care of! We'll be waiting outside for you two, near the corner of Raspail and Edgar Quinet, then we'll all come back here together and go all night!"

"Yay!" yells Christina. "All night!"

"All night!" the others shout.

"Here you go," Stephan says, handing William the pail he's retrieved from the cabinet.

"Much appreciated. As for what goes in it, I'd say sugar and orange juice for stickiness—it would also be nice to add blood. Where's the nearest butcher?"

"At the farmers' market," Stephan laughs. "I've seen guys pouring blood from the meat trays, whacking up whole animals! We'll be able to get entrails as well as blood! Nothing like discarded intestinal walls and organs for upping the fear factor! Bap'll be losing his mind wondering what he's been drenched with!"

"Right," William grins. "What's actually in the recipe is important, but it's what *might* be in it—the great unknown—that'll really unhinge him! How convenient that the market's here to help us mix up an extra nasty concoction! Our enterprise is definitely being aided and abetted by fate!"

"So let's go get some guts!" Stephan says, exiting the kitchen.

Within five minutes William and Stephan are at the market, where a baffled butcher fills their pail about a third of the way with blood and a mishmash of chicken and lamb innards. When they return to the apartment, they add sugar, orange juice, and potato peelings. The pail's placed near the dining table, where it receives many offerings of scraps, including shrimp heads and sea urchin gills, during their meal.

Jean-Marc and Carole, detained by the latter's schedule (she teaches a popular Sunday spinning class), arrive shortly after the meal's commenced. Suffice to say both are as infuriated by the sight of the wound on William's face as everyone else; that they're apprised of the manner in which Baptiste's going to be dealt with and heartily approve. At one point Jean-Marc says, "Fine, douse Bap and sabotage his meeting, terrify him with a huge cop! It's all good, but I still reserve the right to thrash him myself! If I see him again I'll do what I wanted to yesterday, stomp my boot in his face!" At another point Carole says, "It beggars belief that such a creature can exist! Why be petty and spiteful, consumed with envy? Why dwell in resentment, live a poisoned life? What's the point? Bap just plain gives me the creeps!"

As we wind this chapter to a close, we'll check in on William's emotional state: at the same time that he's calmed by the knowledge he's going to be hitting back at Baptiste soon, he's angry at being in the position of needing to hit back; occasionally he touches the tender spot on his face and winces at the discomfort, but that's inconsequential compared with the anxiety he feels on Genevieve's account, when he thinks of Baptiste waiting outside her apartment and wonders if he would've attacked her too; and so he tightens inside with additional resolve, vows the Baptiste problem is going to end. It *has* to end, so he and Genevieve can get on with their lives. Which is to say there's far more that's positive than negative in

William's feelings: when he gazes upon Genevieve, which he can't stop doing, the onrush of joy is such that shimmers spread over his skin and it's as if he's dissolving into the air. He's never fully understood how one can be thankful for needing to look out for someone else as closely as if that person inhabits one's own skin, but he does now and it's beautiful. Genevieve's cares are his cares—Genevieve's problems are his problems—and he's more than equal to the task, not only because the reverse is also true, but because she's a steady influx of energy such as he's never known, as well as a whole new dimension of intuition. Of course he's very close to Christina and Pascale—of course any difficulties they encounter will be his as well—but it's different with Genevieve: more self-evident, more basic—as basic and necessary as breathing. The chemistry between them is like fire stolen from heaven; he's truly left himself behind to unite with a greater whole. The miracle and mystery of love: why Genevieve and no other? and how does he know, beyond a doubt, that it's Genevieve and no other? Why question it? Simply breathe deeply, shimmer in unison with her, and surrender.

Following their meal, William and Genevieve retire to Christina and Pascale's room to take a nap, curled up together on the bed. It's not that they feel tired—both are racing on the adrenalin of love. It's simply that neither have had much sleep in the past forty-eight hours and feel it might be a good idea to obtain some while there's an opportunity. They have quite a night ahead of them and don't want their lack of sleep to catch up with them.

CHAPTER 21

The pail of fetid fluid, triple layered in garbage bags, has been transported via the metro from 225 Rue d'Alésia to 31 Rue Campagne Première. William and Genevieve have briefed her parents on the plan and obtained the keys to the top floor apartments. While ordinarily Genevieve's parents would question the wisdom of spilling foul liquid in the stairwell of their building, they raise no objection after seeing William's face, looking worse—as is the case with wounds that swell and discolor—by the hour. They only suggest that some of the liquid be drained off, as there appears to be enough for three dousings and most of it's going to wind up on the stairs. William, wondering why he hadn't thought of that himself, immediately goes outside and dumps half of the pail's contents into the rain-glutted gutter. By 5:15 PM he and Genevieve are in their places. She's waiting in the unit containing the Roman collection and he's waiting with the pail (its contents concealed by a plastic cover for the time being) on the stairs, just above the second floor landing of the residence of Baptiste's parents. The door of the apartment on the top floor into which he's going to flee has been left ajar.

At 5:47 PM William hears someone ascending the stairs and every muscle in his body tightens—the white marble of the stairway suddenly becomes brighter, crisper; the lines of the stair-edges sharpen, seem to slice into the air. As he flicks the cover from the pail and grips it tightly, tilts it in the direction of the approaching footsteps, he sees, for split seconds in a free-association burst, the edges of the obelisk at Place de la Concorde against the sunrise of yesterday morning—already it seems like weeks ago, a world away: so much has happened in the meantime. Here he is, as tense as a cat stalking prey, on the stairs of the building where the woman he loves grew up—the same woman who was a virtual stranger two days ago. Here he is, dealing with their common enemy—protecting what's already his new family. Here he is, transported into a wholly different life—absorbed in unforeseen feelings and aspirations. All of this flashes upon him lightning quick, then abruptly vanishes. Only one thing's on his mind now: be ready to sling the liquid from the pail with accuracy and dash to the top floor. Maybe it's Baptiste's footfall he hears coming closer and closer, maybe it's not, but he must be ready.

Baptiste, his head tilted downwards, comes into view at the right edge of the stairwell. William waits another second, can feel his bloodbeat pulsing in his temples as everything seems to slow down. It's as if he's hovering half outside his body as he jerks the pail forward—as he watches the arc of dark brown liquid stream through the air, score a direct hit on Baptiste's upper chest, splash into his face. Baptiste jerks himself sideways, drops his umbrella, convulsively grasps at the handrail; then he's shaking his head, frantically spitting again and again, wiping his face with his hands. Then William hears himself yell *Get the message?* as he backs up the stairs, waits for his enemy to spot him. Then there's the flare of hate in Baptiste's eyes and William's racing to the top floor.

Once he reaches the top floor, William shoves at the door of the apartment across the hall and slightly to the right and dashes inside it. He hears yelling—no discernable words—as he shuts the door and it locks itself. Seconds later, thuds descend upon the door, both at head-height and at its base, and William can't help but crack a smile. Not that he's lingering to gloat: he's already climbed the stairs to the skylight and is opening it, cheered by the sound of the rain smacking against its glass. Upon passing onto the roof and closing the skylight and standing, he opens his arms to the darkened sky, turns around and around to take in the storm-obscured panorama of Paris as the wind and rain caresses and calms him. Just what the doctor ordered! A dose of untamed nature! What a balm for the nerves, how soothing to the blood! Ever since being attacked in the morning, William's had Baptiste weighing on his mind; he's been flaring with anger seemingly every other minute, straining at the bit to retaliate and balance matters—chase Baptiste out of his life. How the storm washes that oppressive state away, does away with the sense of being pressed in on himself, all inner claustrophobia! Now he can move on with his new life, surrender exclusively to the joy of getting to know the woman he loves—strengthening their bond!

William treats himself to at least a minute of enjoyment of the storm before approaching the skylight of the second apartment. Then a last look about at Paris (his eye stops at Tour Montparnasse, its lights lifted into the sky as its dark edges vanish within the storm) and a glance across Boulevard Raspail at the café, Raspail Vert, where his friends are waiting—the café's vaguely discernable above the wildly tossing tops of trees in the foreground. Then he's raising the skylight, smiling into Genevieve's uplifted eyes, their ineffably sweet brightness. Then she's scampering up the ladder with a squeal of delight and he's leaning down to kiss her.

"But you're getting soaked!" she exclaims, a charming look of soft-alarm—like that of a little girl who's accidentally stepped on her doll—on her face. "Silly me! I'll get out of your way!"

"Not at all silly," he says. "I've been enjoying the rain! Such a refreshing dousing!"

"A bit different than the one Bap's received, I take it?" she says, jumping from the lower half of the ladder to the floor.

"I got him, all right! A direct hit!"

"I know you got him," she says while assisting him with his descent. "Listen." It's only now that William becomes aware of screaming echoing outside the door from a distance away.

"I don't know if that's good or bad," he says as soon as he's standing beside her. "Bap's obviously lost all grip on rationality, kissed all sense of self-preservation goodbye. What does it portend for the long run if he's too hellbent on getting at me to realize he's sabotaging himself? I sure hope Armand's Samoan friend succeeds in scaring him for good!"

"He's a weakling with no self-control being swept along by the stimulation of the moment!" Genevieve says heatedly, making a dismissive gesture. "When he cools off and sees how his world's shattered to bits—don't forget his dad's already furious, ready to halt the cash-flow—he'll be far too busy trying to piece it back together to think about us! There's nothing like cold reality—as in *Where's the rent coming from?*—for taking center stage! Making trouble for us will be too time-consuming when he has heaps of trouble of his own! And Armand *will* take care of matters from the official end, count on it! And... Sweetie, you know what? *(She squeezes William's arm.)* Let's hurry and hit the streets! I'll call dad and tell him to call Bap's dad and complain about the ruckus he's making! Why not bury Bap deeper, while we have the chance?"

"Deliciously wicked!" William laughs, brushing her hair from her face and gazing upon her with supreme delight. "When Bap's dad sees him going berserk... Hell, I'd feel sorry for Bap if he wasn't the scum of the earth!"

"Please, don't *ever* suggest such a thing again, even in jest," she says, nudging him with her knee. "No pity for Bap, not in our lifetime! But let's go! I've got to call dad!"

They cautiously open the door and peer down the hall to make sure the coast is clear. "So long, my friends," William whispers, saluting the Roman artifacts as Genevieve enables the alarm and they exit the apartment; then they rapidly descend the stairwell on the eastern side of the building to the street. As soon as they cross Boulevard Raspail and step inside the Raspail Vert café, Genevieve calls her father.

"Hi dad," she begins excitedly, motioning for their friends—who've risen to greet them—to be silent. "Do you hear Bap up there? Good, he's still making a scene. Right, we're safe outside now, and... Dad, you're way ahead of me! Have I told you that I love and admire and worship you lately? OK, I'll hang up so you can do it!"

"You didn't even have to ask him to complain about Bap," William laughs.

"He was already itching to do it, waiting for us to be out of there first. He's calling Bap's dad now. What fun that'll be for Bap! He's still up there losing his mind!"

"Tell all," says Stephan, speaking for himself and the rest of the group—Christina, Pascale, Jean-Marc, Carole, and Lucinda—as they crowd close and exchange hugs and kisses.

"Success!" William smiles, raising a fist towards the ceiling. "Bap's been drenched good and proper, a perfect shot! Chest and face splashed with that foul mess! He followed me upstairs and is raising hell, yelling loud enough to be heard by half the building! And he's supposed to be at a dinner party, sucking up to the influential individual who's going to give him an internship!"

"I'd say that internship's been kissed bye-bye," says Pascale. "I don't think there's any *going to* attached to it anymore!"

"Exactly, darling," William says. "That internship's as gone as a pastry down a glutton's throat!"

"Perfect subversion," Christina says, embracing William again. "Congratulations on a job well done! We're proud of you!"

A couple minutes later Genevieve's phone rings and she eagerly answers it. "Hi dad. Really? Alain's gone upstairs, seen Bap's lunacy firsthand? The cops are there? Wow! We got out just in time! And Bap's arguing with the cops? This keeps getting better and better! OK, thanks dad! Yeah, we're heading to Steph's! Bye! Love you!" Then, addressing her friends, "A neighbor called the cops, they went upstairs and confronted Bap; instead of calming down, he started arguing with them. And Bap's dad is there too! It's complete chaos!"

"Not to be alarming or anything," says Carole, "but Bap seems to be beyond certifiable. I sure hope this shoddy business is over, but something tells me it might not be."

"We did the gentle handling yesterday," Genevieve says, "and I'll regret that forever because of his attack on Bill. I was dreadfully wrong to insist upon gentle handling, I was influenced by having grown up with the creep. So now we've hit Bap harder, and he'll be hit harder again by Armand's friend in the morning. He's going to have far too many problems of his own to pester us anymore! But enough of Bap! I'm through with thinking about him!"

"I understand your impatience to banish the creep from your head," Carole persists, "but what if he still won't stop obsessing over you? What if..."

"Sweetie, I know you mean well," Genevieve cuts in, grasping Carole's hands with a smile, "and it's appreciated, believe me. But I'm through with having Bap in my head, he's been there far too long already, and...all right, don't frown...I'll come clean. The sad truth is I put up with Bap's progressively bad behavior for longer than I've let on. For over six months I kept quiet about his sickness and declined to identify it as such, made allowances I shouldn't have—the fact we grew up together wasn't easy to discount. But that's over now, those childhood memories are dead! Any illusions I had regarding Bap's recovery are gone and I'm free! As tolerant as I was when he first began to misbehave is the measure of how much I detest him now! So please allow me to consider the matter closed, I have no more thoughts to spare on his behalf!"

"And it's open season on Bap now, anyway," Stephan says. "If he *dares* try anything, we'll see to it he can't walk! And don't underestimate Armand's cop buddy! I mean, come on! If a huge Samoan was threatening me I'd do everything in my power to keep him from following through on it! Bap would have to be straight-jacket-worthy insane to make trouble after being told by a giant of a Samoan he's on a police watch list! Bap's a coward who's only carrying on now because mommy and daddy are closeby! Two year olds have temper tantrums, and so does Bap! Gen's right! Enough of him!"

"Thank you, Steph," Genevieve says, hugging him. "Onto the wonderful things, as in how blessed I am to have the best boyfriend and friends on earth! I say we get to your place so Bill and I can have our coming out party!"

"And I second that motion," William says. "It's what we've been working for, the right to celebrate with clear heads! Bap was a *chore* to get out of the way first, nothing more! The path to surrender's been blazed, and it's up to us to take it!"

"And we're taking it, all right," Jean-Marc says as he steps towards the door and opens his umbrella; then, addressing Carole, "We'll share this umbrella so you can give yours to Bill and Gen."

"Of course," Carole responds, handing her umbrella to Genevieve.

"But mine's larger," Lucinda points out, extending her umbrella towards Genevieve. "Gen you take mine, Carole you keep yours. I'll share Steph's."

"I gave her mine first and she accepted it," Carole laughs, nudging Lucinda's hand away. "I'll walk naked in the rain before I'll take it back!"

"Fair enough," Lucinda says, flicking at Carole's hair. "I was only trying to give her a *better* one."

"They're both wonderful umbrellas offered in love," Genevieve smiles, unfolding the one given to her by Carole. "The first one I touched is the one we'll use. Thank you both!"

"Girls fussing over umbrellas," Jean-Marc laughs. "It's nice to have things back to normal, with the true priorities taking center stage!"

"Quiet, you," Carole smiles, snuggling against him as everyone steps outside.

"You want a priority?" Pascale asks. "There's only one: celebration, here we come!"

"Celebration, here we come!" shout the others.

Because the Raspail metro station entrances are visible from the residence of Baptiste's parents and our friends by no means wish to be spotted by the enemy and placed at the scene, they walk in the opposite direction up Boulevard Edgar Quinet to the Montparnasse-Bienvenüe station to catch a train. Within half an hour they enter Stephan's building, where we'll join them in the chapter after the next.

CHAPTER 22

Now we'll dial the clock back a few minutes: Alain, having been alerted to the irregularity of his son's behavior by Georges, is ascending the stairs and the amount of his distress cannot be measured as he hears screaming in Baptiste's voice. Heretofore the information concerning Baptiste's unacceptable behavior has been of the third party variety, but now he's face to face with the awful truth and is torn between anger, pity, and fear. Anger because Baptiste was instructed in no uncertain terms to get his act together and report home at precisely 6:00 PM for an important meeting; pity and fear because it now appears he's passed outside of a frame of mind which would allow him to comprehend and heed such instructions. Alain's trembling by the time he reaches the top floor, primarily because pity and fear have gained the upper hand.

Alain can't help but blink his eyes and momentarily recoil at the sight of his son: soiled with brown liquid, flailing his arms and legs at the door of Georges' apartment, yelling threats and obscenities, his face swollen with rage. Then, collecting himself, he calls out, "Baptiste! *Baptiste!*" as he approaches and grasps him by the shoulder. "What's going on? Why are you doing this? Please stop!"

"What?" answers Baptiste, as if at first unaware of who's addressing him. "American son of a bitch ran in here, I'm going to..."

"Baptiste!" Alain repeats. "For God's sake! This is your father speaking! Stop it!"

"Uh," Baptiste grunts, turning to face Alain. "Dad, I...the American threw some stuff on me, see? *(He gestures at the stains on his white shirt and gray sports jacket.)* He ran in here! He's in there and has to be caught and punished!"

"Baptiste," Alain says gently as he readjusts his hand on his son's shoulder, animated exclusively by concern at this point. "You need to come downstairs. Please, we must both go downstairs and sort this out. You cannot be shouting and kicking doors. We're going downstairs now."

Alain gently but firmly turns Baptiste away from the door and leads him to the top of the stairwell; it's when they commence descending that two policemen appear on the landing below them, announcing they've been summoned to look into a disturbance. The cops eye Baptiste suspiciously, and they have reason: he may have resigned himself to his father's guiding hand, but his eyes are rolling wildly and his face is still convulsed with anger and he persists in jerking his head towards the door of the apartment into which William fled.

"Sir," one of the officers says, addressing Baptiste. "I'd like a word with you, please."

This request, instead of exerting a sobering influence upon Baptiste, excites him to renewed fury. "What, you're here for me?" he exclaims, unaware that he's as good as confessed to being the offending party. "What about *him*? The bastard in there? *(He repeatedly jabs his pointing finger in the direction of the unit into which William vanished; then, breaking from his father's hold, he returns to stand in front of it.)* You need to break down this door! I'm not the one causing trouble! I'm not the one you want! The American's in there! He's the one you want!"

"Sir," the officer persists, "were you creating a disturbance?"

"But you don't understand!" Baptiste answers. "He's in there! The son of a bitch! Break down the door, why don't you? You'll see! I'm not the guy who started..."

"Baptiste!" Alain interrupts, now at his son's side again, turning him towards the stairwell for the second time. "Please, Baptiste! You must calm down! Officer, he will stop—I'll see to it. He's coming downstairs, and will settle down. I've lived in this building for over twenty years, and my son grew up here. There's never been a problem, he's a good boy. Please, may I calm my son? He's had a rough time lately."

"Sir," responds the officer, maintaining an even professional tone, "many people have rough times. They do not create public disturbances." Then, addressing Baptiste, "You must either calm yourself or be arrested, those are your options. You must do as your father says, and accompany him downstairs. You must desist with disorderly conduct. There has been no complaint made about anyone besides yourself."

"I'm making a complaint, then!" Baptiste says, raising his voice far more than is advisable. "American son of a bitch threw this stuff on me, ran in there! Smell it? Smell this stuff? He's hiding in there and is afraid of me and right to be afraid of me, doesn't want to come out! And he's probably laughing, because now I'm in trouble and he thinks he's gotten away with it! I don't know his name! Will or something! He's an..."

"If that is true," the officer cuts in, bidding him be silent with an upraised palm and stern glance, "you may make a complaint. But this must stop immediately. We cannot enter apartments without cause."

Georges, who's been following the exchange between father and son and the police from where he's standing at the front of his apartment with the door cracked open a hair, where he positioned himself as soon as Alain ascended the stairs, has had enough of being, however indirectly, brought into the equation by Baptiste and ascends the stairs to the top floor. "Officer," he says, "my name is Georges Clouitier and I've been listening to this discussion from the doorway of my primary residence on the third floor. I'm the owner of this apartment and I can assure you there's no one inside it. Although nothing obliges me to do so, I will open the door and show you—you only, officers. This unruly young man *(He gestures at Baptiste.)* is not to be allowed inside. He must be removed first. I did not call you and make a complaint, but I did call his father. I did not call you out of consideration for his father, who I've known for twenty-five years. His son has no business slinging groundless accusations. His son has been bothering my daughter to an unforgivable degree and also assaulted a friend of hers this morning. In the matter of the assault I, again, chose to inform his father and not involve the police. Perhaps mistakenly, I've entrusted the young man's father with administering appropriate warnings and discipline to ensure that the misbehavior stops. If the misbehavior does not stop charges will be filed, and I'll request that a restraining order be issued against the young man. Now, may we proceed? The young man needs to be removed from the area."

"Georges," begins Alain.

"Alain," Georges cuts him off, "my patience is at an end. Baptiste, who I've known since he entered this world, has become a menace to my family and is no longer welcome in our home. I neither wish to speak to nor gaze upon him again. This must stop and if legal measures are required to see to it that it does, they will be taken. Sorry, but put yourself in my place: you would do the same. Discussion over. Please, officers, inform the young man that charges will be pressed if he does not remove himself."

"But," begins Baptiste.

"Baptiste," his father interrupts in a firm tone, "we are going downstairs to calm you down." So saying, he slips a hand under Baptiste's arm and leads him downstairs, too anxious to think of dispensing parting comments to Georges and the police. To say that he's extremely alarmed concerning his son's unbalanced frame of mind, the irrefutable evidence of which has been presented to him in front of police officers, would be a gross understatement.

"Sir," one of the officers addresses Georges. "As you pointed out, you are under no obligation to allow us inside your apartment."

"Officer," responds Georges, "I'd like you to examine the apartment, and I'll tell you why. In the event that charges are brought against the young man, if he refuses to alter his reprehensible behavior and persists in bothering my daughter and assaulting her friends, I'd like to have you as witnesses. To the effect that the young man perjured himself when he declared someone to be in this apartment. I don't know why he was kicking the door and yelling—I don't know why he's been indulging in any of his recent atrocious behavior—but there's no one in there, and I'd like to prove it."

Georges, although he neither summoned the police nor had any intention of doing so, is glad they're here. He was disinclined to summon the police because of William's involvement; but now William's safely out of the building and there's no evidence he was present, so that's no longer a concern. As for Baptiste, he's more than discredited himself with his antics and Georges isn't worried that anyone's going to consider him a reliable witness. So Georges, while not ordinarily given to perpetrating falsehood, doesn't hesitate to seize the opportunity to further discredit Baptiste. Need we remind the reader that Genevieve's well-being is his number one priority in all circumstances? Because all is fair in war, Georges opens the door of the apartment and bids the officers enter.

"I don't see a soul," says one of the officers, glancing about the single-room unit.

"I'm satisfied," says the other officer, already turning to leave.

Something we've neglected to mention is that the only furniture in the apartment is the stairway—barely wider than an average ladder, but with handrails—to the skylight, a bookcase that extends from floor to ceiling along one of the walls, and a small vanity with a mirror above it and cabinet below it. A dark pink carpet, sitting atop two inches of padding, extends from wall to wall and many large pillows line the walls. It was Genevieve's playroom when she was a girl and hasn't been altered since. It's dimensions are no more than ten feet by eighteen. This is why the officers immediately see that no one's in the room, and why one of them is smiling. It's occurred to him that someone could be on the roof, despite the fact it's raining, and he's more amused than interested; he realizes he could check to see if the top of the stairway's wet to determine if the skylight's been opened recently, but why bother? Besides, he'd be exceeding his authority, given that he's only in the apartment by virtue of the owner's permission. The fact is neither of them care for Baptiste and they're only human. The fact also is that they instinctively respect Georges. It hasn't escaped their notice that, from the moment he appeared on the scene, the tone changed: no one spoke while he was speaking and order was quickly restored.

The apartment having been examined, Georges shuts the door and accompanies the officers downstairs as far as his landing, handing each of them his card as he does so. "I don't anticipate further disturbances tonight," he says, "and, as far as I'm concerned, we're through. The young man may have attacked my property, but he didn't get past the door—I'll let it rest for now. Hopefully, I won't need to contact you in the future, but I would appreciate it if you would hold onto my card just in case. Thank you very much for your help, and drive safe in the rain."

"Thank you, sir," says one of the officers, already descending the stairs. "Goodnight."

"Goodnight, sir," says the second officer, following his partner.

As for Baptiste and Alain, they reach the second floor landing of the latter's residence before Georges admits the officers into the apartment. Once there, Alain finds himself uncertain of how to proceed. The living room is full of guests and he'd rather they didn't see Baptiste in his present state, but what alternative is there? Of course they already have a good idea of what's been going on—it's inescapable. He'll announce that a family matter needs to be attended to, offer regrets, and send everyone home. He'll attempt to reason with his son, get to the bottom of what's bothering him. He'll do all he can in the way of curing his son of what's obviously an affliction. No more threats to cut him off—no more yelling. It's professional help that's needed, he sees that now. "Baptiste, please go straight to the front bathroom and clean yourself up. I'll send our guests home so we can have a long talk. Just know that I love you!" Then, taking a deep breath, he pushes open the door.

"I'll spare you more embarrassment, dad," Baptiste says, beginning to descend the stairs. "I'll..."

"Baptiste, no!" Alain pleads. "I never mentioned embarrassment, I only want to help! Please, come inside with me! *Please!*"

"Goodbye dad," Baptiste says. "I love you too!"

Baptiste springs down the stairs, taking them two at a time, and is soon on the sidewalk and running south on Boulevard Raspail. He steps into the street less than ten minutes after William and Genevieve and the others set off towards the Montparnasse-Bienvenüe metro station—not as close of a near-miss as the previously cited one, since the two parties are traveling in near-opposite directions. He's running more for the sake of running, as if by doing so he'll outdistance the torment in his breast, than because he has a clear idea of where he wishes to go.

Alain, following his son outside and vainly seeking to catch a glimpse of him in the heavy rain, immediately begins calling his cell phone again and again—unaware that it no longer exists—and leaving pleading messages, supportive messages. Likewise, he leaves messages on his home phone. Finally, he races back upstairs to get the car keys and the duplicate set of keys to Baptiste's apartment, passing the officers on their way down as he does so and assuring them nothing's wrong. The officers don't believe a word of it, but continue on their way; after all, they've performed their duty: the matter of the disturbance in the building has been resolved.

Once back in his residence, Alain informs his wife he's driving to Baptiste's apartment and that he'll call her when he arrives. When he does arrive at the apartment he finds it empty and resumes calling Baptiste's cell phone. It's not until he's been there for over an hour that he remembers to call his wife. He tells her he's going to wait until Baptiste comes home and do his best to save him.

CHAPTER 23

We rejoin William and Genevieve and their friends as they step from the elevator at 225 Rue d'Alésia and turn towards Stephan's apartment. Actually, we'll rephrase it as: we rejoin our *merry band*. Because a merry band is finally what they are. The tension of earlier in the day has broken apart like the ice of a frozen lake in spring—their enemy's been vanquished and order restored. They know of the extent of the vanquishing because Georges has already phoned Genevieve and described how the officers examined the empty apartment, and how culpable it made Baptiste appear in their eyes. As for Genevieve's commentary, it was as follows: "Bap's false accusation of Bill being in the apartment is in a police report! A very nice circumstance in our favor—I'd say the disarming of Bap's nearly done! Armand's Samoan cop friend in the morning, informing Bap he's on a police watch list, will be the lock! No more insanity!" And with that, Baptiste had ceased to be a subject of conversation.

"Yay!" Carole exclaims, dashing into the apartment ahead of the others. "I get to put the music on!" She races to the computer, clicks a few times, and dance music's soon filling the air. "Mylene, Buzy, and Zazie remixes!" she shouts, twirling about before extending a leg straight at the ceiling, doing a standing split. "Hey, anyone want an aerobics class? A ten minute limber up? You have an instructor at your disposal!"

"Only ten minutes?" laughs Christina, likewise lifting a leg skyward until she's doing a standing split. "Yeah, surprise! I can do it too! Dance training since grade school, gymnastics in high!"

"Showoffs!" shouts Pascale, grasping her right knee with both hands and bringing it to her chest. "I can balance like this, but... Well, let's see!" And with that she slowly unfolds her raised leg until her toes are pointing at the ceiling. "My oh my! What do you know? I guess those yoga classes have paid off!"

"OK," laughs Lucinda. "Try this one, girls!" Standing on one leg, she bends forward and brings her forehead to her knee, then grasps her ankle and extends her other leg as straight up as those of the others—an inverted standing split.

"Now, that's what I call scenery!" Jean-Marc exclaims. "Aerobics girls are the ticket! And it's nice to see the Americans are as game as our homespun sweethearts! Bicontinental synchronization!"

"Hey, Gen!" William calls. "Sweetheart! Where'd you go?"

"In here," she responds from the kitchen. "I'm getting some strawberries."

"Could you come out here?"

Genevieve starts laughing the second she enters the living room. "Alright, Bill, I see why you called me! Sorry, but I've never been a bendy Wendy—my leg's not going up there! You'll just have to settle for *this*!" She skips forward a couple steps, lunges, and executes three flawless one-handed cartwheels, without a pause between them.

"Settle for it?" William laughs. "Are you kidding? Sheer poetry of motion! I'm in awe!"

"So let's have more motion," Genevieve says, grasping his waist and commencing to dance. As if by silent command the others join in. All manner of dancing's indulged in—there's even a conga line for a couple minutes. Then they're running together in a circle, laughing hysterically.

"Bloody hell!" yells Stephan, coming to a stop. "Time to fill this place up! Eight people does not a celebration make! Lucy, Jean-Marc, Carole! Get on the phones! Start calling! And tell them to bring stuff!"

Carole, encountering resistance from the first person she phones, one of her students, says, "What do you mean you can't come because it's Sunday? Steph's not going to like that!"

Stephan, overhearing, yells, "Damn right I don't like it! Tell that person anyone who makes *But it's Sunday!* excuses won't be invited again! Won't cross my threshold again! Tell everyone it's permanent banishment for no-shows and early departures alike! No one bails on the coming out of Bill and Gen! This is a dictatorship, goddammit, and I make no apologies! And I accept no apologies! They show up and see it through, or it's no go from now on! Tell the excuse makers that!"

"She's decided she can come after all," laughs Carole, punching the end call button.

"A problem for some to celebrate with us because tomorrow's Monday?" Stephan continues, shaking his head in exaggerated disbelief. "Pah! A work or school day? Boo hoo hoo! What's with these people? Parties aren't on a schedule! Festivities aren't restricted to Fridays and Saturdays! There are seven days in a week, for Christ's sake! Are five of them to be wasted? I think not! Going late into the night on a Sunday... What's the big deal? Are we feeding people poison? Nine to five's no excuse! Funeral in the morning's no excuse! Nothing's an excuse! We're young, and don't have families yet! It's not like we're calling anyone with kids! I've gone to rehearsal on no sleep and hung over too many times to count and carried it off without a hitch! I'm not asking anyone to do what I haven't done! I have to pop by the director's office at nine: so what? I'm not throwing tonight away because of it! I wouldn't be able to look at myself in the mirror if I did!"

"Same here," says Carole. "I've not only taught dozens of classes on no sleep, I've gone straight from parties to my classes! Muscle memory always carries me through! I'm an aerobics robot, and there haven't been any complaints! Quite the contrary: there's a reason I have a way above average pay rate! I fully agree, Steph! No excuses! If I can grab a mike and lead eighty people through a crunch or spinning class on zero sleep, then they can go to work or whatever after a fun night!"

"Yeah," joins in Pascale. "Who sleeps? What good is it? Why bother when I can fly on endless adrenalin instead? Mental sharpness is aided by insomnia! An all nighter, then a day of classes... What dedicated student doesn't do it all the time?"

"I have an eight-thirty employment counselor meeting," says Jean-Marc. "Do you hear me bitching about it? Whine, whine, whine! I don't get it! Some people think if they don't get eight hours of shuteye it's a major disaster! I don't even want eight hours!"

"They say car accidents go up eleven percent on the Monday after daylight savings time kicks in," says Christina, "and that heart attacks increase by ten percent during the Monday, Tuesday, *and* Wednesday afterwards! And it's only one measly hour's difference! I don't get that! It's rise and shine differences, to the tune of a lot more than one silly hour, for me all the time, and for virtually everyone I know! The best dance clubs in New York don't open until midnight, and that's to keep the moping daytime drabs, with their precious set schedules, away! And no one with any self-respect arrives before two!"

"And no one with any self-respect's leaving here before dawn!" Stephan shouts. "Thank you, Chrissy! This is now an official not-done-until-dawn party! OK, back on the phones!"

"I *am* back on the phone," says Carole, lifting her phone aloft.

Suffice to say the apartment's packed by 10:00 PM. It should also be noted that, Stephan's declarations notwithstanding, some people are excused from attending. Claire, for instance, is with Armand and has no wish for it to be otherwise. Armand, as an older man with an occupation that involves a great deal of civic responsibility, isn't expected to embrace youthful shenanigans.

Stephan, at the approach of midnight, clears a spot on top of the dining table, climbs thereupon, spreads his arms, and addresses the assembled company. "Silence, revelers!" he shouts. "Silence please! That means you, Cicely! Shut it! *(Within a few seconds all are silent and turn towards him.)* Everyone raise your glasses, honor William and Genevieve! *(Glasses are raised.)* Bill and Gen, approach and ascend! *(William and Genevieve climb atop the table and stand beside Stephan.)* Bill and Gen, I'm honored and humbled to be the one who occasioned your fortuitous meeting! Thank you for being the living proof that my parties serve a higher purpose, the union of bright and beautiful souls! Everyone, drink to Bill and Gen united—two countries united—two continents united! New York meets Paris and falls head over heels! I couldn't be more happy and proud! Drink up! Drain those cups! Together now! Hip hip, hooray!"

"Hip hip, hooray!" the group shouts.

"William and Genevieve," Stephan continues, "everyone knows I like to get up here and yell, but I've never done it to honor a couple before! Why am I doing it now? Because the depth of your affection's readable from blocks away! I don't take love lightly, and I know it when I see it! I hope you understand that! This isn't Stephan putting on a show! This is Stephan dispensing honor where honor's due! All right! Live well, William and Genevieve! Storm the heavens, and be joyful! Endless blessings upon you! Again, everyone! Hip hip, hooray!"

"Hip hip, hooray!"

Genevieve, both blushing and smiling, kisses Stephan on each cheek as William jumps from the table and reaches up to assist her down. She steps into William's embrace, wraps her arms around his neck, and they kiss—albeit gingerly, on account of the wound on his face. *Hip hip, hooray!* the group shouts again, after which William bows and Genevieve curtsies.

"All right," Stephan concludes. "We'll take our eyes off our happy couple now and allow them to mingle freely! Back to what you were doing! Thank you, and on with our night!"

"Stephan," Genevieve says, gazing at him with deep gratitude. She silently mouths the words *Thank You* and he smilingly nods in acknowledgment. Then she and William, after the latter exchanges handshakes and salutes with Stephan, turn to rejoin Christina, Pascale, and Carole.

"Look," Christina says as William and Genevieve approach, "there's a guy doing a handstand on the balcony railing, suspended against the sky! Perfect balance and equilibrium! One slight miscalculation, though, and he tumbles to the sidewalk eight floors down! I'll freely own that we girls *(She taps the shoulders of Pascale and Carole.)* can't hold a candle to that! Our standing splits are a joke by comparison!"

"Now that's courage," says William, having turned to look at the young man who's visible through the sliding glass door. "I admire that unreservedly! Gives me vertigo just looking at him and I'm standing here safe inside! I'm surrounded by four walls with a solid floor under my feet and he's out there looking death in the eye!"

"That's Gilles," says Carole offhandedly. "He's an acrobat in the circus. He'll be out there all night, either balancing or gazing across the rooftops. He once said he only comes to Steph's parties for the balcony, and I'm not sure he was joking. And of course the poor man lives in a ground floor apartment. He says it gives him the creeps."

"Jesus!" exclaims Pascale. "Now he's doing handstand push-ups! To do that eight floors above the concrete with no net takes guts of steel! One off-kilter muscle, and... Do you know how hard those are to do? And it's drizzling, that railing's slippery! And what about the wind? I can't watch anymore!"

"Nothing keeps Gilles off the balcony," says Carole. "See his rubber gloves?—they give him optimum grip. Don't worry, the railing isn't slippery to those gloves. Gilles is a professional, and knows what he's doing. He'll be doing scorpions, curling his feet forward and lifting his head, until half his body's above the sidewalk, instead of perpendicular to the railing. Anyway, no one goes out there when he's there. Mainly because they're afraid of distracting him, but also because it's his religion. He says it brings him extraordinary peace."

"Seeing him in his private world of precarious balance and teasing of death puts matters into perspective," says William. "And I'm only seeing it, not living it like he is. I'm sure he's not afraid of anything on earth or in hell after coming in off the balcony."

"Everyone has their bugaboos," laughs Carole. "Like I said, living on the ground floor makes him uneasy—highly uneasy. No human's free from fear."

"Exactly," says Jean-Marc, who's just stepped up. "We can build all the cities we want, seek to persuade ourselves we're safe inside our architectural wonders, but nothing will ever rid us of primal unease! Society can do its best to sugarcoat the indifferent face of existence with distraction—attempt its media manipulation tricks, drown us in ready-made dogma, give us fancy gadgets to play with—but it will never blind us on the cellular level! The membranes of our cells know there's nothing standing between them and Mother Nature and the passage of time and the metamorphosis of death! Our nerves, try as society might to tap into and regulate them, will always hum in unison with the vastness of the universe—the universe that couldn't care less if we're alive or dead! Take away the show and tell, and what's the one guiding principle behind our economic system? It's to make money by selling us the illusion of safety!"

"Right," says William, pouncing on the subject. "Our weakness is also our strength, as in: which would you rather call master, the mysterious expanses of the universe or the manipulations of modernity? In the end, we can't be bought or sold! Our blood, that fears being spilled every second it's flowing through our veins, won't allow us to be swindled! Buy a fancy apartment, be busy with a career, accumulate trinkets, adopt the fashionable attitudes... It's all worthless window-dressing! No one escapes primal whisperings, the voice of our one and only master! The more people attempt to pave over their depths with purchasable diversion, the more those selfsame depths shiver in protest and propel them towards the clarity of uneasy thoughts! Nature's churning outside the veneer of civilization, waiting to claim us, and that's fine by me! I say it again: our weakness when faced with the majesty of nature is also our strength, because it means the artificial reality of society will never succeed in bending us to its will! Civilization's shoddy manipulations will always fall away and be exposed as a false front when faced with the greater breadth of existence!"

"All right," says Carole, giving a thumbs-up signal, "you've both spouted fine speeches—I'm sure we silly girls agree with you! Right? *(Genevieve, Christina, and Pascale nod while laughing.)* But that's enough! We don't need any more boys will be boys stuff, OK? We just want to dance and play! Come on, Jean-Marc!"

"Sure thing, dollface," Jean-Marc answers. "Can't argue with girl logic, right Bill? We can trash society all night, but a good dance washes everything away! Chit-chat's nothing compared to..."

"Come on!" cuts in Carole, yanking him after her.

Jean-Marc and Carole stroll towards the group that's dancing on the other side of the room, and the others follow. It doesn't take long for Christina and Pascale to find dance partners—they've been trading boys all night—and William and Genevieve likewise start kicking up a storm. They're engrossed in this delightful activity for about half an hour.

Sometime later Christina's saying, "And there's a flying trapeze artist here too. Forgot to mention her, we were chatting earlier. Colette over there. *(She indicates a petite redhead, very sweet of face.)* She says trapeze is no big deal, that lots of French girls do it. Ha ha! Is it true, Carole? Do all the French girls do trapeze?"

"No, but Colette might think they do," giggles Carole. "Trapeze is her world—her addiction. She doesn't think it's a big deal because she couldn't live without it."

"An acrobat defying death on the balcony, a trapeze artist insisting trapeze is nothing special," says William. "You'd never see that at a New York party! I don't know why, but it seems so undeniably Parisian!"

"It's your American imagination choosing to find it undeniably Parisian," laughs Jean-Marc. "You've only been here a couple days, so our town's still a wonderland in your eyes!"

"You bet it is," says William, running his hands through Genevieve's hair, gazing upon her with unconcealed tenderness. "And I don't see that impression abating anytime soon!"

"Nor do I," Genevieve responds, snuggling close to him. "Of course, I'm talking about the wonders of New York!"

"Hey, Jean-Marc," Stephan calls out. "Where's the paper cup? I saw you going at it earlier!" He's referring to a game of hand badminton that was being played with a paper cup.

"On the windowsill over there," Jean-Marc answers, gesturing in its direction.

"And that's another undeniably Parisian thing," laughs William. "Looking around for a paper cup, because there's probably only one in the apartment! Because a paper cup's a freak thing in Paris, where people carry real glasses to parks in the middle of the night and bring them home afterwards! Ha ha ha!"

"Stop mocking us and play!" Stephan says, batting the cup in William's direction.

William, caught by surprise, whacks at the cup too late and it spins off the edge of his hand to the floor. "Bloody hell!" Stephan yells. "If paper cups are so familiar to you, why can't you return service?"

"Shut up and play!" William answers, picking up the cup and batting it back at Stephan, who bats it to Carole. Soon half the people in the room are doing anything and everything they can to keep the paper cup aloft. The cup travels about the apartment, even halfway down the hall towards the bedrooms before returning to the living room, as it careens off fingers and palms, flies in unexpected directions. People rapidly clear the way, or join in, as the cup continues following its erratic course—shouts, clapping, and laughter accompany it wherever it goes. And when it eventually hits the floor a collective groan goes up, as if a supremely tragic event has occurred. Then another round, with more jumping, lunging, and yelling.

Then William's at one of the windows after the cup's tumbled to the floor again, gazing down at the street. "Hey, the rain's tapered off—it's barely misting," he says. "And guess what's on the curb? A box of baguettes!"

"What?" shouts Stephan. "We don't have enough food here? You want to eat old baguettes? Just try! You'll break your teeth! There's a reason they've been tossed—they're rock hard! I would've thought..."

"No no no!" interrupts William. "I don't want to eat them! Christ! Of course not! I want to play ball! Baseball! Yankees!"

"We don't play baseball in France!"

"Cultural exchange!" William persists. "If you can whack a cup with your hand, you can whack a ball with a baguette! We won't play the whole game of baseball! Only pitch and hit and run! Outside with the old baguettes and balls made of wadded up paper! People whack the ball, run to one base! Don't naysay it until you try it!"

"All right," laughs Stephan. "We'll give it a whirl! Outside, people! *(He means their immediate group.)* We'll indulge the Yank!"

We've neglected to mention that across the street from Stephan's building, where the farmers' market was held, is a paved park of sorts with concrete benches and trees in square planters. It's here that our friends intend to play baseball and within five minutes they're approaching the box of discarded baguettes.

"Christ!" yells William, upon seizing one of the baguettes. "They're soggy! Tough as if made of rubber, and acting just like rubber would and flopping about! Not exactly rigid bats!"

"What did you think wet ones would be like?" Jean-Marc asks.

"No matter!" William says. "As long as they don't fly apart in our hands, and these won't! *(He whacks a tree with the baguette.)* Unbelievable! Not a single tear! I'm not sure I want to eat them anymore! I don't need an undigested wad of dough getting bigger and bigger in my stomach!"

"It's a delicate chemical balance," laughs Carole. "If they're eaten warm and fresh, when they tear apart like feathers between the fingertips, then they digest easily and are chock full of nutrients! Wait a bit too long, and the composition changes—they can't be chewed! No need for expiration dates—it's expiration hours! A bakers conspiracy! Have to buy fresh ones every day!"

"Yeah," Lucinda joins in. "It's a special recipe honed by centuries of experimentation, as in making something that's indescribably succulent for a few hours, then useless! Just think: if they lasted even an hour longer, not to mention a whole day, the bakers would be out of a lot of money!"

"That's product development genius, all right," William says. "But the bakers are still missing out on heaps of income! The old ones could be sold off as construction materials! I have a feeling they're impervious to termites, roaches, rats, everything! But, to it! Where's some newspaper?"

"Ahead of you there!" calls out Pascale. "We've made some!" She, Christina, and Genevieve wave their arms aloft, holding paper balls—about softball size—in each hand.

"Play ball!" yells William, assuming a batter's stance with baguette in hand. "Pitch me one!"

Christina, after an exaggerated wind-up, throws a perfect strike over what would be the plate. William swings and misses. "Damn! Tricky floppy baguette!"

"Strike one!"

"Hey, what are the parameters?" asks Pascale.

"If I hit one I run to that tree," William says. "If I get there safe, before you can throw me out, then I get to come back here and keep hitting; if not, the pitcher takes a turn at bat and I field with the rest of you."

"Line's too long," Pascale says. "We're starting another game over here! Come on Jean-Marc, Carole, and Lucy! Four in each group!"

The two groups are soon pitching and hitting—running, laughing, shouting. At one point William's pitching to Genevieve. She makes contact and the ball flies over his head. Stephan dashes to catch it, is too late, and the ball rolls past him towards Christina. Before Christina has time to field the ball and throw it Genevieve dashes to the tree and taps it, crying out with delight. William, having raced to the tree to receive Christina's throw, is amazed anew at the sight of Genevieve—her black hair swishing about her face, the sweetness in her eyes, the radiance of her complexion. And she belongs to him—this beautiful woman, giggling like a little girl! And still so poised, innately elegant from head to toe! The lines of her body, snug in a white cashmere sweater and black leather skirt, are as graceful as waves!

"What?" she asks, widening her eyes.

"You're just so beautiful!" he says, embracing her.

"Hey, lovebirds!" Stephan yells. "No time for that! On with the game! I want a turn at bat!"

A few more minutes of baseball follow, then the game evolves. Jean-Marc, striking out, throws his baguette at the pavement in disgust and kicks it. Soon a game of soccer, with the baguette serving as ball and the space between a pair of stone benches serving as goal, is being played by the males.

"Leave us out, will you?" yells Carole, throwing one of the paper balls at Jean-Marc. Thus, the game evolves again. It's an all out war with the paper balls, everyone for themselves. In between throws is a great deal of scampering to make more balls out of any available paper. Wadded up paper's flying in all directions, no one can stop laughing.

"Do you mind showing a little consideration?" is suddenly heard from across the street. "Some of us have to work in the morning."

Turning towards the source of the voice, our friends are greeted by the face of a thirtyish woman—quite attractive—who's standing in her bathrobe on the balcony of her second floor apartment. Amazement and annoyance occupy her expression in equal measure.

"Sorry," says Stephan, not hesitating to appraise her appearance and make it obvious he's doing so, run his eyes up and down her body while smiling with approval. "We were celebrating the recent union of this lovely couple *(He points to William and Genevieve.)* and got carried away. What's your name?"

"Are you insane?" she responds. "You be quiet now or I'll call the cops."

"You can come upstairs to our party if you'd like."

"I'll take you across my knee, and you won't like it," she shoots back, smiling slightly despite herself. "Now, be quiet—I'm not kidding. Some of us have to work, you'll understand when you grow up and become a man." And with that she turns about and goes inside, sliding the glass door shut and closing the curtains.

"I'm in love!" exclaims Stephan, blowing the woman a two-handed kiss.

"You're in trouble," frowns Lucinda, tossing a paper ball at his head.

"Ew!" cries Christina, wincing in disgust while averting her eyes, taking a few rapid steps away from the curb.

"What?" inquires Carole.

"You don't want to see it!"

"See what?" likewise asks William, advancing to the place at the curb that Christina's vacated. "Ha ha! Priceless! A lamb's head rotting in the gutter! Dead filmy eyes absently staring at nothing! A sacrificial lamb!"

"So what?" says Jean-Marc. "A leftover from the market, probably tumbled out of a vendor's cart. A lamb's head! Whoopee! You silly tourists think everything in Paris is charmed!"

"Mythical significance has nothing to do with tourism," counters William. "The head's a ritual offering, to curry favor with the Gods! A favorable omen, blessing for our gathering!"

"A rotten head's a blessing?" scoffs Pascale, stepping forward to have a look at it. "If it was sacrificed, I think the benefit's expired! I can smell the thing! Anyway, we didn't sacrifice it! It has nothing to do with us!"

"Sacrifice, shmacrifice!" says Stephan, picking up the head by one of its ears, he having slipped his hand inside a plastic grocery bag plucked from the sidewalk. "Anyone want to bat it? Girls, want to take a closer look, see the mess at the neck?"

"There's only one girl who's squeamish about the head," says Pascale, pointing at Christina.

"We French girls have eaten them, as you well know," says Carole. "What's this business about trying to shock is with the lumpy blood stuff at the neck? It's Chrissy who's weird about the head! Here, Steph, let me hold it! Soon as I find another plastic bag!"

"Believe it or not," says Christina, "I've had lamb's head too. I *am* from an Italian family! It's not the head, but the decay that's revolting! Same as a rotten steak! Who plays with rotten meat? Yuck!"

"Point taken," laughs Stephan, dropping the head back into the gutter.

"This is for picking filthy heads up!" Lucinda says, tossing another paper ball at his head. "And these are for blowing women kisses in front of me!" She throws three at once.

And, with that, they resume their war with the paper balls and chase each other back into the building, soon returning to the apartment.

Your humble narrator feels it's time to wind this chapter to a close. He also wishes to state that, while he's done his best to communicate the doings of our friends at the party, he feels he's barely scratched the surface. The rapidity with which they fling themselves from one diversion to another—the various conversations which, in some cases simultaneously, spring up in a second and just as quickly pass onto other subjects, or yield to fresh rounds of play: your narrator admits that capturing a small fraction of the whole is the most he can hope to accomplish.

Suffice to say that when our friends reenter the apartment it's not 3:00 AM yet and a great deal of amusement is still in store and the party doesn't begin to break up until about 6:30 AM. William and Genevieve aren't the first to leave, but they aren't the last either. They've reserved a cab for 7:30 AM and it arrives on time. Accompanied by Christina, Pascale, Stephan, Lucinda, Jean-Marc, and Carole they descend to the sidewalk with William's belongings, say their goodbyes, climb into the cab, and depart for 160 rue du Temple.

CHAPTER 24

When William and Genevieve climb into the cab they're as elated as it's possible for people to be. Not only have they spent the night with their dearest friends and thoroughly flushed the conflict of earlier from their systems, they have each other to themselves for the first time in nearly a day. There's a small infinity in the variety of caresses hands can impart to one another—each finger caressing and caressed in turn, palms twisting and turning and flipping about, thumbs endlessly curling and uncurling—and they immediately sample of this infinity. The gentle explorations of their intertwined fingers reverberate throughout their bodies, ebb and flow in their thoughts, are as seamless and hypnotic as waves oscillating on a quiet shore. The whole of the cab ride is this magical interplay of hands, with only their breathing breaking the silence.

How different this cab ride is from William's last one, on Saturday morning. He notices next to nothing of his surroundings, from the journey east on Rue d'Alésia to the final shot up Rue du Temple and all points between. He could just as well be in a cab in

New York or Tokyo: he's far too absorbed in the world of Genevieve, meshing with her emotion-whirl below the surface of things, to have any interest in the world outside the windows. The surface of things is but a dream: what's real is the energy flowing back and forth between himself and Genevieve, the pull of her undertow—the scent of her hair, impossible to pin down, and electricity of her touch. The cab ride seems to both last for above an hour and to be over in two minutes.

When the cab stops and the driver voices the amount due, the world outside the windows crystallizes again, comes into sharp focus: there are the doors of Genevieve's building. Already William's thoughts are traveling through those doors and up the stairs and into her apartment to her bedroom and heaven in her arms.

It's still a dim day, overcast and lightly misting, when they step from the cab and the driver begins extracting the three suitcases from the trunk, but the scene couldn't be more beautiful in William's eyes—the precipitation-glistened sidewalk, cross of Sainte-Élisabeth rising into the sky across the street, cheerful orange and purple awning of Café A La Tour Du Temple. He inhales deeply, savoring the post-rain freshness of the air.

Then the cab's departed and they're approaching Genevieve's building, she in front. Glancing back at him with a smile, she raises one of her calves behind her, pointing her toes, and giggles.

"So why's the half-leg up gesture an indication of attraction and delight?" William asks, teasing her by means of adopting a clinical tone. "I've always been mystified by that. Obviously it's sex-code, but it seems so arbitrary that it should be sex-code."

"You don't think its pretty?" she asks, turning to face him. She tilts her head down and raises her eyes.

"The word *pretty* doesn't do it justice," he replies, instantly abandoning the detachment act. "It's an extraordinarily beautiful gesture! Your every movement's as beautiful as rippling water, lilies swaying in the wind, seagulls cleaving the sky!" His eyes, complementing his words, are running up her legs to her waist and chest and throat and face and then back down again. His eyes will never tire of relishing the symmetry of her figure—her unfeigned grace and poise. There's not a pretentious bone in her body; nothing, be it as slight as the curl of a finger, that rings false. The very waves of her hair are as effortlessly pleasing to the gaze as wind-patterns on shifting sand.

"Flattery will get you..." Genevieve pauses, smiling as she turns to push the door open. "*Everything!*" And with that she scampers up the stairs, giggling while flicking the hem of her shirt up and down. A couple flights later she, carried away by mirth, accidentally drops the suitcase she's carrying and it tumbles down the stairs, narrowly missing William's feet.

William, bursting into laughter, intentionally drops the two suitcases he's carrying—they tumble down to the other one. "My oh my!" he grins. "Disaster strikes! Whatever will we do? A bolt from the blue sky, how are we mere mortals to cope? The Gods have sent an unfavorable sign!"

"And why unfavorable?" she inquires, reaching under his shirt to tickle him. "The Gods only wanted to free up our hands!"

"The female spin on things is always refreshing," he says, likewise reaching under her sweater to tickle her.

Soon they're at the base of the flight of steps, attempting to gather the suitcases amidst an exchange of tickles. No sooner does one of them pick up one of the suitcases than they're forced by the other to drop it. From there, it spins into attempts to throw the suitcases up the stairs, and finally into grabbing the suitcases and running laughing to her door. Once they step inside her apartment they drop the suitcases and turn towards one another. In a send-up of a flirtatious gesture, Genevieve flicks her hair away from her face, rolls her tongue about her lips, shakes the hem of her skirt, winks, and says, "Hey, soldier boy!" When William makes a movement towards her she swiftly skips to the pair of balcony window-doors and opens them—the long floral print white curtains to the sides of the window-doors undulate in the breeze, their fringed bottoms wisp back and forth on the floor. The flowers on the curtains are scarlet roses and William immediately associates their color with that of Genevieve's lipstick, which they match perfectly. The red of the roses and the red of her lips, the white of the curtains and the white of her sweater, the swishing of the curtains and the swishing of her hair, the black of her skirt and the black of her hair: it all comes together in an impression that freezes time, takes its own snapshot. William will remember Genevieve standing in front of the balcony on that morning until the day he dies.

Genevieve steps away from the balcony, is stretching in the center of the room, lifting her hair over her head and letting it fall, doing a gentle backbend. William's eyes are following the curl of her body upward to the radiance of her face and swishings of her hair and he's about to advance to take her in his arms, when an agitated shape appears from within the bedroom, at the edge of his peripheral vision. At first he doesn't understand: is it another curtain undulating in the breeze? Before he can turn towards the shape it's directly in front of him, approaching Genevieve. What is it? Who is it? It's Baptiste—yellowed of face, absent of expression, unseeingly silver-eyed. Baptiste advancing with a jerky mechanical step, like a machine—soaked to the skin, in the same clothes as when William last saw him, with a large brown stain on his shirt: this information's computed in the space of a second. Then William hears himself yell, feels his feet spring forward—sees Genevieve recoil—sees Baptiste lunge—sees something in Baptiste's hand, a silver thing. The hand's jerking upward, it's holding a knife. A scream—Genevieve screams as she lifts her right leg—as her knee strikes Baptiste in the groin as William seizes him by the shoulders, hits him in the face, stomps downwards at his shins with all his might. Genevieve spins to the floor—Baptiste staggers towards the open window-doors, turns around, drops the knife, is holding his arms in front of his face—is backing up—backing through the window-doors onto the balcony, flipping over the railing, tumbling out of view. William's racing onto the balcony, leaning over its edge, looking—Baptiste's face-down on the sidewalk, crimson's streaming from his head—a purple awning's blocking the view of the lower half of his body.

William's in methodical mode now, all superfluous thoughts and perceptions blotted from his awareness. There's no time for distress or fear, only quick action. The perpetrator out of the picture, he's instantly at Genevieve's side, pulling his phone and headset from his pocket. But the French emergency number: what is it? He only knows it's not 911. Genevieve's refrigerator door—the number's on the door. So he's soon in the kitchen, examining the card with emergency number's on it—all very quickly, but seemingly in slow motion. 112? Is that it? No, that's general emergency. It's the SAMU number he wants: 15. He's already dialing while reaching into the freezer for a tray of ice cubes, is speaking by the time he's unlocking the front door for when the emergency personnel arrive, shortly back at Genevieve's side. He's reciting: stab wound, serious, emergency, 160 Rue du Temple, fourth floor, left at top of stairs, corner unit, number 402, please hurry. Reciting: dead man on sidewalk, send police, do not confuse the dead man with the emergency upstairs—do not mix the two up—please hurry. Still on the phone, he's being coached concerning first aid: staunch bleeding, apply pressure to wound, once pressure's applied do not stop applying it. Patient may go into shock, take preventive measures. Situation: is she conscious? Yes. Situation: how is she positioned on the floor? Fetal. Solution: keep her calm and quiet; if possible, turn her onto her back, elevate feet. He's yanking a pillow from the couch and removing his shirt—easing her onto her back and elevating her feet on the pillow; wadding up his shirt and pressing it against the bleeding. Worries: how does he know he's doing the right thing? He hears: the most harm will be done by doing nothing; do not worry about being inexperienced, follow instructions and all will be well. He's brought ice cubes, place them on the wound or not? It's an option, but applying pressure is more important; and keep her warm; and seek to elevate the wound above her heart. He's yanking another pillow from the couch, slipping it under her waist; he dares not leave her to get a blanket to place over her legs for warmth, must keep pressing upon the wound—must loosen her clothes if possible, loosen the belt of her skirt. Brassiere? He's unable to reach under her to unfasten it while pressing upon the wound, must keep her still. He's speaking to Genevieve: please, sweetheart, do not speak—the ambulance will be here soon. I'm on the phone with them, they're coming. He's asking the person on the phone: how do I know if there's internal bleeding? He hears: he's doing what's best given present knowledge of the situation, and by no means stop pressing upon the wound, but seek to be gentle, must not agitate the wound, open it further. He's thinking: keep pressing firmly but not too hard; keep smiling into Genevieve's eyes, soothing her; keep her calm.

The world's compartmentalized itself, emotions have separated and sorted themselves in order of priority: unwavering attention to the emergency at hand is the one and only priority, there is nothing else in all of existence. There is no time for tears, no time for worry: blot it all out, focus exclusively upon attending to the wound, dispensing comfort, shielding Genevieve from confusion and panic. Stroking her forehead now, speaking: "Gen, the ambulance will be here soon, all will be well. We'll be laughing in this room before the week's done, count on it sweetheart. Count on it."

Dreadful thoughts? William cannot afford to have them. Allowing himself to become fearful on account of the large patch of scarlet—it's right there, on the sweater he's pulled away from the wound—is not in Genevieve's best interest. While he's waiting for the ambulance all is bathed in stark clarity, simplified to the thoughts and gestures necessary to continue to efficiently render first aid. There will be no second chance to do right by his beloved.

CHAPTER 25

After what seems like an infinity of kneeling by Genevieve's side, knowing she has no one but him at the moment—that her well-being's entirely in his hands, the pressure of his palm upon her wound—there's knocking at the door, and William's yelling, "It's open! Come in! The emergency's in here! Come in!"

Three people are soon at his side, bidding him turn the patient over to them. One person's unfolding a wheeled cart, the other two are examining the wound. An OK is given and Genevieve's lifted onto the cart, wheeled to the door, and carried downstairs to the ambulance. William's following close behind, at first not fully understanding what the man who examined her is saying. Then he gathers that a more thorough examination will be conducted in the ambulance. "In the ambulance?" he's asking himself. "Why not a hospital?" He instantly knows what his new task is: to convince the paramedics by whatever means necessary—reason, pleading, cajolery—that Genevieve's injury is serious, and she must not be allowed to languish in the ambulance. Once she's been placed in the ambulance and the door's about to be shut, he tells the man at the door to please, for God's sake, take her to a hospital and give her the care she needs. The man, saying he must attend to the patient, directs him to the attendant who's still outside—the man who unfolded the cart, who's also the driver—and shuts the door. The driver, ascertaining William's an American, explains that, in France, the hospital arrives on scene; that the man he just spoke to, who's treating Genevieve, is an emergency specialist physician and all the equipment he needs is in the ambulance; that the woman's a fully qualified nurse, experienced with assisting at operating tables; that the operating table itself is in the ambulance. William's listening to the words, but not allowing himself to believe them. "A hospital, in there?" his mind's asking. "Does he know what he's talking about? Is this a misfit ambulance crew?" He hears himself tell the driver paramedics are unqualified to diagnose serious medical conditions. He hears in response: "As I said, the man is a fully trained emergency specialist physician, not an emergency generalist. He is exploring the wound to determine the course of treatment, which will be administered shortly. In any case, she is safe. She is not in danger. Her wound is not life-threatening." Then the driver turns away from him, as if in response to someone's summons.

Not life-threatening. William's turning the words over and over in his mind, not sure if he should trust them—dare abandon his vigilance, surrender to relief—when another man approaches from behind and asks him if he would mind answering a few questions pertaining to the deceased. The deceased? At William's back are policemen who have been attending to the inert Baptiste—a circumstance he's been unaware of, so singlemindedly has he been focused upon looking out for Genevieve.

When William turns around he sees a long black bag being lifted into a second ambulance: only now does the sequence of the attack return to his recollection, it having been shoved aside as unnecessary to know, like everything else not having to do with tending to Genevieve. Then he's listening to himself answer one of the officer's questions: "The deceased was hiding in my girlfriend's apartment and stabbed her with a knife. She's in the ambulance, bleeding." No longer able to ward off the distress—overwhelming sense of vulnerability, violation, shock, and fear—that's been hovering in the background of his feelings and threatening to engulf his awareness from the moment the attack occurred, he feels tears flood his eyes and blur his vision, sobs start to choke him. The unkind phrase *Genevieve's been stabbed!* echoes in his head, flares in his nerves. He witnessed the horror and immediately consigned it to the realms of the unreal; but now it's crystal clear, tying searing knots of dread in his chest.

"Sir," the officer's saying, "I know it's hard. I wish I didn't have to question you now but I do, both concerning the diseased and the assault. Take all the time you need."

Genevieve cannot and will not die! is what William hears shouting in his head. His sudden recollection of the attack has thrust the comforting words of the ambulance driver aside: the sight of Genevieve's blood-soaked sweater surges into his mind's eye, as vivid as a scream. A rapid-fire sequence of pictures, probably less than a second in duration, whips through his awareness: their first shock-glance of secret recognition at the lake, first intimate touching of hands north of Montsouris Park, first kiss at the Opera; the dinner with her parents, their time together on the roof, their first night in each other's arms... No! No! No! He *cannot* lose her! She's his breath, his heartbeat, his pulse! She's the hum of the nerves under his skin, his place of emotional habitation, his life! She's why he'll be happily greeting the promise of each new day for the rest of his life! "What *are* they doing in there?" he hears himself demanding of the officer as he chokes back his sobs, gesticulates frantically at the white vehicle with the blue stripe and words SAMU DE PARIS upon it. "She's been attacked with a knife! Don't they know it's serious? Please make them go to a hospital! If I lose her, I'll die!"

So the SAMU way of doing things is explained to William again, this time by the police officer—a person he's more willing to trust. While listening to the officer's reassuring elucidation of SAMU doctrine, and what's being done at this moment— Genevieve's being diagnosed and treated by a fully certified doctor, no less skilled and experienced than those at hospitals—William's watching picture after picture of the health and beauty of Genevieve spin through his head. "So she's all right?" he asks when the officer finishes speaking. "She's really all right?"

"I've been told she is," the officer responds. "Why don't we get an update?" He calls to the driver, bids him approach, and puts William's question to him.

"She's fine, sir," the driver addresses William. "We'll know the particulars shortly. Rest assured, she's out of harm's way." He doesn't mention that he's already told William as much: he's very accustomed to dealing with distraught people.

"Thank you! *Thank you!*" William says with immense relief, finally allowing himself to wrap his emotions around the good news.

Then William's answering more questions, informing the officer the assault weapon—the knife—is on the floor of the living room upstairs and hasn't been touched; that the deceased dropped it there after stabbing his girlfriend; that he struck the deceased in self-defense, to save his girlfriend's life; that the deceased had been hounding her, and many witnesses will attest to the fact. Yes, that's correct: he struck the deceased, but that's all—he did not push him out the window. The deceased stepped backwards through the open window, and fell over the balcony railing. The deceased was waiting in the apartment, he wasn't invited. How did the deceased get in the apartment? William has no idea: he wasn't invited, that's all he knows. The bruise on William's face? The deceased is responsible for that as well—he struck him in front of Sainte-Élisabeth yesterday morning and ran away. Yes, right there, across the street—he was stalking his girlfriend, waiting for her outside. The deceased was a problem for a long time, many people will swear to it. His girlfriend's parents were aware of the problem, and placed warning calls to the parents of the deceased—all will be borne out. Again, he has no idea how the deceased came to be in his girlfriend's apartment—all he knows is he wasn't expected to be there, could never be wanted there. Yes, the deceased fell out the window—he wasn't pushed.

Suffice to say William answers quite a few questions, some of them more than once. Then the officer informs him he has no more questions at present, but there may be more in the future, and he'll need to provide the names and contact information of the witnesses. It would also be helpful if he instructed the witnesses to contact the police and refer to the case number, which will be provided shortly. Then he's asking William for the names of the assault victim and the deceased, and the nearest of kin of each. It's then that William realizes he hasn't called Georges and Catherine yet, or anyone else.

But now the doctor's at the door of the ambulance, smiling. "Good news," he's saying. "The patient does not have an intra-abdominal injury. Only local anesthesia is being used. She'll be returning to her apartment within the hour. You did well."

Dares William believe it? Will Genevieve really be upstairs soon, recuperating in her own bed? What energy stirs to life in his bones! He's recollecting how Genevieve kneed Baptiste in the groin: she saved her own life! Yes! His fit and toned sweetheart struck her assailant quickly enough to prevent the knife from going too deep! And then he realizes for the second time that he hasn't called Georges and Catherine, and pounces upon his phone.

"Mrs. Clouitier?" he begins. "This is Bill. Right, Cathy—please listen. Gen's safe. She's OK, being tended to by the SAMU, but... She's OK! All's well, I assure you! She'll be in her bedroom in an hour, the doctor said so. Baptiste was in the apartment and attacked her—stabbed her with a knife. Yes, Gen's OK, doing fine, completely safe! She's being fixed up in the ambulance, won't have to go to the hospital. Don't worry about Baptiste—he fell off the balcony, he's dead, it's over. The knife didn't penetrate far, there's no intra-abdominal injury. The police will be calling. We're in front of her building. Good, see you and Georges soon. Again, don't worry. Gen is safe, and it's over. Bye."

Then William's calling Christina's phone, speaking to her and Pascale. They'll soon be on their way, as well as alerting others. Before he hangs up he approaches the officer who questioned him and obtains the case number, so his friends can start relaying it. When he hangs up he informs the officer his girlfriend's parents will be here shortly, as well as some witnesses to the past behavior of the deceased. Then he's standing at the back door of the ambulance, waiting for it to open. He'd very much like to be admitted immediately, but knows it's best to stay out of the doctor's way.

Left to his own devices, William's thoughts are far from pleasant: now that he knows Genevieve's safe, his worst fears are free to gratuitously torment him. Thoughts of the merciless *What if?* variety descend upon him, as in *What if Bap had attacked when we both had our backs to him, and we weren't able to deflect the blow?*; as in *What if he'd used a meat cleaver instead of a knife?*; as in *What if I was watching them zip Gen into a...?* But then he's shaking those thoughts off, reprimanding himself—saying he ought to be counting his blessings and offering thanks, instead of imagining worst-case scenarios that didn't happen. But it's not easy for him to exclusively focus upon the positive, given the circumstances: cheating death doesn't mean thoughts of death aren't going to haunt him, especially where Genevieve's concerned; reflections concerning the fragility of life aren't going to be easy to keep at bay; his thankfulness for the happy outcome will be accompanied by shuddering for awhile.

As he continues standing at the ambulance door, intentionally facing away from the activity at the recent location of Baptiste's body, William's struck by the dismalness of this day: the gray of the sunless sky, heavy shroud of mist and fog. He also reflects upon the utter indifference of surroundings to the creatures that inhabit them: Sainte-Élisabeth church couldn't care less if every person in Paris were alive or dead.

"But stop!" he admonishes himself again. "I must be strong for Gen! I need to see her through this, keep her spirits up! She's alive—wonderfully alive—and how dare I allow gloom to envelop my feelings! Strength begets strength! Will I be smiling when I see her again? Of course I will! I'll be swooning with delirious joy! I'll be offering thanks to high heaven! I'll *be* in high heaven!"

"Gen's safe and I'll be seeing her soon," he continues. "She's safe, and it's not even serious—a non-penetrating wound, no vital organs touched! The doctor said so, and he's a real doctor—blessed be the SAMU! So stop bemoaning what might've been, and embrace what *is*! God, I can't wait to gaze into her eyes and hold her hand and let her know how much I love her! I can't wait to be strong for her and celebrate life with her and show her how indispensable she is!"

Then it's but a hop, skip, and a jump to William's next thought: *I can't wait to make Genevieve my wife!* Reaching into his pocket for his keys, he begins detaching them from the ring and slipping them back into his pocket, one by one. Once the ring is free of the keys, he clenches it in his right hand and waits for the ambulance door to open. He's dizzy with a mixture of impatience, jitteriness, and delight.

CHAPTER 26

William's still waiting for the ambulance door to open when Catherine, who ran straight to her Citroën after his call and started driving before phoning Georges, pulls up and parks the car on the sidewalk in front of Sainte-Élisabeth. She's been allowed to do so after explaining to the police that she's the mother of the girl in the ambulance; otherwise, she would've been rerouted down Rue Dupetit-Thouars along with the rest of the traffic.

"Bill," Catherine calls out the second she steps from the car. "How is she?"

"She's fine," William answers, embracing Catherine as she strolls up to him. "I'm going crazy waiting to see her, but she's all right. A shallow wound, thank God. She'll be going upstairs before too long." He's so fixated upon proposing to Genevieve that he wonders if it shows on his face; he's happy and relieved that Catherine's arrived, but it's also awkward.

As for the conversation which follows: of course Catherine's relieved and thankful at the same time that she's worried and distraught; of course she can't wait to see Genevieve, and fires question after question at William; of course she waves the police officer away when he approaches her for information, explaining he'll have to wait until after she sees firsthand that her daughter's safe.

Then the ambulance door opens and the doctor announces that the wound's been cleaned, sutured, and dressed, and the patient's well on her way to being as good as new. William, craning his neck to catch a glimpse of Genevieve and fairly dying to strengthen their bond with his question, barely indicates he's heard the doctor's words. Then his body's following the movement of his neck and he's stepping into the ambulance, flushing at the sweet brightness—the palpable touch—of Genevieve's eyes, swimming in her radiant smile, grasping her outstretched hard, bending to kiss her. She, concerned on account of the bruise on his face, says with alacrity, "Be careful honey! That's very tender! It won't do to disturb it!"

"You're worried about my face?" he asks, looking at her with loving amazement. "After what you've been through?"

"What, this?" she says, pointing at her stomach with one hand and waving the other in dismissal. "It's nothing."

"It's not nothing, Gen, I..." he begins, unfolding his clenched hand to reveal the key ring. "What I was...Genevieve, I..."

"What, dear?" she says, widening her eyes.

William's looking at her as if stunned: here before him, smiling and incomparably beautiful, a living miracle, is the love of his life—she who, for scattered dreadful moments as she lay bleeding on the floor, he feared he was on the point of losing. (Never mind that he dared not acknowledge such fear at the time.) But he hasn't lost her, and he's not going to lose her—he's going to cling to her as if his life depends upon it, because it does. The love brimming in her eyes, warmth of her hand as she clasps his hand, energy radiating from her ravishing face... These things instantly dissolve his trepidation, make it seem pointless and silly. The nurse is there, the doctor is there, Catherine is there: William's blind to their presence. It's only he and Genevieve in the ambulance and he must pull her close and keep her close, hold onto her for all he's worth. "Genevieve, will you marry me?" he asks, holding the key ring between his forefinger and thumb and raising it to her eyes.

"With all my heart, William," she replies without hesitation. "Yes, William! Yes!"

And then he's slipping the key ring onto her finger, kissing her again as her joyfully intoned *With all my heart!* echoes in his ears: the music of her voice and touch of her lips and electricity of her presence—magnetic surge of their shared affection—is the extent of his perceptible world. All that matters is that his world has become what it *must* be. All that matters is that Genevieve will be his wife.

Love is accorded unconditional respect by all good people. And so Catherine (even though she hasn't had a chance to greet her daughter), the doctor, and the nurse discreetly withdraw and close the ambulance door behind them to allow William and Genevieve to enjoy their special moments in privacy. Catherine and the nurse are almost ashamed of themselves for having been present during the proposal; they also feel privileged to have witnessed it and have very moist eyes. Catherine may not have had a chance to greet her daughter, but she's clearly perceived that all is well; and now all is well beyond her wildest expectations.

The doctor, being a man accustomed to keeping his emotions under wraps for the sake of adhering to his professional standards, finds himself moved despite himself. "That's a first," he says, smiling. "My heartfelt congratulations, ma'am."

"Thank you," replies Catherine, taking his hand. "And you know what, doctor?"

"What, ma'am?"

"They met on Friday and if anyone had told me I'd want my daughter to marry a man she's only known for three days, I would've told them they were insane. But I couldn't be happier."

"Under these circumstances, I'd say three days count for a lot more," says the doctor. "They've been through something most couples never encounter in a lifetime. In my professional opinion the young man accorded himself exceptionally well. He did all the right things as well as could be expected. And he wanted to kill me when I said we were going to patch your daughter up in there, he didn't understand our way of handling emergencies, it had to be explained. He obviously cares for her deeply."

"An American," Catherine smiles. "Poor Bill! He had no idea what a SAMU is, and must've been going crazy wondering what you were doing to my precious. And, doctor, as a mother, I thank you from the bottom of my heart!"

"You're very welcome, ma'am. It's my job."

As for William and Genevieve, they spend close to five minutes wordlessly gazing into each other's eyes with hands joined, fingers curling and uncurling—silently exchange vows.

Genevieve's the first to revert to the spoken word. "So now, for the rest of our lives, we'll be saying we became engaged in an ambulance?" she smiles. "We'll be telling our children that?"

"Sorry if there are unpleasant associations with our engagement, honey, but I couldn't wait. After what happened, after fearing the worst... Look, you're *all* that matters to me! I *had* to make you mine!"

"I was *already* yours, darling! Now and forever! And although there's nothing nice about why we're in this ambulance, there's only joy here now! To ask me to be your wife after what happened took courage! Turning a negative into an overwhelming positive is a bright and beautiful thing, and a special skill! I admire you, and will tell the story of our engagement with pride!"

Following another couple minutes of silent mutual appreciation, Genevieve says, "But I'm surprised they're letting us do this, we're tying up a valuable SAMU. Maybe we ought to free it up? I'd also like to prove to myself I can walk."

"Absolutely, honey," William says, rising to open the ambulance door. "Your bedroom's a much nicer place to be." When he opens the door and announces that Genevieve's ready to go upstairs, Catherine's eye is the first one he catches. He doesn't need to voice the question that stamps itself upon his face.

"Of course you have my blessing," Catherine says. "You already know that." Stepping forward and opening her arms, she embraces William as he leans down, adding, "Welcome to our family."

As soon as Catherine releases him, William hears, "As a father, I couldn't want for more in a son-in-law," as Georges clasps his hand in both of his, gazes meaningfully into his eyes—a look that expresses his pleasure and affection far more effectively than words could. "Gen's always had a head on her shoulders, something she demonstrates again and again, and now she's surpassed herself in her choice of a husband." Needless to say, Georges arrived while William and Genevieve were in the ambulance.

"Hi mom and dad," Genevieve smiles, raising herself to her elbows. "Or should I say hi again, mom? We didn't mean to chase you away!"

"Sweetie," Catherine says as she and Georges step into the ambulance, "you did nothing of the kind. I couldn't be happier, I'm so proud of you! I..." She breaks off, tears of joy welling in her eyes, and kisses her daughter.

No sooner are Georges and Catherine joining their hands with those of their daughter and William and reaffirming their approval than a loud *Hear! Hear!* is heard. Christina, Pascale, Stephan, Lucinda, Jean-Marc, and Carole jump into view at the door of the ambulance from where they've been concealing themselves alongside it. *Hear! Hear!* they shout again, clapping enthusiastically. All of them of course instantly dropped whatever it was they were doing at word of the attack and hastened here. Stephan and Lucinda were at the Comédie-Française, Jean-Marc was meeting with an employment counselor, Carole was teaching an aerobics class. All of them gave "family emergency" as their reason for leaving, and it's the truth: blood ties or not, Genevieve is family.

Then the doctor reenters the ambulance and, mindful of medical priorities, requests that matters extraneous to them be put on hold. Speaking to Genevieve concerning routine follow-up wound care as William and her parents listen, he explains when and how to change the dressing and clean the wound, what to look for when inspecting the wound, and adds that if discoloration or pus appears to contact the clinic immediately. He also says the sutures will be removed on the following Monday and hands Genevieve an appointment card. Then he reiterates that the wound, although received in a frightful manner, is not serious. Therefore the patient, he smiles, has no reason to "sit on her duff." Then he tells of a soccer player he surgically treated for a hernia, who was at practice later on the same day kicking balls. While he doesn't expect her to be at the same level of physical conditioning as a professional athlete, he does expect her to exercise every day and maintain a positive attitude. Then he says no antibiotics are required and names an over-the-counter painkiller that's an option if she experiences overmuch discomfort. Lastly, he officially releases Genevieve from his care and tells her she'll be able to walk to her apartment.

Supported on each side by William and Georges, Genevieve rises and takes a couple steps, declaring as she does so, "It feels good to be on my feet."

"That's the spirit," the doctor says. "You keep up that positive attitude and you'll be running around in no time. A good half of the healing process is the eagerness to heal. The desire to heal manifests itself and the body follows suit."

"Thanks again, doctor," Genevieve says, stepping from the ambulance onto the pavement, William and Georges still at her side. Her friends crowd around and accompany her to the door of her building, offering congratulations on her engagement and praising the Gods she's out of danger. William and Georges continue with her up the stairs as Stephan and Jean-Marc follow. The women remain outside because there's police business to attend to.

CHAPTER 27

Realizing that Baptiste's demise needs to be addressed as quickly as possible, the women approach the investigating officer and provide testimony concerning his history of unsavory behavior. Catherine doesn't mince words when describing how her daughter asked them to bar Baptiste from their home, and the subsequent conversation between her husband and Baptiste's father; nor when describing Baptiste's attack upon William, and the second conversation with Baptiste's father, during which legal action was threatened. Lucinda and Carole are very forthcoming concerning the manner in which Baptiste's been hounding Genevieve; Christina and Pascale add their more recent observations. In addition, the names of many more witnesses are provided: Lucinda and Carole have spoken to some of them and the word is being passed along. (The first person Carole called, of course, was Claire. Claire's already told Armand that sending his Samoan compatriot to put the fear of God into Baptiste is no longer necessary.)

Then the women and the men trade places: Georges, William, Stephan, and Jean-Marc return to the sidewalk as soon as the women arrive upstairs. Likewise, names and testimony are provided. Then the officer ascends to the apartment to question Genevieve and review the incident on scene; both she and William describe what transpired within the apartment—where Baptiste was hiding, where the assault occurred, where William struck him, why the window was open, how Baptiste fell out of it.

Over the next twenty-four hours over two dozen witnesses come forward to testify concerning Baptiste's behavior in general and on Saturday morning in particular, when they went to great lengths to peaceably separate Genevieve from him. Baptiste's parents likewise concede there was a problem—devastated as they are, they cannot escape the truth. In the mourning father's words: "It was like my boy caught a virus, became ill. The way he was behaving... That wasn't Baptiste. The way he was looking at and speaking to me the last time I saw him... My boy wasn't there." Also, the staff of Café A La Tour Du Temple, having recognized the body of the deceased as being that of the unstable young man of twenty-four hours ago, provide crucial testimony: to the effect that he was in the café and they were afraid of him, such was his disordered state; that he exited without paying the full amount of his bill and attacked William in front of Sainte-Élisabeth and ran away. The entire history comes out, including William's dousing of Baptiste on the stairs. Concerning the latter incident, the police take the occasion to explain to William that he should've reported the assault and allowed them to handle it instead of taking matters into his own hands. At the same time, they concede it appears that nothing would've cured Baptiste of what ailed him—the evidence of such is becoming more incontestable the more they investigate. The pattern of Baptiste's behavior is one they're familiar with: attraction to someone who's uninterested, and unwillingness to accept it; increasing instability, isolation from beneficial social influences; eventual despair and desperation, acts of harassment and violence. Happy outcomes are extremely rare in such cases.

We're sure the reader's wondering, along with the police and everyone else, how Baptiste came to be in Genevieve's apartment.

About three months ago, when he still had virtually unlimited access to Genevieve's family, he repaid their trust by pilfering one of the two spare keys to her apartment that her parents kept in a bureau drawer, assuming it wouldn't be missed. Then he began to worry it might be missed after all and his motives misconstrued, so he copied the key at a hardware store and returned it to the drawer. In his deluded mind, he'd hit upon the idea of surprising Genevieve in the fashion of a character in a romance novel, impressing her with his extraordinary daring, by letting himself into her apartment on the sly and revealing he was no longer content to be her friend. But then came the distressing alteration in Genevieve's behavior towards him, such that he began to suspect she might not be receptive to such a course of action. Why was she suddenly less forthcoming with confidences, and unwilling to reveal why? Why did she often seem less than pleased to see him? Why would her face cloud when he surprised her on the sidewalk or in the hallway of her school after class? Why was she acting as if she preferred the company of others, constantly surrounded by people who disliked him? So he'd put his confession-of-affection plan on hold, feeling it would be best to wait out what he could only feel was temporary capriciousness. It was so unlike Genevieve, these displays—however subtle—of displeasure towards him, and he was certain they'd soon be a distant memory. He was sure he'd soon reawaken her to who her one and only true friend was; that order would be restored and their closeness would return; that things would again be as they were when they were younger and had no secrets from one another.

But the new Genevieve, instead of standing aside to allow the old Genevieve to return, was becoming more assertive. Always, there were excuses why she couldn't be alone with him, engage in social activity apart from the people who didn't like him. She no longer sought out his company of her own accord, regardless of the circumstances. At the very most she'd say adequate things when speaking to him, as if he was an acquaintance instead of a friend; and her adequate words were becoming increasingly strained, occasionally verging on impatience. Any smile she dispensed upon him was merely the practiced smile of a receptionist—there was little warmth in her smile, only what appeared to be concealment of thoughts he might not find appealing. So Baptiste had resolved to be more attentive, more insistent; after all, he reasoned, a man must win a woman—show her he's willing to endure difficulty, impress her with his faith in their eventual union.

The reader's familiar with the thunderclap Saturday night, when Baptiste's father informed him complaints had been leveled against him by Genevieve and he was no longer welcome in the Clouitier home; how Baptiste had passed out on the couch, tossed and turned in troubled sleep, and awakened early Sunday morning, still in a state of shock. As for the copy of the key to Genevieve's apartment: Baptiste had placed it in the coin purse of his wallet then and there because, one way or another, he was going to gain access to her and disprove the slander that he was convinced her friends were spreading about him, make things right with her again. Then he'd arrived on the street outside Genevieve's building and seen her with William in the window and his plan had been annihilated; from that point on, he'd assuredly ceased to be counted among the sane. He'd attacked William in the manner that's been described, and run as fast as his feet could carry him.

And yet, as highly unhinged people are occasionally capable of doing, Baptiste had pulled himself together adequately enough to make a reasonable attempt at self-preservation. He'd managed to grasp the seriousness of his father's outraged words pertaining to his attack upon William and the Clouitiers' anger, comprehend the precariousness of his situation. So he'd obtained some sleep, dressed appropriately, arrived at 31 Rue Campagne Première on time for the ultimatum meeting, and was climbing the stairs. Alas, past actions—especially if they be ugly ones—often come back to haunt their perpetrators, and sooner than they anticipate: as the reader knows, that's when William doused Baptiste with the foul liquid. The final stroke, as they say: when Baptiste ran away following the dousing, left his father standing at the landing of the family home, it was on account of finally understanding beyond a doubt, in every hidden nook of his disturbed heart, that the thing that *had* to happen—his coming to happy terms with Genevieve—was *never* going to happen; that his one and only hope and desire was a fantasy, and all was lost. His last words to his father, "Good-bye dad! I love you too!" were the last words he uttered to anyone, the last instance in which he was capable of voicing ordered thought.

Baptiste had dashed down Boulevard Raspail to the Denfert-Rochereau metro station, as oblivious of the rain as he was unclear in his conscious thoughts, functioning on blind impulse alone. After reaching the rail platform he'd waited under the bright lights, absently watched blurred glares slide about the white bricks of the tunnel's ceiling—watched a white and light green westbound line 6 train slide into view in front of him, seen its doors open, stepped inside. He hadn't realized, in some distant vaguely conscious place inside him, until several stops later that he was on the wrong train. At La Motte-Picquet Grenelle he'd exited, then boarded a northbound 8 train and circled around the long way to Place de la République. (That he'd been capable of eventually arriving at his destination was doubtless due to his being a lifelong resident of Paris: again, we stress that he was operating entirely on automatic pilot, directing himself from a place that was for the most part removed from conscious thought.) For the duration of the line 8 ride he'd stared blankly at the air in front of him, deaf to the chatter and blind to the movements of the other passengers. Once outside at Place de la République he'd walked down Rue du Temple to Genevieve's apartment, turned the key in its door, stepped inside, and stood in the middle of her living room for several minutes, motionless except for the rise and fall of his chest. Then he'd gone to the kitchen, plucked a knife from the counter, and taken it to her bedroom and sat on the edge of her bed. His head was empty of thoughts and images while he sat there, his mental faculties being too paralyzed to conjure either. It was as if he was in a waking coma—as if his reflexes resembled those of a plant that functions solely via sensory stimulation, as in opening its leaves in the morning in response to the sun's rays. Then Baptiste's sun arrived in the morning and he was propelled to his feet by the sound of her voice and he followed the sound of her voice to the living room and aimed the knife in his hand at her stomach. Did he feel Genevieve's knee strike his groin, feel William's fist hit his face, feel William's boot strike his shins? Did he know he was backing out of the open window-doors, falling over the railing of the balcony, tumbling to his death? These are questions we're unable to answer.

Suffice to say the clincher in arriving at the truth to the satisfaction of the police was that the copy of the key to Genevieve's apartment was found in Baptiste's pocket, and its age and origin were determined. (The hardware store's name was on the key, and the store had a record of the transaction.) Imagine the shudder which ran through Georges and Catherine when they were told of the key: that Baptiste, known to them since he was born, could have copied Genevieve's key three months ago with the intention of harming her! Needless to say, they had no means of knowing what Baptiste's original plan was; given that he'd attacked Genevieve with a knife, how could they—or anyone else, including his own parents—not suppose he'd intended violence from the start?

Long story short, as spelled out in the police report: the deceased was not invited to and had no business being in the assault victim's residence; he engaged in unlawful entry, using a copy of a stolen key. Once there, he assaulted the victim with a weapon that was the victim's property—a weapon with his fresh fingerprints on it. He was repelled by the victim and her boyfriend, then went onto the balcony of his own volition and fell to his death. Because it's unclear whether Baptiste accidentally or intentionally plunged to the sidewalk, impossible to prove either way, his death is ruled accidental. On Thursday morning the case is closed.

Now that we've covered the matter of official police business with regard to Baptiste, as well as provided clarification of his motives and movements, we're free to remind the reader that Genevieve's newly returned to her apartment, very happy to be home. We join her as she's seated on her bed with her back to a mound of pillows, sipping spearmint tea while surrounded by her friends. "Are you sure I don't owe our engagement to stressful circumstances?" she's asking William with a smile. "Are you positive I didn't land you on a wave of pity, because of this mark on my tummy? Tell you what, I want to be absolutely fair: when I'm fully healed and life's returned to normal, I'll let you off the hook if you'd like. I'd rather not catch a man because of medical-emergency-rebound!"

"And that's another reason why I'll never stop loving you," William answers. "Your courage in the face of adversity—your sense of humor despite stressful circumstances! Catch me? Every man should be so lucky! There's no pity, darling, only gratitude that you've deigned to accept me! Gratitude that, out of this mess, I've received the best gift a man could hope to receive—an *amazing* fiancée!"

"Whew!" says Pascale, addressing the others. "Steamy in here, don't you think? Maybe we ought to give the lovebugs some privacy."

"We'll stop!" responds Genevieve. "Bill and I are happy you're here, believe me! We were talking about it when the police officer was here—we don't want to be alone, not because we're not happy but because of the other thing that happened. We'll have to come to terms with that other thing soon enough, but not now. You're our buffer zone against haunting thoughts and we want what's good to shine bright and not be clouded, it being so soon after our engagement."

William, eager to divert the conversation to more cheerful matters, says, "Darling, I'm afraid that ring's a bad fit—it's all I had when I asked you to marry me. We need to get you a proper engagement ring. Chrissy and Pas, I'm sure, would…"

"Of course," cuts in Christina. "We'd be honored to be sent on the sacred mission, we'll pick out a dandy ring!"

"You bet!" affirms Pascale.

"And are we French girls to be left out?" asks Carole, indicating herself and Lucinda.

"The more decision-makers the better," says William. "It's a bi-continental engagement, it ought to be a bi-continental choosing of the ring."

"Loose it may be," Genevieve says, holding up her hand and twirling the key ring about her finger, "but it's not coming off until it's replaced! And I can assure you this would be my one and only engagement ring if it was a snug fit and I didn't have to guard every second against it slipping off! It's a wonderful engagement ring, an example of the resourcefulness I admire in my man, and I'm going to string necklaces and bracelets through it and wear it for the rest of my life! I'll get to wear two engagement rings at once, what a lucky girl! And nothing pleases me more than knowing my fitted ring will be chosen by the four of you! I'll treasure it more than if I chose it myself! A maximum participation ring!"

"Sweetheart," Carole says, gently patting Genevieve's head, "I'll say it again: I'm so happy for you! It's a delight to see you this way!"

"I love seeing love!" Lucinda says.

"Doesn't everyone?" puts in Stephan, who's been curiously quiet.

"So let's measure your finger," says William, grasping Genevieve's hand.

"Measure it?" laughs Carole. "Silly, all we need to do is take one of her rings as a sample."

"Right, I knew that."

An appropriate sizing-ring having been located, the four girls leave for Place Vendôme with William's credit card. "Lots of jewelry stores there to choose from," Carole explains to Christina and Pascale. "We'll not only find the optimum ring, we'll be able to play the stores off against each other to get the best price."

The girls having departed, William turns to Stephan, "Steph, as the man who brought Gen and I together, without whom it would've never happened, I'd be honored if you'd be my best man."

"I'm the one that's honored," Stephan answers, shaking his hand, "and of course I accept. But I'm thinking some of your lifelong friends back home might be upset."

"Don't worry about them, they'll understand. Without you there's no wedding so, obviously, you're my best man. And, besides, I have a number of lifelong friends: how would I choose from among them? Draw straws?"

"Assuming my say-so counts—I know it's a man thing," puts in Genevieve, "I'd say Bill's logic is irrefutable, and that his friends back home will unanimously approve."

"Of course your say-so counts," William says. "Everything about you counts, from the fingernail of your pinkie to every last hair on your beautiful head, and..."

"Come here," Genevieve interrupts, flushing with delight. "Have a sip of my tea."

In the meantime, Georges and Catherine have been preparing two large pots of bouillabaisse in the kitchen; as the morning progresses, the scent of seafood, garlic, tomatoes, thyme, and saffron grows stronger. Jean-Marc and Stephan carry the coffee table in the living room to Genevieve's bedroom, arrange place settings on it, and distribute pillows on the floor to serve as seats. A bed tray's provided for Genevieve. Shortly after 2:00 PM the bouillabaisse is ready. Catherine sets a large bowl of it in the center of the coffee table, and begins ladling portions out.

Minutes later as William partakes of the succulent fish, prawns, calamari, and tomatoes at the coffee table with Genevieve nearby in her bed, Georges and Catherine on either side of him, Stephan and Jean-Marc across from him an overwhelming sigh of relief and thankfulness overcomes him at the same time that the unkind events of the morning—the attack, his kneeling by Genevieve's side as she lay wounded, the wait for the emergency crew—return to his recollection and cause him to shudder. He fought, and he fought well, and now this cozy scene is his reward. How wonderful to have become engaged to the woman of his dreams, and welcomed into a new family! And how horrible it is that she could've been taken from him—irrevocably lost—a mere six hours ago! Had Genevieve—his brave wife-to-be—not raised her knee in self-defense as quickly as she did; or had the knife been aimed higher, at her heart... No! He will *not* think about such things now! He will *not* think about how close he may have come to making funeral arrangements instead of wedding plans! He *will* push this sudden awareness of his mortality—the frightening fragility of life—away, and help himself to another bowl of bouillabaisse and gaze upon his beloved and rejoice in her smile!

CHAPTER 28

Following their meal, everyone—with the exception of Georges and Catherine, who quietly read and chat together at the table in the kitchen with the door shut—retires for some much needed sleep, Genevieve and William in her bed and Stephan and Jean-Marc each on a couch in the living room. It's not until after 8:00 PM that the four girls return with Genevieve's engagement ring, they having put their hearts and souls into the enterprise. As for the ring, it's platinum, the most durable metal—almost as durable as deep abiding love. Twin rows of diamonds, as fiery as stars in a dark sky, are imbedded in the ring proper, in a channel setting. The ring's been chosen for sleekness and simplicity of design—its graceful lines draw the eye to them by their very unobtrusiveness—and to be worn side by side with Genevieve's future wedding band without clashing. Genevieve, being a self-assured and balanced woman, dislikes ostentatiousness and this is a ring suited to her personality. Nor does she, being a physically active woman, want a ring that's likely to snag on clothing or scratch skin: very few of her rings have prong settings, and she rarely wears those that do.

The four girls, having neither eaten since morning nor, excepting during the metro rides to and from Place Vendôme, been off their feet, are both famished and exhausted when they arrive. Instantly aware of the aroma of the bouillabaisse, the second pot of which has been kept warm for them, their mouths moisten and stomachs tighten with anticipation. Nevertheless, it's straight to the bedroom they go, Carole announcing with pride, "Here you go, Bill!" as he groggily opens his eyes. She hands the ring to him before he's half awake.

Lucinda, returning to the living room, rousts the sleeping Jean-Marc and Stephan. "Get up, slouches! The ring's arrived! We haven't slept yet, so no pity for you! Up! Up! Up! The occasion demands it!" As she's waking them Georges and Catherine emerge from the kitchen.

Everyone's assembled in the bedroom when William extracts the ring from its gold-trimmed scarlet velvet box and places it upon Genevieve's finger, saying as he does so, "Genevieve, please accept this humble token of my love for you—my love which I *know* will grow stronger with each passing day."

"Thank you, William," she says in a hushed tone as she clasps his hand in both of hers. "I pledge to be worthy of your love, and to return your love and make us both strong and joyous in our love. I love you so much I'm dizzy with it!"

Then they kiss, the others quietly applauding as they do so.

"But just look at it, Bill!" Genevieve says, lifting her ring finger. "I couldn't have picked out a better ring if I had a month to do so, and they did it in a day!"

"They've translated your style to a ring, all right," William says, "and I'm not even sure how I know that. It's just obvious at a glance, a perfect match in all aspects. The mission was entrusted to the right people. Come here, you! *(He grabs Pascale by the wrist, pulls her to him, and embraces her.)* And, you! *(He embraces Christina.)* Thank you!"

Genevieve's likewise embracing Carole and Lucinda and thanking them; then she's embracing Christina and Pascale as William's doing the same with Carole and Lucinda; then there's so much simultaneous embracing and kissing going on among the group that it's beyond the capacity of your humble narrator to keep track of each instance: suffice to say joy is shining in the eyes of all.

"But have you eaten?" Catherine asks the four new arrivals. "There's a pot of bouillabaisse for you."

"We're *dying* of hunger, hallucinating about food!" Carole exclaims.

"Smells so good my tummy's banging in me like an unborn baby!" Lucinda says, circling her hand about her stomach.

"Then be seated and served," says Jean-Marc, gesturing at the coffee table upon which four places have been set. "Steph and I are your devoted waiters, at your beck and call, ready to indulge your every whim. We shall return presently with the bouillabaisse, prepared by master chefs Georges and Catherine."

"Mom and dad, isn't it beautiful?" Genevieve says, smiling from ear to ear as she extends her hand towards them, twitching her ring finger.

"The girls accomplished their mission, and then some," says Georges. "If anyone deserves a feast and pampering, they do."

"Absolutely stunning!" says Catherine. "The lines compliment the diamonds and accentuate their fire effortlessly—remarkable! An engagement ring's for life and this will last for several! I'm so happy for you!"

"Steph and Jean-Marc, come take a look!" Genevieve says after they return with a bowl of bouillabaisse and set it on the coffee table, leaning forward with the eagerness of a little girl as she presents her hand. Both voice enthusiastic approval of the ring before filling the bowls of the girls and distributing slices of sourdough bread for dunking. Then they're busy preparing a salad of avocados, oranges, mangoes, and grapefruit at the vacant end of the coffee table.

Chatter and laughter fills the room as the girls dig into their bouillabaisse and William and Genevieve begin a game of gin on her bed and Georges and Catherine spread two decks of cards on the floor for a game of double solitaire. Soon the attention of all are upon the latter as they begin slamming cards down on the two piles, each eager to score more points: shouted advice and cheering erupts at such volume and with such urgency that anyone overhearing them would think they're watching a soccer match on TV.

Then Genevieve's saying, "Bill, will you get the bracelet that's in the red box in the second drawer from the top over there? I want to add my first, and equally precious, ring to it." After William hands her the said bracelet, a gold chain one, she removes the key ring from her finger—where it's been since it was placed there in the ambulance—and separates its fold and slips it inside one of the bracelet's links. "Now, it's an engagement bracelet!" she announces, placing it on her wrist and holding up her arm. "An engagement ring and an engagement bracelet! How lucky can a girl get?"

About a half hour later the girls, having finished dining and commenced to pick up their dishes, are prevented from doing so. "Oh no you don't!" says Stephan, taking the bowl from Christina's hand. "You've exerted yourselves beyond the call of duty—selflessly accomplished an important mission! You will *not* be looking after yourselves tonight, that will be the duty and pleasure of Jean-Marc and I! You, as victorious soldiers, shall be showered with glory and perhaps, in serving you, we shall taste of some small part of your glory! Now, reseat yourselves! Allow us to clear the table! And allow us to massage your poor tired feet, if you so desire! In short, your every wish is our command!"

"All right, then, on your knees!" Carole says to Jean-Marc, giggling as she points to the floor.

"Certainly," he responds, kneeling before her. "Anything else?"

"No," she laughs. "I was just seeing if the wish is our command stuff was true and it looks like—maybe—it is! I can't speak for the others, but I won't take advantage, even though I should! You may rise, sir!"

"Thank you, your grace! And now we'll clear these dishes."

"Actually," puts in Lucinda, "we'd rather you unfolded the sofa bed so we can collapse on it. We haven't slept for...I can't even remember when I last slept."

"You poor dears!" Catherine exclaims, bringing her hand to her forehead. "We'll get the bed ready right away! Shame on me for that oversight! All night at Stephan's and all day finding a beautiful ring! My God! I'm going to treat you all to dinner at the restaurant of your choice on the night of your choice! Jean-Marc, will you unfold the sofa? Stephan, will you reach up here *(She opens the closet.)* and grab the blankets? I'll take care of the pillows."

The king-sized sofa bed in the living room is unfolded and four sets of blankets and pillows are arranged upon it. The girls distribute themselves comfortably, each taking a quarter of the bed, and Catherine tucks them in. Then the living room lights are turned off and everyone else returns to Genevieve's room and the door is shut. The dirty dishes, having been transported to the kitchen sink, will be allowed to soak until morning.

"So, sweetheart, are you ready to meet my parents by phone?" William asks Genevieve as soon as everyone's resettled in her room. "I'm calling them now to give them the good news. It's approaching one in the afternoon there."

"Ready?" she smiles. "Nervous and flustered are the words, I think! I'm as ready as I'll ever be!"

"Misplaced nervousness, I can assure you," he says. "As the girl who's claimed my undying love and devotion, you'll never be able to do wrong in their eyes. For that alone they'll instantly love you, no questions asked. Especially my mother, who was starting to worry if I'd ever get—quote-unquote—*serious* in a relationship. And then, once they get to know you, they'll love you for who you are, aside from you being my fiancée. So, please, no worries! Anyway, I'm dialing now so you won't have time to think about it— mom first, dad's at work. *(He punches the speed-dial for his parents' home number.)* Hi mom. Yeah, surprise! Yes, mom, everything's all right, don't worry about that! In fact, I'm in heaven, as I've never been before, and that's why I'm calling! And you? Good, I have news you'll want to hear—serious good news—but want dad on the line first. Hang on a moment, I'll do a flash so we can have a three-way, be right back. *(He punches the flash button on his phone, then the speed dial for his father's work number.)* Dad? Hi, it's... Yeah, all's well—couldn't be better! Wait, I'm going to patch mom in, she's on the other line—I have good news that I want both of you to hear at once. *(He punches the flash button again.)* Mom?

OK, dad's on the line, so here's the news: I've met the most wonderful girl on earth, and am getting married! You heard me! Married! Wait, she's right here—speak to her! Yeah, I know I'm putting her on the spot, but how else am I to do this? I'm doing it fast so thinking doesn't get in the way! Here, I'm giving my beautiful fiancée the phone!"

Genevieve, who hasn't anticipated being handed the phone so quickly, at first hesitates, flinging her hands up in a wait signal, a charming look of mild alarm on her face; but then she smilingly shrugs her shoulders, grabs the phone, and says, "Mr. and Mrs. Bergen?"

"Please call me Bianca," William's mother says, at once gently and breathlessly. "I'm here with Hal, Bill's father. We're both delighted to meet you and, silly Bill, he hasn't told us your name."

"Genevieve, Mrs. Bergen...sorry...Bianca."

"Hi Genevieve," says Hal. "Very pleased to meet you."

"Me too," Genevieve answers. "I'm so happy to meet you, Bill's standing here, he..." she trails off, too nervous to speak.

"I'm afraid our son, bless him, could've done this a bit better than he has," Bianca says, her voice sympathetic and kind. "Poor you! You're talking to your fiancé's parents seconds after they've received the good news, and you have no idea what we're like! Rest assured, Genevieve, we're on your side and couldn't be happier!"

"We're not going to grill you," laughs Hal. "Relax. And if it's any consolation, I'm here in my office fidgeting in my chair—this is no small thing on either end. I certainly don't want to make a bad first impression."

"A new family's starting up, of course it's *huge*!" Bianca says. "The bride and the parents of the groom are meeting by phone—none of us want to botch it!"

"Ha ha ha!" Genevieve laughs, surprised and alarmed at herself the instant she does so. "I mean...sorry..."

"Thatta girl!" Bianca says. "Laugh at the situation, it *is* a little crazy! Actually, it's *big* crazy! But don't apologize! We may be the parents but, as Hal said, we're squirming too! It wouldn't do for our new daughter to think we're weirdos! Ha ha ha!"

"Guess what?" Genevieve says, becoming more comfortable by the moment. "Bill's laughing! *(She addresses William.)* Yeah, very funny, doing this to us! You're enjoying yourself, aren't you?"

William, coming to the phone while Genevieve continues to hold it, says, "OK, I'm laughing, but... Look, it's like I said at the get-go: how else go about this? Build it up with a lot of talk so you have time to think too much and get self-conscious? In my humble opinion, that wasn't the way. I know all of you, give me some credit. I knew it wouldn't take long for you to calm each other down."

"He has a point," Hal says. "Maybe he's laughing, but it's not his fault we're in California instead of Paris. I'm certainly happy to be speaking to you, Genevieve, that's the bottom line."

"I'm happy about it too, Hal and Bianca!"

"Which doesn't mean Bill's going to get away with laughing at us," Hal chuckles. "What do you say, Genevieve? Feel like playing a prank on our son with us after we meet in person?"

"Sure," she giggles, very relaxed now. She lightly pokes William in the ribs.

"I'll gladly be your prankee and take my lumps," William says, he having his ear close enough to the receiver to hear. "Far from complaining, I'll only offer thanks." Need we say he's jumping out of his skin for joy? The rapidity with which his fiancée and parents have bonded, helped each other through this awkward situation: how could there be a more favorable start to familial relations?

"No prank shall be played upon you," Genevieve finds herself saying. "Your parents are wonderful—you didn't exactly throw me to the lions! Sorry, Hal, you and Bianca are so nice...I don't see how I can punish Bill for introducing us."

"Genevieve, I love you already," says Bianca. "Hal and I have always wanted a daughter and we're convinced Bill's chosen the best one in the universe!"

"You've got that right," Hal says. "Genevieve, with all my heart I say: welcome to our family!"

"Thank you Hal and Bianca! Thank you so much!"

"So guess what?" William says, gently twisting the phone from Genevieve's hand. "The first round went so well, I'm going to do it again. Guess who's here? Genevieve's parents are in the room, and they've heard our side of the conversation. No, dad, I didn't plan it this way! How could I? I haven't planned anything, there's zero premeditation! You think there aren't butterflies in my stomach too? When I said I was doing this fast to avoid too much thinking I wasn't excluding myself! I'm plenty nervous! But at least this time I'll tell everyone's name first! OK, Genevieve's parents are Georges and Catherine, they're fabulous people. I'm giving them the phone. Georges and Catherine please meet my parents, Hal and Bianca." He hands the phone to Georges, who shares it with Catherine.

"Hello Hal and Bianca," Georges says. "Cathy and I are very pleased to meet you."

"And Bianca and I are delighted to meet you, Georges and Cathy," Hal says. "Your daughter's a wonder in our eyes already, she handled herself flawlessly in a difficult situation. What I mean is that the situation stopped being difficult very quickly."

"Thank you, Hal," Catherine says. "We couldn't be more proud to welcome your son into our family. He has our unconditional blessing, we've had something of a betrothal ceremony here. We've been thanking our lucky stars all day that William will be taking our only daughter as his bride."

"Thank you, Cathy," says Bianca. "As I said to Genevieve, we've always wanted a daughter and our son has provided us with one who's surpassed our fondest hopes."

"Thank you, Bianca," Catherine continues. "We deeply appreciate that, and look forward to meeting you in person."

"And the same with us," says Hal; then, seeking to break the ice a bit more, he adds, "I don't know about you, but I'm a little—shall we say—overwhelmed by the uniqueness of our situation, meeting by phone when our families are uniting."

"We're feeling it," laughs Georges. "Parents of a century ago didn't have to meet by phone and feel each other out with their voices!"

"Exactly!" Hal likewise laughs. "But I must say, if I may presume so, that it's nice to experience the situation with kind and reasonable people."

"You took the words right out of our mouths," says Catherine. "Good God, Georges and I are feeling very fortunate indeed! Parents don't always mirror their offspring, we have a story that's far too close to home pertaining to that—an opposite story, as in the offspring being bad. *(Georges, uncertain if the subject of Baptiste should be brought up at this time, taps his wife's wrist and looks at her questioningly; gently tilting her head in the affirmative, she indicates that she's going to proceed with it.)* Georges, I think we ought to tell them now, don't you?"

"I agree," Georges answers, first of all because there's nothing else he can say and also because he realizes, with the assistance of the look in his wife's eyes, that something as serious as the chaos of the morning should not be concealed from William's parents simply because they've just met them: full disclosure is best from the outset.

"Please do tell us," Bianca says, detecting the apprehension in their tone. "Whatever the trouble is, we're behind you. We're family now. Your troubles are ours."

"First of all," Catherine says with fervor, "your son accorded himself as well as anyone possibly could under trying circumstances, and may have saved our daughter from bleeding to death."

"My God!" Bianca exclaims. "Is Genevieve all right? She sounded so above the clouds, so…"

"She's all right," Catherine hastens to interrupt. "Absolutely all right! Everything's divine, I can assure you! Don't worry! But now, please let me tell you a story."

And so Catherine relates the Baptiste episode in its entirety, leaving nothing out. Hal and Bianca, needless to say, are by turns quivering with rage and exhaling with relief as the tale enfolds— frequently interrupting with questions, exclamations, and thanks to God. Tragedy has one thing in common with wedding announcements: it unites people and, given that the two situations have been combined, the four parents are soon the best of friends. Their conversation continues for nearly two and a half hours, well after serious matters have been discussed and put to rest, no one wishing to end it. In the end, William and Genevieve doze off to the reassuring sound of their parents happily socializing.

When they say goodbye to Hal and Bianca after midnight, Georges and Catherine briefly awaken William to let him know his phone's on the nightstand and that they're leaving and will return in the morning. "You understand, of course, that we're only a phone call away," Georges says. "Don't hesitate to call us for any reason at any time." Catherine, seeing Stephan and Jean-Marc are asleep on the floor by the coffee table with only pillows for comfort, covers them with blankets before she turns out the lights.

CHAPTER 29

We rejoin William, Genevieve, Christina, Pascale, Georges, and Catherine on Tuesday at the approach of noon. Stephan, Lucinda, Jean-Marc, and Carole have departed on account of assorted responsibilities and will return in the evening. Georges and Catherine arrived shortly after 9:00 AM with croissants and a platter of cheese and fruit, and only a few crumbs remain. Nothing of note occurred during the night at Genevieve's apartment because all present slept as if drugged.

Being too exhausted to dwell upon the disturbing aspects of their day was a godsend for William and Genevieve—sleep was a much needed refuge. Because, fortunate outcome or not, an assault will generally return to haunt those who were on its receiving end: it's as if disaster delights in reminding people that it can strike without warning, at any time. And one of life's cruel ironies is that, as soon as adequate sleep is obtained to restore equilibrium to the body, clarity is also restored to one's mental faculties, such that one becomes aware of whatever gnawing recollections are present. And so, as our otherwise happy couple chat with the others in

Genevieve's bedroom, they become increasingly aware of unpleasant flickerings, related to Baptiste's attack, in the background of their thoughts.

As long as William and Genevieve are with her parents and Christina and Pascale, their uneasy stirrings remain submerged, unable to claim the bulk of their attention. But then it's time for the first change of the dressing and examination of the wound, and William accompanies Genevieve to the bathroom. The dressing's removed, there's the wound staring her in the face: in and of itself it's not frightful to look at—it's no more than an inch long, clean, flawlessly sutured—but it's a memory-trigger. Genevieve starts and shudders, jerks her gaze away, as clear recollection of Baptiste's attack, the sight of the person she's known since infancy approaching her with a glaring crazed look and a knife, surges into the forefront of her awareness. "Sorry, Bill!" she exclaims in a tremulous whisper, cupping her hands over her face and beginning to sob.

"Honey," William says, gently wrapping his arms around her, "you cry all you want, you have every right! You are so brave—you are so strong! Please, sweetheart, no apologies! And no shame! Let it out! I'll kiss your tears! I'll kiss them, kiss them, kiss them!"

"What can I do? Can I come in? What do you need?" Catherine asks in a rapid-fire burst, speaking from the other side of the door.

"Of course you can come in, mom," answers Genevieve, stifling her sobs. "It's only a weak moment."

"Would you please stop that," William says, clasping her hand. "You are *not* weak! You are *not* to cast aspersions upon your courage! You kicked that bastard like an Amazon! You're my Goddess, and... My God, after what you've been through... And I'm not exactly free of thinking about it either, don't suppose that for a second! We're only human!"

"If that son of a bitch wasn't already dead, I'd kill him myself!" Georges shouts, stepping into the bathroom at Catherine's heels. "If I could, I'd bring him back from the dead so I could personally send him to hell! Falling out of a window was too good for him! He got off easy!"

"Georges," Catherine says, "I'm not sure that's helpful under the..."

"It's helpful, mom," Genevieve interrupts. "See? I'm smiling! That's my dad talking and I love it!" She lifts her chin and purses her lips, by way of indicating her father should present his cheek for a kiss, which he does. Then she kisses her mother.

"OK," Georges says, "you two make my princess shipshape, then we're going to air this out! Therapy in the bedroom! It's always helpful to talk about it!"

"Dad," Genevieve says, reaching for his hand. "As a couple, maybe we need to face this alone. There won't always be people sheltering us, so we've got to learn how to handle things ourselves. I'm not afraid to, and Bill isn't either."

"Don't be so eager to face things alone," Georges smiles. "There'll be plenty of opportunities for that, believe me, and more than you'll want. So use us, Gen, while we're here—don't be afraid to. I'll see you in your room, we'll slice and dice this thing there. *(He addresses Christina and Pascale, who've been at the door ready to render any needed assistance.)* Come on, girls. We'll go wait for the brave couple."

William and Catherine assist Genevieve with washing the wound in mild soap and water and placing a new dressing upon it. That done, they accompany her back to her bedroom, where she finds her bed pillows fluffed and the blankets placed in order. As she's climbing into bed Georges—eager to get straight to the business of talking things out—exclaims, "And Bill's banged up too! To think that that sick son of a bitch attacked both of you! They say we're not supposed to speak ill of the dead? Rubbish! A viper in a bird's nest, that's what he was! Nurtured by us in part, trusted by us... Damn it to hell! *(He slams his fist on the arm of the chair he's sitting in.)* He won't be missed! His death is his own doing, he willed his own end, and far better his death than... All right, I don't need to spell it out! Let's stick to facts: no one feels sorry for him, OK? And no one *(He glances meaningfully at William.)* blames himself for fighting back on Sunday!"

William, caught by surprise, involuntarily glances away, at a loss for ready words.

"I knew it!" Georges exclaims. "You're berating yourself for letting him have it on the stairs, wondering if it made matters worse and led to the attack! Listen to me: that bastard was beyond recovery! No prank made any difference! And don't forget that's all it was: a prank! Nothing like the blow on the face he gave you! He got off easy with that too!"

"I can't hide from you, can I?" William says, quickly recovering himself and meeting and holding Georges' gaze. "Of course I've been wondering if I'm to blame. Was the dousing necessary, a good judgment call? Did I unwittingly place Gen's life in danger, by aggravating the situation and pushing Bap over the edge? In retrospect the dousing comes off as gratuitous showboating, to soothe my ego and show off in front of my friends."

"Nonsense!" shouts Pascale. "Here, take a look at yourself! Wait, where's that mirror? *(Catherine grabs Genevieve's hand-held mirror from the top of the highest dresser and hands it to her.)* Thank you, Cathy! Now, look at yourself! See what Bap did to you? See *that*? And you're telling me fighting back was gratuitous? I was there, remember? None of us were at peace, we couldn't enjoy the Sunday brunch! The matter had to be redressed, we all had a share in it! It was a good plan! Humiliate the worm without causing physical harm, sabotage his big meeting with the law firm guy, bring some serious stress into his life! No more kid gloves, as on Saturday morning! All of us were in on it, get that through your head! You knew it then, so remember it now! How could we know he was psychotic? Real life psychotics are a rarity, thank God!"

"She's absolutely right," Genevieve says. "I was in on it as much as you were! So what if you're the one who pulled the trigger? We all supplied you with the gun! Gratuitous showboating? You were defending yourself, and defending me! It was my apartment he was shadowing—he was shadowing me! You took a bullet for me, sweetheart *(She points to his face.)*, and I love you and enough of blaming yourself for what's only in your imagination!"

"And I third that motion," Christina says. "Billy, I'm proud to say I tossed a couple handfuls of table scraps in that bucket, along with everyone else! We all made the concoction, remember? We all wanted a piece of the action! Bap snuck up behind you, hit you, and ran away! That's the act of a cowardly scaredy-cat! Then he's in here with a knife? And he strikes with the knife? And we were supposed to piece that together in advance? Impossible! No precedent! Not a chance could we know he was that far gone! And, as far as that goes, how did he get in here? Crawl in through a window? It's too high. Drop down from a balcony above? I don't think so. Did he have a key?"

"Chrissy," Georges says hastily, "you are one bright girl and have said more than you know. Of course we've all been wondering how he got in here. In part, I started this conversation because I wanted dialogue about this business going on so I wouldn't be dropping a bomb from out of the blue. I was going to wait until later but you've asked the question, so I'll answer it now. Long story short: the police called us this morning and we know how the assailant—that's what I'm calling him from now on—got in here. A key to the apartment was found in his pocket. It was a copy of a key he stole from us at least three months ago."

"What?" Genevieve gasps, a shiver gripping her spine. "How...?"

"He took one of your spare keys from the dining room bureau and copied it, then put it back," Georges continues in a willfully controlled and even, gritting-of-his-teeth, tone. "He copied it three months ago. We know this because the name of the hardware store where he copied the key was on it. The store had a record of the payment with the date. The assailant paid with his credit card, not troubling to cover his tracks—something that, to my mind, bespeaks the unconcern of utter lunacy. The fact he had the key for three months also bespeaks cold-blooded premeditation. If I've been irritable this morning, now you know why. If I've been going out of my way to show no regrets for the assailant's demise, that's the reason."

"He had it for three months?" Genevieve says. "For three months he...?

"For three months he smiled at us while having that key!" Georges shouts, no longer able to restrain himself. "For three months he attended gatherings in our home and enjoyed our hospitality while having that key! So no one feels sorry for him! No one expresses regret to his family, the name of which is now poison to me! And, Bill, it's another reason why you need to stop second guessing the dousing on the stairs! Listen to the girls, and listen to me! Cathy and I had a part in the dousing too—we sanctioned it! You won't see me second guessing that, especially in the light of this key business! And think about this: say I called the police Sunday, had him arrested after he assaulted you... Assuming he was locked up at all for a first time offense, he wouldn't have been locked up for long; and once he was released, what then? Think about that! If anything, the dousing shook him up and made him careless and helped cause him to botch what he was probably planning from the get-go!"

"God!" Genevieve exclaims. "To think that the boy I grew up with—laughed on the playground with, made sand castles on the beach with—would grow up to... *(She pauses, shudders.)* Now, when I think back on the way he started looking at me weeks ago I can see the offness in his eyes, and it scares me to death! And just now, in the bathroom... I saw it again, dad—saw him coming at me with the knife in my own living room, where by all rights I ought to be safe! Saw the insanity in his eyes! I know it's over, but... God!" She cradles her head against William's chest, starts sobbing again.

"Sweetheart, that's what I was afraid of," Georges says gently. "It's not only your body that's wounded, your psyche is too; but you know what? As I've known since you were knee-high and never tire of saying, you're a very strong girl. You're already talking about it, and were able to get a good night's sleep. Pumpkin, we were so happy to see you sleeping soundly when we looked in on you this morning. And, the important thing is, you're not bottling it up. It'll go away, but not overnight and one's going to take it lightly. My God, it's not easy to be attacked, regardless of the happy ending; and the ending *is* happy, we know you know that. Your fiancé is here, we're here, Chrissy and Pascale are here, you have many devoted friends. The happy ending, as the days go by, will shove the shock away. Your upcoming wedding will drown out the unwelcome noise of your delayed reaction to... All right, I won't elaborate. The fact is there's nothing but good here now, and...

Honey, you just cry and cry all you want: tears are like bathing in a pristine spring, with the difference that you're being washed from the inside. And words may only be words in and of themselves, but when words are birthed by feeling, accompanied by emotion, they become magical incantations. Digging down for the troubling feelings and attaching them to words and voicing them in front of loved ones does wonders for shortening healing time. Your loved ones are here and we're not going anywhere, so take advantage of us. We'll stay here all night until tomorrow night and the next night, if we need to. Out with it, sweetheart."

"Oh, Dad!" Genevieve says, reaching for his hand. "I don't want to be mining this thing like some drama-queen, and try people's patience!"

"All right," Georges says, caressing the back of her hand, "that's both good and bad. Good because you're self-possessed enough to—however misguidedly—be concerned for our welfare, as if that's an issue. Bad because you're holding back when you shouldn't be. So out with it, Gen—I'm not dropping the matter until you do. I know you, honeypie, so I'm going to hold firm."

"OK," Genevieve says, sitting up straight and evening out her voice, willfully pulling her nerves together. "It's this. The memories of the innocent days, when Bap and I were kids, keep coming back and contrasting with the final result! *(She starts quivering with anger, as if despite herself.)* The final result as in that creep waiting here, in my own bedroom, and then coming at me with a knife because I could no longer abide his presence! Because I, quite simply, insisted on being my own person, instead of the one he wanted me to be! Because I was fed up with the false coincidental meetings, the suffocating clinging, the unending jealousy, the demeaning lie! Of all the shoddy disgusting... *(She pauses to catch her breath, gather her thoughts.)* So he stole my key and copied it three months ago? What sick garbage was in his head? He's given me a pretty clear idea! He fell out the window on his own, but I'm almost sorry I didn't push him! Copying my key, coming in here, ruining a beautiful morning after Bill and I had been up all night at Steph's, celebrating our love and having the time of our lives? How dare he, the sick creep? He's dead, and I'm glad! I'm glad of it, and feeling guilty for being glad! You see? I'm glad he's dead but I grew up with him, and..." She breaks off, looking at her father.

"Right," Georges says, "that's the nefarious way of the recently departed, especially if one's known them for a long time—they seek to fight the living as if they're still alive, don't want to relinquish their hold. There *is* such a thing as ghosts, but it's we who create them—they don't exist apart from us. Ghosts exist solely by virtue of our memories and it's within our power to make them disappear. Ghosts live as long as they're able to creep into our recollection, distract us from the life before us, and vanish the moment we forget them. The dead thrive on demanding that their demise be come to terms with, to however great a degree they're responsible for it. And make no mistake: the assailant's death was his own doing. He's dead because he wanted to claim you for himself, when he had no right to do so: he took the only way out. He made it into a you or him situation, not you. If someone's hellbent on taking the path of self-destruction the *only* option is to get out of the way. And if that path of self-destruction happens to lead straight through someone else, then that someone else had better wake up and defend herself before it's too late. And you did that, darling, and are therefore alive and surrounded by people who love you. William loves you, as you do him, and you'll make each other as happy as you both deserve. The love between you two... It takes my breath away, Gen! Daughter, you're alive and radiant with life, so chase the ghosts away! *(He stands up, waves his arms, shouts.)* Begone, ghosts! You are not welcome here!"

"Begone, ghosts! You are not welcome here!" the others repeat.

"Theatrics aside, though," Georges quickly resumes, "I know the healing's not going to be a walk in the park. As I said, we'll stay here as long as needed. No pampering, mind you, simply loving care. Gen, I know you're not finished speaking."

"Copied my key!" Genevieve repeats, shuddering; then she's looking at William, "Honey, if you hadn't come into my life, what then? He probably lets himself in here while I'm alone is what! Maybe it would've happened Sunday morning, after he was told to stay away from me, and was shadowing me instead! And I would've been screaming bloody murder, cursing him like I've never cursed anyone before! And then what? He would've grabbed one of my kitchen knives and come at me when I had no man to protect me! My God! Of course I'm glad he's dead, and to hell with feeling guilty about being glad! Childhood? That's a long gone dream! Bap changed, became a...he became a monster! Is that my fault? No! I didn't ask him to become sick and entangle me in the sickness, force me to defend myself, so why should I feel guilty? If I could order matters differently and have him turn out to be a decent human being, I'd do so in a heartbeat! Is it frightening that he changed? Horribly so! But... *(She shakes her head, then composes herself and smilingly frames William's forehead with her fingers.)* Darling, we're alive and in love and the threat to our love is gone! The enemy who wanted to separate us is no more! Guilt? It's stupid to feel that way! We're alive, dearest! Alive!"

"From now on we'll be guarding each other's privacy," William says, caressing her cheeks. "No one will be able to maintain the illusion for a second that we're available to be used in any way! We've staked an exclusive claim upon one another, and there will be *no* sharing! My God, I still can't believe my good fortune!"

"*Our* good fortune," she corrects him, leaning forward for a kiss.

"*Our* good fortune," he echoes, joining his lips to hers.

After about a minute of respectfully looking away, trading smiles with his wife and Christina and Pascale, Georges brings up another matter he considers of paramount importance. "The strong will always veer towards the positive, build new fires out of old ashes," he begins, "and the two of you are proof positive of that. And not to douse the happy flames, but Bill has more airing to do before I'm going to be quiet—quiet for today, that is. *(William involuntarily winces.)* All right, Bill, I'm fairly sure you've guessed what's coming, and I apologize in advance. I apologize, but will proceed nevertheless. You were here when the assailant attacked our precious—you saw it all, lived it all. You saw our dear Gen wounded and you tended to her until the ambulance arrived. That's more trauma than anyone deserves, and I won't even try to imagine it. You have our undying gratitude, and...I know you're carrying the shock inside you, that it's bothering you. We're family now, please bring it out. And yes, honey *(He grasps Genevieve's hand.)*, I know it's going to bring back some ghastly moments, but better in front of us than when you're alone. Again, I know this isn't easy—God, I know—but confronting the haunting images hastens their departure: it's an infallible law. Facing off isn't pleasant, but looking away isn't an option: looking away only means the ghastly things will be able to approach unbidden, without warning, during your vulnerable moments—blindside and terrify you when you're least prepared to deal with them. Please, Bill."

"If I end up with a father-in-law half as wise as you, I'll count my blessings every day," Christina says softly. "He's right, Billy, we're all here to help. We're all so close to you that whatever you say it will be as if we're talking to ourselves."

And on that note we'll begin a new chapter, where William will comply with Georges'—and, by implication, everyone else's—request.

CHAPTER 30

"As I said, I can't hide from you," William begins, smiling at Georges, "and I don't want to, because you're right: confronting nasty recollections stops them from festering. It's been in my head ever since waking up, seeking to undermine my joy in our engagement—not succeeding, mind you, but definitely making repeated attempts. As Gen said, we had a wonderful time at Steph's—how can one not have a wonderful time at Steph's?—and were as happy as a couple can be. The cab ride home, all by itself, was bliss such as the Gods would envy, and make them want to be mortal. Simple hand holding, our... OK, that's private. The point is we arrived here delighted beyond measure, all the stress of dealing with the *problem* was gone. Gen went to the windows and opened them to let the wind in; the wind was fluffing her hair... Then our delight's shattered in an instant: I'm watching that diseased creature appear from out of nowhere and attack her. Then Gen's...sorry, Gen..."

"Darling, I'm fine," Genevieve breaks in. "We're going to exorcise the aftershocks together. We haven't covered the minutes after the attack, me on the floor—my mind was something of a blank, actually. It seems like there should be a great deal of thinking in that situation but there isn't much at all, so preposterous does the idea become that one's been senselessly assaulted—the situation becomes unreal, starts to resemble a dream. It's not easy to describe. Maybe it's that one's too alarmed to be alarmed, if that makes any sense. Anyway, sweetie, please continue—we'll go back to those moments together. Mom and dad and Pas and Chrissy are here—they'll help us shoo the darkness away. And you're here, honey, as you were then, thank God."

"My pillar of strength," William says, grasping her hand; then he, as it were, dusts himself off—shakes his head a bit, opens his eyes wide—and continues, "OK, one moment all is heaven on earth, the next I'm pummeling the creep for all I'm worth and then he's out the window and gone, and... Next I'm on the phone with the emergency woman, she's talking me through first aid—I'm positioning you to ward off shock, staunching blood, doing my best to keep you calm. I didn't have time to be aware of being afraid, but afraid—terrified—I certainly was. Crystal clear this morning, especially in the shower—doubtless because I was alone—was all the fear I buried while looking after you. And I can't stop thinking about the thin margin of error, asking myself if it's only by a miracle that I managed to look after you the right way. There's no room for a mistake when... It scares me to death in retrospect! All the fear I couldn't afford to be aware of while administering first aid keeps coming back to collect some sort of debt! And then there's the interval right after they placed you in the ambulance, and I'm arguing with the driver—I thought they were going to let you die in there! It was as if I'd been thrust into the bottom of a grave, when I was pleading with him and not understanding they were treating you straightaway—I was watching all my hopes die and my life die and... Gen, neither of us deserved that! The sick bastard! I'm glad he's dead too!"

"Come here," Catherine says, opening her arms as she seats herself beside William on the bed. "I want to thank you again—I'm so grateful I could cry. *(She hugs William tightly and doesn't let go while speaking to him softly, as if they're the only people in the room.)* First of all, Bill, the end result is the measure of your accomplishment, and the end result is clasping your hand as I monopolize you—you and Gen have a bright future. I was there when the doctor praised you, remember? And his eyes said more than his words—he *admired* you, and we're talking about a man who sees these things every day. A thin margin of error? That's a margin you were careful to respect, and you didn't step outside of it—no, you didn't. Listen to me: of course it's scary, but focus on the positive—focus on the actual: you, without any experience of handling a serious medical situation, knuckled down to the task and succeeded as well as anyone possibly could. You *had* to knuckle down to it, and so you did. No couple should be put through such an ordeal, but you were put through it and you emerged with the highest marks, and the everlasting gratitude and affection of a mother who dotes upon her daughter. As a mother, I know my Gen will be in good hands—the best hands a mother could hope for. Yes, Bill, the best, and... *(She tightens her hug for a few moments, quivers with the force of it.)* As I said, Bill, deal with the facts of the matter, because the facts are all good and confirm your bravery and presence of mind: you were up all night and happy, then disaster struck and you triumphed. Those are the facts, so embrace them—think about them when the fear returns." She slowly unwinds her arms, sweetness brimming in her eyes.

"No one's naive enough to think the hurting will be gone overnight," Georges adds, "but, as Cathy says, embrace the positive outcome: as the days go by the fear will weaken, and finally dissipate. Brushes with death, close or otherwise, don't easily depart from the recollection. Even events that were only the possibility of a brush with death, instead of actually being so, are capable of creeping back when one least expects it, and stinging. Death's a tireless enemy and the living must constantly fight back: such is the nature of life. One must fight for mental stability, emotional equilibrium—it doesn't always come easy, especially following a shock such as you've sustained. But life's instinct is also to seize the happiness that's at hand, and hold it tight and not let go. And you've done that. A proposal in an ambulance, the doctor told us that was a first. You're both fighters, as has been incontestably proven, and you'll just plain get fed up with fear's revisitations and be done with them before... It may seem farfetched now, but I predict that in less than a month the aftershocks will be gone. Which isn't to say I'm taking anything for granted: we're going to do this all week—talk about it until you're sick of it, and then some. Because, when you start to get sick of it, that's the beginning of the end. Gen, you mentioned..."

"It's the attack itself that keeps returning," Genevieve breaks in, anticipating her father's line of questioning, "far more than me being on the floor afterwards. I keep seeing Bap's inhuman expression, the hate in his eyes! This from someone I grew up with, who populates my earliest recollections! Once upon a time happy memories, now poisoned ones! That same childhood Bap turning out bad, it's insane! All his oppressive clinging for weeks, then the fury! He, really and truly, wanted to end my life! And for what? For declining to be his...whatever he wanted of me, it wasn't anything that's healthy! I didn't mean him any harm, I just wanted to be left alone; but he meant me plenty of harm for wanting to be left alone! I was being punished by an emotional cripple for exercising my free will! I think it infuriates me more than it scares me, and it scares me plenty! But, as Bill said, we'll be guarding each other's privacy from now on! A relationship is an *Off Limits!* sign, to keep the Baps of this world away! Obviously, it was the fact we grew up together that made him think he owned me! But there won't be any more open doors to this girl, because Bill's slammed them shut and locked them! *(She snuggles close to William, wraps an arm about his waist.)* And you know what? Now I realize that when I think about being on the floor after the attack, with Bill beside me, what I most feel is comfort and reassurance—there's very little fear. My beloved was looking after me—my guardian angel was keeping me alive! I had faith in him, and he did me proud! The attack was terrible; but then the assailant was gone, and Bill was beside me... Bill, you make me feel so *safe*!" she cries, kissing his left cheek. "And the ring's beautiful—*beautiful*! Look at it, everyone!" she cries again, extending her ring hand. "The undying flare of the diamonds is a perfect compliment to the undying flare of our love! Dad, sorry, but I'm through with dealing with aftershocks! What are these aftershocks when held up to the bonfire of our love? Paltry annoyances are the aftershocks, no different than pesky mosquitoes on an otherwise divine day in the Bois!"

"Honey," Georges says eagerly, overjoyed at his daughter's healthy attitude. "You're right, we're through for today."

"Only for today?" Genevieve says. "Honestly, dad, I don't know if Bill and I will have the patience to do this again. Do you really want me to be whining all the time?"

"Of course I don't want you to be whining," Georges says with a smile, "and you know it. And I think you also know there hasn't been any whining today—that's just your way of baiting good old dad. What I want is for you to be doing what you're doing, getting impatient with my program. The idea's to get this sort of dialogue going so you become comfortable with it. Then it can pursue its own course, work itself out—it becomes as natural as water seeking its own level. I'm only seeking to bring the power of self-healing into the forefront of your awareness—not merely as a plausible theory, but as something known to be true by your blood and nerves. You know about muscle memory: there's also emotional-reflex memory, as in automatically stressing the positive after unpleasant occurrences. Anyway, maybe we'll reconvene tomorrow and maybe we won't. At this point, it depends on you two—I'll certainly grant you that."

"So you wanted to put it in our heads," William says, "and there won't be any scheduled sessions after all? I understand perfectly, I'm feeling it. What I mean is that this talk's been very healthy—it's definitely kick-started the healing process. And, Gen, I'm with you one hundred percent—we can fly solo now. And, Cathy, I'm never going to forget what you said—thank you. I still can't believe how blessed I am to be a part of this family."

"I merely stated the truth," Catherine says, "and don't need to be thanked for that. As I said, you have my undying gratitude and respect. And you and Gen will learn soon enough that when the pain comes all you'll need to do is gaze into each other's eyes to melt it away—you won't need any hugs from me. Actually, what I think I meant to say is that you already know that." Then, addressing her husband while grasping his arm and nodding towards the door, "I think it's time we do our chores, don't you?" She's referring to the preliminary dinner preparations.

"By all means," Georges says, standing. "Onto the chores."

"When I said the aftershocks would be gone in a month," Georges says as he and Catherine enter the kitchen, "I don't think I did the lovebirds justice. They're so in love and exploding with it the aftershocks will probably be gone in a week. They're too impatient to start really getting to know one another to put up with obstruction. That bit about mosquitoes in the Bois was vintage Gen—priceless! Neither of them can talk about what ails them without ending up in each other's arms: if that isn't beauty, I don't know what is! Time heals all wounds, but love heals them faster!"

"I couldn't agree more," smiles Catherine, kissing her husband. "Now, could you please hand me the big wooden bowl? Where are the endives and leeks?"

In the meantime, Christina and Pascale are rising from their seats in the bedroom. "We're going to leave you two alone," the former says. "Aside from getting the distinct impression that four's a crowd, I'm sure they can use a hand in the kitchen."

"Salad assembly line," laughs Pascale as they turn towards the doorway. "That's always fun! And you two have fun too!"

"Can you use us?" Christina asks as soon as she and Pascale step into the kitchen.

"Please use us," Pascale adds.

"What do you think, Cathy?" Georges asks his wife as he winks at the girls. "Can we use them?"

"They came to the right place if they want to be used," Catherine laughs; then, addressing the girls, "See those vegetables on the table?"

"Be sliced and diced in a jiffy," Pascale says, clapping as she advances to the table. "All you have, throw them at us."

"Heap them up, we'll whack the pile down," Christina says, grabbing a knife from the counter, Pascale having claimed the one on the table.

And so the girls begin cutting up over a dozen varieties of vegetables, tossing them into two large wooden bowls, as Georges and Catherine begin shucking corn and lining two large baking trays with some of the husks. Into the baking trays they'll add the corn cobs as well as potatoes and a couple dozen clams. To these will be added the lobsters Stephan and Lucinda are bringing, Georges having given them the money for the lobsters in the morning. They're engaged in lively conversation, frequently punctuated with laughter, while tending to their tasks.

William and Genevieve, hearing the merriment in the kitchen, exchange looks that say they'd like to be a part of it. "It's been over a day now that I've been stuck with this," she says, pointing at her stomach, "and you know what? I'm feeling much better—*much*! The doctor said the danger wasn't in being active, but in being a slug, right? If a guy can have a hernia operation in the morning and kick balls in the afternoon, I can help with dinner."

"Then let's go," he says, rising from the edge of the bed and extending his hand to her.

"As I said, sweetie, I'm not a cripple," she smiles, ignoring his hand and climbing from the bed on her own.

"What took you so long?" Georges says matter-of-factly, betraying no surprise whatsoever, when William and Genevieve appear at the threshold of the kitchen. "Gen, you can help the girls chop—get a knife. Bill, why don't you peel the potatoes? The peeler's beside them."

"I don't think it took us very long, dad!" Genevieve says, poking him as she extracts a knife from a drawer. "And don't think it's lost on me why you told me to grab a knife! I know you're testing me!" Then, seating herself at the empty chair at the table, she begins carving a green pepper.

"I didn't think I'd slip that by you," laughs Georges. "The point is you're surrounded by reminders of the attack that mustn't be allowed to trigger negative reactions. Never forget that the said reminders, whether they be knives or something else, are only objects; and that the location of the assault in your living room, as well as the sidewalk where the assailant met his end, are only places. Objects and places are neither alive nor malicious—it's only mistaken human perception that grants them such qualities."

"Georges," says Catherine, tugging at his sleeve. "Weren't we through with this for today?"

"I just want to be sure Gen's on the path to letting go of the shock," he answers. "Am I wrong to bring it up again? Better now than later—psychic tumors, the merest chance of them, must be acted upon quickly, as with physical ones. Bill, take a look at your fiancée—chopping away with a knife that's identical to the one she was cut with. That's what's known as strength and fortitude."

"Georges!" cries Catherine.

"Cathy," he responds, holding up his hands in a mitigating gesture. "If it's overkill, so much the better—that'll mean they don't need any of this." Then, addressing William and Genevieve, "The *only* thing that matters is the love you bear one another. That alone is what you rely upon to emerge from this business happy, with heads held high! Love and life soldiers on! All else is an illusion!"

"I think we know that, dad," Genevieve says. "Didn't we agree that Bill and I will be handling this from now on? Maybe I'll break down and cry again, maybe I won't; maybe a nasty flashback knocks me to my knees, maybe they're powerless from now on: either way, Bill's with me and we're going to be just fine!"

"I know that, sweetheart," Georges smiles, "so I'm done. You're both now officially released by Dr. Dad. No more sessions unless you request them, and by no means be ashamed to request them. Never hesitate to call. Now come here, lovebug!" he concludes, opening his arms.

Beaming with delight, Genevieve rises from her chair, albeit gingerly, and crosses the kitchen to her father. "I love you dad!" she cries as he enfolds her in his arms.

CHAPTER 31

At the approach of 6:30 PM Stephan, Lucinda, Jean-Marc and Carole arrive with sixteen lobsters. The lobsters are promptly divided between the two baking trays and placed in the oven. That done, Catherine begins preparing the dipping sauce—butter, chopped garlic, lemon and lime juice, and assorted herbs—for the lobster.

In the meantime, the others are readying the living room for their feast. It's been decided that, rather than dividing people between the dining table and sofas and floor, everyone will sit on the floor. Newspaper's spread upon the hardwood and places are set in a circle, each with a pillow for a seat. An empty tub, for the lobster scraps and other trash, is placed in the center along with a vase of long-stemmed white roses and four bottles of chardonnay. The coffee table, still in the bedroom, is moved back to its place in front of the largest sofa. Upon the coffee table are placed the two bowls of salad, a loaf of sourdough bread, a wheel of brie, and vinaigrette.

By 8:00 PM all are seated on the floor with a plate of lobster, clams, corn on the cob, and potatoes before them on a rose print placemat. In addition, each have a salad bowl, a dish for the butter dipping sauce, a finger bowl with a lime wedge impaled on its edge, a set of silverware, lobster crackers and picks, white linen napkins in brass rings, and gold-trimmed wine glasses. Genevieve, eschewing the bed table that's been set up for her on the couch—William was to sit beside her with his plate in his lap—has joined the others on the floor. "I'm only aware of a little tightness down here," she says, referring to the sutures on her stomach. "It smarts a bit if I laugh too hard, but doesn't mean I don't want people laughing. Laugh away, I'll gladly take my lumps. I won't go against the doctor's advice and overpamper myself. I have no intention of succumbing to *invalid syndrome*. If he was here, I'd want him to be proud of me."

"We're all proud of you," William says, "but there's no reason for you to be unnecessarily uncomfortable. I'm sure the doctor wouldn't begrudge you a seat on the couch. Just say the word and we're there."

"I won't be saying that word, sweetie, because sitting on the couch would mean being a little bit apart from this comfort and joy. As positive feelings greatly contribute to healing, being in the middle of the bunch is a better cure." She leans her head on his shoulder.

"You're right about that, honey," he responds, running his fingers through her hair. "It's *very* cozy here! And I know I sound touristy, but I don't care—I'm still tickled to death at your way of doing things. Dinner effortlessly becomes a special ritual, whether it be on newspaper on the floor or in a park after midnight. Every detail's always in place, done without a second thought—roses in a beautiful vase, napkin rings, finger bowls. Your refinement suggests permanency, and seems to freeze time. Not to mention that the food's always as succulent as it is healthy. Very comforting, indeed!"

"What?" cries Jean-Marc, grinning. "You're still acting as if you're in a museum, on the outside looking in, after getting hitched to a Parisian doll? After being swept into local events, triumphing in conflict? OK, OK," he pauses for a moment, acknowledging the mild looks of warning being darted at him by everyone not named

William and Genevieve. "But you know what I mean! You're engaged to the finest that Paris, and therefore the world, has to offer so I'd think you'd start acting like it! A vase of flowers, finger bowls... It's our way, no big deal! Some would say we waste too much time with details! I don't agree, because they've been part and parcel of my life since birth and are—yes, I'll admit it—*comforting*! A way of making our special moments, shared in good comradeship, more memorable! But they're nothing to *gush* over! How long is it going to take for you to casually slip into our way of life, stop raving about it? Not that you've been here long, but... Damn, Bill! After what you've been through, I'd think you'd be assimilated!"

"My," says Carole, "what pearls of wisdom have tripped off your tongue! So profound were they, I'm still not sure which side you're arguing from! You mock Bill for admiring our manners, then say you like them as well! You chide him for not having adjusted yet, then acknowledge he's barely been here!"

"Jean-Marc," Genevieve says, "Bill's only been here since Friday! Let's see you go to New York and be assimilated in four days!"

"I don't think you're going to win this one," Stephan laughs, addressing Jean-Marc.

"No, he's not!" Genevieve laughs; but then she's immediately touching her stomach. "Ow! As I said, it only hurts when..."

"Are you..." William begins.

"Fine, sweetie," she resumes. "Only a slight twinge, gone now, all's well. But, as I was about to say... If my darling wants to *gush* over our beautiful dinner, then you let him, Jean-Marc! Bill, if the roses and fingers bowls and napkin rings please you, then by all means allow them to do so and don't let a cynic derail your joy! Rather, my sass-mouthed friend *(She points at Jean-Marc.)* ought to be ashamed of himself, for not enjoying his culture through your eyes! I, for one, find your wonder wonderfully refreshing!"

"I only meant that I'm surprised he's still analyzing things when he's already one of us," protests Jean-Marc. "We've welcomed him to our way of life with open arms, so I'd think he'd surrender to it instead of admiring from afar! You in particular, Gen, have given him the go-ahead to be as Parisian as he wants to be! Bill, you ought to allow yourself to be happy, instead of wondering why you are!"

"What?" William cries. "I'm not happy now? Are you nuts?"

"You know what I mean!"

"Sure," William says, raising his glass to Jean-Marc, "I'm a New Yorker who, by the infinite grace of God, is going to be allowed to be a Parisian, and for some peculiar reason you think I ought to—or that it's actually possible for me to—transition immediately! You're underestimating the amount of awe I feel, the magnitude of my gratitude! I'm still pinching myself every second, so to speak, to confirm it's not a dream! Yeah, I'm gushing, all right! And I don't care how naive and silly my words sound, because it means life's sweet! Sweetness of life's worth all the cleverness ever spoken and, if you want to laugh at me, go right ahead! Life's sweet, very sweet, and here's my life!" he concludes, kissing Genevieve.

"Bravo!" Jean-Marc shouts, clapping. "I avow myself beaten and, given the result, I know I didn't want to win!"

"That's our new couple working together," laughs Stephan. "Arguing with one is the same as arguing with two! Everyone, a toast to our happy couple! *(Glasses are raised.)* To Bill and Gen's engagement!" The others clink their glasses together and drink.

"Our turn," Georges says. "From a mother and father to their daughter and son: may our united families grow and prosper, in love and honor and respect and joy. May your journey through life be enriched by your union, and heaven's bounty be apparent during every moment you share. Above all, may you be ever more joyful as the years fly by!" Again, everyone clinks their glasses and drinks.

"So sweet!" Genevieve says, blowing kisses around the circle; then, addressing William while gazing out the window at the cross of Sainte-Élisabeth, flaring in the light of the setting sun, "Speaking of our union, honey, guess where I'd like to have our wedding ceremony?"

"Hmm, let's see...that's a tough one," he answers, following her gaze to the cross. "In Sainte-Élisabeth?"

"Smart man," she smiles. "The church and legend of Sainte-Élisabeth have brightened my days for two years, so there's no place I'd rather have our wedding ceremony. The gentle princess Élisabeth, known for founding hospitals and miracles of healing. And guess what? Élisabeth's the patron saint of young brides!"

"Really?"

"Yes, darling. We became engaged at the doorstep of the patron saint of brides! Is that a favorable omen, or what? As for our wedding..."

"Entirely up to you, honey. I'm ready to get married tomorrow."

"As am I, my dear. But I have friends and relatives who'd be upset if we went ahead without them. Sorry to say, I've been raised to play to a large gathering—it's expected of me. Actually, strike that, I'm not sorry at all: it's with great pride that I shall become your bride in front of a large audience. I wouldn't want it any other way."

"Nor would I, sweetheart, now that you've spelled it out. Not to mention that my parents would never forgive me if they weren't a part of it. It's with great pride that I shall show off my radiant bride, the larger the crowd the better. I'll savor every second of our marriage in Sainte-Élisabeth."

"Our marriage *ceremony* will be in Sainte-Élisabeth," she clarifies. "Our actual marriage will be—here's another cultural difference for you—conducted in the town hall by a representative of the mayor of Paris."

"Huh?"

"Laïcité, my dear," she continues. "The separation of church and state is official policy in France, and marriage falls under the state's authority. Religious ceremonies are meaningless in the eyes of French law, only civil ones count. So we'll be at the town hall first, to get legally married, then at Sainte-Élisabeth to get religiously and dramatically married. We'll have *two* weddings!"

"Only makes it more exotic," William laughs. "With all due respect, Jean-Marc, it's another reason for me to be tickled to death! It's fun to be surrounded by new, and unexpected, customs!"

"Some people would say annoying customs," Jean-Marc says. "Here's something else: you can't get legally married outside of Paris—not that it's a problem in your case—because at least one person must reside in the town where the marriage takes place. Add that needless bit of bureaucracy to your exotica!"

"Shush, you!" Genevieve says; then, turning to William, "As to when, I'd say late September or early October.

"Not in the summer?"

"A lot of people leave town for the summer, sweetie. We wouldn't have the full turn-out we deserve."

"Right, silly me."

"But I appreciate your eagerness, honey. Believe me, I share it, and then some."

"Good," Georges cuts in, "I'll take care of the arrangements. Bill, I trust early autumn will be acceptable to your parents?"

"Any date will be acceptable to them, especially my mother," William smiles. "And come to think of it... Gen, how do you feel about flying stateside next week to meet them?"

"Try to tie me down!" Genevieve exclaims with a sudden movement, immediately wincing slightly and gently touching her stomach. "Owie! I keep forgetting!"

"Careful, honey," William says, placing a hand on her shoulder. "We don't want you hurting, and we want you healing on schedule."

"I'm fine, sweetie, don't worry. As I said, there's a bit of tightness in my tummy, but it's not intrusive. Or maybe I should say it's not intrusive enough. Because I'm starting to forget about it, and so I laugh or twist a little too abruptly, and there's some smarting. In fact, it's amazing, the difference between yesterday and today. I don't feel I'm tempting fate by saying I'm well on the mend. After all, the doctor *did* stitch me to perfection! As for flying stateside, how about next Tuesday?"

"Maybe I shouldn't have said next week," he says. "There's no reason to rush the trip, considering..."

"Don't worry about me, darling," she cuts him off. "Next Tuesday won't be too soon, *considering* that I could take the trip tomorrow! The sutures come out on Monday, then I'm officially—signed and sealed by the good doctor—a free woman! Free to fly to America and meet your parents!"

"*Our* parents," he smiles.

"Of course, *our* parents. I can't wait to meet my new mom and dad."

"I'll make the reservations, then."

"Don't concern yourself," says Georges, winking. "I've got it. Company account, secretary will handle it. It's on me."

"Thanks, dad," Genevieve says before William can protest. "So nice, we appreciate it."

"Thanks Georges," William says. "Very nice of you."

"My pleasure."

"And I hope you know you're *required* to stay put at my place," Stephan says, addressing Christina and Pascale. "Bill may have gotten you in the door, but we're family now. That is, assuming you're not also flying back to America."

"So nice," Christina says. "Thank you, Steph! Pas and I aren't flying out before our time's up! Not a chance of that!"

"Steph, you're an absolute sweetheart," Pascale says. "As Chrissy said, we want our full six weeks of Paris, and thanks so much."

"Maybe I ought to start shopping around for a Frenchman?" Christina laughs. "That way, I'll have a lifetime in Paris option too!"

"Just keep attending Steph's parties, it'll happen," Lucinda says.

"And they'll be attending them," Stephan says. "They won't have a choice!"

"We're not in Paris to sleep!" adds Pascale.

Suffice to say that lively conversation continues throughout the meal; that, after the remaining lobsters are split in half and portioned out and consumed, the men volunteer for cleanup duty and carry the dishes to the kitchen, as well as dispose of the newspaper; that, far from being thought of as a chore, cleanup duty's transformed into a raucous assembly line game of washing, drying, and stacking that lasts less than half an hour. In the meantime, the women begin playing cards, either gin or double solitaire, on the floor. Then Claire and several others, secretly alerted by Carole (who's called from the bathroom) that now's a good time, stop by bearing gifts and cards. Only Claire stays on, however: those that accompanied her, although welcome to stay, perceive the intimate nature of the gathering and don't wish to be in the way, they not being of the, shall we say, *inner* inner circle. Among the gifts is a pitcher of coconut water and container of coconut meat, recently extracted from fresh coconuts and meant to be consumed immediately. Everyone partakes of the coconut as the card games and conversation continue.

"I hate to exercise the rights of an injured person and shoo everyone out the door," Genevieve announces at the approach of midnight, "but I'm feeling a bit tired and would like to turn in soon."

"Sure," her father says, glancing at her with amusement.

"Right, dad, I can't fool you—that's not the real reason. The real reason's that I *love* exercising the rights of a newly engaged girl and would like to be alone with my fiancé!"

"Are you sure you don't want Chrissy and I to stay?" asks Pascale. "We'll be more than happy to sleep on the sofa bed."

"Absolutely," affirms Christina. "We'll be inconspicuous, you'll have your room to yourselves."

"Thank you," Genevieve says, clasping each by the hand, "but it's not necessary. I'm fine and would like to enjoy what healthy people enjoy: privacy."

"Of course you know our phones will be turned on all night," Carole says. "There not a one of us who won't come running the second you ask."

"I know that, sweetie, and it's greatly appreciated—I'm blessed with the best friends on earth. But I don't plan on calling. The doctor told me not to afraid to have faith in the power of the body to heal and, far from being afraid of it, I'm feeling it happen. I believe it wholeheartedly and am being proven right. So I'd like to reap the rewards of healing and be alone with Bill."

"We're out the door," Georges says with the easy authority that comes natural to him, making a sweeping gesture towards the exit. "We'll expect you two, and anyone else who cares to join us, for dinner tomorrow night."

"Absolutely," Genevieve says; then, addressing the others, "I'd love to see you at dinner."

"Of course," Carole says, speaking for herself and Jean-Marc. Christina, Pascale, Stephan, Lucinda, and Claire also happily accept the invitation.

Following farewell kisses and embraces, everyone files onto the stairs, where Georges says he'll be driving them home, if they don't mind being squashed like sardines in his car. William and Genevieve, upon closing the front door, find themselves alone for the first time since Monday morning.

CHAPTER 32

William couldn't be happier as he and Genevieve stroll from the front door back to the living room; but then he starts, experiences an inner jab, at the sight of the bare hardwood floor: his thoughts unexpectedly whip back to the last time they were alone there, the agonizing wait for the ambulance to arrive.

"I know, sweetie," she says, seeing his thoughts on his face, "it's hitting me too. I glanced towards the bedroom and my nerves jumped, as if half expecting that *thing* to come out of there again, and... But you know what? Something beautiful is hitting me as well, and that's our good fortune—the miracle of our love."

"Our paradise is the foremost thing on my mind, believe me," he says, stepping inside her arms and grasping her gently. "We'll chase the ghosts away together, my dear." As he joins his lips to hers he slides his fingers through the waves of her hair—her hair lightly brushes against and tickles his face as the room wafts in and out of his awareness. Soft shivers engulf her body and are soon reverberating within him—racing up and down his spine, flaring in his nerves. Every second of their embrace and kiss suggests a small infinity: it's as if William's about to step outside of time. Their kiss is an emotional womb—soothing mood-caress, nourishing infusion of energy—and he's being whirled into a place where his feelings effortlessly rearrange themselves in order of priority. An overwhelming sense of security sweeps over him: he realizes there's no conflict that he and Genevieve can't overcome with their united wills.

Following a signal between them that neither would be able to pinpoint or explain, they step apart and are holding hands, gazing at one another in rapt appreciation. "I love you *so* much!" he says, squeezing her hands.

"And I love you too *so* much!" she responds, her eyes intensifying with silver light, at once trembly and insistent.

"More, sweetheart," he says, wrapping his arms about her and slipping his hands into her hair again—joining his lips to hers again—tasting of the sweet suspension of time as the room whirls out of focus again. Then he's softly caressing her cheeks as they continue to kiss; and she's returning the gesture, stroking sparkles into his neck and left cheek and forehead, staying clear of the bruise on the right side of his face.

"We'll be together from now on with no interference," he says when they step apart again. "We thought so twice before but failed to account for Bap weaving his sickness into our lives. What I mean is that as long as he was out there our lives didn't fully belong to us, through no fault of our own. But now our lives *do* belong to us, and that's not going to change! Sorry...maybe I shouldn't have brought Bap back into the picture."

"Honey," she says, seizing his hands, "as dad said, we absolutely cannot keep things bottled up. If Bap must be mentioned for awhile, so be it. Far better that than to have him lingering on the tips of our tongues, accumulating in our thoughts, and infecting our feelings. And, as I said, he isn't absent from my thoughts, either: I grew up with him, and he came out of the bedroom with a knife!"

"OK, then, Bap's not out of our systems yet," he says, caressing her fingers. "I was right to bring him up after all. He stole our beautiful Monday morning from us, plunged us headlong into terror and stress, and we haven't had to deal with it alone and we ought to. What I mean is that we're without our buffer zone of friends, so let's earn our lasting peace together. It's our first time alone since our ordeal, so let's come to terms with being alone and celebrate being alone and reap the benefits of being alone! Let's celebrate our lasting union by annihilating the recollections of Bap!"

"Absolutely!" she says heatedly. "Why should Bap be mentioned for awhile? I was wrong when I said that. We're together now and we're strong, so there's no reason for us not to succeed in vanquishing the flashbacks! I don't want to be saying stuff like it's our second or third time alone since the attack! I want our first time alone to be the end of Bap! I'm sick of Bap seeking to hijack our feelings, making us flinch at the sight of our own bedroom! Sick of it, and..."

"Why not recreate Monday morning?" William breaks in, freeing one his hands from hers and gesturing at the balcony. "Recreate how it was after we arrived from Steph's and had no idea the *thing* was here? We can emotionally revise Monday morning, stamp the present upon it—stamp our love and our engagement and our bright future upon it once and for all! So what if we shudder a bit? We'll confront those shudders and wash them away for good! I say we do it, I have implicit faith in you."

"Yes!" she says without hesitation, seizing his free hand again and squeezing tight. "Wonderful idea, honey! Let's finish dad's work here and now! Enough of Bap's revisitations, he needs to be buried and forgotten forever! How do we begin?"

"I say we start outside on the sidewalk, so it's like we just climbed out of the cab. Wait, maybe you..."

"Maybe I can't handle it, because of *this*?" she completes his sentence, glancing at her stomach. "Not so, honey, don't concern yourself on that score! As I keep saying, I'm already *so* much better, healing up real quick! We're going to the sidewalk, OK?"

"OK, Gen," he says, wrapping an arm around her waist. "Onto the sidewalk, then we come back here. You go to the balcony windows, as you did on Monday, and open them—so beautiful, that gesture—and turn towards me..."

"Let's go!" she smiles, pulling him towards the door. "We'll go back to Monday morning, all right, and reclaim it for ourselves forever!"

Suffice to say our couple are soon on the sidewalk; that Genevieve, recalling how she raised one of her legs behind her on Monday morning, does so again; that William, as captivated by the gesture as he was the first time, again delights in lauding her grace and beauty; that, as they climb the stairs to her apartment, the full force of the joy they felt on that morning returns to them when they remember throwing his suitcases up the stairs, tickling each other, laughing uncontrollably.

Needless to say the tickling and laughter aren't repeated on account of Genevieve's wound; but they're smiling from ear to ear, every bit as dizzy with anticipation as they were on Monday, when they reenter the apartment and advance to the living room.

"I remember doing this!" she says, beaming with delight. She flings her hair back, rolls her tongue about her lips, flicks the hem of her dress up and down.

"And then, when I was about to grab you, you scampered to the windows with the cutest angelic tease-look on your face and pulled them open. I remember that crystal clear—what you were wearing, the glow of your skin, the aura of energy that surrounded you. The very air was alive and crackling, my dear!"

"I remember it crystal clear too, sweetie! Your stance, the love in your eyes, how fresh and alert you were—especially, how your eyes were touching me from the inside out! I remember the electricity leaping between us when I came over here and flung these doors wide, like this, and the breeze and rain-mist washed over me, and I turned towards you again with no intention of scampering away a second time!"

"Yeah, it was crystal clear that tease-time, brief as it was, was over! I was about to gather my prize—you were so stunning it was bending the air! Dear, that's when... No, forget that! We're not going in that direction! *(He steps to her, wraps his arms around her.)* What matters, darling, is that the emotions are the same and we're back at Monday morning after arriving from Steph's! I'll never forget how you looked then, and I'll never forget how you look *now*! I love you Genevieve!"

"And I love you, William! I love you so much it's a storm—a peace-dispensing storm!" she says, bringing her lips to his.

After kissing for close to five minutes, they pause to gaze in joy at one another while softly caressing each other's faces. William's the first to speak. "Let's be sure of our kill, honey," he smiles. "This is Monday morning again and it's also Wednesday morning now, and *all* morning's are going to belong to us, on our own terms, from now on! We're going to kill off bad associations for good, so it's only happiness we feel when we're in this room!"

"You bet we are, sweetie," she says, bringing her lips to his again.

After at least another ten minutes of unbroken kissing—soft, lingering, hungry, blissful kissing—they smilingly step apart. Gently tilting her head towards the couch, Genevieve asks William with her eyes if he'd like to sit there. "By all means, love of my life," he answers aloud, whereupon they step to the couch arm in arm, seat themselves, and cuddle.

"So that's how couples fight back, and *win*!" William says a couple minutes later, raising a fist to the ceiling. "No monster came out of the bedroom, and *never* will again! It's you and I who're here as we're meant to be, with our love and lives before us! In place of monsters is peace and privacy, the God given right to be *us*!"

"I mean, it's unbelievable!" she says, clutching his arm as she turns to him with fire in her eyes. "As long as Bap was alive every moment we spent together was borrowed time: is that insanity, or what? And now that he's gone... Any threat to a couple's right to love, of course they want it gone; and if that threat won't gone except by dying, then... It was his choice, and I'll—we'll—shed no tears!"

"Of course not! Gen, I hope you're not..."

"Feeling guilty? No, I'm not! I'm only airing it, and hopefully for good! I conjured up that phantom so I can send it to wherever phantoms go to die! Why feel guilty for being overjoyed, alone at last in peace and security and knowing it will last, with my wonderful man? The not shedding tears stuff popped out because I want

Bap's memory extinguished! I want him gone into oblivion, all his ties to my memories dissolved, and... But why am I getting worked up? That's not how to get him to disappear! I want to be indifferent! As dad said, ghosts perish when we ignore them!"

"Honey, you get as worked up as you need to," he says, caressing the backs of her hands. "Getting worked up is often very beneficial, a purge. The storm-waves of emotion expend themselves, then fall into calm water—flatten out. Indifference is sometimes only possible after an outburst. The outburst swings back on itself, becomes annoyed at its cause: the waste of time and energy is suddenly crystal clear, and liberating indifference follows."

"Thank you, sweetie, you're so right! You always turn negatives into positives, which is one of the many reasons I love you—reasons I can't begin to count!" She nestles her head against his chest.

"Always remember that I'm your bottomless well into which you're to pour all that bothers you," he says, caressing her temples. "I'll always treasure your confidences, receive them as precious gifts, because they'll be a measure of our faith in one another, the depth of our affection. Never hold anything back because you deem it unpleasant: whatever lingers in you also lingers in me; the well-being of one of us is the gauge of the well-being of both of us, because we're inseparable. And, honey, I'm explaining this to myself as much as to you—I've never experienced love like ours before. Until meeting you I always felt there were places inside me that no amount of confiding could reach, matters I had no choice but to resolve alone."

"That's because you were alone," she says, raising her head and smiling into his eyes. "You're not alone now—you'll never be stuck with resolving matters alone again. A good wife doesn't allow that to happen. You can discuss anything with me, I'm a part of you, that's the miracle of love—two merged personalities, a single bottomless well. But now I'm echoing you, aren't I?"

"As wonderful an echo as any man could hope to have," he says, lightly grazing her lips with his. "And now I need to follow my own advice, unfortunately—I didn't want to bring this up, but it's best I do. The reason I flinched when we came in here after saying our good nights. It's funny how I didn't think about it during dinner, when we were on the very same floor. But, then again, there were so many good things happening—our wedding plans and flight to the states." He leans towards her to kiss her.

"Honey, go ahead and say it," she says, gently placing her fingers on his forehead. "Please follow your own advice."

"OK, Gen, here it is: I've never felt more helpless in my life than when I was kneeling beside you, listening to the woman on the phone while doing my best to tend to your wound—those awful slow-motion moments when I wasn't able to be sure I was helping. I put my terror on hold, to keep it from getting in the way, but it was definitely there. I'm bothered by the thought that it was only by luck that I did the right things. My whole life was at stake and I could've let it slip away. That's what troubles me more than anything else."

"Helpless?" she cries with unconcealed incredulity, turning completely towards him and grasping him firmly by the shoulders while looking at him very seriously. "You were the opposite of helpless! Listen to me: as I said during dad's probing of us it's the attack itself that's bothered me—I wasn't spinning things when I said I don't feel fearful when I think about being injured with you beside me. Your voice was flowing over me, darling, and you were gently and efficiently tending to business—your voice was so soothing, your touch was so stabilizing. Your expression I recall as being very intent, deeply focused, and that's comforting as well. And love was shining in your eyes—shining through our troubles, steady and clear! Yes, sweetie, it was! Bill, that's one recollection I'll never fear, and that's not wishful thinking talking—that's my confidence in you talking, the fact I had no doubt—that's right, dear, *no doubt*—that I was in good hands and safe. I won't call it a beautiful memory, but aspects of it are beautiful—the confidence I feel, safety I feel, when bringing it to mind are beautiful. That's something you need to remember when it returns to you. Again, rest assured that you were *not* helpless! That's an unkind trick of your imagination! You were praised by the doctor—everyone knows you did all that you could and did it well! Please, I don't want to hear you say you were helpless again! Talk about those moments by all means if you wish, but don't spin things against yourself, especially because it's a lie! The truth is...I won't repeat myself. You *know*, don't you?"

"I know it when you explain it," he answers, kissing her cheek. "And you're right: I need to let that go. An aftertaste of helplessness and fear when you're sitting here safe beside me, well on the mend, is nuts! Pointless mind games that..."

"All has turned out well, sweetie, that's the bottom line," she cuts in. "That's what you focus on! It's turned out heavenly, you know it and I know it and our parents and friends know it! Darling, ours is a fairytale with a happy ending! OK, I just wanted that out there, I didn't mean to interrupt. I'm glad you've told me what you have, Bill, and anything else that needs to be said, you say it."

"I'm done with it, honey. I just want to live our fairytale, reap the rewards of our love. I just want to do you proud."

"You do me proud by simply breathing, by looking at me—I live in your gaze."

"As I do in yours," he says, wrapping his arm about her as she rests her head on his shoulder. They sit side by side for nearly half an hour, silently savoring their mutual bedazzlement.

Later on, when they remove the dressing from Genevieve's wound and she's gazing upon it for the second time, she suffers no flashback attack—her attention's solely focused upon washing it and applying a new dressing. Shortly after 2:00 AM they climb into bed, where they eagerly resume their demonstrations of affection.

CHAPTER 33

"Good morning, dearest fiancé," Genevieve says when they stir in bed on Wednesday as noon approaches. "I knew it would be heaven on earth to wake up on our first morning all by ourselves as an engaged couple."

"Heaven doesn't begin to describe it," William says, thrilling to the touch of her lips as he leans across her and kisses her. His eyes spin between her face and the waves of her hair and the sun streaming through the aquamarine curtains, bathing all in blue light.

"I can already tell I'm even better," she says after they finish kissing. "The doctor told me I'd heal fast, and he was right! Look!" She slides to the edge of the bed and pivots her feet to the floor in a single flowing movement.

"I'd be very surprised if you weren't moving around like a feisty cat. After all, you've had two whole days!"

"But what about your face, honey?" she asks, jumping to her feet. "Owie!" she yelps, wincing and freezing. But then she's immediately annoyed at the interruption and repeats the movement—

not quickly, but faithfully. Then she begins slowly leaning from side to side at her waist.

"Gen, healing's one thing, but pushing it's another. I didn't mean to imply you should be jumping around, it's no small thing having a cut like yours. Forget what I said about cavorting like a cat, it was irresponsible. I shouldn't have joked about the two days."

"Irresponsible?" she responds, widening her eyes as she continues to stretch. "I think I know when my man's teasing me—teasing me in a positive way. You're only encouraging me to do what the doctor said, not be afraid to move. I need to refamiliarize myself with the effected muscular area, reclaim it as a comfort zone. My tummy muscles need to reacquire their flexibility, and a pinch now and then's only to be expected."

"Agreed," he says, standing to take her in his arms. "But please no more sudden jumps. We're going to be active today, that's important, but we're not going to leap about, OK?"

"OK, honey. But enough of me. How's your face? The bruise is receding."

"The tightness is almost gone, no more twitches of discomfort," he says, making a dismissive gesture. "Before long, I'll only know it's there when I look in the mirror."

"Well, don't be like me and forget about it too much," she smiles, tapping his shoulder. "You'll make an impulsive movement and get a jolt!"

"Gen, that's not funny—don't minimize the seriousness of your injury, we still need to monitor it. And there's no comparison between your injury and my face, don't think that for a second. It's only a bruise on my face, nothing's punctured, it's not a big deal. We're not going to worry about me, OK?"

"But I have the last say in that, sweetie," she says, seizing his hand and leading him into the living room. "I haven't forgotten what you said last night, when you twisted your beautiful behavior—your flawless rescuing of me—against yourself, and spoke of feeling helpless. Does that need to be addressed again? Do you want me to lie on the floor? We could, and maybe should, reenact that. We only reenacted the moments before the attack—that's right, *the attack*: I can say those words without flinching, they no longer have a nasty hold on me. I'm going to lie on the floor, OK?" They're standing at the place where the assault occurred.

"Gen, it's not needed," he says. "There's already a world of difference between this morning and last night. Last night we found ourselves without our buffer zone of friends and family for the first time, and handled it—faced off with being alone, celebrated being alone. I've already made an adjustment, and so have you: the attack no longer frightens you, and those moments of looking after you no longer frighten me. How is it that we've been cured so quickly? All I can say is that it's miraculous how one's deep quiet places, secret emotional reserves, rise to the surface during sleep and wash one free of bad associations and attendant trepidation. And I'm sure our first truly secure night alone together had a great deal to do with it. We awakened entwined—so magical's your embrace, so delightful it is to open my eyes and see and feel you wrapped around me. It's not farfetched to say our physical closeness mirrored our psychic closeness as we slept: our energy was meshing under the surface, washing away the residue of inner shocks, freeing us from flashback attacks. I *know* it's true!"

"You bet it is, darling," she smiles, wrapping her arms around his neck. "Our wounds will heal—your face will clear, my tummy will lose its scar—and be forgotten. Likewise our psyches are healing, and the inner... I was about to say inner *shocks*, but that's granting them too much power—they're already going going gone! You're so right! A night of sleeping with you is the most miraculous medicine on earth! Yes, *finally* we've had our first night alone together in safety, knowing the one opposition to our well-being's gone, so of course we're feeling pristine inside! My uneasiness of yesterday morning's already a phantom-thing, as if felt by a different Genevieve! And I'll prove it! I'll lie right here, at the exact spot of the attack, and curl up on my side! I'm not afraid, and know you aren't either!"

"But it's not necessary, honey," he says as she slips to the floor and assumes the fetal position she was in following the assault.

"I'm sure it isn't, but..."

"The aftershocks are *so* over, sweetheart!" he breaks in, his voice ringing with joy. "This is *our* room for sure! *Our* home! *Our* life! The only thing on my mind is how beautiful you are! The lines of your body are sheer poetry, and the light's dancing on you! I'm going to dance on you!"

William joins Genevieve on the floor and, far from harking back to the emergency of Monday morning, he's solely engrossed in enjoying her company. At the end of their intimate interval, however, he says, "Dearest, you asked me if my unease of last night needed to be addressed again and now I ask you the same. What crosses your mind when you glance at our bedroom? Do you still see the monster there?"

"No, my dear, I don't," she smiles, rising to her knees. "There are no more monsters, it's over and done with. We can love to our heart's content, no monsters will be emerging from our bedroom! As you said, this is *our* home! *Ours!* There's no place in it for ghosts! Now what do you say: how about a nice breakfast of salmon and eggs?"

"Sounds good to me," he laughs, running his hand up and down her back as she stretches in response.

Once they're in the kitchen, William sets the table and prepares the broiling tray for the salmon fillets, Genevieve instructing him what herbs and spices to add as she busies herself with poaching eggs. Inside of forty minutes they're seated across from one another at the table with plates of salmon and eggs before them. The eggs are resting on a smear of cream cheese with fresh basil, slivers of leeks, and capers added; sprigs of parsley and cilantro garnish the whole.

For a few moments William, as it were, steps outside of himself to relish the sight of the sunlight streaming through the rose-print curtains, splashing Genevieve's silver silk nightgown with streaks of carmine and pink—the nightgown that's clinging to and highlighting the symmetry of her body, adding radiance to her face. Then he catches himself saying, "Are we going to mention this is our first breakfast alone since Sunday, when Bap smacked me outside? No, we're not! Actually, what I mean is that this is the first and last mention—a half-mention! And, OK, maybe I shouldn't have mentioned it at all; but I just want to further confirm our victory—confirm there's no trepidation hovering in the background."

"Certainly not," she says, capturing one of his legs between her ankles under the table. "This morning belongs to us alone. That's a given from now on, no more sickies waiting with delusions outside! No more hovering phantom-things!"

"Certainly not," he says, caressing her shins with the toes of his non-captured foot.

"Breakfast is served, you know," she smiles. "Why don't you try your eggs?"

"My fiancée's more beautiful than a flower, so the eggs are of secondary consideration," he says, brushing a stray tendril of hair from her face.

"Oh!" she exclaims, a charming look of mild panic on her face. "I forgot to put flowers on the table!"

"Ha ha! Is forgetting flowers a high crime in France? Let me assure you they're not needed. As I said, *you're* the flower!"

"I'll be right back," she says, rising and going into the living room. Upon returning with some roses that she's plucked from the large vase on the coffee table, she places them in a small vase, fills it with water, and sets it in the center of the table. "There," she giggles, "now I can eat!"

"Come here, dollface," he says, leaning across the table to kiss her.

The salmon and eggs are followed by a salad of chopped tomatoes, avocados, and green peppers; for dessert it's a bowl of kefir with blueberries. After their meal they repair to the living room for tea and cuddles on the couch. Early evening arrives in a flash.

Then, with William in attendance, it's Genevieve's first shower since Sunday, she having restricted herself to washings of her face and extremities the day before. She's healing remarkably well, with no complications, and, following the shower, changes the dressing on her wound quite matter-of-factly. Later on, when she emerges from the bedroom (William, already dressed, is waiting in the living room), she's seen to be wearing a light green sleeveless halter neck dress with a wisp of a white scarf tied about her upper right arm, white stockings, and silver heels. Her only jewelry is her engagement ring and engagement bracelet: perhaps the reader will recall that the latter is the gold chain bracelet which her original, stand-in, engagement ring (William's old key ring) has been placed upon.

"How am I assembled?" she asks, turning about.

"Assembled?" he laughs, rising from the couch to embrace her. "That's a dry way of describing an immaculate vision! Count on a French girl to be the definition of elegance, and say she's assembled!"

"It's nothing," she says, flicking her hair back and shaking it from side to side.

"I beg to emphatically differ, sweetheart," he says, running a hand through her hair, "You're more flawless than the diamonds on the ring and I can't wait to show you off in the streets."

"Nor I you," she says, caressing his neck. "Shall we go?"

CHAPTER 34

William and Genevieve emerge from the Raspail metro station shortly after 7:00 PM, where Christina, Pascale, Stephan, Lucinda, Jean-Marc, Carole, and Claire are waiting for them, they having arranged the meeting earlier in the day.

"Genevie," says Carole as they exchange greeting-kisses, "it's refreshing to see you so...so refreshed! You look like you're ready to take three of my classes in a row!"

"There's positivity in my life to burn," Genevieve smiles, gesturing at William before exchanging kisses with the others.

"And the ghosts?" Christina asks, recalling the conversation of the previous afternoon. "Sorry, I'm just checking."

"Not to worry, Chrissy," William says. "We've vanquished the ghosts, a night together did that. There's so little room for ghosts in our lives we can mention them now and laugh!"

"No surprise there," Stephan says. "You're a couple that so blatantly belongs together and are invincible together it's obvious at first sight from halfway down the block! Of course you've already vanquished..."

"All we ask," Genevieve cuts in, "is that ghosts not be alluded to again. Not because we're afraid them, but because we have better things to think about. Ghosts are *boring*!"

"We're past our psychic healing phase," William says, "or at least the public version of it, and good riddance! As for bodily healing, that's coming along nicely too—which doesn't mean we're going to expect Gen to do a cartwheel today."

"Of course no cartwheels today," Lucinda says, wrapping an arm around Genevieve. "We're going to look out for her, whether she likes it or not."

"I thank my lucky stars every day for the friends I have," Genevieve says, patting Lucinda's shoulder. "But aren't we going for a stroll? I might not be able to do cartwheels, but I'd sure like to walk."

"How about through the tree-tunnel of Rue Émile Richard, then circle around to Boulevard Raspail again?" Jean-Marc suggests. "It's not too long, not too short."

"I'd say that's perfect for an exercise-hungry girl who can't do cartwheels yet," Genevieve smiles.

Inside of a minute the group's rounded the corner of Boulevard Raspail and Boulevard Edgar Quinet, turned left onto and commenced to stroll south on Rue Émile Richard. The latter cuts through Montparnasse Cemetery and is framed on both sides by its walls. It's a single-lane one-way overtly pedestrian-friendly street: wide walkways are on each side of it and account for more space than that allowed for vehicles. Rows of large trees are also on each side, such that their limbs intersect above the street and form a leafy ceiling, concealing the sky. This is what Jean-Marc was alluding to when he referred to Rue Émile Richard as a tree-tunnel.

"Take a look, Pas," Christina says, gesturing to the left and right. "The walls of this cemetery are *much* lower than those of Père Lachaise! We could easily boost and pull each other over by ourselves, we wouldn't need a male to hoist us, or rope to climb down! It's nice to know we tackled the more difficult cemetery on our first night! This one looks like it's for amateurs!"

"Compared to Père Lachaise, Montparnasse Cemetery *is* for amateurs!" Stephan laughs. "It's all flat ground inside, no sharp alterations in grading at any point! And laid out like a grid, no hidden nooks and crannies, no possibility of getting lost! No guards posted at any of the tombs! No barriers, barbed wire or otherwise, at the top of any part of the wall! Any place on the wall is as easy to climb as this area here! Rest assured, everyone's aware of the degree of difficulty of Père Lachaise, amount of moxie required to tackle it during a fierce storm! People can't stop talking about your adventure, it's becoming the stuff of legend, and I'm always going to feed that! You're the fearless American girls!"

"If it was an ordinary night I'd climb this wall in a second and make my own comparison," Pascale says. "But nothing's going to get me to rumple my dress before dinner with Gen's parents!"

"That's another reason your legend's growing," Claire smiles. "People note your flawless fashion sense, refined and delicate manner, then try to compute the nighttime scamping among graves in thunder, and climbing down walls on a rope! The contrast adds to their fascination! It's a finicky-girls-gone-wild thing!"

"Right," Lucinda says. "You were immaculately dressed on the night of the adventure! Talk about a memorable entrance!"

"Except for the hiking boots," Christina laughs. "Rather clunky, those!"

"As if any of the males noticed that!" Carole says. "We petite things have already got to beat 'em off with a stick! And there you were, in wet dresses, not one curve concealed! Ha ha ha!"

"Delicate flowers who go cemetery romping in storms," Jean-Marc says. "A lot of people already think New York must be an insanely wild place, and you've helped that along!"

"Yeah, the grass-is-greener syndrome," Pascale says, "and all because we made a memorable entrance by accident!"

"It's not as if we planned on turning up at the party in drenched dresses," Christina adds. "We were silly tourists having fun!"

"You know as well as I do your adventure falls far outside the typical tourist agenda," Stephan says. "It falls outside of *any* agenda!"

"Meaning it might start a whole new agenda," Jean-Marc says. "I, for one, am ashamed of myself—I've been trumped by Americans in my own town! I think I'm not going to easy in my mind until I'm in Père Lachaise at night during a storm!"

"Don't take it so hard," William laughs. "Like Pas and Chrissy said, it was accidental. We didn't consult the weather report and say, *There's going to be a storm: let's hightail it to Père Lachaise!* That excursion was planned weeks in advance, when we were in New York. That's where I got the headlamps."

"Plans, shmans!" Stephan shouts. "I say we take a detour over the wall right now!"

"Sure," Lucinda says, "that's why we're dressed nice for you, to get mussed and dusty! You heard what Pas said! If *she's* not going over, none of the girls are! I'm not scuffing these shoes!"

"Lucy dear," he says, "I'm sure you know I meant Bill and Jean-Marc and I. Of course I don't want girls getting rumpled, or shoes scuffed, or hair out of place!" He flicks her hair.

"Careful, sir," Lucinda responds; then, quickly breaking into a grin, "So go on! Have fun!"

"Not going to be far, Lucy dear—we'll be walking with you, the only difference is we'll be on the cemetery side."

In less than a minute William, Stephan, and Jean-Marc boost and pull each other to the top of the wall and lower themselves into the cemetery. Judging by how quickly their voices recede into the distance, they've decided to race from the wall towards the interior.

"Hey!" Carole calls out after about five minutes have elapsed of not hearing from the men, as the women continue walking south. "I thought you were going to stay alongside us!" Then, upon receiving no response, she calls again, "Jean-Marc! Steph! Bill!"

"Just boys being boys," Genevieve says. "Probably chasing each other around, or they're over at the circle of the angel of eternal sleep or paying their respects to Baudelaire. They'll be back."

"It's best to ignore them," Pascale says. "They'll soon wonder why they're not missed and come running!"

"Exactly," Claire says. "It's a ploy to pique our curiosity, and make us yell for them like their mommies used to do! Boys are always attention starved!"

"And that's the thanks we get," is heard in Stephan's voice, "for toiling to obtain flowers for our flowers!"

No sooner is Stephan finished speaking than blossoms of all shapes and colors—tulips, chrysanthemums, daisies, snapdragons, geraniums, violets—begin raining down on the girls as he, William, and Jean-Marc toss them over the wall.

"Ooooo!" cries Carole, as a flurry of geraniums land in her hair and on her dress and spill to the ground at her feet. "A scarlet shower!"

"Now, aren't you ashamed?" Jean-Marc smiles, he having been boosted to the top of the wall by the other two.

"We're moved and delighted!" Carole exclaims.

"I'm speechless," Claire says, curtsying.

Soon William and Stephan are seated alongside Jean-Marc. "And now for the grand finale," the latter says, producing a plastic bag and turning it upside down and shaking it, whereupon another whirl of blossoms rains upon the girls' heads. Then the three of them descend to the ground.

"A flower princess!" Jean-Marc laughs, referring to the amount of blossoms in Carole's hair.

"We're all covered in colors," Pascale says. "Thank you!"

"You were already covered in colors," William says as the girls busy themselves with gathering the blossoms on the ground. "A lovelier group of girls in bright summer dresses I've never seen!"

"Yeah, girls who dress summery are the ticket," Jean-Marc says. "There's a fireworks' display worth of color here, mixed in with sleek body-lines! Sheer heaven!"

Genevieve's light green ensemble has been described. As for the others, Lucinda's dress is vermillion; Christina's dress is violet with white polka dots; Claire's dress is white with bright red and green v-stripe patterns; Carole's dress is aquamarine with purple and gray floral prints; Pascale's wearing a silver dress with scarlet lace fringe. Needless to say, they're tastefully accessorized: we'll dispense with the details because it would take too long to list them.

After the girls have each gathered a handful of blossoms, they assist one another with arranging a number of them in their hair. When they're through their hair's splashed with the colors of the rainbow, particularly where it frames their faces.

"Now that's what I call a perfect picture of springtime in all its glory!" Stephan says, sweeping his arm towards the girls.

"We thank you again," Genevieve says, the other girls nodding in accord.

"The pleasure's ours," Jean-Marc says. "It's nice to stroll around town with stunning visuals!"

"Shameless flatterer," Carole giggles, embracing him.

"Yeah, laying it on thick always goes down well with the girls!"

"Nothing thick about it," William says, kissing Genevieve.

"Not at all," echoes Stephan, likewise paying tribute to Lucinda.

"Darling," Pascale says, addressing Christina. "We definitely need to go on a man hunt, find Frenchmen for the rest of our stay!"

"That's a given," Christina laughs. "The sight of all this love's heating the atmosphere, and I'm going to need to cool off *sometime*!"

"You'll have a fine opportunity tonight at Sergio's," Lucinda says, glancing at them from over Stephan's shoulder.

"We know that," Pascale says, rubbing her hands together.

"Sure you're not up for it, Gen?" Carole asks. "You'll never convince me you're an invalid."

"Honey," Genevieve smiles, "I'm a newly engaged girl who's dizzy with the joy of it, remember? I told you Bill and I..."

"Just teasing, darling, I know where your priorities lie. I said that to let you know how fresh and healthy you look!"

"Yeah, you were grabbing the flowers as fast as we were," Claire says. "I knew the Gen I know and love would bounce back overnight!"

"It *is* getting increasingly—amazingly—easy to forget this thing," Genevieve says, touching her stomach.

Your humble narrator again pauses to point out he can only hope to capture a small percentage of a group conversation, since different things are often being said simultaneously and constantly spinning off into sub-contexts. Suffice to say that our friends, chatting and laughing the while, reach the end of Rue Émile Richard and turn left onto Rue Froidevaux, where they stroll alongside the southern wall of the cemetery, then turn left again onto Rue Victor Schoelcher, which they follow north until it terminates at Boulevard Raspail; that, once on Boulevard Raspail, they continue north and are soon at the corner of Rue Campagne Première, across the street from where they began their walk and a few yards from number 31, where Genevieve's parents reside.

"So," William says as they approach the art deco door of steel and glass, "the last time I opened this door I had no idea I'd be engaged to the girl of my dreams less than a day later! My entire life's completely rearranged itself for the better since Sunday!"

"Right, sweetie, we're traveling at the speed of light," Genevieve says, caressing his neck. "A complete stranger arrives from New York on Friday, and now that complete stranger's as close to me as the beat of my heart and I'm insanely in love with him! God, I *love* life!"

"I love life!" William yells, raising a fist to the sky.

"I love life!" the others echo as they begin filing inside the building. Soon they're boisterously ascending the stairs.

Then, when our group reaches the second floor, the wholly unexpected occurs: the door of the Grashelle residence opens and Baptiste's mother, Solange, appears with tears in her eyes. Genevieve, instantly afraid, clutches William's arm. William, instantly protective, switches locations with Genevieve so that he's standing between her and Solange. The others freeze in their tracks, ready to intercede if needed.

"Please, Genevieve," Solange says softly, not daring to step from the doorway. "I was by the door and heard you coming up the stairs, I wasn't waiting, I...I mean you no harm, Genevieve, I've been your friend since you were born, always..." She breaks off, quietly sobbing, and lowers her eyes towards her feet.

Genevieve, uncertain what to do, casts a worried glance at the others. She's still fearful, but also feels pity tugging at her breast; alongside the thought that this is the mother of he who tried to kill her is the thought that this is a person who has, indeed, always been her friend and is obviously hurting deeply. She hears herself say, "I'm not sure what you want from me, Solange."

"Poor Baptiste was ill," Solange says, still very softly while staring at the landing. "I...I hope you bear me no ill will, Genevieve. I bear you none. I'm a grieving mother, I almost wish I could die. I just wanted you to know I only wish good things for you, that I'm sorry. I would like you to know that Alain and I are... This is so hard." Again, sobs interrupt her.

"Solange," Genevieve begins, taking a step towards her.

"Gen," William says, squeezing her hand.

"It's OK, sweetie," Genevieve says as she crosses to where Solange is standing; then, addressing the latter, "I don't bear you any ill will, Solange, and... Baptiste, he... You're right, it's so hard. I'll never be able to imagine how you feel."

"I only...only wanted to make a gesture," Solange says, her lips trembling as she forms the words. "Maybe we'll be able to talk again someday. I know it will never be the same, but maybe our families can talk again someday. That's all I wanted to say, Genevieve."

"That's possible, Solange," Genevieve says, still uncomfortable. "I mean, I would think our families will speak again. I know you've always been my friend. I've always been your friend."

"Thank you, Genevieve," Solange says, still hesitating to raise her eyes. "That's all I can ask, that's all...all I wanted to say."

Genevieve, seeing Solange's profound misery, feels her unease melt away; before she half knows what she's doing, she wraps her arms around Solange's shoulders.

"You've always been the sweetest angel," Solange says at a near whisper. "Thank you, Genevieve, you'll never know what this means to me." Then, as if afraid to accept too much of Genevieve's gesture, she gently extricates herself from her arms and retreats into her home and quietly closes the door.

When the door shuts the others instantly surround Genevieve with worried and questioning faces. "I'm OK," she says, wiping a trace of moisture from her eyes as she begins ascending the stairs. "She told the truth: we were very close until her son started acting up, and I began avoiding their family so he'd have fewer opportunities to bother me. It's all so insane. The family that's been closer to my family than most of my relatives can't turn to my family in their hour of sorest grief because their son wanted to harm me."

"Harm you?" Carole interjects. "He wanted..."

"Shss, please," Genevieve cuts her off. "Bill and I are dealing with that, *have* dealt with that, and don't need to be pouring salt in wounds that are healing. What applies here is that Solange is a victim too, but that it'll take awhile to get past our opposite poles with regard to the deceased—I don't know if we ever will. I'll mention our talk to dad, but I'm through with it for now. What I mean is I'm glad I saw Solange because the hurt on their end's an unaddressed issue, but I don't feel it's my area—I can't afford to make it my area. It's for the parents to blaze the trail of family reconciliation."

"Are you sure it doesn't need to be addressed now?" William asks. "I don't want you burying anything that might be capable of returning to bother you. You've known her your whole life, and were close before the nonsense began: that's not easy to ignore, regardless of what her offspring turned out to be."

"Don't worry, sweetie, nothing's being buried," she answers, gently sliding her fingers across his left cheek. "I have my own wonderful man to look after, remember? I have no inclination to take on the emotions of other families, because I have my own family. I will help Solange, though—I'll suggest a thing or two to dad. But we're here for a nice dinner, you know! Why don't we have our dinner?"

"Absolutely, darling," William says as they open the door.

CHAPTER 35

"Cathy," Georges calls to his wife as the girls step from the hallway into the dining room, where he's putting the finishing touches to the table settings, "six Floras, as radiant as the dawn, have arrived for dinner."

"You're looking good yourself, dad," Genevieve says, embracing and kissing him.

"Gen, you're a revelation," Georges says, stepping back to gaze at her. "Seeing you so happy is the best gift two proud parents could ever receive!"

"That's for sure," Catherine says, stepping into the dining room from the kitchen to greet everyone. "A daughter sparkling with health and joy, what more could dad and I want? Bill, we've always had it so easy with her! Gen could've raised herself!"

"That's not true, mom," Genevieve says, kissing her mother. "Not by a long shot. I'm the one who's had it easy, because I'm blessed with the best parents in human history! And now I'm blessed with the best fiancé in human history!"

"And you're proof that Paradise can be regained," William says, caressing Genevieve's arm.

"You were spot on, honey," Catherine says, addressing her husband. "Our kids are too eager to love one another to put up with obstruction."

"That's the deal in a nutshell," Genevieve says. "There's no room for anything but love!"

"It's a basic chemical reaction," William laughs, "as when a heavier liquid is poured into a bottle and forces the lighter liquid out of the top until completely displacing it. The energy of our affection easily displaces would-be obstructions!"

"Together, we're a force field that enemy emotions can't penetrate," Genevieve smiles, crossing to the dining table. "But there *is* something that needs to be dealt with: mom and dad, everyone, could we sit for a bit? I wasn't going to do this now, but on second thought feel there's no better time. You know what I mean, right sweetie?"

"I know," William answers, "and agree. It's fresh in our minds, best to deal with it before it lingers too long."

"So go ahead, Gen," Georges says.

"OK, dad and mom, it's this: it goes without saying that Solange and Alain are living in hell, they've lost a son and can't turn to their best friends. Our families have been close enough to eclipse the influence of relatives. These are two people, your dearest friends for my whole life, who..."

"I don't know that we need to mention them," Georges interrupts. "All that matters to me is the well-being of my family, getting past the doings of that sick assailant. And you're doing that—actually, as far as I can tell, you've done that and I'm very grateful and relieved. I don't care about anything else. I'm not going to worry about the parents of the assailant!"

"Please, dad, will you allow me to finish?"

"All right, Gen, please finish—I'll listen."

Genevieve relates the details of her encounter with Solange on the stairs. At first there's a mixed look of anger and alarm on Georges' face—twice, she must again ask him to be silent. Towards the end of her recountal he's considerably calmer, and more thoughtful concerning the subject. Genevieve concludes by saying, "Do we always know where the ghosts are hiding, dad? Because of how close our families have been, don't you think there might be feelings that are unaccounted for, lingering in hidden places? Maybe I'm wrong, given the situation, but I would think a twenty-five year friendship isn't to be dismissed overnight—that you could at least speak to them. Solange was very decent and has no illusions. She knows as well as we do it'll never be the same as before. She also said she wanted to die, and that was too believable and scared me. I don't think you believe, any more than I do, that Solange and Alain had anything to do with Baptiste's behavior. He turned on everyone, violated everyone's trust."

"Listen to our daughter, Georges," Catherine says. "She's right. I don't see myself inviting them to dinner, but I don't see a reason to refuse to speak to them either. You know in your heart that Baptiste plain and simply became ill and they had nothing to do with it. We've shared with them for over half our lives, and their son is dead."

"Exactly," Georges responds. "There's always going to be that double-edged truth standing between us: we're glad the assailant is dead because of what he tried to do, and the assailant happens to be their son. How are we going to bridge that chasm?"

"Honey, no one's suggesting it's not going to be an uncomfortable relationship from now on. What Gen's suggesting, and I agree with her, is that we make an overture of sympathy."

"All right, I'll grant they're not at fault for what their son became and what he did. It cuts me to the quick to acknowledge it, but I helped raise that kid too. I'm sincerely devastated that he became sick, but I will never lie to myself and imagine I regret his demise—I don't regret his demise one bit. Now, can we honorably socialize with them under those circumstances? I would think not."

"But can we peaceably coexist with them under those circumstances and show some understanding for their loss?" Catherine asks. "I would say yes and that it's vastly preferable to ignoring them for the rest of our lives. Obviously, we're devastated that their son became ill: that's a sentiment we share with them, and a starting point. As Gen asked, do we always know where the ghosts are hiding? I'd think an offer of sympathy would help with disarming the ghosts, wherever they're hiding. Do you really want jabs of discomfort in the pit of your stomach every time you think of Alain? Because think of him you certainly will."

"What can a man do when the women he loves want something?" Georges asks, smiling at the others; then, addressing his wife, "All right, Cathy, you call them first. Harsh words were spoken by me, it would be best if your voice was the first they heard."

"Of course, honey. I was going to suggest that myself."

"We'll talk and see how it goes. I make no promises, though. A lot will depend on them."

"Indeed it will," Catherine says, rising to her feet. "A wrong word or misplaced sentiment and I'll be the first to hang up. Gen, is there anything you'd like to add?"

"I'd say the subject's been covered, mom. I'm glad you're going to call them."

"Good," Catherine says, "onto brighter things. I love your flowers."

"Then have some," Genevieve says, picking up her bouquet from the table.

"I think I know how to adorn my wife," Georges laughs, intercepting the bouquet. "Cathy, undo your hair." Catherine pulls the pins from her hair and allows it to fall free. Georges, using the girls as reference, places over a dozen blossoms in her hair, making sure many are in the waves that frame her face. "Now we have seven Floras," he smiles.

"Thank you, dear," Catherine says, kissing her husband.

"And *that's* going to be us when we're grown up," William says, addressing Genevieve while gesturing at her parents. "Truly an inspiration and model to live by!"

"You *are* grown up," Catherine says, "and more than you know. The way you two have buoyed each other up and are united and strong is an indication of great things to come. You only need each other for inspiration."

"Words that only confirm you're the best role models on earth," Genevieve says.

"But I need to get a bowl for these," Catherine says, referring to the bouquets of flowers lying on the table. "Let's get this show on the road."

"I'll get the bowl, honey," Georges says. "It's going to be heavy."

In a couple minutes Georges returns with a large crystal punch bowl filled with water and places it in the center of the dining table. After everyone tears the remaining portions of the stems from the blossoms, they place them in the bowl, where they float on the water and their colors shimmer among the bowl's facets.

"That gives me an idea," Claire says, setting some flowers among the crystals of the chandelier above the table, where their colors also flicker among the facets.

"Beautiful," Genevieve says. "Now we're doing springtime justice."

"Bet you can't guess where the flowers came from," Carole says, addressing Georges and Catherine with mischief in her eyes.

"Judging by the shortness of their stems and lack of wrapping and the fact each of you had an uneven handful, I'd say they were filched," Georges laughs.

"Right so far," Carole says, clapping. "Where from?"

"You didn't," Catherine says.

"I didn't because I'm a girl in finery," Carole answers. "It's the boys who raided the cemetery!"

"OK," Catherine responds, laughing. "We didn't need to know that! We *are* parents, remember? We're supposed to discourage such shenanigans!"

"Which, of course, is why you're tickled pink," Carole says with glee.

"All right, I'd say the sea bass is about ready," Catherine says, stepping towards the kitchen.

"Be happy to help," Carole says, following her.

"Happy to have you help," Catherine smiles over her shoulder.

Although it's of no great importance to the progress of our narrative, we'll mention that Catherine and Carole are very close. This is partially because Carole's adopted Catherine as a second mother, her parents being in Lille. It's also because Carole's able to bring out Catherine's playful side: when they're together they often carry on like little girls. Such was the stress of the past two days, they refrained from such behavior. Now that the stress is past, they're soon to be heard loudly chatting and giggling. In the meantime, Georges and Stephan open a couple bottles of Pinot blanc and begin filling glasses at the dining table.

By 9:15 PM everyone's digging into the fillets of Chilean sea bass and stacks of steamed vegetables on their plates. During dessert, as they're partaking of watermelon sorbet and strawberries, Georges clinks on his glass with his spoon, waits for silence, and announces he's booked a Sunday, October 17, wedding date at Sainte-Élisabeth church—Genevieve's squeals of delight are accompanied by enthusiastic applause on the part of the others. Even Catherine, it turns out, didn't know.

"A dad and husband likes to spring a surprise now and then," Georges smiles.

Shortly after the dining table's been cleared, William calls his parents to inform them of the wedding date, then passes his phone to Georges, who immediately says he'll call back from his landline so he and Catherine can speak more comfortably. The two pairs of parents spend over two hours in highly enjoyable conversation, as on the first occasion they spoke. In the meantime, William and Genevieve and the others pay a visit to her old playroom on the top floor, open its skylight, and begin ascending to the roof.

"I suppose I could mention this is the first time I've been in this room since Sunday, when someone was kicking the door," William smiles, nudging Genevieve, "but I'll let it pass. I wouldn't dream of pointing out the difference between the lunacy of those moments and the sanity of these moments! No, ma'am, I'm not going to allude to that at all!"

"Nor am I," she laughs. "I won't contrast my being on tenterhooks on Sunday, when I was in the Roman room down the hall and hearing lots of screaming, with the freedom I'm feeling now! No, sir, I won't do that at all!"

"Betrothed couples and their games," Stephan winks at the others as he starts climbing the mini-stairway to the roof.

"Better games than being caught in the quicksand of unsavory past events," Jean-Marc says. "Playing games means they're buoyed up by the emotional bounty of the present, being swept towards and embracing the future."

"I couldn't have phrased it better myself," William says, following Genevieve up the stairway.

"Wow!" Christina says, turning around and around to take in the view from all angles as Genevieve steps onto the roof. "Gen, you're one lucky girl! A playroom with a stairway to heaven! I don't envy many people, but I envy you! What a fabulous childhood you had!"

"I've been coming up here since I was two, when dad carried me," Genevieve responds, "and it never gets old! I lose my breath every time I see this, as if it's my first time!"

"I'm certainly losing my breath," Pascale says. "Have you ever slept up here? I would've."

"Funny you should ask that," Genevieve grins. "The answer's yes, of course! And it usually isn't intentionally. It's not difficult for me to be lulled into a gentle hypnotic state when I'm on my back gazing at the sky at night: one moment I'm watching the patterns the city lights make on the clouds, the next I'm out. More than once I've awakened with the sun in my eyes the next morning, momentarily wondered what I was doing up here."

"I can vouch for sky-hypnosis, the tricks the light-patterns play," Claire laughs. "Gen and I nodded off up here two winters ago, snug in our coats after dinner. Because of that we missed *Romeo and Juliette*, my favorite ballet! We had third row seats!"

"I'm all for putting sky-hypnosis to the test," Pascale says, reclining onto her back.

"Why not?" Genevieve says, following suit. Soon everyone is on their back, gazing at the sky.

"Clouds drifting by, constantly splitting apart and recombining, dissolving and rematerializing," William says, "are definitely hypnotic, strangely consoling."

"A mirror of the mutability of life," Stephan says. "The clouds are saying, *Don't fret over unexpected setbacks, because the scenery will switch and you'll be drifting free again. Always have faith in beneficent rearrangement, the elimination of obstacles to happiness: it's as inevitable as the changing of the tide."*

"Right," Jean-Marc joins in, "the glorious impermanence of things! Some people are distressed by the temporality of life: why? I don't understand that attitude! Temporality applies to everything: it means bad things can become good things, that boredom can swirl into bliss!"

"And that's why contemplating our mortality in Père Lachaise was comforting," Christina says. "We have one life and it's unpredictable—constantly in flux—and can be taken from us without warning, so why not just relax and roll with it? Our situation can't be changed, so just laugh and play! Disaster will strike, that's a given, and those who are armed with this perspective will more easily overcome it! And that's very pertinent now! Bill and Gen are the living proof! They were being chased by ghosts yesterday, and today have kissed those ghosts goodbye! Isn't that so, Billy?"

"Right, my dear," William answers. "The clouds above twist and turn and rearrange themselves according to the wind patterns, and so do people rearrange themselves according to the patterns of their feelings, and those of the special people in their lives. Virgil's right: love conquers all things."

"Love conquers all things, and cemetery frolickers have an invaluable perspective on love," Stephan says. "I've stared into the shafts of shattered and abandoned sepulchers, seen smashed caskets in the dirt, and understood that the wonder and miracle of love's not to be taken for granted, ever."

"Which is why you generally have a new girl in bed every week," Lucinda laughs.

"Uh-oh," Claire shouts. "Lucy's making a play for permanent relationship status!"

"If that were true," Lucinda counters, "you certainly wouldn't say it aloud!"

"I'll admit I've been curious," Pascale says, emboldened by the levity with which the subject's being treated. "Steph has this reputation of having a revolving bedroom door, but I've only seen him with you. Of course it's none of my business..."

"We're an on and off," Lucinda smiles, "and it suits us both just fine. Next week? Who knows? Nice insertion of *none of my business*, by the way."

"Ha ha ha! Yeah, that *was* transparent! I..."

"Pas, we're family!" Stephan cuts in. "Everything's all of our business, if the subject crops up. If something isn't anyone's business, then don't air it. Those are the unspoken rules! As for having a revolving bedroom door, I don't see how that's a strike against love—I'm *always* in love! Love's different with each different girl, and I embrace that! Love's a kaleidoscope, as ever changing as these clouds, and I surrender to all its nuances and colors!"

"Amen to that," William says. "Love's a kaleidoscope and I have a kaleidoscope fiancée in whom all of love's nuances and colors shine bright. Her multifaceted personality is infinity on earth."

"Sweetheart, I still can't believe I'm marrying into this," Genevieve says, tapping his forehead.

"And I..." William begins, then interrupts himself. "We'll have plenty of time to be private later, honey."

"Indeed, we will. And right now this is in-the-bunch time."

"We're not policing you!" Pascale says.

"Certainly not!" Carole seconds.

"We know that," William says. "But we're here to watch the sky, right? Watch the clouds drift by, change shape with every shift of the wind and bend of the city-light, and drift with them in our heads—seem to float upwards and join them, be released from earthly concerns, become sleepy sleepy sleepy."

"Sleepy sleepy sleepy," echo the others, excepting Christina, in a low tone.

"I'd rather admire magnificent Paris," Christina says, rising to her knees. "Sorry to break the spell, Billy, but I can't help it! I'm a virgin rooftopper, and don't want to sleep!"

"That's OK," Carole laughs, sitting upright. "I don't either!"

"Preach all you want, Billy and Jean-Marc, about the downsides of modern civilization," Christina continues, "but I defy you to say Paris at night in this corrupt day and age isn't beautiful!"

"I know my town's stunning," Jean-Marc says, sweeping an arm across the skyline while still on his back. "Centuries have come and gone, new buildings have been built upon the ruins of the old many times over, and it's as if Paris is striving to pull away from the earth and soar into the sky as lights glitter as far as the eye can see. It's as if, subconsciously, we've created a representation of infinity."

"One of my earliest memories is of San Francisco at night," William says. "In kindergarten all my drawings were of city lights. I've always thrilled to the sight of cities, day or night, and if that's inconsistent with my aversion to the manipulations of modernity so be it. I flow as the clouds flow, and take pleasure in beauty as my inner pinwheel dictates. And what, after all, are the impositions of modern civilization when held up to love? Love's the most effective antidote to falsity there is."

"Absolutely," Carole says; then, addressing Jean-Marc, "Do you agree, sir?"

"One of your standing splits instantly annihilates all attempts by our manipulative civilization to subdue me," he responds. "Does that answer your question?"

"Yes, sir, it does," she says, promptly rising and executing a standing split.

And on that note, dearest reader, we'll allow our friends to continue to enjoy each other's company on the roof and simply say that at about 12:30 AM everyone, excepting William and Genevieve, board the metro and take it to the Belleville station, not far from the party at Sergio's apartment at 17 Allée Louise Labé, where they enjoy his hospitality until the metro reopens shortly after sunrise.

We'll also mention that Pascale, successful in her endeavor to find a Frenchman at the party, returns with one to Stephan's apartment. Christina, having been asked out on a date for the following night by a Frenchman of her own, is equally as pleased. William and Genevieve spend the night in her old bedroom, where numerous objects from her childhood are on display. These objects inspire questions from William, the result of which is that they pass half the night sharing anecdotes from their childhoods, something they haven't had occasion to do yet. Almost as enjoyable as the actual swapping of anecdotes is the realization that there's still much they don't know about each other, in the matter of factual details, and how delightful it will be to fill in the blanks.

CHAPTER 36

Dearest reader, there's little remaining of our adventure that needs to be described in detail. By way of summarization, we'll mention that William and Genevieve attend dinners and parties on every night leading up to Monday, primarily at Stephan's but also at Jean-Marc's and Claire's apartments; that another nighttime excursion to Montsouris Park takes place, on Saturday, and Genevieve experiences no difficulty in entering and exiting via climbs of the fence, assisted as she is by strong arms; that a picnic is spread on the slope of lawn between the lake and the statue, *Les Naufragés*, and a spirited game of Frisbee ensues; that, although Genevieve sits out the game on account of still having sutures on her stomach, she's able to laugh to her heart's content without feeling any discomfort.

We'll also mention that Catherine obtains a medical postponement for Genevieve's exams from the doctor on Thursday—a request he happily fulfills, once he knows the real reason for it is Genevieve's engagement-related trip to New York. Also on Thursday Catherine calls Solange; following a few preliminary words on the part of the women, Georges and Alain join the conversation and the four of them speak for about fifteen minutes. While neither set of parents are overly comfortable during the conversation, all are relieved afterwards at having had it. In fact, it was far easier to speak again than they'd thought possible; any serious apprehensions that they, and Georges in particular, had beforehand that inappropriate things might be said have been put to rest. Twenty-five years of friendship is, indeed, difficult to thrust aside. On Friday Catherine and Solange speak again and on Saturday they meet for lunch, during which they manage to smile. Healing between the two families, with the tacit understanding that their relationship has been forever altered, will be spearheaded by the women.

On Monday afternoon Genevieve's sutures are removed, as scheduled, and she's a free woman. Judging by the facility with which she executes a couple celebratory cartwheels the moment she's outside on the hospital lawn, she's reobtained, if not 100% of her physical capabilities, then an amount very close to it. That night, there's a quiet gathering at Stephan's, with their closest friends in attendance, where William and Genevieve say their goodbyes, as their flight to New York leaves at 10:25 AM. They spend the night with Georges and Catherine, where they've already deposited their luggage, and Catherine drives them to the Orly Airport in the morning. Not only does their flight depart on time, they have a row of three seats to themselves.

About three hours after they've lifted off from the Orly runway Genevieve's resting her chin on William's shoulder as they're gazing out the window. "So now we're above instead of below the clouds," she smiles, "watching them drift over the blue of the sea instead of under the blue of the sky."

"A complete flip-flop," he laughs. "Very appropriate! Here I am, headed back to New York barely a week after arriving in Paris for a six-week vacation I'd planned for half a year, and I'm deliriously happy about it! And speaking of wonderful and unexpected life-upside-downing events: how long was it between when we first saw each other and became engaged? What I mean is, when was the first time we truly saw each other?—in other words, were *awakened* by each other? I don't count our technical first meeting at

Steph's, right after I arrived and was only thinking of snatching a nap."

"Nor do I," she answers. "The first time I saw you, your one and only priority was collapsing in your room. Not to mention that you were with Chrissy and Pas and it would never occur to me to wonder if you were available. Plus I wasn't looking!"

"I don't even count the party at Steph's after returning from Père Lachaise," he continues. "There were too many distractions, I was meeting a lot of new people, getting to know Jean-Marc. Sure, I noticed how delightful to the eye you are and the sweetness of your disposition, but I wasn't looking either. I was with Chrissy and Pas."

"I remember you chatting with Jean-Marc mostly because Bap was causing trouble and drew my eye in your direction. I saw how bright and self-assured you were, noted your broad shoulders and upright stance, but the Bap problem was uppermost in my mind— that and getting to know Chrissy and Pas, who were with me. It wasn't until we circled around to Steph and Lucy at the lake in Montsouris and we suddenly stared at each other and froze that you struck me differently, from out of the blue. That's when I first saw you in a way that astonished me. My knees grew weak, and I mean that literally—it was a benign seizure, inner imbalance that was delightful and mildly disturbing. I saw your surprise too, but didn't dare read anything into it. That's definitely when we first saw each other, at around four in the morning Saturday. If we're going to count the hours between first sight and our engagement, we start there. That's why you asked, right? You wanted to confirm that I'd start the countdown from the same place as you!" She grasps his hand and squeezes.

"Confirm?" he smiles, reaching for her other hand and beginning the dance of fingers they always delight in. "There's no confirmation involved, darling! I'm just enjoying hearing you say what we already know, as in of course that's our love at first sight moment, when the veil was lifted from our gaze and we were jolted awake! I'll treasure that moment, as magical as anyone could hope to experience in a lifetime, for the rest of my days! I can't begin to describe it: your startled beauty, electric surprise, as shimmers shoot up my spine and engulf me in mists of unformulated yearning! You're so right: it sprang on us from out of the blue! A clash of wonder and desire, with no promise of anything coming to fruition, and no ability to be clear about what I wanted! I didn't know much about you, aside from your wish to shed that unwanted shadow! The voices of the others faded and the trees and lake disappeared and I was alone with you, and stunned! I've since wondered how that worked itself into happening."

"It happened because our hidden places were busy making their own decision without our knowledge," she says, rubbing her thigh against him. "It seems crazy to me that we were near each other on the couch at Steph's and the picnic blankets in Montsouris and you had no discernable effect upon me, and then there was this spontaneous revelation, but that's what happened. Our energy sensed what eluded our conscious awareness and bided its time for a bit and accumulated, then broke to the surface all at once and took us by storm! Sweetie, we weren't given a choice!" Giggling, she kisses him on the cheek.

"That's for sure," he laughs, returning her kiss. "Falling in love wasn't our decision! Cupid aims his bow and shoots his arrows, and we mere mortals obey! But how wonderful it is to obey Cupid! How wonderful to be unexpectedly seized by love, with no preliminary warning—no opportunity to prepare! When our love first surged to the surface at the lake it was too strong for us to wrap our understanding around it! But the seed of understanding had been planted and it didn't take long to sprout!"

"I love how our friends were looking at us after our second experience on Avenue René Coty, when I grabbed your arm like this," she says, grasping his arm with both hands. "We got away with surprising each other in secret the first time, not so the second! Obviously, our hidden places were getting impatient, because it happened less than an hour after the first time and was a lot more physically expressive and couldn't be concealed from others!"

"We were less surprised the second time—I was smiling inside as much as I was amazed, and able to do *this*," he says, seizing one of her hands again. "I remember looking up at the sky between the rows of trees and not caring that our friends were catching wind of what was going on. Seeing the looks on their faces was like gazing into a mirror and helped me confirm what I was feeling. And by the time we'd ditched the pest and taken the cab to the Opera we were already caught in the current and couldn't fight it! Not that we wanted to fight it, do anything but surrender!"

"I'll remember that morning at the Opera forever, honey. Our feelings for one another were surging into the foreground, *demanding* we attend to them! Our first kiss was made *necessary* by our meshing emotions, sympathetic electrical fields! The sun was rising and our love was rising! It's fitting that the Opera's always been a favorite place of mine—it's a *sacred* place now! And Chrissy and Pas are the greatest sweethearts on earth, the way they put me at ease right away and further opened the floodgates."

"Floodgates is right," he says as they intertwine both sets of fingers again. "By the time we were forced to separate because you had to get some sleep and collect yourself before broaching the subject of Bap's behavior to mom and dad, I was clearly—self-awarely—in love! Saying goodbye at the Opera was agony! Waiting all day was agony! I barely slept, but wasn't tired; and when I was walking from Steph's that evening to see you again, have dinner with you and mom and dad for the first time... My emotions were spinning far too fast for me to feel I was staying abreast of them. I wasn't confident about being able to handle my emotions, because I'd never had such an experience before—never been seized from the inside out so completely so swiftly. Of course I was shimmering with joy, but could I reason about it, control it? No! But I'm telling you the moment I was standing before you again, embracing you again, everything fell into place in my feelings and I was as centered as it's possible for a person to be!"

"I was in two worlds at once when I sat down to speak to mom and dad that evening. I'd been rehearsing that scene in my head for awhile—what I'd say, how I'd seek to make it go smoothly—and was having trouble staying focused because you were uppermost in my mind. Mom discerned my altered state and, as soon as the banishment of Bap business was over, said I looked like a man had caught my fancy! I was too wildly in love to be able to hide it! And then when I called you to invite you to dinner, the sound of your voice on the phone swept through me like a million electric particles of sand! As long as we were apart on that day, it *was* confusing—deliciously so, but still confusing—and as soon as we were together again, it wasn't confusing at all! We needed each other to complete each other, and be inwardly calm! That's love!"

"It *is* incredible how quickly we came together! I'd be highly skeptical such lightning-quick understanding, as in a couple uniting for life over an interval of *hours*, is possible had we not accomplished it! So let's see: how long was it from our benign seizure at the lake to our engagement in the ambulance?"

"OK," she smiles, "from about 4:00 AM Saturday to about...I'd estimate it was around 9:00 AM on Monday, although I wasn't exactly checking the time in the ambulance."

"I was dealing with pre-proposal jitters, and a few other things I won't mention by name," he says, "so noticing the time wasn't an option. It may have been a bit later, but I'd agree 9:00 AM's the time if we're rounding to the nearest hour. So from 4:00 AM Saturday to 9:00 AM Monday's fifty-three hours. It's fifty-three hours, give or take about an hour, that it took us to become engaged after opening each other's eyes in Montsouris!"

"And the total time involved, between technical first sight and our engagement: noon Friday to 9:00 AM Monday? That's sixty-nine hours. Not bad for how long it took us to go from complete strangers to betrothed! And from noon Friday to 4:00 AM Saturday is sixteen hours: that's how long it took our subconscious impressions to break to the surface, start waking us up!" She playfully pokes him in the ribs and slings a leg across his lap.

"Not bad is right," he says, wrapping his arms around her. "And on second thought, what's so incredible about it? Considering you're my drop dead gorgeous one-and-only that I thought only lived in fairytales, it's only fitting sixty-nine hours is all it took for us to be engaged!"

"And you're my astoundingly handsome prince charming! I'm sure the Fates arranged our marriage when we were born!"

It's here that our couple indulge in a great deal of what might be termed lovey-dovey talk—verbal confectionery that's immensely gratifying to them, rich with love and trust, but that might come across as silly to people happening to overhear, especially if they be of an uncharitable disposition—while exchanging an abundance of kisses and caresses. Finally, William's mirthfully tossing Genevieve's hair about as she squeals with delight and tickles him. A number of their fellow passengers turn in their direction: most are amused, but a couple are irritated.

"Shss," she whispers, grinning from ear to ear. "Good people aren't supposed to be disruptive on planes."

"Right," he says, lowering his voice, "we're the unruly children the parents can't control."

"We'll show them we're also capable of picture perfect decorum," she says, straightening herself in her seat and smoothing her dress, sliding her hands from her waist to her knees. As Genevieve does so William's briefly absorbed in one of his step-outside-of-himself experiences—relishing the sight of the waves of her hair as they spill down the sides of her smiling face; and how snug she is in her dress, delicate her hands are, effortlessly graceful she is.

"What, honey?" she inquires, widening her eyes in amusement.

"I'm admiring the gift I've received," he answers. "I've met the girl of my dreams and discovered untold emotional riches—the joy of cherishing someone who's an extension of myself and growing with her! In fifty-three miraculous hours this new world was discovered and fought for and obtained by us! That's something of what I was thinking. Plus I love the way you dress!"

"Being alive's going to be luscious beyond belief from now on," she says, flinging her hair behind her shoulders. "We're a fully united couple, secure in the blanket of our love, surrounded by a high wall of emotional cohesion! No one will scale our wall and intrude upon our joy, and that's our miracle! You're my miracle, honey! I'm in awe of the feeling of security that encloses me when you're near, and also when we're apart and I think of you! Your breathing's my breathing, and I'll never stop shimmering at the wonder of it!"

"And I'll never stop gazing in amazement at your wellspring eyes, marveling at the way the air hums when you're beside me!" he says, passing his hand through her hair. "You're my miracle, and I can't wait to introduce you to my friends and show you my town!"

"And I can't wait to meet your friends and see your town! And to think it's only hours away, a whole new world!"

"We'll be in Central Park this afternoon. I'll show you our obelisk, Cleopatra's Needle, then take you to Turtle Pond and Belvedere Castle; afterwards we'll rent a rowboat and drift on The Lake, then have dinner at The Boathouse and walk through Bethesda Terrace and the Mall and eventually emerge on Fifth Avenue. Then it's Bergdorf Goodman, if it's still open, where I'll buy you your first New York dress, and after that... Actually, who knows how our day will play out? I'm sure we'll be doing a lot of on-the-fly stuff! The only *mandatory* event is the party at my friend Don's place tonight, where I'll proudly present you to everyone!"

"But the Central Park tour sounds wonderful," she says. "I'll love every moment! Cleopatra and castles and lakes and boats... We *are* in a fairytale, sweetie! And it'll be delirious heaven to meet your friends, and especially my new mom and dad when they arrive on Friday! I'm jumping out of my skin!"

"New York's going to be a waking dream, now that you're in my life," he says. "I'll be discovering my town all over again, as I see it through your eyes and through our love! As you said, a whole new world's only hours away! And Friday can't come soon enough: I can already picture your new mom and dad, who already adore you, beaming with immeasurable delight at their first glimpse of you in the flesh! And guess what? For the first time in my life I'm savoring every second of being cooped up on a plane! Being cooped up's no longer possible as long as you're with me! My feelings are flowing further than the distance between the sea and the sun, while centered upon you and you only!"

"You're my wild new wonderful incredible world, all right," she smiles, wrapping her arms around his neck. "Our future's a dream come true—a dream I never knew I had until meeting you."

Pulling each other closer with bliss and laughter in their eyes, William and Genevieve join their lips together again.

About the Author

Robert Scott Leyse was born in San Francisco, grew up in various locales about America, lived in Paris for a spell, and now resides in Manhattan. He has worked as a New York cab driver, on the night shift, and has over a dozen years of experience in the legal field. He has three novels out, *Liaisons for Laughs: Angie & Ella's Summer of Delirium* (July, 2009), *Self-Murder* (April, 2010), and *Attraction and Repulsion* (June, 2011).

Visit him online at: www.robertscottleyse.com

Breinigsville, PA USA
18 January 2011
253473BV00002BA/9/P